THE LADY VIXEN

"I'll take care of you. All you have to do is be waiting for me with open arms when I come in from the woods at the end of a hardworking day."

Anger gave Fancy the strength to jerk away from Chance's possessive fingers. Glaring up into his warm brown eyes, she snapped, "I can take care of myself. I'll not be beholden to any man."

"The hell you say." His voice was harsh now. "You're beholden to every man you take home with you. You're depending on the money he'll put on your pillow before he leaves."

For a moment outrage nearly blinded Fancy. Then, hardly aware of her action, she felt the palm of her hand sting as it connected with a lean cheek. As he stared at her, dumbfounded, she wheeled around and walked away.

"Didn't you offer her enough money, Chance?" the barmaid taunted him loud enough for everyone to hear. "She's not called Fancy for nothin'. She comes high."

Fancy

NORAH HESS

LEISURE BOOKS   NEW YORK CITY

A LEISURE BOOK®

September 2006

Published by

Dorchester Publishing Co., Inc.
200 Madison Avenue
New York, NY 10016

ISBN 0-8439-3783-1

The name "Leisure Books" and the stylized "L" with design are
trademarks of Dorchester Publishing Co., Inc.

Printed in the United States of America.

Visit us on the web at www.dorchesterpub.com.

To Robert Carpenter,
who urged me to write Fancy.

Chapter One

Washington, 1855

The tinny, raucous sound of the scarred and out-of-tune piano fell silent with the last chords of "Camptown Races." For the next fifteen minutes, the taxi dancers could have a respite from the heavy logger boots that had been tramping on their aching feet for the past hour.

Nineteen-year-old Fancy Cranson limped across the sagging wooden dance floor, her short red dress swishing around her knees as she made for the roughly constructed benches lined against one wall. She sat down and leaned her head against the unpainted wall of Big Myrt's dance hall with a sigh of relief. Taking a lace handkerchief from the low vee of her bodice, she dabbed at her damp forehead where short, pale blond hair stuck to the smooth skin.

After a moment she leaned forward and kicked off her slippers. After nudging them under the bench, safe from careless feet that might kick them across the floor, she began massaging her right foot through its black mesh stocking. Her arches ached from the height of her high-heeled slippers and her toes felt as if they were ready to drop off her feet from being tromped on by the heavy boots the rowdy lumberjacks wore. She didn't know which hurt the most, her feet or her waist, where rough, callused hands had gripped tightly as she was hopped and swung around in a wild dance.

But there wasn't much Fancy could do about it. Any man who approached her with a ticket in his hand had bought the privilege of dancing with her for ten minutes, whether she wanted him for a partner or not. If she refused, Big Myrt would show her the door.

And she needed this job, for a while at least. So she tolerated the drunks and the rough, bearded loggers who tried to look down the front of her dress, held her too tight, and made crude propositions to her.

Five weeks ago, when her father was killed in a logjam, she had been devastated. And when she counted the money they had kept in a cracked cookie jar, she could have cried all over again. The legacy left to her by big Buck Cranson was twenty-one dollars and sixty-two cents.

That was not counting two horses, four rooms of furniture that had seen better days, and the care of her cousin Lenny.

All their logger friends had rallied around her, lending their support in whatever way they could, but Fancy knew she couldn't sponge off them the rest of her life. She had offers of marriage but turned them all down. Most of the men were as old as her father, and the others felt like family, she had known them so long. She couldn't feel romantic about them.

Her only hope was to somehow get together enough money to get Lenny and herself to San Francisco. Fancy's sister Mary lived there with her husband and young son. In Mary's letters, which arrived every month or so, she always urged Fancy to join her, writing that jobs were plentiful. Mary assured her she would have no problem finding work in a restaurant or as a maid in a fancy house on Nob Hill. But city life didn't appeal to Fancy, and she hadn't given the idea any thought until now.

Fancy still wasn't enthusiastic about going to San Francisco, but it would be wonderful to see Mary after all these years. She knew life hadn't been easy for her sister; although her husband loved her dearly, Jason Landers was a drifter, moving from job to job. Fancy could always tell when things were tight with them: Young Tod would be put on a steamer and sent upriver to spend some time with Grandpa Buck and Aunt Fancy. After two or three months, Mary would write that they should send her son home. She and her father would know then that the couple had managed to get back on their feet again.

It had been nice having Tod with them. Through the long visits they had gotten to know the little fellow, and they missed him greatly when he was gone. The last time he had been sent to them, around six months ago, he was a sturdy little fellow with a genial nature.

One thing bothered Fancy a great deal: Why hadn't Mary come to their father's funeral? She had sent a letter off to her sister immediately after the accident; it should have arrived the same day. Mary would have had plenty of time to see her father one last time.

The only answer Fancy could come up with was that Jason had moved on to a different job, and the letter hadn't reached Mary. So what was Fancy to do now? she asked herself. She might not hear from her sister for months.

The answer came one day when she accidentally overheard a conversation between two loggers. "You ain't worth spit today, Sam," one of the men had complained. "I bet you was over at the Dawson camp dancin' last night."

"Yes, dammit, and I'm plumb tuckered out today."

"Used up a week's pay, didn't you?" the man said in disgust.

"Just about," Sam said with a sigh. "It don't take long to do it. A man has to pay pretty good to dance with them girls."

"Yeah, and they probably make more money in a week than you do bustin' your ass gettin' the timber cut and hauled to the sawmill."

"They make the money all right," Sam agreed, "but it sure is nice dancin' with them."

The next day Fancy had packed and made arrangements to have her belongings hauled to the Dawson camp. Two days later she had moved into a small house and become one of Big Myrt's girls. She had been dancing for two weeks now.

Fancy came out of her preoccupation at the sound of shrill laughter. She wasn't surprised to see black-haired Pilar come strutting from her room, followed by a thick-set, red-bearded lumberjack. As the Mexican dancer shoved several bills down the front of her dress, Fancy couldn't blame the men who thought that for a price she would take one of them to one of the rooms leading off the big hall and entertain them during the 15-minute break.

The old adage about birds of a feather ran through Fancy's mind. The men had naturally thought she was like the other dancers, who made most of their money that way; it was the main reason they were there. Pilar, however, liked bedding the men and took one to her room at every break.

On the dance floor Pilar was vivacious, ever smiling. But the women who worked with her knew it was all a facade. Beneath those sparkling black eyes and that wide smile was a spiteful woman. None of the dancers liked her; most hated and feared her.

Fancy disliked the Mexican woman intensely. They had clashed over a man recently—Chance Dawson, the owner of the lumber camp. Fancy scanned the milling lumbermen who waited impatiently for Luther, the piano player, to start pounding the keys again. She didn't see the broad-shouldered, whip-lean body of the man who was the reason Pilar had come after her with a knife.

Of course Chance could still come, Fancy reminded herself. It was still early—early for the dancers, at least. They didn't start working until midnight, and the clock on the wall said it was only a few minutes to two. He might be playing poker with some of the married men in camp and would come around later.

As Fancy massaged her other foot, she recalled the first time she had seen Chance Dawson. She had been dancing here for exactly a week when the handsome, brown-eyed man approached her with a strip of tickets in his hand and a devilish twinkle in his eyes. She had felt her heart slam against her ribs when he handed her the tickets and swept her onto the dance floor. Never before had a man made such an impact on her. Living in a lumber camp ever since she could remember, Fancy had known scores of men, but none had ever stirred her interest.

When he asked, "Where did you come from, angel face?" as he smoothly swung her around the dance floor, his hand light on her waist, she couldn't make her tongue move to answer him immediately. Finally she was able to answer him breathlessly.

"I come from Tumwater, about ten miles down the river."

He had looked down at her with a quizzical smile. "What made you leave that camp and come here? Don't they pay the men good wages there?"

Fancy wasn't sure she heard mockery in his voice so she answered, "I'm sure they get the same wages as the men here do."

"Then you must have fallen in love with one of the lumberjacks and he went away and left you, so you decided to move on. Am I right?" The slim fingers tightened slightly on her waist.

"You're partially right," Fancy's lips curved in a wan little smile, remembering how she had adored her big lumberjack father.

"So, you're grieving for a lost love." The tone said that was no big deal, that love was of no great importance. He stroked a finger down her cheek, then lifted her chin. Smiling wickedly, he said softly, "I can make you forget that man ever existed."

Fancy shook her head, a sadness coming over her face. "There's not a man alive who will ever make me forget him. He will always be in my heart."

Fancy felt the logger's displeasure at her words in the way he jerked her up against his hard body and said curtly, "We'll see."

They had danced in silence then, but he was still holding her tighter than she allowed any of the other men to do. It felt good to be held against a hard chest. That was another thing she missed since losing her father: the way he held her close when she was hurting about something.

It was almost time for a rest period when Chance whispered huskily in her hair, "Do you want to show me your room, cuddle a bit?"

Fancy caught her breath and looked up at him with hurt and surprise in her eyes. "I don't have a room here," she answered coldly. "I don't live on the premises. I have my own little house."

"Hey, that's better yet," he said smoothly. When the piano music stopped on a discordant note, he ordered softly, "Get your wrap and let's get out of here."

"I can't leave here until the place closes at five o'clock," Fancy answered stiffly, pulling away from him. "Big Myrt would fire me."

"Let her fire you." The grip he had kept on her arm tightened. "I'll take care of you. All you'll have to do is be waiting for me with open arms when I come in from the woods at the end of a hard working day."

Anger gave Fancy the strength to jerk away from his possessive fingers. Glaring up into his warm brown eyes, she snapped, "I can take care of myself. I'll not be beholden to any man."

"The hell you say." The voice was harsh now. "You're beholden to every man you take home with you. You're depending on the money he'll put on your pillow before he leaves."

For a moment outrage nearly blinded Fancy. Then, hardly aware of her action, she felt the palm of her hand sting as it connected with a lean cheek. As Chance stared at her, dumbfounded, she wheeled around and walked away.

The burly loggers had stared after Fancy, hard put not to roar with laughter. They were wise enough, however, to bite their tongues and pretend not to have seen their boss get walloped by the new dancer that every man jack of them lusted after.

Chance Dawson—the owner of the lumber camp, Fancy later learned—started toward the door, his eyes black with anger and finger marks rising on his cheek. He was stopped by Pilar, her hand on his arm. "Didn't you offer her enough money, Chance?" she taunted him, loudly enough for everyone to hear. "She's not called Fancy for nothin'. She comes high."

Chance shook her grip off his arm and made no reply to the catty remark as he strode out of the dance hall and into the night. It was then, without warning, that Pilar had snatched a stiletto from beneath her garter and lunged at Fancy, screaming that she had better keep away from her man.

The raging dancer was in for a surprise. For all her delicate looks and slender body, Fancy was strong and just as swift as the woman bent on stabbing her. Relying on tricks learned from her dead father, Fancy grabbed Pilar's wrist, jerked it behind her back, and brought her arm up until the knife fell to the floor. Then she brought the screeching dancer to the floor, where she gave her a sound beating, blackening Pilar's eye and cutting her lip.

When the loggers, who had watched delightedly, thought Pilar had had enough they dragged Fancy off her. The Mexican gave Fancy a wide berth since the incident. Nevertheless, the other dancers warned Fancy to keep an eye on her and to be very careful when she was alone; Pilar would seek revenge one way or the other.

Luther, rail thin and somewhere in his fifties, came and sat down beside Fancy. Flexing his long fingers, he said, "I'm afraid I'm getting rheumatism, Fancy." Leaning his head back against the wall, he added, "I can't pound the keys like I used to."

Fancy liked the sad-eyed man very much and suggested sympathetically, "Your fingers probably only need a rest. Can't you afford to take some time away from the piano?"

Luther gave a short bark of laughter. "On what Myrt pays me? I can't afford to take one day off, never mind a couple of weeks or so. Besides, she would soon replace me with some other piano pounder."

"Are you sure about that? I've seen a softness in her eyes when she looks at you."

"Girl, you've got to be blinder than a bat if you can see any kind of softness in that woman. Did you ever hear the way she talks to me? Just like I was some kind of useless old dog that got in her way."

Fancy grinned and asked, "You mean like the way she sees to it that you get a big, hearty meal every night while none of us dancers gets so much as a cup of coffee? It doesn't look like table scraps that you wolf down."

"That's because she knows she's paying me starvation wages," Luther muttered, a flush coming over his pale face. "She probably figures it's to her benefit that I have a decent meal every day, so I can move my fingers with more energy."

"But maybe she's feeding you for a different

reason," Fancy pointed out with a teasing grin. "Maybe she thinks that a good hot supper every night will keep you here where she can keep an eye on you."

Luther shook his head, amusement in his eyes. "You're quite a romantic, aren't you, Fancy?"

"No, I'm not; I just know what I see."

"Hah!" Luther snorted. "You can't see that Chance Dawson can't keep his eyes off you even when he's dancing with another woman."

"You're out of your head! He hasn't been near me since I slapped his face."

"That doesn't mean he wouldn't like to. It was his male pride you hurt, not the face you slapped."

When Fancy made no response Luther remarked, "None of those yahoos in here interest you romantically, do they?"

Fancy shook her head. "I'm afraid not. Anyhow, I'm not here to find a man to become interested in. I took this job to earn enough money to get me to California, where my sister lives. As soon as I've done that, I'll be leaving."

"I'll be sad to see you go," Luther said sincerely. "You're the first lady I've been around in a long time. You don't see many of them in saloons and dance halls. You bring back memories of my youth."

"Thank you, Luther." Fancy patted Luther's hand. "You're the only gentleman I've met since coming to this camp."

The loud clanging of a cowbell interrupted their conversation, signaling that the break was over. Luther gave Fancy a crooked smile, then stood up and made his way toward the piano. Fancy pushed her feet back into her slippers as a bearded logger rushed up and pressed a ticket into her hand. With a resigned sigh, she allowed herself to be led in among the others, who were stomping and hopping to the tune pounded out by Luther.

She lost count of the many partners who shoved and pulled her around the uneven floor, but the small leather pouch strapped around her waist bulged with tickets. When she turned them over to Big Myrt at closing time she would receive a good amount of money in exchange, to be added to the old cracked cookie jar hidden in her small house.

Hours later, as Fancy was whirled around the room by a man whose face she hadn't bothered to look at, she glanced out a grimy window. A sigh of relief feathered through her lips: The eastern sky was turning pink. The cowbell would be rung any minute now, announcing to the loggers that the dancers would be leaving.

She thought of Cousin Lenny, who would be waiting outside to walk her home. He would have their little house nice and warm, and there would be water heated for her in which to soak her aching feet.

Fancy's lips curved in a gentle smile as she thought of the child trapped in a man's body. When Lenny was eight years old he had become ill with a bad case of measles that almost snuffed out his young life. And though he had recovered, his mental growth had been retarded, and his genitals were also affected. Fancy thought the latter was a blessing: If he was always to be a child, it was good that he would never desire a woman.

Now, at twenty-one, he was big and strong, yet very gentle. To look at his handsome face from a distance, one would never know of his handicap. Although fluent, he never spoke of things that would interest an adult. He was more apt to ask someone if he would like to play with him.

Lenny adored Fancy and would fight for her to the death. He was very affectionate, and some of the hugs he gave her when he was caught up in excitement almost broke her ribs.

Fancy remembered with sadness the day Lenny had come to live with her and Big Buck. He was sixteen, but his eight-year-old mind was filled with grief and bewilderment. His mother had run off and left her husband and son when Lenny was four years old, and now the father who had raised him had been crushed to death by a Douglas fir that hadn't fallen in the direction it was supposed to.

Fancy left off her unhappy reflections when,

at last, Big Myrt rang the bell the dancer had been waiting to hear. Freeing herself from her partner, she got in line with the other girls to hand in her tickets.

Big-boned Myrt, with her painted face and red-dyed hair, was rough-spoken and rough-acting, but she was scrupulously honest with her dancers. She never tried to cheat them and didn't allow the loggers to paw them if the women were averse to it. She kept it strictly business between herself and the dancers but she did have her likes and dislikes. She had liked and admired Fancy from the beginning. The young woman minded her own business, was a hard worker, and was dedicated to her simple-minded cousin.

Myrt disliked Pilar intensely. That one was a vicious troublemaker, man hungry and lazy. She intended to get rid of her before winter set in.

Fancy stood in the doorway for a moment before stepping outside, sniffing the odor of sawdust and pine bark drifting up from the mill yard down by the river. She was reminded of her father and her eyes grew moist. She determinedly pushed the memory away and stepped outside. She looked toward the corner of the roughly constructed building and saw the shadowy figure of Lenny waiting for her. Fancy waved to him, and he came forward like a friendly puppy, asking her if her feet hurt as he

25

put an arm across her shoulders.

"They're killing me, Lenny." She said what he wanted to hear. "Do you have warm water waiting for me to soak them in?"

"Oh, sure I do, Fancy," the big man assured her as they turned down the path that led to the small house tucked in among a stand of tall Douglas fir. "And I put salt in the water just like Uncle Buck used to put in his footbath. Remember how he'd always say that it drew the tiredness out of his feet? I sure miss him, Fancy."

Leaning on Lenny's strength as she limped along, Fancy said with a catch in her voice, "I know you do, honey. So do I."

"Don't cry, Fancy," Lenny coaxed anxiously. As though to console her, he added, "I've got a pot of coffee brewed and eggs and bacon laid out ready to fry as soon as we get home."

"You're a good fellow, Lenny Cranson." Fancy smiled up at him.

Lenny's pleased laughter rang out as he and Fancy entered the house and closed the door behind them.

Chance Dawson, on his way to the mill, had paused among the towering pines in the hope of catching a glimpse of Fancy as she left the dance hall. He despised himself for lurking around like a green boy wanting to approach a girl yet not doing it for fear of rejection.

Never before had he been so drawn to a

woman, and he had known many in his thirty years. And he wasn't the only man in camp who practically drooled every time he saw her. Half his crew went around like lovesick puppies. Every time he saw one of his men dancing with Fancy, he wanted to smash the man in the face. He knew the thrill they were experiencing. He had known it too, that one time he had danced with her. Her body had been so soft and supple, molding perfectly with his. She had smelled fresh and clean, with just a trace of rose scent in her hair; not like the heavy, cloying odor of cheap perfume the others wore, trying to cover up the odor of an unwashed body.

Chance realized now that he shouldn't have rushed the new dancer; had he given her time to get to know him, she might be in his house—his bed—right now. But his rashness had been brought on by the unacceptable thought that one of the other men might find favor with her first.

Finally his long wait was rewarded. Fancy stood in the doorway. She stood there for a moment, and in that instant he made up his mind to approach her, to apologize for acting like an ass the first time they had met, to ask her if they could start all over. When Fancy stepped outside he moved forward; then he came to an abrupt halt, a dark scowl coming over his face. A man had emerged from the shadows and was walking hurriedly toward her. The distance was too great for him to hear what was said between them when they came together, but he could clearly see the arm that came around Fancy's shoulders.

"So," he swore under his breath, "she doesn't want to be indebted to a man, does she? It sure as hell looks like she's depending on that one." And who was this man? Chance asked himself as the pair moved away, the man's arm still around Fancy's shoulders. Where did he work? He wasn't one of Chance's crew, and the next camp was nearly twenty miles away down near Puget Sound.

A thought occurred to Chance that made him swear again. Maybe the man didn't work anywhere. Maybe slender, delicate Fancy supported him. There were women who loved their men so much they'd do that for them.

Chance's hands clenched into fists as he watched the pair move off through the trees, Fancy leaning into the man, as he looked down at her, smiling and talking. When he threw back his head and laughed at something Fancy said before they entered her house and closed the door, Chance wheeled around and strode away. He was torn between wanting to put his hands around Fancy's lovely throat and planting his fist in the handsome man's mouth.

An hour after returning home, Fancy lay in bed, her stomach pleasantly filled and her feet aching a little less. She listened to the distant sound of a saw biting its way through a huge pine log. It was a sound she loved, a sound she had grown up with.

Did Mary miss all the racket that went on around a lumber camp? She wondered again why Mary hadn't attended their father's funeral.

Fancy's lids grew heavy and soon she was drifting off to sleep, lulled by Lenny softly singing "My Old Kentucky Home" as he cleaned up the kitchen.

Chapter Two

The morning was crisp and clear, and a sharp wind blew through his jacket as Chance looked down on a logjam in the river. Breaking up logjams was a dangerous business. He had lost his father to such an operation in '53.

He had buried the loved and respected man next to his second wife, who had passed away two years before from pneumonia; then after staying on alone in Placer County for a year, Chance had moved on.

It had been a day like today when he stocked a canoe with enough provisions for a few weeks and headed upriver, looking for a likely timber camp. After a week he had found this spot and sent for his ax men. Timber men, like cattlemen in the early 1800s, paid little attention to who might own the land on which the great trees grew. To those hardy men's way of thinking, whoever got to a place first owned it—or, at least, the timber. They weren't interested in the land.

Winter wasn't far off when Chance's four men arrived, and the first task he gave them was to build a shelter for the crew that would come later: teamsters, choppers, scalers, sawyers, and swampers. It took a week to put up the long building, and though there was nothing attractive about it, it was well built, with tight caulking between the logs and a roof that wouldn't leak.

In the center of the room the men had built a large fireplace that gave off heat in three directions, and above it they had cut a hole in the roof so the smoke could escape. Bunks were built along two walls, and at the end of the long room they had knocked together three rough tables and benches to go with them. Later a grindstone would be placed in a corner. It would get a good workout once the choppers, with their double-bitted axes, began to fell the huge Douglas firs. Across from the emery wheel a water barrel and a bucket would be installed in which the men would wash up in the cold weather.

The day the loggers' quarters were finished, the schooner that plied the river connecting the communities around Puget Sound delivered a load of heavy equipment, and a sawmill was set up. Arriving with the gigantic saw were teams of mules and oxen and Chance's stallion. And some thoughtful person had added a cow to the lot. Many of his crew were married, most of them having children. The mothers would be thankful for the daily milk.

The axes were put to felling more trees, which were dragged by oxen to the sawmill. There the logs were sawed into lumber, one tree yielding enough boards to build a four-room house.

The cookhouse went up first, a building almost as large as the crew's quarters, for there had to be room for the cook's bedroom, not to mention a space for the big cookstove that would arrive with the cook, as well as a worktable and shelves to hold plates, cups, and platters. All the cooking utensils would be hung on the wall next to the stove.

Chance's house went up next. It would be larger than the others that would be springing up among the tall trees for the married men. His place had to have office space where the men could come to express grievances—of which there were always many—settle arguments among themselves, and receive their wages at the end of each month.

Before the men started on the small houses where the men with families would live, another large building was erected. This would be a dance hall, the domain of Big Myrt, a longtime friend of Chance's, and her dancers. This structure would contain Myrt's quarters and a series of small rooms for her girls, who would be arriving shortly after the crew did. The rest of the place would be the dance hall where, for a price, the loggers could be with the young women.

Now, a year later, as Chance let his gaze sweep over his camp, noting the smoke rising from the chimney of each building, he thought of his own cold quarters, where he hadn't bothered to light a fire to ward off the chill. He was seldom in the house except to sleep. With the exception of old Zeb, his cook, and Big Myrt, he had no close friends. He got on well enough with his men during working hours, but other than that he seldom socialized with them. The emptiness of his life hit him. All he did was eat, sleep, and work.

But that wasn't the case with his men: They seemed to live full lives. This was a close-knit camp. Interposed with their hard work they found time to visit each other in the evenings, have gatherings on Sundays when the sawmill was shut down, picnics in the summer and small parties in the winter, when the winds blew out of the north and snow lay a foot deep on the ground.

Although he was never invited to any of their doings, Chance was proud of his men and their families. The wives were decent women, and most were hardworking. Some had found ways of earning extra income for the family. Some washed the bachelors' clothes, Chance being one of the men to avail himself of the aid, while another wife who was handy with needle and thread mended the loggers' shirts and trousers, which were always being torn by brush or the branches of fallen timber.

There was even a new bride among them, who had been a schoolteacher before marrying a scaler. When the men went off to work each morning, leaving their quarters empty, she held classes for the eight school-age children. Her students would be coming along any minute now; the little girls with faces bright and eager would be hurrying, while the boys would be dragging their feet, their faces scowling.

Chance broke off his amused smile to give a wide yawn. He had stayed up late last night, playing cribbage with three loggers who were short of money until payday and couldn't afford the price of dancing with Myrt's girls. Those men who could buy tickets had napped from after supper until midnight, when the hall opened. They would have had sufficient rest then to put in a hard day's labor when the place closed at dawn. It was his habit, also, when he knew he was going to dance a few times with the girls, to take one of them to her room during a rest period.

But he hadn't gone there often lately. He knew with certainty that he should stay away from the place. He doubted if he could stay away from Fancy Cranson even if it meant taking a chance of getting his face slapped again. She entered his mind a dozen times a day, and his nights were filled with dreams of her, dreams that were so erotic, he would awaken with a hard arousal in his hand.

Almost as disturbing as his overwhelming desire was the feeling that Fancy reminded him of someone—a woman he knew, or had known. Maybe a girl from his youth.

"Hey, Chance, how long are you gonna stand there starin' at them logs?" a cracked voice asked from the doorway of the cookhouse. "I can't keep your breakfast hot all day."

Chance turned around and looked at the wizened face of his cook, affection in his eyes. Old Zeb was more than a cook to him. He had been doctor, nurse, adviser, and countless other things over the years. He couldn't remember a time when the ex-sawyer hadn't been a part of his life.

Ten years ago, when the dreaded cry, "Whip the saw!" rang out, everyone knew that a tree trunk was splitting. Men dropped axes and ran. The tree might not fall in the direction in which the sawyers had intended. And that had been the case then. On its way down, the tree had hit another one, and the large trunk had whipped around as though it was a young sapling. When it finally lay still, the earth shuddering beneath it, Zeb lay on the ground, his legs pinned beneath one of the huge branches. When the men rushed forward, three of them lifting the tree limb off Zeb and two dragging him free of it, his left leg had been broken in two places. The nearest doctor was fifty miles away, and Chance's father had set the breaks the best way he could. The leg had mended, but Zeb was left with a decided limp. His days of working timber were over. Seth Dawson had persuaded his longtime friend to become the camp cook.

When Chance walked into the cookhouse, Zeb placed a plate of ham and eggs and fried potatoes on the table before him. "Looks like we're gonna have a nice clear day for a change," he said as he poured coffee into the cup at Chance's elbow.

"About time," Chance answered; then he dug into the plate of steaming food. It had rained off and on for the past three days.

A few minutes later Chance pushed his empty plate away, drank the last of his coffee, and stood up. "I'd better go check on the men down at the river. There was quite a logjam there earlier."

"I expect it's been broken up by now. You've got an experienced crew workin' for you."

Chance mumbled a reply. His attention had been caught by the man who had just walked out of Fancy's house. He recognized the big, handsome fellow with the basket as the same one who had met and walked home with her a week before. His eyes widened in a stare when the man placed the basket on the ground, pulled a wet dress from it, and carefully spread it over a rope that had been stretched between two trees.

As he watched, disbelieving, two more dresses followed, then a pair of men's long-johns. A dark scowl came over Chance's face when delicate ladies' underwear was hung alongside them. As shirts and trousers joined the other articles of clothing, he looked at Zeb, a question in his eyes.

Zeb shrugged his shoulders. "I don't know who he is. All I know is that he came here with that pretty little Fancy girl. Keeps to himself, always stays around the house."

"He doesn't look sick or crippled. I wonder why he hasn't asked me for a job."

"Maybe he's just downright lazy. It don't seem to bother him that a woman is supportin' him. He sure is a handsome feller, ain't he?"

"Well, handsome or not, he's got no pride, that's for sure." Chance snorted his indignation. "You'd think he could see how beat Fancy is when she leaves that dance hall."

Zeb slid Chance an amused look from the corner of his eye. He'd never seen his young friend so riled up over a woman before. He turned his head away from Chance so the irate man wouldn't see the wide grin that tugged at his lips. It appeared that Chance Dawson had finally fallen for a woman—and had fallen hard.

Zeb managed to pull a semblance of sobriety to his face before responding to the muttered remark. "I agree," he said, "it ain't easy bein' a dancer, havin' your toes stepped on, makin' men keep their hands where they belong. But I reckon Fancy loves her man enough to do it. They seem awful fond of each other," he continued, jabbing at Chance. "He waits for her at the dance hall every mornin' and walks her home. They hug and he keeps his arm around her as they walk along, with him talkin' forty to the hour."

"There's no figuring women," Chance said, disgruntled. "She's such a fiery little piece, I'd never in the world think that she would work so hard to support a big, strong, healthy man."

"I guess when the love bug hits a person it makes him do a lot of crazy things," Zeb said, sliding Chance another amused glance.

Chance gave a disgusted snort. "I doubt if love has anything to do with it." He stepped outside and started to walk away, then paused when he saw a horse and rider coming up the trail from the river. The stranger reined in beside the cookhouse and said to Zeb, "I'm lookin' for Chance Dawson."

"I'm Chance Dawson." Chance stepped forward. "What can I do for you?"

"Are you kin to Jason Landers?" the man asked.

Chance nodded, apprehension gripping him. What had Jason done now? he wondered before answering. "He's my stepbrother. Why do you ask?"

"I'm afraid I have some bad news for you."

Chance waited, his body tense.

"Landers and his wife drowned this morning, trying to cross flood waters down by Puget Sound."

The blood left Chance's face and his stomach clenched. He felt Zeb's supporting hand on his upper arm as he choked back the denial that sprang to his lips. It was impossible to believe that Jason's laughing and carefree face was stilled forever in death . . . and Mary, too, with her gentle ways.

He choked back the lump in his throat and managed to say, "They had a young son; is he gone also?"

The stranger shook his head. "He's all right. The way he tells it, the mare he was riding refused to go into the water, which was lucky for him. His ma and pa's mounts were caught in an undertow and were swept downstream. I'm sorry to tell you this, but it's doubtful their bodies will ever be found."

"How'd you know where to find Chance?" Zeb asked.

"One of the loggers in Al Bonner's camp recognized the Landers name and said he thought you were related to him." The man looked at Chance.

Chance pulled himself together and said, "I'll go get my nephew just as soon as I can saddle up."

"You'll find him at Al Bonner's camp, down near Puget Sound. Do you know where it is?"

Chance nodded and struck off running toward the shed where he kept his stallion.

The stranger turned to Zeb and asked, "Do you know where Fancy Cranson lives? The boy said she was his aunt, and that she was living in Dawson Camp."

"Yeah, she lives here." Zeb stared goggle-eyed at the stranger. "You say she's kin to the boy too?"

"Yes. The boy is all broken up about his parents and keeps crying for her."

"Fancy lives right over there in that little house." Zeb pointed to the one with the red curtains.

Chapter Three

Fancy blinked sleepily as she was shaken awake. "What is it, Lenny?" she asked, almost in a cross tone. She was sure she hadn't been sleeping more than half an hour.

"I'm sorry, Fancy," Lenny apologized, "I know you're tired, but there's a man here who says it's very important that he speaks to you."

"Who is he?" Fancy sat up, knuckling the sleep out of her eyes.

"I don't know. He's a stranger. He's waiting for you in the kitchen."

"Lenny," Fancy scolded, "you know you're not to let strangers come into the house."

"I'm sorry, Fancy." Her cousin looked crest-fallen. "I forgot."

"It's all right." She patted his broad shoulder as she slid off the bed and reached for her robe.

"But try to remember the next time."

Fancy tied the belt around her trim waist and walked into the kitchen, wondering what the early caller wanted with her. When the stranger gawked at her sleep-flushed face and tangled curls, she frowned and said crisply, "I'm Fancy Cranson. What do you want to talk to me about?"

The stranger gulped, his adam's apple bobbing as he got out, "I'm right sorry, miss, but I'm afraid I have some bad news for you."

Fancy knew immediately that the the news had to do with Mary. "What has happened to my sister?" she asked in a low, shaky voice as she clutched the back of a chair so tightly that her knuckles turned white.

It was clear that the young man didn't want to relay to Fancy the same news he had blithely given Chance a short time ago. It took him two starts before he got out, "I'm sorry, miss, but she and her husband drowned this morning trying to cross a flooded river."

For a moment, Fancy was sure she was going to faint as everything around her began to spin. "Oh, no!" she cried out brokenly. "Not Mary." She sat down in the chair she had held on to and laid her head on the table. Harsh sobs shook her slender shoulders. The young logger helplessly watched her, crushing his hat between his hands.

Lenny, wringing his hands and crying

44

because Fancy was so upset, searched his mind for ways he could help.

He remembered that his Uncle Buck used to put whiskey in his coffee when he was upset. So he grabbed the coffeepot off the stove, poured some of the still-warm coffee in a cup, and then, before the logger's surprised look, he splashed in a good amount of the whiskey Fancy kept for medicinal purposes.

Lenny placed the cup at her elbow and coaxed gently, "Here's some coffee, Fancy. Drink it, you'll feel better."

Fancy mechanically took the cup and raised it to her lips. Taking a hefty swallow of it, she caught her breath as the whiskey's fiery strength burned its way down her throat. Coughing, she gasped, "Lenny, why didn't you tell me you poured half a bottle of whiskey in this coffee?"

"No, I didn't, Fancy," Lenny denied, pounding her on the back. "I only put a half cup in it. That's how much Uncle Buck used to put in his coffee."

Fancy gave him a wan smile. "I know, honey, but your Uncle Buck was a big man and used to drinking whiskey. Still, I do feel better, and that's what you had in mind."

Fancy found that the alcohol had blunted her shock enough for her to ask about the details of the tragedy and the welfare of her nephew.

When she had been told the same story that

had been relayed to Chance, she thanked the messenger and ushered him to the door. His staring made her nervous, and besides, she must get dressed and hurry to Tod. The poor little fellow would be beside himself with grief. The small Landers family had been very close, and losing his parents must be overwhelming for him.

"Fancy," Lenny said as she started toward her bedroom, "have cousin Mary and Jason gone to heaven like Uncle Buck did?"

"Yes, honey, that's where they are now. But we've still got Tod. He'll be living with us. You'll have company now while I sleep, someone to pass the time with."

Lenny's face lit up and he said excitedly, "Me and Tod will have lots of fun. I'll let him play with my wooden rifle."

Fancy shook her head. How sad it was to hear this big man talking about playing with a toy gun. She had often wondered about God's master plan. What reason did he have for Lenny's simplemindness? And now, why take a little boy's parents away from him?

Fifteen minutes later, when Fancy had hurried into a riding skirt and heavy woolen shirt and had laced up her boots, she called her cousin into her room. He sat down on the edge of the bed and watched her coil her hair into a loose bun at her nape.

"I'll probably be gone most of the day," Fancy

said, glancing at his mirrored reflection. "Make sure you stay in the house until I get back, and don't let anyone in. And be real careful if you cook something to eat."

"What if I have to go to the privy, Fancy?"

"Well, of course you can go there. Just don't linger. Do your business and come straight back to the house. And don't forget to bar the door behind you."

Planting a kiss on Lenny's cheek, Fancy left the house and half ran to the long, low stable building that housed the animals. As she bridled her little mare, then threw a saddle on her back, she noticed that Chance's stallion was gone. Minutes later, she was guiding her little animal into the river at the same spot Chance had used a half an hour earlier.

At the river's deepest spot, the water reached the mare's chest and Fancy automatically kicked her feet free of the stirrups and pulled them up to hook around the back of the saddle as the animal began to swim. In the back of her mind, as though in a fuzzy dream, she could hear the loggers calling back and forth to each other, the ring of an axe, the thunder of a tree hitting the forest floor. None of this really penetrated her brain. Her whole being was wrapped up in grief for her sister.

Mary—sister, friend, and mother—was gone, gone forever. Mary, who at age ten had taken over the care of the three-month-old baby she had named Fancy.

Their parents hadn't wholly approved of the name, but they had promised their firstborn that she could name the expected baby if it was a girl. The story went that Mary had taken one look at the small pink face topped with pale blond hair and exclaimed, "Oh, my, isn't she the fanciest little thing you ever saw!"

She had looked up at her parents' beaming faces then and said solemnly, "Fancy shall be her name." Mother and father had looked at each other with pained expressions, then shrugged their shoulders in surrender.

Sarah Cranson had never completely recovered from the delivery, and that winter, in her weakened condition, she caught pneumonia and passed away in a matter of three days. Consequently, Mary was the only mother Fancy had ever known. And now Fancy would be mother to Mary's son.

It was high noon when Fancy rode into the Bonner mill yard situated on the shores of Puget Sound. She inquired of a young teenager, probably the cook's helper, where she could find the owner of the mill. He directed her to a small, square building, saying that Mr. Bonner was in his office.

Fancy reined the mare in under a large pine and dismounted. As she was looping the reins over a branch, Bonner's office door opened and

Chance stepped outside. "Damn," she muttered. "Just my luck he'd be visiting here today."

She and Chance spotted each other at the same time, and after giving her a hard look, he walked over to her and demanded, "What are you doing here?"

Temper flared inside Fancy. It was none of Chance Dawson's business why she was here. He had no jurisdiction over her movements. She could go where she pleased, when she pleased.

"I could ask you the same thing," she retorted, her voice sharp, her face flushed.

"I have important business here." Chance glared down at her defiant, upturned face. "What about you? Do you have a lover in this camp, too, one that no one knows about?"

Fancy wanted to slap the sneer off his lips as she snapped heatedly, "That is none of your business."

Chance saw the pain in her dark blue eyes and wondered about it. As he was mulling its cause over in his mind, a tall man, somewhere in his mid-fifties, walked up to them.

"Chance," he said, "are you ready to go see your nephew?"

Nephew? Fancy looked startled, and an alarm went off in her brain. Surely Bonner didn't mean Tod. When the two men started walking away, she grabbed the older man's arm. "Are you talking about Tod Landers?"

"Why, yes, I am." Bonner gave her a searching look while Chance frowned impatiently. "Are you Fancy Cranson?"

"Yes, I am. I'm Tod's aunt. I just got the news of my sister and brother-in-law's drowning."

Bonner's lips curved in a relieved smile. "I'm sure glad you're here. The boy is in a bad way. He's been crying for his Aunt Fancy. Come on, I'll take you to him. He's in the house with my wife."

Chance, his body stiff from shock, stared at Fancy, dumbfounded. He had known that Mary had a younger sister, but other than that he knew nothing about her. He now realized whom Fancy reminded him of. He couldn't believe he hadn't seen it before. It must have been Mary's brown hair, he supposed, for otherwise they looked very much alike. They had the same fair skin and even features, the same delicate build and dark blue eyes. But where Mary had been sweet and soft-spoken, Fancy had a fiery nature.

And he mustn't forget the moral differences between the pair, he reminded himself. Where Mary had married the first man she had kissed, only God knew how many men had kissed Fancy's red lips or made love to her lush body.

When Bonner and Fancy disappeared into the house a few yards from the sawmill, Chance shook himself free of his immobilized state and hurried after them. If Fancy Cranson, with her loose morals, thought she was going to take over the rearing of his nephew, he'd soon put that notion out of her head. But as soon as Chance walked into the Bonner living room, he knew it wasn't going to be easy separating young Tod from his aunt. He had arrived in time to see the little fellow give a broken cry and throw himself into Fancy's arms.

Holding him close to her breast, Fancy let the youngster cry, stroking his head all the while. When only an occasional shuddering sob shook his narrow shoulders, she lifted his face and gently kissed his cheek before taking the handkerchief Chance handed her and wiping Tod's eyes and face.

"Would you like to talk about it now?" Fancy asked softly, sitting down in a chair and pulling the boy onto her lap. "It's up to you, honey. Sometimes it helps to talk about what is grieving you."

After a couple of hiccuping moments, Tod nodded. "I think I'd like to talk about it, Aunt Fancy."

"Then go ahead," Fancy said in the same soft tones as she pressed his head down on her shoulder.

"We started out for Grandpa Buck's house the same day Ma received your letter telling us about his accident. Ma cried and cried, and so did Pa and I. We were just about ready to cross over into Washington when the wagon hit a great big rock and busted two of the wheels. Pa didn't have any spare ones with us; wheels cost a lot of money, and the broken ones were beyond repair.

"Pa unhitched the mules and took our supplies and blankets from the wagon and we headed out again, Ma and Pa riding the mules and me on our little mare.

"A couple weeks later, fairly into Washington, we ran out of supplies and Pa didn't have any money to buy more. We lived off the land until we came to a little town where Ma got a job washing dishes in a small restaurant. At the end of the week, when she got paid, we brought provisions and started out again."

Tod gave a ragged sigh before continuing. "We made good time for a week, but then it began to rain. It came down in sheets and we were sure thankful when we came upon an old abandoned shack. We stayed there for four days, waiting for the rain to slacken. When it slowed to a drizzle, we started out again."

Tod paused as though preparing himself to go on with his story. Fancy understood and tightened her arms around him in a comforting way.

"Our spirits were high. Pa was saying that in a couple of days we'd be with you and Lenny. Then"—Tod paused again to choke back a sob—"we came to the river. It was running high and wide from all the rain. Ma suggested we ride along the bank until we found a stretch not so deep. But Pa said it looked safe enough where we were and he rode his mule into the water. Ma's mule followed his.

"But the little mare, Suzie, didn't want to wade into the river, and no matter how hard I thumped her with my heels and yelled threats at her, she wouldn't budge. I looked up to call out that Suzie wouldn't follow them, and at that moment the mules were caught in an undertow that swept them downriver. Pa slid off his mule and fought his way to Ma, and she had just slid into his arms when they were both sucked under the water.

"When they didn't come back up, I started screaming and screaming. Two of Mr. Bonner's men heard me and came running. They yelled that I should ride upstream about half a mile where I could cross safely."

Tears ran down the boy's cheeks again. "Poor Pa," he sobbed, "he was wrong." His tone said that it wasn't the first time his father had made a wrong decision.

In the silence that followed, Chance knelt down in front of Fancy and the emotionally spent boy sitting on her lap. When he stroked a hand over his nephew's blond hair, Fancy said grudgingly, "This is your Uncle Chance, honey."

Tod gazed gravely at Chance. "Pa talked a lot about you. He used to tell me about the things you two did when you were young."

"Do I look so old now?" Chance teased.

"No, I guess not." Tod didn't sound too sure as he studied his uncle's face, then said, "You don't look at all like my Pa."

"That's because we're stepbrothers. We always felt closer than that, though."

"I'm glad you came, Uncle Chance." Tod slid off Fancy's lap and into Chance's welcoming arms.

Chance hugged the small, wiry body, swallowing back the lump that welled up in his throat. "I came as soon as I got the news," he said. "My camp is only about twenty miles from here."

Tod released Chance but kept an arm around his shoulder as Tod asked Fancy, "How did you get here so fast?"

"I live in the same camp as your Uncle Chance." Fancy smiled at him. "I moved there after your grandfather was killed."

"With Lenny?" Tod asked anxiously.

"Of course with Lenny. You don't think I'd go off and leave him, do you?" Fancy playfully tweaked his nose.

"No." Tod grinned. "I know how much you love him. Ma was fond of him too," he added sadly.

A tiny nerve ticked in Chance's jaw. Didn't this family care that Fancy was living with this Lenny person without benefit of marriage? Perhaps they were thankful that she had settled down to one man, that she no longer spread her favors among God knew how many men. Maybe they thought that in time she would marry the handsome, lazy lout.

Tod dropped his arm from around Chance's shoulder and went to lean against Fancy. "Can we get started to your house, Aunt Fancy? I'm pretty tired."

"Of course, honey." Fancy stood up. "We'll leave right now."

Chance jumped to his feet, his brow creased in a frown. His voice was calm, however, when he said, "Tod, would you like to go with Mr. Bonner and let him show you where to water our mounts before we head for my camp?"

"Come on, son," Bonner laid a hand on Tod's shoulder, sensing the tension that had suddenly sprung up between Chance and the beautiful woman.

As soon as the door closed behind Bonner and Tod, Chance stared down at Fancy with eyes as hard as flint. "If you think that innocent kid is going to live with the likes of you, you're as dumb as the oxen that pull the logs through the woods."

Fancy, her eyes sparkling with indignant anger, jumped to her feet. "What do you mean, the likes of me?" she demanded. "What about yourself, drinking and carousing, bringing women home with you? What kind of conduct is that for a child to see? My dancing for a living isn't going to hurt him."

"What about that Lenny you all seem so fond of?" Chance retorted. "What's the boy going to think when he sees you crawl into bed with him every day? Do you think that's good moral teaching for him? And another thing—I have never brought a woman into my house."

"Ha!" Fancy snorted. "Tell that to your oxen. They're dumb enough to believe you. And for your information, I don't sleep with Lenny. He has his bedroom and I have mine."

"With a worn path between the two rooms," Chance said contemptuously.

"I should slap your hateful face for that remark," Fancy ground out, "but I don't want to soil my hands. I'll just consider its source and ignore it."

A smug smile curved her lips. "You know that Tod is expecting to live with me. He'll probably even insist on it. What's more, he needs to be with a female relative right now. With me he can cry over his loss whenever he feels like it and not be embarrassed. With you he would hold it in for fear his big logger uncle would think he was a sissy."

"I would never think that." Chance glared at her. "What about your precious Lenny? Can the boy cry in front of him?" Chance sneered. "That lazy lout is as big as I am."

"Lenny is a very sympathetic person and Tod knows it. Lenny would cry with him. And he's not a lazy lout, you big dumb ox."

"Why hasn't he asked me for a job then? Why does he let you support him?"

"He hasn't asked to hire on with you because I told him not to. And it's none of your business if I support him. Anyway, how did we get on the subject of Lenny's working? We're supposed to be discussing Tod's future."

"As far as I'm concerned, it's settled. He'll be living with me," Chance stated, finality in his words.

"Like hell, he will!" Fire sparked in Fancy's eyes. "He's my sister's son, and I'm going to raise him."

"He's my brother's son, and it's up to me to see to his welfare." They were standing toe to toe now.

"Jason wasn't your blood brother"—Fancy narrowed her eyes at Chance—"so you have no jurisdiction over my nephew."

"All right," Chance said, moving away from her, "so he was my stepbrother. But we were raised together, and I always felt like he was a blood brother. I know he'd want me to raise his son."

As they argued back and forth, both holding fast to their determination, Chance began to worry that Fancy's claim was too valid to ignore. She was, after all, a blood relative, and at such a tender age the boy did need a woman in his life.

But dammit, how could he stand by and

watch the boy being raised by a woman whose morals were those of an alley cat? He walked over to the small window and stared thoughtfully outside. When Fancy made sounds as though she was leaving, he swung around to face her.

"There may be another alternative," he said reluctantly.

"And what is that? Put him in an orphanage?" There was contempt in Fancy's voice.

"No, damn you!" Chance almost shouted. "Let him live with both of us."

Fancy stared at him as though he had lived in the woods too long and had lost touch with reality. "And just how do we do that?" she asked. "Surely you aren't suggesting that we get married."

"Hah! Not in your lifetime, lady. I'd never be interested in another man's leavings."

"I suppose that every time you take one of the dancers to bed, she's a virgin."

"I wasn't talking about marriage, and you know it. My thought is that we move into my house, since it's much larger than yours. We'll all live together."

"And how many bedrooms does it have?" Fancy gave him a cool, cynical smile.

"It only has two, but with you working nights and me working days, we could use the same bedroom and Tod could have the other one."

"Tod and Lenny, you mean." Fancy's eyes dared him to say no.

She wasn't surprised when he snarled, "Like hell I'll have him living in my house, the two of you carrying on when I'm not around."

"We do not carry on, as you put it," Fancy snarled, her fists on her hips. "Lenny is—"

"Aunt Fancy," Tod called from outside, stopping Fancy in mid-sentence, "are you about ready to get started?"

The question of Lenny was left hanging as Fancy turned and walked outside, Chance following her.

A pretty young woman with sad eyes, about half Bonner's age, stood with him and Tod beside the waiting mounts. "This is Clare," Bonner said, proudly introducing the woman. "My wife."

Fancy smiled at the wife, wondering why she had married a man so much older than herself. There were so many young men around to choose from. Then Bonner was boosting her into the saddle, and she thought no more about it. She had more important things to think about.

Chapter Four

As Chance, Fancy and Tod left the muddy banks of Puget Sound and began climbing up the mountain, riding single file on the narrow trail, Chance's thoughts were on the father of the youngster riding behind him.

He recalled the day, a week after his seventh birthday, when his father brought home a new wife, along with her son. Jason was a friendly little boy, two years older than himself, anxious to be made welcome and to be friends with his new stepbrother. Unlike Chance, Jason was fine-boned and at least two inches shorter than his stepbrother. Even then Chance had known that he must look after the new addition to his home.

He had done so as the years passed, fighting Jason's battles first with small fists, then large ones as they became teenagers and grown men.

Jason had always been a dreamer. Unlike Chance, he had never been interested in the rough life of a logger. Growing up, he had always talked of going to San Francisco, where he would make his fortune. Chance had never been able to pin him down as to how he planned on accomplishing this. He learned later that Jason had no idea how his wealth was to be made.

When Jason was in his mid-twenties, their father sent Jason on an errand to a logging camp at Tumwater. After a three-week absence, with no word from Jason in the meantime, the whimsical young man finally returned. But not alone. He brought with him a wife—pretty little Mary Cranson.

Mary adored her husband, and when he said that he wanted to move to San Francisco, she readily agreed. Chance remembered clearly the morning they boarded a steamer that would take them to that fast-growing city. Mary's teeth had chattered from the cold wind blowing off the Sound, but there was a happy glow on her face as she clung to her husband's arm. And Jason could hardly contain his impatience to get aboard and start the big adventure that was to bring him great wealth. Just before the new husband and wife stepped upon the gangplank, Tom Dawson pressed a roll of money into his stepson's hand and wished him and Mary the best.

Ten months went by without a word from the newlyweds. Nan was worried sick, her imagination running wild. Jason and Mary had been attacked by Indians, they had been killed by robbers, for wasn't San Francisco overrun by riff-raff and cutthroats? Finally, to ease his stepmother's mind, Chance decided he'd go to San Francisco and look for the pair.

The day before he was to leave, a letter arrived from Jason. He wrote that he and Mary had a two-week-old son named Tod. He went on to write that he had finally found a good job clerking in a mercantile. He ended the short letter writing that the three of them were in good health and promising to write more often. As Nan folded the letter back in its envelope, he and his father looked at each other, their expression saying that they were wondering how many previous jobs Jason had grown tired of.

Later it was proven that their suspicions were correct. Nan answered her son's letter, sending it to the business address he had given. Two weeks later it was returned with the message that Jason Landers no longer worked there. Nan sighed and shook her head sadly.

Over the years they had heard from Jason sporadically, always asking for a loan of money, and always from a new place of employment.

Poor, weak Jason, Chance thought as his stallion followed the trail that wound among the pines, he had never found the riches he had dreamed of. He hoped that young Tod had inherited his mother's character, that he had some of the fight in him that his Aunt Fancy possessed.

And thinking of Fancy and her fiery temper, Chance dreaded the fight that lay ahead when they arrived at camp. She hadn't said yes or no to his suggestion that they all share his house. He knew that she was against it, for he had told her that he was not going to allow her lazy lout of a lover to live in his house. If she wanted to continue carrying on with the man, it would have to be somewhere else.

With an irritated jerk of his shoulders, Chance pushed away the unwelcome thought of Fancy and her lover in bed together and tried to ignore the sharp jab to his midsection. He angrily told himself that it was nothing to him who the little slut slept with.

His unpleasant thoughts were interrupted by the ringing sound of an axe biting into wood and the shouts of a driver urging oxen along a skid road leading to the White River, which flowed into the Duwamish near Seattle. The logs would be skidded into the water there, and when they reached Puget Sound they would be hoisted onto barges and shipped to San Francisco. Camp was just a short distance away.

When shortly the three of them rode into the clearing among the pines, Fancy grimaced as she heard the laughter of camp wives and bits of sentences. They all shunned her, as they did the other dancers. It wasn't fair, but she really couldn't blame them. The other dancers weren't all they should be. Actually the majority of them were no more than whores, and she couldn't really blame the wives for assuming she was just like the rest. And the men in camp probably thought the same. Certainly Chance Dawson did.

And strangely, that hurt. She couldn't explain why it hadn't angered her when the other loggers propositioned her, yet when Chance offered her something more than a quick tumble in bed she had become incensed. Had it been his arrogance in taking it for granted that she would jump at the chance to live with him until he tired of her? She refused to believe that his good opinion was important to her.

Fancy sighed softly. She did miss the companionship of females though. All the women in the Tumwater camp had liked and respected Buck Cranson's daughter. She was used to running in and out of their homes, having them drop in on her. In this camp, with the exception of Molly Jackson, the young wife who taught the children, the women just looked right through her. Molly smiled when they passed each other, but she was always in the company of other wives, who hurried her along as though she would be contaminated if she stopped to chat.

Fancy dismissed her neighbors from her mind when they came to the path leading off to her house. "Turn here, Tod," she said. "That's your new home straight ahead."

"Now just a damned minute." Chance wheeled his stallion to block Tod's mount. "I thought it was understood that we were all going to live in my larger house."

"Maybe that's the way you understood it, but I didn't." Fancy kneed her mount around her nephew's so that she faced Chance. "So just move out of our way and let us get home. I'm sure Tod is hungry and tired. I know that I am."

Keeping a tight rein on the stallion, he ground out, "Look, let's not go through that again. My nephew is going to be raised in a decent home. I'll not have him see—"

"See what?" Fancy's eyes sparked blue fire.

"Tod is going to need a man's guidance as he grows up," Chance said, ignoring her question, "not the mollycoddling he'd get from you. What could you teach him? How to dance?"

"I could teach him how to be a decent human being," Fancy shot back. "That's more than you could do."

Their voices had grown louder, and it took a second for the broken little cry to penetrate the angry words Fancy and Chance were hurling at each other. They turned their heads to look at Tod, to see that tears were running down his cheeks.

"Please don't yell at each other," he sobbed, knuckling his wet eyes with grubby little fists.

"Oh, honey, I'm sorry." Fancy nudged her mare closer to the boy's so that she could lean over and put her arms around his narrow, shaking shoulders.

"I love you both, Aunt Fancy. Why can't we all live together?" Tod looked at her with large, bewildered eyes. "We could be a family."

Fancy gazed at her sister's child, the fire dying out of her eyes as she realized what the little boy wanted—and needed. A family again, a mother and father figure. Her shoulders sagged in defeat. For his sake it looked as if they must live with the smug-looking man, for a while at least. The length of time depended on how well she could get along with the arrogant beast.

She gave Chance a bitter look and said, "I'll go get Lenny and meet you at your house."

"Hold on now." Chance grabbed the mare's bridle when Fancy would have moved out. "I meant what I said about him. I'll not have your—have him living under my roof."

"But why not, Uncle Chance?" Tod looked puzzled. "Lenny is real nice. He's no bother at all, is he, Aunt Fancy?"

Chance looked helplessly at the small tear-stained face gazing up at him so earnestly. How was he to explain to this innocent child that he couldn't allow his aunt to carry on her licentious affair with this Lenny person?

While he was searching for the right words, trying to ignore the satisfied look on Fancy's face, her door flew open and an excited voice called out, "Toddie! I've been waiting all day for you to get here."

As Tod scrambled off his mount, Chance watched Fancy's lover lope toward them, a wooden rifle in his hand. His eyes narrowed when his nephew threw his arms around the big man's waist and hugged him. He decided on the spot that he didn't want this lover of Fancy's in his camp. Tod was much too fond of him. The boy hadn't greeted him, his uncle, with that much enthusiasm.

As Chance looked on, Lenny handed the toy gun to Tod, saying excitedly, "You can play with it all you want today, Toddie, then tomorrow we'll share it."

"Thank you, Lenny." Tod's small hand stroked over the smooth pine barrel. "We'll have lots of fun, just like we used to." He hugged Lenny again.

"I knew he'd be glad to see me, Fancy," Lenny said, treating her to a wide, boyish smile.

"You were right, honey." Fancy leaned over and ran an affectionate hand over his dark hair. Chance's face wore a mixture of surprise and chagrin when she straightened up and looked at him, her lips twisted in silent laughter. "Meet my cousin Lenny, age eight," she said in a low, cool voice that Lenny couldn't hear.

"You little bitch," Chance grated out. "You deliberately didn't explain about your cousin. You looked forward to letting me make an ass of myself, didn't you?"

"Let that be a lesson to you, Mr. Know-It-All." She let him see the amusement in her eyes as she reined the mare around and headed her toward his house. "Don't be so fast to jump to conclusions from now on."

Chance stared after the slender, straight back, the proudly lifted chin, and let loose a string of swear words that made Tod and Lenny gape at him.

When Fancy stepped through the back door of her quarters, she could only stand and stare. She guessed this was supposed to be the kitchen, but the room was completely bare. There was no cookstove, no table or chairs. She walked across the floor to a row of cupboards, and each door she opened revealed only empty shelves.

She went through the entire house then, Lenny and Tod's footsteps ringing hollowly as they followed at her heels. Only one room held any furniture—a bed, a dresser, a wardrobe, and a night stand. A kerosene lamp stood on the small table, its chimney smoked black. The bed covers had been carelessly smoothed over the mattress, the sides hanging uneven.

"There's no furniture in this house, Fancy," Lenny said, pointing out the obvious.

"Where are we supposed to sleep?" Tod asked. "I didn't see a stove in the kitchen and I'm starved."

"I know you are, honey. So am I." Fancy hugged his shoulders. "I bet Lenny has a big pot of stew waiting for us at our little house." She smiled at Lenny, and he nodded his head eagerly.

"It's been cooking real slow all afternoon, just the way you showed me."

"Good. Come on, fellows, let's get out of here and go eat."

Chance was sitting on a tree stump when the three stepped outside, a look of waiting on his face—waiting for Fancy to explode. Ten minutes ago it had hit him that his house wasn't set up for housekeeping. He had been so intent on making sure his nephew lived under his roof that everything else had escaped his mind.

"Look," he said, standing up when Fancy came stamping toward him, "I know the house is empty, but until we get your furniture moved in you can have the bed and the boys and I will sleep on the floor in bedrolls. And we can eat supper in the cookhouse. Zeb's a fair cook. We won't go hungry."

Fancy wasn't surprised at Chance's suggestion. If the circumstances were different, if they were on amicable terms, it would be the perfect solution. But they were far from being that, and not so much as a frying pan of hers was going into his house. She had no intention of staying for more than a month, and she'd have a devil of a time getting it back when she was ready to leave.

"You're out of your mind if you think anything of mine is going in there." She jerked a thumb toward the biggest house in camp. "A hundred yards from here are two comfortable beds and a big pot of stew waiting to be eaten. The fellows and I will be there until you get what's needed in that empty barn."

"Just don't settle in too cozy," Chance snapped, giving in because he knew the little spitfire was right. "I'll take a steamer down to Seattle tomorrow and bring back what's needed."

"Good." Fancy pushed the wide-eyed Tod and Lenny onto the path that led to her place. "After we've eaten, I'll make out a list of things for you to buy."

Before she followed her cousin and nephew, she added with a thin smile, "I hope you can afford all that's needed to make a comfortable home for your nephew."

"Don't worry about that, Miss Priss." Chance glared down at her. "Just make out your damn list."

Fancy looked at Chance through lowered lashes. He looked calm and in control, but she knew that inside he was furious with her. She couldn't resist giving him one last jab. Lifting

71

her blue gaze to him, she said with sham thoughtfulness, "I think maybe I should go with you. You'd probably think that half the articles I want are unneccessary." Before he could fire back a cutting remark, she wheeled and walked away, amusement lifting the corners of her mouth.

Chance watched her go, wanting to follow her, to grab her and shake the smirking smile off her face. But before she entered the house and closed the door behind her, his thoughts had taken a different turn. He wished instead that he could draw her into his arms and kiss the mocking lips, appease a portion of the hunger she aroused in him.

He stamped off toward the cookhouse, frustration chewing at him. To feel those red lips crushed beneath his wouldn't be nearly enough. Only complete possession of that soft, slender body would bring the relief his aching loins cried out for. He feared he'd made the biggest mistake of his life, insisting they live under the same roof. He would probably go around with a perpetual arousal pressing against the buttons of his fly.

He shoved a hand into his pocket before entering Zeb's domain. That sharp-eyed old coot never missed a thing.

"Zeb," he said, entering the kitchen and sitting down at the long table, "did you know that this Lenny living with Fancy is . . . not very ma-ture, that mentally he's around my nephew's age?"

"I've suspected somethin' was strange there. Fancy keeps a close eye on him all the time. I thought maybe he was hidin' from the law. I just now found out different." He shook his head. "It's a shame a nice young woman like her has to be burdened with the chore of lookin' after him. It costs a lot to feed and clothe such a big feller."

"I'm sure she'll earn enough to do it," Chance remarked sourly.

"I don't know." Zeb scratched his whiskered chin. "A woman don't make much money dancin' with them big-footed loggers. I have a feelin' Fancy has a hard time makin' ends meet sometimes."

"She has other ways of making money," Chance said with a curl of his lips.

"I know what you're sayin', but I think you're dead wrong. I ain't seen no men 'round her house."

"That doesn't mean anything. She could always take one into a room back of the dance hall."

"I'd know about it if she did. The men like to brag about the women they take to bed. If one of them was lucky enough to get Fancy, he'd trip over his tongue tellin' about it."

"Well, don't be surprised when some of the

loggers from Tumwater start showing up, knocking on her door."

"What was she and your nephew and her cousin doin' over at your house? They didn't stay very long."

Chance could have resented Zeb's questioning him about something that was none of the old man's business. But the cook had been a part of his life for so long that he seemed like family, and Chance answered him as he would his father.

"She was looking the house over to see what it needs in the line of furniture. I never brought anything in but my bedroom stuff. For my nephew's sake, we'll be living in my house when I get it set up."

With a frown, Chance added, "I've got to waste a whole day tomorrow taking her to Seattle to pick out what she thinks she needs to fix up the place."

Although Chance sounded annoyed, Zeb felt that actually his friend and boss was looking forward to a day spent with the little beauty.

He kept his suspicions to himself, and in the silence that developed Chance rose and left him, walking toward the river.

Chapter Five

Fancy lay on her side, watching the red ball of the morning sun slowly rise and shine through the tall Douglas firs. Wood smoke from Zeb's cookstove wafted through her open window, mingling with the delicious odor of frying bacon. The loggers would be leaving their quarters soon, crowding around the long table in the cookshack, wolfing down whatever the cook put before them.

Her eyelids felt heavy. She hadn't slept well last night. She had barely drifted off to sleep when Tod left Lenny's bed and crept in beside her. The poor little fellow was missing his parents, she knew, as she pulled his small body into her arms and pressed his head down on her shoulder. He had clung to her all night, making it impossible to get into a sound sleep. And in between the short naps there would creep into her mind thoughts of the trip to Seattle with Chance.

A whole day spent with Mr. Better Than Thou would be a nerve-racking time, she told herself now. She didn't know how much of his sarcasm and insults she could take before slapping his hateful face. She refused to remember how every pulse in her body became throbbingly aware of him every time he came near her and how she felt a fluttering in the pit of her stomach.

Putting Chance Dawson firmly from her mind, Fancy carefully untangled herself from her sleeping nephew and slid out of bed, her feet fumbling for her slippers. Then, slipping on a robe that had seen many better days, she moved quietly through the house and into the kitchen. She wanted to make out a list of what was needed in the empty house before the boys got up and started their endless chatter. She brewed a pot of coffee, then sat down at the table with paper and pencil in front of her and a steaming cup of coffee at her elbow.

Furniture for all the rooms, including a kitchen range, was jotted down first. Linens, dishes, flatware and cooking pots came next. The list was long by the time she added all the food staples that were needed. As she sat back, stretching her cramped fingers, the sun had fully risen. The boys were beginning to stir, and she could hear the loggers approaching the cookshack.

As she folded the sheet of paper and slipped it into her pocket, a devilish smile glittered in her eyes. Chance Dawson was going to howl like a wolf when it came time to reach into his pocket and pay the high price it took to make a comfortable home for his nephew. He'd be sorry he had insisted on helping to raise Tod.

She had biscuits baking in the oven and was frying thick slices of ham when Lenny came into the kitchen, his hair tousled and a wide smile of greeting on his face. Fancy returned his smile and said, "Good morning, honey, did you sleep well last night?"

"I slept real good, Fancy," Lenny answered as she poured warm water into a basin for him to wash up in. He looked at her anxiously then. "I hope I didn't crowd Toddie. I see he's sleeping in your bed this morning."

"You didn't crowd him, Lenny," Fancy assured him as she handed him a towel to dry his dripping face on. "Tod was missing his parents and needed comforting."

Lenny nodded in understanding. "I felt that way when Uncle Buck died." As he stood in front of the small mirror fastened on the wall, raking a comb through his hair, he asked, "How come I didn't get to sleep with you then?"

"Because you're a big fellow. Tod is just a little boy." Her cousin's pleased smile told Fancy she had given him the right answer.

Tod came into the kitchen then, a smile on his face, his spirits having risen with the sun. When he had washed his face and combed his hair Fancy put hot biscuits, crisp ham, and fried eggs on the table. She waited until the boys had eaten before she told them her plans for the day.

"Tod, your Uncle Chance and I are going to take a steamer down to Seattle to buy furniture and other things we'll need for his house. The two of you will be alone all day." She reached across the table to lightly grip Lenny's hand as she said, "Lenny stays alone quite a bit and knows the rules I've set down. You must do as he says, Tod. That means staying in the house until I return. There are a lot of wild animals moving about in the woods. It's not unusual for bears to come right into camp."

"We can go to the privy, Toddie," Lenny told him solemnly. "But we musn't linger, right, Fancy?" Fancy nodded. "We just do our business and get right back to the house, right, Fancy?"

Fancy nodded again, hiding a little smile. Lenny took seriously everything she told him.

Chance was roused from sleep by the sound of the loggers' loud voices as they tramped into the cookshack. He gave a low groan. As had happened every morning for close to a month now, he awakened hard and needing.

He sat up in bed, swearing under his breath. He was going to put an end to this tonight. He would go to the dance hall, buy a fistful of tickets, and take Pilar to her room. And not only tonight, he was going to do it every time the mood struck him. He didn't give a damn how much that little blue-eyed witch curled her lip when she saw him lead the Mexican off the dance floor.

By God, a man had his needs.

His mood was surly when he entered the cookshack half an hour later, having waited until the crew had eaten and departed. Zeb looked at his frowning face and speculated silently that Chance could have used a woman this morning before leaving his bed.

"How do you want your eggs?" He brought a bowl of them over to the stove.

"I don't care," Chance grunted, taking up a biscuit and spreading butter on it.

"How's your nephew this mornin'?" Zeb cracked three eggs into the skillet of hot bacon grease. "I guess the little feller is still broken up over his parents."

"I imagine he is, but I haven't seen him since Miss High And Mighty whisked him away to her house. I'll go over there as soon as I finish eating breakfast. I expect Her Highness will be waiting with a list as long as my arm."

"You know how women are. They want things to be real nice."

Chance made no response as he picked up his fork and jabbed at the center of one of the eggs Jeb had placed in front of him. It still griped him that Fancy refused to move her furniture into his house. Her insistence on keeping it, as well as the house, didn't look as if she intended staying under his roof very long. He wondered what she had in her devious little mind.

"Good morning, Zeb," called a friendly voice from the doorway. Both men looked up; Zeb's face creased in a wide smile, but Chance looked at Fancy through narrowed eyes.

"My, my, you put a rose to shame this mornin', Fancy." Zeb stood up and pulled a chair out from the table. "Sit down and have a cup of coffee with us. I know you've had breakfast. I smelled your ham fryin'."

Fancy looked at Chance, her eyes carefully blank as she asked, "Do we have time?"

Chance nodded at Zeb. "Go ahead and pour her a cup."

The sun, shining through the window, bathed Fancy in a golden glow, striking lights off her pale hair. As she sipped her coffee, Chance stole glances at her from the corners of his eyes, thinking that the old man was right. Her beauty did put a flower to shame.

"So, you're gonna spend some of Chance's money in Seattle today, are you?" Zeb asked, returning the coffee pot to the stove.

Fancy grinned. "I sure am." She patted the

small silk bag she had removed from her wrist and placed on the table. "I have a long list in here."

"You plan on fancyin' up the place, I take it." Mischief sparkled in Zeb's eyes.

Fancy caught the sly glance the old man shot at Chance, and she joined in the fun. "When I'm finished with that empty barn, it will be equal to any place on Nob Hill in San Francisco."

"Boy, Chance," Zeb said in mock seriousness, "she's gonna empty your pockets in Seattle today."

Chance muttered some incoherent word, and Fancy and Zeb winked at each other. They were getting to him. Then Chance looked up and caught them.

"You two are certainly in high spirits this morning," he growled, and standing up, he walked toward the door. He paused there to say to Fancy, "Meet me down at the river in five minutes."

"Yes, sir." Fancy saluted him smartly. With a muttered curse, Chance struck off toward her house.

"I've seen him in better moods." Zeb grinned, watching the angry strides Chance was taking.

"Well, I never have," Fancy said in a sour voice. "It's always snap and snarl where I'm concerned."

"You must have riled him sometime or other. Chance is right partial to pretty wimmen."

81

Amusement flickered in Fancy's eyes. "I must have," she said, remembering how she had vexed the handsome logger the first and only time she had danced with him. She had ruffled the rooster's feathers by refusing to be his private whore.

She finished her coffee and rose to her feet. "I'd better get down to the river. It would be just like him to go off and leave me. I'd hate to leave it up to him to purchase what he thinks it takes to furnish a home."

Zeb watched her walk down the path leading to the river, thinking to himself that Chance was going to find it hard to get his way with that little lady.

His gaze narrowed when Big Myrt stepped out of her quarters back of the dance hall and called out to Fancy. Now what did that old ex-whore want to jaw at the girl for? Surely she wouldn't yell at Fancy for failing to work last night. A woman couldn't go dancing the day her sister died.

Fancy also wondered what Myrt wanted. "I'm sorry about your sister, Fancy," Myrt said kindly.

Fancy was too surprised to respond. When Myrt went on to say that if she needed to take a few days off from work it was all right with her, Fancy finally found her tongue.

"I'd appreciate one more night off. I expect you know that Chance and I have a nephew in common. He and I are going to Seattle today to purchase furniture for his house." Fancy paused, looked down at the ground, then back up at Myrt. "Because his house is bigger than mine, we'll all be living in it. Everyone's tongue will be wagging about this time tomorrow."

"Let them wag, Fancy," Myrt said, an old resentment in her voice. "It will last for maybe a week, then something else will happen that will give them new fodder to chew on. I've put up with vicious tongues for half my life. After a while you develop a hard shell that people's words can't penetrate."

"I expect so. It's just that I'm not used to it."

Chance was approaching them from the direction of Fancy's house and they said goodbye. Fancy watched Myrt disappear into her quarters, knowing that she had a friend in the big woman, but knowing also that outwardly nothing would seem changed between them. There was too much jealousy among the dancers for the dance hall owner to show favoritism to one.

"Was that old bat chewing you out for not dancing last night?" Chance demanded, his tone cold and threatening. "What did she say to you?"

"She was very nice. She extended her condolences about Mary and said that I should take as many nights off as I need."

"You're damn right you can. You don't need

to work for her anymore."

"I certainly do," Fancy flared, turning stormy eyes on him. "Nothing has changed just because I'll be living under your roof. I'll not be dependent on any man unless he's my husband."

"You're not likely to get one with that sharp tongue of yours, so prepare yourself to work for a long time." Before Fancy could make a sharp retort, he said, "Come on, let's get going."

Fancy fell in behind him, thankful that she had worn her dark blue woolen dress and a lighter blue shawl wrapped around her shoulders. Autumn was approaching, and she knew it would be quite chilly out on the water.

When they reached the river, Fancy sat down on a tree stump while they waited for the vessel that would take them to Puget Sound. She passed the time watching the booms of logs that jostled down the Columbia to the whining mills.

This has to be the most beautiful country in the world, she thought, looking east to the Cascade Mountains, then west to the Olympias, then dropping her gaze to the green rolling hills. She caught sight of an old Indian woman digging clams out of the sand. She wondered what tribe she was from. There were two tribes inhabiting the area—the Chinooks and the Haidahs. She thought the elderly woman might be a Haidah from the shape of her broad face. Neither tribe was friendly toward the whites.

A lumber schooner was making its way up the

river when Chance spoke behind Fancy. "Come on, let's get down to the shore and be ready to board. The captain doesn't like to be kept waiting."

Fancy gave the long lumber boat making its slow way toward shore a skeptical look. Its cabin looked so dilapidated that she was half tempted not to board it. Then she saw a black-and-white cat sitting in a sunny spot, calmly grooming itself. Surely it wouldn't be so contented if the vessel was unsafe.

Chance was striding ahead of her, and when the schooner edged alongside the shore he jumped up on it. When he went directly to the pilot and stayed there, ignoring Fancy standing on the bank, she knew he wasn't going to help her board. She stood there, fuming inside. There was no way she could leap up on the log carrier in her full-skirted dress.

She was almost in tears when from behind her a male voice asked, "May I assist you onto this big beauty, miss?" She swung around and gazed into the sparkling eyes of a handsome, swarthy-faced stranger. "Your companion seems to have forgotten you." Even teeth flashed in a white smile.

"It appears the boor has." Fancy returned his smile. "I would appreciate it very much if you would give me a hand."

"My pleasure, miss." The dark-haired man stepped forward and, placing his hands on her waist, lifted her up and stood her on the deck.

Fancy gave a breathless little laugh, and with twinkling eyes she said gaily, "Thank you very much, kind sir."

Chance turned his head at the sound of Fancy's laughter and scowled at the man gazing up at her. Chance started to step forward, then stopped himself. It was his fault that she had needed the stranger's help. He had intended to help her after a while. He only meant to make her wait a minute, take some starch out of her. He should have known that some man would come along to aid her. There would always be a man anxious to get his hands on her.

To his relief, the schooner began to move and Fancy's new admirer stepped back from the shore. When she took a seat near the black-and-white cat, she lifted a hand to the stranger and waved to him, calling, "Thank you again."

"You're more than welcome," he answered, walking alongside the schooner. "I'd like to help you again. Do you go downriver very often?"

"I'm afraid not," Fancy called loudly as the vessel pulled out into the middle of the river, leaving the handsome stranger looking after them.

"Do you know who that man is?" Chance asked the captain as they got underway.

"I know him to see him. He's been working for Al Bonner. He's a scaler, I think."

No more was said between them. The captain

had to be careful to keep out of eddies and avoid drifts floating down the river.

Fancy spent the time watching the scenery slide by as the schooner moved slowly along. She gazed at the towering Douglas firs, so big it took twenty mules to drag some of them to the sawmill. Several times she saw deer standing in patches of fern so tall that the animals were almost hidden in the lush foliage as they stared curiously at the schooner. Once they passed a bear at the river's edge, his great paw dipping into the water to scoop up a fish.

With the exception of one old Indian who lifted his hand in greeting to them, she saw no other sign of human beings. It was claimed that there were only four thousand whites in Washington Territory. She supposed it wasn't surprising that she saw none in the pine wilderness.

In a short time the schooner was nosing its way into the muddy shore of Puget Sound, where a few wooden houses and a hotel stood. Fancy wondered if there would be anyone around who would help her disembark, when Chance jumped ashore and held up his arms to help her down. Surprised, she leaned toward him, not knowing that he had caught sight of three men and a woman coming toward them and knew that each one of the men would be more than willing to help her ashore.

Chance started to swing her to the ground,

then noted the ankle-deep mud he stood in. He paused a split second; then, his hands still gripping her waist, he carried her over to the wooden walkway and set her on her feet. Before she could thank him, he was hailed by one of the men.

"Hiya, Dawson." Al Bonner walked up to them. He nodded a greeting to Fancy, then asked, "How's young Tod coming along?"

"He's doing about as well as you'd expect, considering everything," Chance answered. As he and Bonner switched their conversation to timber, Fancy took a close look at Clara Bonner. She had been too upset yesterday to pay much attention to anyone. The young wife would be exceptionally pretty if she didn't wear that pouty look and took more pride in her appearance. Her brown, shoulder-length hair was lank and oily, and her dress was wrinkled as though it had never felt the heat of a hot iron. There were food stains on the front of her bodice and sweat stains under her armpits.

Why had she married a man twice her age? Fancy wondered. Women were scarce here in the northwest and there were any number of young men she could have chosen as a husband. Fancy opened her mouth to speak to the unhappy-looking woman, but without a word Clare Bonner turned around and walked away from them.

She's as unsociable as that lot back at camp,

Fancy thought as she tried to ignore the two
men accompanying Bonner, who were openly
ogling her. But since there was no place she
could go to escape their hungry eyes, she stood
where Chance had put her and watched a small
steamer approaching the Sound. When it came
on in and chugged up to the shore, Chance
stopped talking to Bonner and walked over to
stand beside her.

When a narrow wooden ramp was let down,
Chance helped her to step up on it and kept his
hand on the small of her back as she climbed
the steep ramp, not removing it until the crusty
old captain helped her step onto the schooner.
Chance stepped up beside her and, taking her
arm, led her to a group of women and children
sitting on bales of hay. The older women spoke
to Chance with friendly warmth while the teen-
age girls blushed and gave him shy smiles.

Does he know everybody in Washington Territory? Fancy wondered as Chance said, "Good
morning, ladies, can you make a spot for this
young lady to sit down?"

"We sure can," a buxom woman of middle age
spoke up, nudging a young boy of around ten
to move over. Without any introductions,
Chance turned and walked away.

Fancy returned the curious, friendly stares
directed at her, thinking how fresh and bright
they all looked. She thought that they were farm
women, strong and healthy from the active life

they led, although it might be an arduous one. She knew that as the loggers cleared the forest, farmers moved in, working from dawn to dusk, clearing the land of brush and tree stumps before plowing and seeding.

She left off her scrutiny of her companions when a little girl exclaimed, "Look, Mama, there's that strange woman we see in the woods sometimes."

"Shhh, don't point," the little girl was told as the women turned their heads to look in the direction the child had pointed.

Fancy looked also and was surprised to see that it was Clare Bonner who had drawn their attention. "In what way is she strange?" she asked the woman who had made room for her to sit down.

"I don't know if strange is the right word to describe her. I would say unfriendly, like she was mad at the world. She spends most of her time wandering around in the woods—in the daytime that is. No one goes there after dark.

"I feel right sorry for her. Her pa made her marry Bonner to settle a debt he owed him. I must say, though, Bonner is awfully good to her—crazy about her, in fact."

So, Fancy thought, that explains a lot about Clare Bonner's behavior.

"Are you ladies going into Seattle to shop?" she asked when Clare had disappeared into her house and the steamer moved out into the middle of the river.

From then on until they landed in Seattle, the women were like a bunch of magpies. They gave their names and explained that they were going to Seattle to sell their garden produce. They also told Fancy that they supplied Chance's cook with eggs, butter, bacon, ham, and fresh meat at the butchering time, which would be arriving soon what with cooler weather setting in.

"Do you ever have any extra milk?" Fancy asked, thinking of Tod. Heads were eagerly nodded, and she made arrangements to have a gallon delivered at camp every other day.

The steamer was suddenly pulling in to shore, and everyone stood up. Good-byes were being said and invitations issued when Chance appeared beside Fancy. His voice was curt as he said, "Come on, let's go," but he had a warm smile for the farm women.

Chance pointed over Fancy's shoulder and said, "Down at the end of the street you'll find Stevens's household emporium, and across the street from it is Johnson's mercantile. You should find everything you need between the two stores." He stressed the word need. "I'll meet you back here at three o'clock sharp."

He walked on then and was halfway down the muddy street when Fancy called after him, "You forgot to give me some money."

Without breaking his stride, Chance called

back, "Tell the shopkeepers to put everything on my tab."

Fancy walked into Stevens's emporium and sniffed the scent of new wood, paint and varnish. Her eyes widened at the sight of rows and rows of furniture in the long room. She spent over two hours walking down the narrow aisles looking at dressers, chests, wardrobes, kitchen tables, small tables, chairs of all kinds, china cabinets, and sofas. Everything was plain but well made.

With each room in mind, Fancy started her selections. The young clerk followed her about, his eyes growing wider and wider as her order grew larger and larger. Finally he excused himself to go have a word with his boss.

Fancy smiled to herself as Mr. Stevens approached, a polite but uneasy look on his face. "Are you a newlywed furnishing your new home, young lady?" he asked, shooting a fast glance at her left hand.

Fancy looked at him and smiled, then deliberately avoided answering his question. "You would think so, wouldn't you."

"Yes . . . well, you've chosen quite a few pieces for a single woman."

"Do you really think so?" Fancy asked, still smiling.

"They're going to cost you a good chunk of money." The frustrated man looked pointedly at the small, flat bag on her wrist, which couldn't possibly hold enough money to pay for her purchases.

"That is likely true." Fancy looked away from the man, afraid that she would laugh in his face.

"I only deal in cash," Stevens said doggedly.

With an effort, Fancy controlled her mirth as she looked at the red-faced man with an expression of wide-eyed surprise before saying in a voice that was near tears, "But Chance Dawson told me you'd put the cost of everything on his tab."

This time she was really hard put not to laugh out loud at the change that came over the man's face. She thought for a minute that the wide smile that replaced his grim look was going to split his face.

"Of course, in some cases I make exceptions," Stevens hurried to say. "I have no fear that Mr. Dawson won't pay his bills. Are you sure you have everything you want? I have some lamps and pictures and other little gee-gaws that pretty up a house."

Fancy shook her head. She left the store while the elated storekeeper was totaling up a bill that would make Mr. Chance Dawson blink.

Out on the mud-encrusted wooden sidewalk, Fancy's stomach rumbled. Looking up at the sky, she saw that it was well past lunch time.

But where to eat? she wondered, looking around. Perhaps the hotel she had passed earlier had a dining room. She nodded her relief when she stood in front of the two-storied building and read the sign in the window which stated that special for the day was fried chicken and all the trimmings, with apple pie for dessert.

She walked up the two steps to the narrow porch and, pushing open the door, went inside. When her eyes became accustomed to the dimness, she ignored the avid stares from the men sitting in the lobby as she passed through it and into the dining room.

A rosy-cheeked farm girl wearing a white apron and a small ruffled cap perched on top of her head smiled shyly at Fancy and led her to a corner table. "Will you be having our special?" she asked as Fancy sat down and removed her gloves, then slid the small bag off her wrist.

She shook her head. "Just a beef sandwich and a cup of coffee."

The waitress moved away, and Fancy grew uneasy as she glanced around the room. All the other diners were men, and worst of all, she saw Chance sitting with three other men only a couple of tables away.

Their eyes met, but there was no recognition in his. His cool gaze seemed to look right through her, as though she wasn't even there. She looked away, feeling her face flaming with anger. It would appear that Mr. Chance Dawson didn't want to acknowledge the common little dance hall girl in front of his fancy friends. She vowed that someday she would bring him to his knees.

However, a few minutes later, when Chance and the three men had finished their meal and stood up, he walked over to her table and asked brusquely, "Have you finished your shopping?"

"I have not," Fancy answered just as curtly. "I still have to visit Johnson's mercantile."

Chance stood a moment as though he wanted to say something further; then with a brief nod, he moved on to join his friends, who were waiting for him just inside the door. The three were eyeing her with interest and one made a grinning comment to Chance. He shook his head and made a dismissive motion of his hand as though she was of no importance. Her sandwich was brought to her and she bit into it, although her appetite had deserted her. She could have been eating wood chips for all that she tasted the tender slices of meat.

Fancy left most of her lunch on her plate, but drank the coffee. She half wished that it was whiskey in the cup, for suddenly she wasn't so brave about the heavy-handed way she'd spent Chance's money.

"But I didn't buy one thing that wasn't necessary for that empty house of his," she muttered under her breath, her fighting spirit returning.

Fancy's courage faltered again when she approached the pier; behind her a boy trundled a cart filled with the supplies she'd purchased at the mercantile. A furious-faced Chance paced back and forth as he waited for her. She glanced at the steamer, and her eyes widened a bit at the pieces of furniture stacked in its center. It looked like so much more than it had in Stevens's emporium.

"I'm ready if you are," she said cheerfully, as though Chance's face didn't resemble a storm cloud.

"Ready for what?" Chance roared, advancing on her. "Ready to feel the weight of my hand on your runty little ass? Are you sure you don't want to go back to Stevens's shop and buy the few pieces you left there?"

That Chance would even consider laying hands on her person struck fire off Fancy. She glared up at him and bit out, "Look, mister, did you think that all I was going to buy was a bed, a kitchen table, and chairs? Maybe you can live like that, but my nephew isn't going to. I'm going to make a home for him, a comfortable home. If you don't want to be a part of it, then have the furniture taken back to Stevens and Tod can live in my house. And furthermore, Chance Dawson, don't you ever even think of laying a hand on me."

"Look here, missy," Chance retorted, "I want Tod to have a nice home, too, but you know damn well you bought more stuff than was neccessary just to spite me."

"I did not! You'll see that once everything is in place."

Chance opened his mouth to continue the hot exchange, then threw up his hands in surrender. He was swearing under his breath as he hopped up on the deck and strode across it to stand beside the captain. Fancy stared at his broad back. She had won the battle, but the fighting of it left her shaking inside.

And this was only the first of many she was sure would follow as she and Chance tried to live under the same roof.

Chapter Six

Fancy stepped out of the dance hall and stood a minute in the pink dawn. She breathed deeply of the fresh air, clearing her head of the tobacco smoke that hung so heavily in the big room.

She lifted her gaze to the fir trees marching up the mountain—ponderosa pines that towered hundreds of feet in the air and Douglas firs, one of which was so huge it could produce enough lumber to build four ordinary five-room houses. They reminded her of cathedral spires in the heavy fog rolling in from the river.

From off the river came the honking of geese, then the flapping of many wings. The geese had been flying south for several days now. The first chill days of autumn were upon them. Winter would follow shortly, the first one she would spend without her father. And poor little Tod.

It would be his first winter without his parents.

Her eyes were damp with the memory of her sister when Lenny's big figure came hurrying toward her. "I'm sorry if I'm late, Fancy," he puffed, "but I was busy making Toddie's breakfast and laying out the clothes for him to wear to school."

Chance had asked Molly Jackson if she would take on another student and she had readily agreed. Tod wasn't too enthusiastic about it, but Lenny thought it was wonderful that his little friend could go to school and read all the books there. He enjoyed so much having someone read stories to him.

"You're a little early, aren't you, honey?" Fancy asked gently, slipping her arm through his. "The sun isn't up fully yet. School won't start until the loggers have cleared out of their quarters."

"I know that, Fancy. I just want to make sure Toddie isn't late on his first day at school. Miss Molly might not like that and then she wouldn't let him come no more."

"Has Chance left yet?" Fancy asked as they neared the house.

Lenny nodded. "He's been gone since the hour hand was on the five and the minute hand on the three." After a pause he said, "He's real nice when you get to know him. He's going to take me fishing later this morning. Just me and him."

"He is?" Fancy sounded surprised. "You didn't ask him to take you, did you, Lenny?"

"No, I didn't, Fancy. I was pouring him a cup of the coffee I had made for you and he smiled at me and said would I like to go fishing with him." Lenny pushed open the kitchen door, adding, "I haven't been fishing since Uncle Buck left us."

Tod looked up from his seat at the table when they walked inside and gave Fancy a sleepy smile. "Good morning, honey," she said and ruffled his hair. "I see you're about ready for school."

Tod nodded, then yawned, and Fancy gave him a sympathetic smile, then stifled a yawn herself. She didn't have time to get sleepy yet. She had a lot of work ahead of her. The new furniture had been carried into Chance's house yesterday, but most of the pieces hadn't been placed where she wanted them. Zeb had promised to help her move them around today.

Even though the furniture wasn't hers and she'd not have the care of it for very long, she was excited. Although her own little house was cozy and comfortable, nothing matched in it and everything was years old.

Fancy had just finished eating breakfast when Lenny announced from his post at the window that the kids and Miss Molly were on their way to the loggers' building. She gave Tod a bracing smile. "Are you ready to go, honey?"

Tod gave a nervous nod of his head and followed her out the door, with Lenny bringing up the rear.

Fancy was surprised to see Chance waiting beside the cookhouse. He gave her a brief nod, and then gave his attention to Tod, his gaze sliding over the boy's clean shirt and britches, his scrubbed face and neatly combed hair. Fancy clenched her jaw. She shouldn't be surprised that he'd be here to make sure Tod looked presentable. Damn the man for his poor opinion of her.

"You all ready to get some learning pounded into your head, Tod?" Chance joked with a warm smile.

"I guess so. I'm a little nervous though."

"There's no need for that." Chance stepped closer to Tod, shouldering Fancy out of the way. "You'll like Molly. She's real nice, a perfect lady." He looked at Fancy, as though comparing her to the teacher.

Before Fancy could make a biting retort, Molly Jackson approached them, her students tagging along behind her. With a warm smile on her face, she said, "Good morning, Chance. Is this my new student?" She smiled at Tod.

"Yes, my nephew Tod," Chance said proudly, placing a possessive hand on Tod's shoulder.

Molly looked at Fancy, and with a genial smile said, "You're his aunt, aren't you? He looks like you."

Fancy smiled back. "His mother and I looked a lot alike and he takes after her."

"It's so sad about his parents," Molly said as Tod struck up a conversation with a couple boys around his age. He was paying no attention to what the adults were saying. "I would like to extend my condolences to you on the loss of your sister."

"Thank you." Fancy's eyes grew moist. No one but Big Myrt had offered her any word of sympathy or comfort. None of the camp wives had come to her to say they were sorry about her sister. And Chance had only insulted her, claiming that she wasn't fit to raise her nephew. She had cried her tears alone.

Chance had noticed Lenny standing off by himself, a yearning in his eyes to be a part of the group. Walking up to Lenny, Chance took his arm and led him up to the schoolteacher.

"Molly," he said, "shake hands with Lenny. He's going to be my fishing partner today."

Molly's eyes grew gentle as she looked into the handsome, guileless face of a child trapped in a man's body. "I am very happy to meet you, Lenny." She offered her hand. "Aren't you lucky to be going fishing with Chance?"

Lenny nodded proudly. "Besides Toddie, Chance is my very best friend."

After they had all laughed softly at Tod's solemn remark, Molly looked down at her students, who were still standing around her, and said, "Well, I guess we'd better get to our lessons, children. We're not going to learn much out here in the woods gabbing."

She looked at Fancy and said, "Maybe when you're all settled in Chance's house, you'll invite me over for a visit some afternoon."

Fancy was so stunned that she couldn't answer right away. One of the camp wives wanted to come calling on her? Didn't Molly care that she wasn't married to the man she'd be living with?

"I'd be happy to have you," she finally managed to get out. "What about day after tomorrow?"

"Fine." Molly smiled, then led the children away. Tod looked back and waved to Lenny, calling back that he'd see him soon.

Fancy turned to go to Chance's house and was startled to see a pleased look on his face. But even as she wondered what had brought that about, his face resumed its usual stony grimness. She silently chastised herself for momentarily thinking that her making a woman friend had pleased him. He couldn't care less whether she had a friend of any sort, man or woman.

Her sour thoughts were interrupted when Zeb called from the cookhouse window, "I'll be able to help you in about fifteen minutes, Fancy. Just as soon as I get my sourdough to risin'."

"What's he going to help you with?" Chance

frowned down at Fancy.

"To move some furniture around," Fancy answered shortly.

"There's no need to bother Zeb. I'll do it."

"Thank you, but I've already made arrangements with him," Fancy persisted stubbornly.

"You little mule-headed vixen, haven't you noticed how crippled up he is? He shouldn't be pushing furniture around. Anyhow, since I paid for the damn stuff, I'll handle it if I want to."

Fancy knew that Chance was right about Zeb's infirmity and grew angry at herself that he'd had to point it out to her. It seemed that lately she hadn't been thinking clearly about anything. "Have it your way," she snapped.

"I intend to," he snapped back and headed toward his house. She glared after his broad back, calling him some very uncomplimentary names under her breath.

Then, just before Chance stepped up on the porch, he turned around and called to Lenny, still looking yearningly after Tod and the other children, "Come along, son. You can give us a hand. The sooner we get this done, the sooner we can go fishing." Suddenly, most of Fancy's anger left her. She couldn't stay mad at anyone who was nice to Lenny.

She started to follow Chance, then swerved to take the path to her own house. Inside her kitchen, she gathered up her broom and mop and a scrub pail in which rested some rags and a bar of lye soap. Although Chance's house had hardly been lived in, most of the floors were encrusted with mud, and the windows were grimy.

As she approached her new, temporary home, Chance stepped out onto the porch, followed by a man who made her start and stare. It was the stranger who had assisted her onto the timber schooner yesterday. Catching sight of each other at the same time, they both smiled in pleased recognition.

"Well, hi there." The stranger's twinkling eyes ran over her curves in the faded work dress. "Do you work for Dawson too?"

Fancy shook her head, but before she could deny working for Chance he broke in almost with a snarl, "No, she doesn't work for me. She lives with me."

Fancy stared at Chance incredulously. How could he say such a thing? How dare he let this stranger think something that wasn't true? She set the pail and mop and broom down, intent on making it clear she wasn't living with Chance in the way he made it sound.

"Now look here, Chance," she began, but he talked over her.

"This is Gil Hampton, Fancy, my new scaler." He held up a folded piece of paper. "He comes with a good recommendation from Al Bonner." Chance spoke so fast that Fancy couldn't get in a word. Then Hampton, his smile gone, was answering.

"I should have known you belonged to some man," he said jokingly, but disappointment was plain in his eyes.

"But you're mis—" The rest of her sentence was broken off as Chance brushed past her, speaking gruffly to his new man.

"You can store your gear in the men's quarters; then I'll show you where we're working today." He stepped off the path, motioning Hampton ahead of him.

As Fancy fumed, her eyes sending darts at Chance's back, Lenny cleared his throat in an attention-getting sound. Chance paused and turned around. "Would you like to come with us, Lenny?" His voice was soft.

Lenny nodded his head eagerly, and Hampton smiled at him and said warmly, "Come along then, big fellow."

Fancy watched the three walk away, a pleased smile on her face. Although it was plain Hampton was a ladies' man who wouldn't hesitate to infringe on another man's territory, whether it be wife or lover, there was a sincere warmth about him, a caring for people such as Lenny. Most men would have ignored her cousin.

Pilar would climb all over him, she thought. Gil was just the type that would appeal to her.

Fancy picked up the pail and cleaning tools and entered the house. Dirt and dried mud flew before the broom as she swept out the rooms. She had just finished mopping the kitchen floor when Chance and Lenny returned. Chance put Lenny to unpacking the dishes, pots and pans, cautioning him to be very careful of the china-ware. He looked at Fancy, who had just re-turned from tossing out the pail of dirty water, and said gruffly, "Come on, let's get everything where you want it."

The room she would take turns sharing with Chance needed only the new dresser moved to a wall across from the bed, and she was satisfied with the placement of the furniture. Once she made curtains from the material she had bought at Johnson's store and spread a couple rugs on the floor, the room would be warm and inviting.

It was in the sitting room, where the furniture had been placed mostly in the middle of the floor, that Chance became disgruntled. Fancy had him move the sofa twice and rearrange the chairs half-a-dozen times. Finally, his face flushed with aggravation and sweating from ex-ertion, he turned on her.

"Are you purposely working my hind-end off? I've spent at least an hour here listening to your 'I don't think I like the sofa there. Move it in front of the window.' Then when I lug it over there you say, 'No I think you'd best put it in front of the fireplace. It will be too cold by the window in the winter time.' And the chairs I refuse to move one more time."

Fancy hid her smile as Chance stamped out of the room. Had she subconsciously made Chance move the furniture more times than neccessary? Had she been getting back at him for letting the new man think she was living with the timber boss?

Deep down, she knew that she had as she followed Chance into the kitchen. He was going to learn that she would fight him with any means available.

Zeb entered the kitchen at the same time Fancy did, a platter of sandwiches cradled in one arm, a pot of coffee in his hand.

"That sure looks good, Zeb," Chance said as they sat down to eat their first meal at the new kitchen table. After they had eaten and Chance had smoked a cigarette, they went back to work. Two hours later everything was placed where Fancy wanted it. Chance didn't say it, but Fancy knew by the look he tried to hide as he glanced around that he was quite pleased and proud of the way his home looked now.

She wondered how long it had been since he'd had a bright, comfortable place to come home to. She felt a stirring of pity for him, then quickly repressed it. This man needed no one feeling sorry for him.

And, she told herself, she'd best not get too attached to Chance's home. As soon as she had sufficient funds, she and the boys were going to slip away from here.

Fancy was making up the boys' beds when she heard Chance say to Lenny, "Let's go catch those fish, big fellow." She gave a big sigh of relief. She would have the house to herself long enough to have a good hot bath. She couldn't remember when she had felt so sweaty and grimy. She planned on dancing tonight despite Myrt telling her to take all the time she needed before returning to her job. Her little hoard of money wouldn't grow if she didn't work.

Fancy carried the new washtub into the bedroom, then made two trips to the cookshack for pails of hot water. After she had cooled it a bit with a bucket of cold water, she dropped a bar of rose-scented soap into the water. Then, with a sigh of relief, she stripped down to bare skin, picked up a flannel washcloth, and stepped into her bath.

She sat soaking until the water grew cold, then climbed out and dried herself off. When she had pulled on fresh narrow-legged bloomers and a camisole, her hours of strenuous work hit her. She looked at the bed. It looked so inviting. As she dragged the tub of soapy water through the sitting room, a glance at the mantel clock showed she had time for a short nap before Tod came home from school. A minute later, she lay curled on the bed she had made up a little over an hour ago.

Fancy

Fancy stirred, gave a soft little sigh, and nestled closer to the fingers stroking her cheek. In her half sleep she murmured a whispered word, then made a fussing complaint when the warm presence was removed. A rough hand was shaking her shoulder then, and she came out of her half dream with a start. Her eyes flew open, and she stared up at Chance's frowning face.

"Are you about ready to get up?" he asked gruffly. "The boys came home hungry, and you hadn't even started supper."

Fancy continued to stare at Chance. Had he been caressing her cheek? She lowered her lids against his cold features. There was no way in the world he would give her a tender touch. It had all been a dream. Wishful thinking maybe? the little voice inside her whispered.

No! she denied silently and felt angry with herself for having had such a thought, even in a dream. When she caught Chance staring at her breasts through the thin material of her camisole, her voice was sharp and cross as she snapped, "You can roll your eyes back into your head now."

Chance narrowed his gaze at her and said contemptuously, "Don't act the shy virgin with me, Fancy Cranson. There have been plenty of men who have gazed at those beauties, and in a bare state at that."

His untrue remark stung. Sitting up and hugging her knees to her chin, hiding her *beauties*, she shot back, "It's certain you never will."

"It won't be the death of me if I don't," Chance retorted as he stamped toward the door. He paused there a minute to say, "I let the boys eat with the loggers this time, but don't make a habit of not cooking for them. I don't intend hiring a woman to come do your job."

Fancy hopped out of bed, her eyes furiously searching for something to throw at his hateful, arrogant face. Her glare fell on her hair brush, and grabbing it up, she threw it at Chance just as he closed the door behind him. It crashed against the doorframe and clattered to the floor. Still in a rage, she jerked a dress over her head, picked up the brush, and swept it through her hair, smoothing out the tangles. She then went looking for the cousins.

As she passed through the sitting room, where two lamps had been lit, the clock struck eight at the same time her stomach gave a hungry growl. She couldn't believe she had slept so long.

And where were the boys? Had Chance kept an eye on them? Lenny sometimes got very venturesome, going for walks and getting lost. From the corner of her eye she caught sight of a dim light shining from the bottom of the second bedroom door. Since losing his parents, Tod liked a light burning while he slept. For

Lenny's sake, the wick was always turned low. Were the boys in bed?

She found them there, sound asleep. With a rush of tenderness, she walked quietly over to the bed, bending to raise the flame in the lamp. Had they washed up before retiring? she wondered. Both faces were shiny clean. Had they used soap and water on their own, or had Chance seen to it? She felt a twinge of guilt for her uncharitable thoughts of him. He had seen to the boys, after all, and had allowed her to get some rest.

She gave one last look at the two sleeping faces, Lenny sprawled on his back and Tod curled on his side, then lowered the flame in the lamp, leaving the room in a soft glow.

As Fancy left the room, closing the door quietly behind her, her stomach growled again. Would Zeb have any leftovers? she wondered.

The smell of wood smoke was strong in the quiet intensity of the fog-filled evening as Fancy made her way to the cookhouse. It was quite cool and everyone had either a fireplace or a stove lit.

Zeb suddenly appeared in the doorway of the cookshack, the lamp light behind him framing his bony frame. "I been waitin' for you," he said as she walked up to him. "I held back your supper before the hogs came tramping in."

"Thank you, Zeb." Fancy smiled at him. "I

sure am hungry," she said, following him inside.

"I'm not surprised." Zeb placed a big bowl of beef stew on the table, then sliced a thick piece of bread from a sourdough loaf. "Lenny wanted to wake you up to have supper with them, but Chance said to let you rest."

Fancy halted a forkful of meat halfway to her mouth. She couldn't believe that Chance Dawson had cared whether or not she got some rest. Surely Zeb had misunderstood him. But she wasn't about to question the old cook, maybe make him think that it was important to her if Chance showed an interest in her well-being.

"How did the fishermen do? Did they catch any fish?" Fancy asked later when she had scraped her bowl clean and Zeb had poured her a cup of coffee.

"Yeah, they had pretty good luck. Brought back a string of trout." Zeb grinned. "Lenny could hardly contain himself, he was that excited. He caught three big ones. They're over there splashin' 'round in a pail of water." He jerked a thumb toward a dark corner. "The kid sure took a likin' to Chance, didn't he?"

Fancy didn't like hearing that, but she knew that it was true. Lenny was like Chance's shadow whenever he was around. It would be hard on Lenny when she took him away from here.

"Don't you agree?" Zeb asked when she made

no response to his remark.

"Oh, yes." Fancy gave a start before answering. "He misses my father, and now he has Chance for his hero."

"Yeah, boys need to have a man in their lives. Lenny and Tod are lucky to have Chance. He'll raise them right."

Fancy gazed out into the darkness, wishing that the old cook hadn't pointed that out. Chance had angrily said the same words, but she hadn't allowed herself to dwell on them.

Her small chin was resolute. She'd not consider the future now either, she told herself. There were a lot of young men who had been raised by their mothers and they had turned out fine. Her father was one. There was no law that said there must be a man in every household. She knew of plenty of homes that would be much better off if there wasn't a man within ten miles of them.

She and the boys would be just fine, she was sure of it. Right now she must get back to the house, put on her hated short red dress and paint her face and prime herself to spend five hours dancing with the loggers. Chance, no doubt, would be wanting to go to bed before long. She would go to her house and wait until midnight, when Luther took his seat at the out-of-tune piano.

Chapter Seven

There was no sound coming from the mill yard as Fancy started the short walk to the dance hall. The big saw was shut down when darkness fell.

She'd been back dancing for a week now, and a sort of routine had been set up in the Dawson household. Sometimes she and Chance would pass each other on the path, he going to have his breakfast with the loggers, she returning from the dance hall. They would say a crisp "good morning" to each other, not missing a stride.

But every evening around six o'clock, they met at the supper table. There they listened to Lenny and Tod chatter away as they ate whatever she had prepared. Sometimes Chance joined in the boy's talk, either gently teasing or soberly serious, depending on the topic.

Fancy had little to say, for it was man-talk mostly that went on between the three males. She became more and more aware of the importance of Chance being a part of Lenny's and Tod's lives. She worried about how the boys would react when they left the Dawson camp and the big lumberman. She glanced at the big house, wondering if Chance had gone to bed yet; perhaps tonight he would stay up until the dancing started. He had only visited the hall once since she'd gone back to work. He had danced with a couple of women, but most of his tickets had gone to Pilar. He hadn't taken her to her room during rest period, however, much to the dancer's obvious disappointment.

Fancy told herself as she walked along that she didn't care that he hadn't even looked at her, much less asked her to dance.

An owl flew across the moonlit clearing into the deeper darkness of the tall pines as Fancy neared the cookshack. "Off to the salt mines, are you, Fancy?" Zeb spoke from the dark doorway of his domain.

Fancy looked up and smiled at the old cook sitting in the shadows, puffing on the pipe that seldom left his lips even if it wasn't lit. She walked over to him and sat down on a chopping block just outside the door. "Yes, I'm afraid it's time for me to get my feet stepped on for the next few hours," she said, giving Zeb a crooked grin. "I've got to earn my living."

"Couldn't you earn more, and much easier, if you hired on at one of the fish canneries?"

Fancy shuddered. "Good Lord, no! I couldn't stand handling the slimy things all day. I have been thinking about trying my luck in San Francisco though. Maybe work in a dress shop or as a housekeeper for some rich folk up on Nob Hill. Actually, I planned on going there right after my father died. When I first started dancing for Myrt, I only intended to work long enough to earn passage money for Lenny and me. I thought we could live with my sister and her husband until I found a place to work. Then . . ." Her voice trailed off.

Zeb gave her shoulder an awkward pat, knowing that she was reliving the day her sister drowned. After a short silence, Fancy sighed. "I'd miss the mountains though. The big timbers and rivers and Puget Sound. They're all I've known since I was born."

Zeb nodded in understanding. "Most of my life has been spent around some tract of timber or other. I don't believe that I could stand bein' squeezed in with a bunch of people.

"But, Fancy, I can't see no future for you and the boys here. With the exception of Chance, there's not a man workin' here is worthy of marryin' you. And you and Chance get on like a cat and dog."

Fancy made no response to the obvious and

changed the subject. "You've had a new man for meals lately, haven't you?"

"Yeah. Gil Hampton. Seems a nice enough feller. Good lookin' too. I guess the girls at Myrt's are probably fightin' over him. There seemed to be a coolness between him and Chance though."

"I noticed that, too, and wondered why Chance hired the man if he didn't like him."

"Hampton's a good scaler, I heard, and Chance needs an extra one," Zeb said.

But the cook silently thought to himself that the tension between the two big men was caused by the beauty perched on his chopping block. Chance tried hard to hide it, but the little dancer had him going around in circles. He felt threatened by Hampton where she was concerned.

"Well, I'd better get going." Fancy sighed. "Myrt raises Cain if any of us are late."

"I heard her raisin' hell with Pilar before. Told her to go take a bath, that she smelled like a whore."

"Myrt doesn't mince words, that's for sure." Fancy chuckled. "I don't want to give her cause to slash at me with her sharp tongue, so I'd better be on my way."

Fancy could hear the rumbling of male voices as she neared the dance hall and she grimaced. Ahead of her lay five hours in which she'd be clutched by callused hands and subjected to the odor of unwashed bodies and stale sweat. Not to mention the struggle to keep a respectable distance between her and her partners. That was hard to do sometimes. For if a man was determined to hold her against his burly chest, she had to catch Big Myrt's eye and signal that the man was out of order.

Myrt was good that way. If a dancer didn't want to be mauled, the big woman didn't allow it to happen. If a woman didn't mind having her partner rub against her, that was all right with Myrt too.

Fancy wasn't sure, but she believed that she was the only one who asked for help occasionally. It didn't happen often, for most of the men had learned, and accepted, that she wouldn't allow any sort of intimacy between them. But there were a few too stubborn to give up.

The men were milling around in the big room when Fancy stepped inside. She knew they were waiting impatiently for Luther to appear and sit down at the piano. Then, not unlike a herd of stampeding buffalo, at the first discordant note they'd make a rush for the dancers. She walked across the floor to join the other dancers sitting on the long bench, feeling the male eyes watching her every step.

As she sat down and tugged at her short skirt, trying to cover her knees, she heard Pilar asking excitedly, "Has the new man come in tonight?" When they all shook their heads, the Mexican's lips drew down in a pout. "I can't imagine what's keepin' him away. He hasn't got a wife."

Fancy, too, had wondered why the good-looking man hadn't shown up at the dance hall. He went somewhere though. She had overheard Chance and Zeb talking about the scaler, wondering where he got off to every night.

"I want you women to know that if he ever does show up, he's mine." Pilar patted her thigh where the stiletto was concealed beneath her dress.

"What if his interest should lie somewhere else?" The woman speaking looked pointedly at Fancy.

Pilar tossed her head, her black eyes narrowing. "He won't. Once he gets the big freeze from her, he'll welcome my warm arms."

"And hot legs," the woman sitting next to Fancy muttered in an undertone.

Fancy hid a grin, then glanced up and looked straight into Gil Hampton's eyes. He wore an expression of surprise and pleasure and started across the floor toward her just as Luther began pounding the piano.

Reaching her, he gave her a wide smile, and picking up her hand, he placed two long strips of tickets in it. "And when these are gone, I'll buy some more," he said as he pulled her up and into his arms.

The men who had been close behind Hampton began to grumble, muttering dire threats.

Hampton looked over his shoulder at them, and with a genial grin said, "I'll let you men dance with her once in a while." And while the men still muttered among themselves, he swung Fancy out onto the dance floor. Neither one was aware of the furious hatred directed at Fancy from a pair of flashing black eyes.

Fancy was pleased to find that Gil Hampton was a graceful dancer and didn't attempt to draw her up against his body. She was relieved that most of her dancing tonight would be with him. Her poor toes would get a rest.

"I can't believe that Dawson is allowing you to dance here and let other men hold you in their arms." Gil looked down at her as they circled the room, his eyes serious.

"Chance Dawson has nothing to say about what I do. He gave you the wrong impression, saying that I live with him. The truth is that Chance is Tod's uncle and I am the boy's aunt. When we argued over who should raise him after his parents' deaths, we finally concluded that for the time being we would all live under the same roof, each sleeping alone. Other than that, there is nothing between us."

"Are you sure? He acts very possessive about you. If ever I had a pair of threatening eyes glare at me, it was when he said you lived with him."

"I think you imagined it. He doesn't think too highly of me—or the way I earn my living."

The buzzer sounded, announcing that it was

a rest period. Hampton looked down at Fancy as though debating whether to ask her something. Then, as though deciding that the answer would be a cool no, he sighed under his breath and released her. After thanking her for the dances, he ambled across the floor and stepped outside. After taking a deep breath of the clean night air, he walked down to the river. He stood there a long while, looking across the water, a worried expression in his eyes. When he thought it was about time for the dancing to resume, he turned and walked slowly back to the dance hall.

He arrived only seconds before the fifteen minutes were up. When the buzzer sounded again, he stood back while several men practically fought to be first to thrust a ticket into Fancy's hand. Several times during the next few hours, he claimed Fancy, but he danced with Pilar also, reading the invitation in her eyes and the way she rubbed her body against his.

At last the sky pinkened in the east and the dancers were free to leave as the loggers set out to work.

Fancy breathed little puffs of steam on the cold air as she stepped outside and wrapped her arms around her body. It had turned much colder during the night, and a sharp breeze blew in off the river. All the weather signs pointed to an early winter.

Away in the distance came the cry of a loon

in the early morning air, making Fancy feel colder for some reason. "Brr . . . it's cold, Lenny," she said when the large figure stepped away from the corner of the building.

"It's not Lenny," Chance said, moving into the light shining from the cookhouse window.

"Where is he?" Fancy stood still, her eyes narrowed suspiciously. "He always comes to meet me. Did you tell him not to this morning?"

"I did not." Chance glared back at her. "Tod was telling Lenny all that he had learned yesterday at school, and the kid was so interested in it, I asked him if I should come meet you and he said that was a good idea."

"Well, I don't agree," Fancy snapped and stamped off toward the house, the red skirt swishing angrily a couple of inches above her knees. Chance followed her, his eyes riveted on her shapely calves and graceful ankles.

Gil Hampton, standing off to one side, watched Fancy and Chance. He couldn't hear what they were saying, but he could tell by their expressions that they were having an angry exchange. He wished he knew just how it was with those two. He knew how Dawson felt. The man was head over heels about the fiery little dancer, but he couldn't make up his mind about how Fancy felt about his boss. She denied vehemently that anything other than dislike existed between them, but if that was true, how could Dawson upset her so?

Norah Hess

Hampton made up his mind about one thing. He was going to court the beauty. But when Pilar came up to him and slid her arm in his, an invitation in her eyes, he decided that in the meantime he would enjoy tumbling this one.

Chapter Eight

Fancy awakened later than usual. It was nearly two o'clock according to the little clock ticking away on the small table beside the bed.

She hadn't slept well, not that deep sleep that truly refreshed the body. When she had climbed into bed this morning and pulled the covers up around her shoulders, the blankets still held Chance's body heat, and his scent was strong on the pillows. When she had finally dozed off, her sleep had been filled with dreams of him, dreams in which he had held her in his arms and made love to her.

Fancy gave a disgusted grunt and slid out of bed, telling herself that hunger must have made her have such foolish dreams. Her stomach was grumbling like a hungry bear's.

She picked up her robe from the foot of the

bed and shrugged into it, then searched for her house slippers. She found one where it had been accidently kicked under the bed; the other was lying beneath one of Chance's heavy boots. She hurriedly snatched it up. The small slipper and the large logger's boot looked too cozy together, too intimate.

Fancy walked into the kitchen and felt the coffeepot. It was still warm from a small fire in the range that must have being burning all day. She took a cup from the cupboard and filled it; then, after shoving a piece of wood into the range, she placed a skillet atop the black surface. Fifteen minutes later, she put a plate of ham and eggs on the table.

When she sat down to eat, she saw the slip of paper propped up against the lamp in the center of the table. It read, "Molly has invited Lenny to attend school with Tod."

That's very nice of Molly, Fancy thought. If Lenny enjoyed listening to the children's lessons, it would give her peace of mind, allow her to sleep better. Lenny almost always listened to what she told him, but sometimes he forgot and would wander away from camp.

The corners of her lips tilted. Maybe now they wouldn't have to eat fish every other day for supper. To entertain Lenny, Chance took him fishing at least three times a week. She wouldn't let herself think, or admit, how nice that was of Chance.

Fancy

As Fancy sipped her second cup of coffee, she gazed out the window. It was a beautiful Indian summer day, the sun bright, the air brisk, and the sky blue. A few minutes later as she washed her breakfast dishes and the skillet, she decided she'd ride up the mountain and take advantage of the short time before winter set in with its freezing weather and deep snow. Besides, she hadn't ridden Beauty since arriving here four weeks ago. The little mare needed to stretch her muscles.

Fancy made up the two beds, swept out the kitchen, then dressed in a riding skirt and a heavy flannel shirt and pulled on her logger's boots. When she had laced them up and cuffed her woolen socks over their tops, she brushed her hair and braided it into a single thick plait.

The mare strained at the reins, wanting to run as they neared the mill yard where rows and rows of aromatic raw planks were stacked shoulder-high. But the little mount soon changed her mind about a run when Fancy urged her up the mountain. It was a rough, rock-strewn trail that did not lend itself to a gallop.

Fancy pulled Beauty in at a cleared spot that overlooked the valley, the river, and the Haidah Indian village. She could not see the Chinook tribe that lived farther down the river.

A fine blue veil of smoke hung over the village, coming from many cook fires. As her eyes ranged around, she wasn't surprised to see and hear the cawing of crows. It seemed that there were always flocks of them hovering over Indian villages. She saw three women come up from the river and walk off in three different directions. They carried baskets on their backs, supported by a wide band around their heads. She imagined that fish filled the woven-reed vessels.

Her gaze fell on a group of children darting around, playing some game as they laughed and called out to each other. And though it was approaching November, the little ones still ran around with no clothes on. A sturdy people, she thought as she lifted the reins and urged Beauty on. And a very religious people also, she remembered from the time when she was around sixteen and had happened onto a group of Indians chanting to drive away the evil spirit from a sick man as he lay dying.

She could still see him lying on a woven-grass mat surrounded by women beating on a deerskin drum and giving out a monotonous wail. She had heard later that it was an old chief the women had chanted over and that after he died, he had been placed in a canoe and hung high in a tree. Scattered throughout the mountains were a number of canoes suspended in the large fir trees, trees that were never touched by the loggers out of respect for the mummified chiefs inside the canoes.

But not always out of respect, she thought. Some loggers left those trees alone out of fear. Should they be caught bringing one down, they would die a horrible death and they might also send the tribe on the warpath.

The position of the sun alerted Fancy that it was time she headed back down the mountain to start the evening meal. She decided that for a change of scenery, she would take a different route. She was soon sorry that she had. The new way was boulder-strewn and full of narrow crevices where the mare could break a leg.

Finally, the way became so steep and rough that Fancy was forced to dismount and walk, letting Beauty pick her own way. They were nearing the foothills when the mare gave a nervous snort and began to pull against the reins looped around Fancy's arm.

"What is it, Beauty? Do you see a snake?" Fancy looked around on the ground and behind her.

Alarm shivered up her spine then. Only yards away, its yellow eyes glaring at her, stood a female cougar, a cub at her side. Fancy knew that ordinarily the big cat would pose no danger, but this one had a new baby and might attack at any minute. There was nothing more vicious than a mother mountain cat.

Fancy watched in hypnotic fascination as the big cat crouched down on its belly, its tail swishing from side to side. As it began to creep toward her, closer and closer, she could see the muscles in the thick neck and shoulders moving under the sleek skin. She let out a piercing scream when, with a snarl, the beast gathered its muscles to spring at her.

Her sharp, shrill cry hadn't died away when the crack of a rifle split the sudden deathly quiet. With a last baring of its fangs, the cat and her cub turned and moved on up the mountain.

With every muscle quivering, Fancy looked toward the spot where a puff of gunpowder was wafting up among the pines and saw Gil Hampton. He was hurrying toward her, his rifle in his hand. He reached Fancy and caught her in his arms just as her knees gave out and she started to fall.

Gil held her close, murmuring soothing words as he stroked her hair. When her trembling stopped, Fancy moved her head from where she had pressed it against his chest, and with a wan smile pulled herself out of his arms. "I thought for sure my time had come," she said in a shaky voice. "Thank you, Gil, for not letting it happen."

Hampton wanted to reach for her, to pull her back into his arms. She had felt so good nestled up against him. But caution warned him not to. He reminded himself that he must go very slowly with Fancy Cranson. When she did come to him, it would be worth the waiting.

"I'm glad I decided to go squirrel hunting this

afternoon." Gil smiled down at her. "I'm afraid that otherwise pretty little Fancy wouldn't be dancing tonight."

Fancy shivered. "Let's get out of here," she said with a tug at Beauty's reins. Hampton took her elbow, steadying her as they descended the mountain.

As they walked into the camp half an hour later, Fancy saw Chance leaning in the cook-house doorway and her heart skipped a beat. Although he looked so controlled, she knew he was furious. His face was set in stern, rigid lines as he straightened up and stalked toward them.

Ignoring Gil, Chance's eyes whipped contemptuously over Fancy. "I thought it was understood that you'd stop your whoring if I allowed you to help raise Tod," he gritted through his teeth.

Before Fancy could angrily respond, Gil took a step forward. "You contemptible cur," he snarled. "Don't talk to her like that. She doesn't deserve it, and she just had a frightening experience."

"Is that so," Chance snorted dersively. "Couldn't you satisfy her?"

Before the words were barely off Chance's tongue, Gil's fist hit him in the mouth. Chance sat down hard, shaking his head. Then, his eyes reckless and dangerous, he jumped to his feet and plowed into Gil.

As the two big men tried to destroy each

other, a crowd gathered round, flinching every time they heard the smack of flesh on flesh. Chance's split lip was bleeding, and Gil's right eye was beginning to swell.

Fancy darted around the grunting, sweating pair, yelling, "Stop it! Stop it!" In her agitation she got too close to the pair and caught a fist on her chin. She stood a second; then her eyes rolled back in her head and she tumbled to the ground, unconscious.

The fighting came to an abrupt end as everyone gasped loudly. In the silence that followed, both men stared down at the small figure, a stricken look on their faces. When Gil took a step toward Fancy, Chance pushed him away. Kneeling down, he scooped her up into his arms. As he started walking toward his house, Fancy's head lying limply on his shoulder and her legs hanging over his arm, it looked for a moment as if Gil would follow them. Zeb caught his eye and shook his head slightly.

With his fists clenched at his sides, Gil stalked off toward the mill yard. As he walked past the dancers, Pilar reached out a hand to him. Her eyes sparked fire when he brushed it aside and walked on.

The sudden laughter of children being dismissed from their lessons caught everyone's attention. As Molly's students spilled out of the men's quarters, Pilar's eyes fastened on Lenny's handsome, smiling face. She studied him, her eyes narrowed in thought. After a moment, she turned and walked toward the dance hall, a cunning smile twisting her lips.

A cold wetness on her forehead brought Fancy swimming back to awareness. Her lids fluttered open, and she gazed into Chance's worried brown eyes. "Are you all right?" he asked, his voice rough with emotion.

"I think so." Fancy felt her chin where a dark bruise was beginning to appear.

"I'm sorry you got hurt. I don't even know which one of us hit you." He grinned down at her. "Didn't your pa ever tell you to stay away from fistfights?"

"I knew better, but all I could think of at the moment was getting two idiots to stop fighting."

"One idiot, Fancy," Chance corrected her. "I was the idiot. I shouldn't have said what I did, and I'm very sorry about it." He pointed to his cut lip. "I deserve this."

Fancy nodded her head. "Yes, you do."

Amusement flickered in Chance's eyes at her ready agreement. "Do you want to tell me what your bad experience was?"

Fancy stole a glance at him. Was he sincere in wanting to know what had happened to her? There was genuine caring in his eyes, so she briefly told him what had happened up in the mountains. "If Gil hadn't come along when he did, I'd have been clawed to death by that cat."

Chance's face paled beneath his tan. The

thought of this lovely soft body being mauled by a wild animal, those lovely blue eyes closed forever, was unbearable.

"I see that I owe Hampton an apology as well as a thank-you," he said in a low voice.

"There's no need to thank him," Fancy said flatly. "I've already done it."

Chance knew what she was telling him—that he had no more right to thank Hampton for saving her life than he'd have if it had been one of the other dancers.

He stroked a gentle finger across her bruised chin. "Are you ever going to forgive me for what I said to you?"

As if you'd care whether I do or not, Fancy thought dully before looking him in the eyes and saying coolly, "I doubt it. It was uncalled for and I don't trust people who are always ready to think the worst of another person."

Chance sat another moment on the edge of the bed; then, dropping the washcloth into the basin of water, he stood up. "Lie there and rest while I make us some supper," he said, his tone void of expression.

"I'll make supper." Fancy started to sit up.

"No, you won't," Chance said firmly. "You've been through a lot today. You just lie there and rest until it's time to eat." He left the room, closing the door quietly behind him.

Fancy stared up at the ceiling, wondering what to make of this softer side Chance had shown her. It had to be guilt, she decided. For although she had caught him looking at her with desire several times, she knew he didn't care for her as a person.

She breathed a long sigh, thinking that she had made the biggest mistake in her life, agreeing to live in the same house with such an unpredictable man.

Chapter Nine

Fancy softly hummed "Camptown Races" as she rubbed a sheen into the sitting room furniture. It seemed strange to feel so alert at this early hour. Ordinarily at this time of day she would be dead tired and eager to get to bed.

But she hadn't worked last night, knowing that today, Saturday, Molly would be coming for her visit. She wanted the house to be spotless and to have time to bake a couple of pies, one for the family's supper and one to serve with the coffee she and the school teacher would drink as they chatted.

She had baked pies upon rising this morning, and at the moment they were hidden away in the top shelf of the cupboard, out of the boys' sight. Those two had eaten breakfast, then gone off to pursue whatever they had planned for the day.

Fancy stepped out onto the porch to shake out her dust cloth, and after giving it a couple of good cracks, she noticed Chance coming toward the house. Because she had stripped her bed and hadn't gotten around to washing the linens, there was no place for Chance to spend the night except with his crew. He had griped loudly about it, complaining that he'd get precious little sleep with all the snoring in the bunkhouse, not to mention the stench of sweat and dirty socks.

Her lips twitched in amusement when he walked over to the porch and stared up at her. His eyes were bloodshot from lack of sleep as he stated darkly, "Let it be known right now, under no circumstances will I ever sleep with my men again. I would rather sleep in the shed with our horses."

"You could have slept with Pilar." Fancy went back into the house and Chance followed her.

"I thought about it," Chance said, then added slyly as he watched her face, "but I saw your friend Hampton go to her room."

If that bit of news bothered Fancy, it didn't show on her face. Her only response was a calm, "Why didn't you challenge him to a fight? Let the best man sleep with her."

Lenny and Tod came rushing into the house, imploring Chance to take them up the mountain to look for the golden eagle that they had learned about in school yesterday.

Chance's face showed plainly that he didn't like the interruption, that he wanted to continue on the subject of Gil Hampton. But with two pairs of eager eyes watching him, he had to content himself with a departing remark. "I wouldn't have had to fight for her. I'd only have to crook a finger at her."

As he trailed the boys outside, Fancy was tempted to pick up a piece of stove wood and hurl it at his arrogant head. What he said was probably true, though, she thought as she resumed dusting the furniture. She did hope that Gil didn't become too involved with Pilar. He was a nice man, and only trouble would come from a relationship with the hot-tempered dancer.

Gil Hampton groaned low in his throat as Fancy's slim fingers stroked and fondled him. He whispered her name as he reached for her, his maleness hard and wanting. His eyes snapped open and he jerked awake when Pilar sat up screeching angrily, "If you say her name again, I swear I'll kill her!"

Gil raised himself up on his elbows, blinking away his dream of Fancy. He glanced down the length of his naked body at his arousal, which was losing its rigidness. He became aware of the closeness of the small room, the heat, the odor of spent passion. His throat was dry, he had a godawful taste in mouth, and his head felt as if it might roll off his shoulders.

How much whiskey had he drunk last night? He remembered old Zeb taking him into the cookhouse and putting a piece of raw meat on his eye, then giving him a glass of whiskey. He had then given him some advice.

"It's best you leave the little beauty alone, son. Regardless of what you may think, she's not like the other dancers. She's decent and she has simpleminded Lenny to take care of as well as her nephew. She's not the sort of female a man sleeps with for a couple months, and then goes off and leaves. Men marry the Fancy Cransons of this world."

Zeb gave him a searching look. "Do you have that in mind? Can you settle down and support a ready-made family as well as the other younguns that would come along?"

"Is that what Dawson has in mind for her?" Gil asked, wanting to hit Zeb for his brutal frankness. The cook knew as well as he did that he could barely support himself.

"I don't know what Chance is thinkin,' " Zeb said. "I don't think he knows himself. But there's one thing I'm sure of—he's not gonna let another man step in and steal her while he's tryin' to make up his mind. They have the boy in common, which is a big plus on his side if he ever wakes up and realizes Fancy's worth. I know he's dyin' to bed her."

Gil had known as he sat in the cookhouse, holding the piece of meat to his eye, that he had been given good advice. Fancy Cranson wasn't for the likes of him. He thought of the years when he had wandered from one timber camp to another, never staying put longer than a few months, growing restless, moving on . . . and leaving broken hearts behind him.

His lips twisted in a rueful grimace. It was ironic that when he finally found a woman who could change all that, she wasn't the least bit interested in him.

Common sense told him it was time to move on, that only trouble waited for him here. But would it be wise to leave at this time of year? Timber bosses wouldn't be taking on new crew members with the threat of winter slowing down the workload of felling trees and getting them to the river and sawmill. They would be letting men go instead of hiring more. In fact, if he weren't careful, Dawson might tell him his services were no longer needed. It would be a good excuse to keep him away from Fancy.

Gil stared up at the ceiling. There was another reason he couldn't leave here at the present.

Pilar jabbed him in the ribs with a sharp finger. He turned his head and looked at her pouting face. She was a good bed partner, so he'd avoid tangling with Dawson again and spend the winter months with his second choice.

Her crisp blue muslin dress swishing around her ankles, Fancy walked over to the kitchen window and looked outside. Soon Molly would appear on the path that led to Chance's house. She always referred to the snug building as belonging to him. She knew it would never be her permanent home. How could it be? She and Chance Dawson could barely look at each other without quarreling, let alone give Lenny and Tod the stability of a loving home, which both boys needed. Especially Tod. It was important at this time in his life that he have a solid foundation of love and security.

As much as she hated to admit it, Chance was very good with her cousin and their nephew. Lenny adored him, and it was going to be hard on the man-child when she took him away from here.

But that wouldn't be for a while yet. Snow could start falling any day, and all the trails out of the mountain would become impassable. Besides, her savings hadn't grown as rapidly as she had hoped, although that should change, what with Chance providing the food she cooked each day.

When she and Chance had finally come to an agreement about their living arrangements, a part of it had been that Chance would support them all and that she would cook, clean, wash and iron.

She directed a derisive laugh at herself. What it boiled down to was that she was working for bed and board. She'd like to see Mr. Chance Dawson hire a woman who would work so cheaply.

But to be truthful, she didn't mind. She liked being a homemaker. When Mary had married and gone away, she had left her young sister to take over her duties. The chore had sat lightly on Fancy's shoulders. She hated working in the dance hall and yearned for the day she could turn her back on it. Thank God her father didn't know how his baby daughter was earning her living.

Fancy glanced out the window again. As she watched for Molly to appear, her attention was caught by three figures walking toward the river: Chance and Lenny with Tod keeping pace between them. Each carried a fishing pole, and Tod held in the crook of his arm a can of bait, probably small pieces of salt pork begged from Zeb. They hadn't stayed up the mountain very long, she thought. Tod had probably gotten tired. She supposed she should thank Chance for taking the boys off her hands today. She and Molly could visit without being interrupted by them.

But *was* Molly going to call on her today? she wondered. She had expected her an hour ago.

Maybe the young woman had thought it over and decided she shouldn't associate with a woman who lived with a man out of wedlock. Or perhaps the other wives had advised her not to get chummy with one whose morals, seemingly, weren't like their own.

Fancy was about to turn away from the window when she saw Molly emerge from the pines and take the path to Chance's house. After giving the kitchen a fast, appraising look—the bright flowered curtains she had made, the white cloth on the table with a bowl of autumn wild flowers in its center—she hurried to open the door.

"I'm afraid I'm late, Fancy." Molly puffed a little as she stepped into the kitchen and removed a lightweight shawl from her shoulders. "I was just getting ready to leave the house when Sukie Daniels came running up, crying, her dress ripped and one eye turning black. I had to take her in and try to console her."

"My goodness, what happened to her?" Fancy took the knitted garment from Molly and hung it on a peg next to the door.

"Oh, the poor thing," Molly said as she pulled a chair away from the table and sat down. "Every time her husband George gets drunk, he wants Sukie to go to bed with him. She's been refusing lately because that's when he's careless about getting her with child. They already have eight, and Sukie is nearing forty and doesn't want any more. George goes into a rage, then, and beats her something awful. He's a brute of a man. Nobody likes him."

"Is she still at your house then?" Fancy placed one of the apple pies on the table and turned to take the coffeepot off the stove.

"Oh, no. She went back home when she saw George stagger over to the dance hall. He'll pay one of the dancers there to take him into her bed."

"Poor woman. That must make her feel awful, knowing that her husband is going to another woman's arms."

"Not Sukie." Molly laughed. "She'd like it just fine if George never came near her bed." She put her fork into the slice of pie Fancy had placed before her and added with a grin, "If my Frank should even look at another woman with lust in his eyes, I'd clobber him with a stick of wood."

The coffee cups were refilled twice as the afternoon wore on. The two young women gossiped and laughed, speaking of their youth, the places they had lived before. Then Molly began to fill Fancy in on her neighbors.

Some of what she said surprised Fancy. There was Alma Bandy, in her early thirties, pretty and on the plump side, who was sneaking behind her husband's back and sleeping with one of the sawyers.

"Opinions are split among the women on the right or wrong of Alma's cheating," Molly said.

"Half of them think that Bill Bandy should be told about what's going on, while the rest say they can't much blame Alma, Bill being so fat and stinking to high heaven. Alma claims that since they got married ten years ago, he hasn't taken a proper bath with soap and water. In the summer, according to her, he occasionally wades into the river and sloshes water over himself."

A slight shudder rippled over Fancy. "I can't imagine going to bed with a man like that."

"Me either." Molly spooned sugar into her third cup of coffee. "Bill Bandy should be married to Blanche Seacat for a month. That straightlaced, Bible-spouting harridan would soon straighten him out. She'd give him a crack across his head with her broom, then scrub him herself."

"I take it Blanche has a husband," Fancy said.

"Yes." Molly nodded. "Poor old Victor. Nodody envies him. He's so browbeaten, he doesn't even get his pay envelope handed to him. Blanche waylays Chance every payday and demands her husband's wages. It really gripes Chance to hand over Victor's hard-earned wages to Blanche, but what can he do? I think he's half afraid of her too. After all, if she lit into him with a stick, how could he protect himself? Chance Dawson would never strike a woman."

Fancy nodded, believing that to be true. Chance might cut and slash a woman with his tongue, but she felt that he would never lay a hand on a woman in anger. Not even herself.

"Do the Seacats have any children?" she asked.

"Yes, believe it or not." Molly laughed. "Everyone is amazed that Blanche let Victor into her bed at least three times to produce their three daughters, who are the spitting image of their mother. They have the same thin, mousy colored hair, little pale brown eyes, thin pinched lips, and can keep up with their mother when it comes to spouting Bible verses. They're fifteen, sixteen, and seventeen, and for all their religious talk, they're man crazy." Molly looked at Fancy and said soberly, "I think you should keep an eye on Lenny when they're around."

"Thank you for warning me, Molly," Fancy answered, "but the young ladies would get no response from Lenny. The fever that impaired his mental growth also affected the sex urge that happens to the normal male. In that respect, he's just an innocent little boy."

"I thought that might be the case, but I wanted to warn you, to be on the safe side. He's such a handsome fellow. . . . "

"But to get back to Blanche Seacat. I can't help but feel sorry for her. She, and everyone else in camp, knows that whenever Victor can scrape enough money together he visits one of the dancers. It must cut her pride to pieces."

Fancy agreed, then asked with a chuckle, "Do

we have any normal couples in camp?"

"Oh, yes. There's Ina and Odie Snyder. They're a real nice couple. They're in their mid-forties and always ready to help a neighbor. Then there's Mavis and Henry Bedloe. They're real nice, in their late thirties with three school-age children."

After a slight pause, Molly grinned and said, "I musn't forget Peter and Clarence. They live in the house back of mine."

"Why do you speak of them as a couple?" Fancy looked puzzled.

Amusement sparking her eyes, Molly answered, "They claim to be brothers and wanted a place to themselves. But it's suspected that it's not brotherly love they share, if you get my meaning."

"You mean . . ."

"Exactly. But they're very nice men and make good neighbors."

"I'm wondering what the rough loggers think about that," Fancy said.

Molly shrugged. "As you might expect, at first they taunted and tormented the pair. Then one day Peter waded into three of them with his axe, and he and Clarence are left alone now. My Frank says they're real hard workers. I guess they've been together for years. They're somewhere in their forties."

"I don't understand it," Fancy said after a while, "but how people live their lives is their own business as far as I'm concerned."

"That's how Frank and I feel too," Molly agreed. "We don't poke our noses into our neighbors' business, and we don't allow anyone to pry into ours."

Fancy had been waiting for Molly to ask some leading questions about her and Chance. She relaxed. Molly, at least, wasn't going to ask any personal questions. Had her new friend purposely made that remark to put her mind at ease?

"Your kitchen is so warm and inviting, Fancy," Molly said, her gaze traveling over the bright room, taking in the pretty dishes in the pine hutch, the polished sheen of the big black range with its deep warm-water reservoir. "I haven't seen one like it since I left my parents' home."

"Thank you, Molly." Fancy's tone said she was pleased at the schoolteacher's praise. "Would you like to see the rest of the house?"

"Yes, I would. Then I've got to get home and start Frank's supper."

Molly's complimentary remarks about the other rooms were sincere. There was one moment that could have been awkward. They had left Tod and Lenny's room and had entered the other bedroom, which she and Chance shared. Molly was admiring the quilt on the bed when Fancy saw her robe lying across the foot of the bed. She had forgotten to hide it away in the wardrobe. That would have been all right if a pair of logger boots had not been sitting in a corner, a wide belt of Chance's lying on top of them. And if that wasn't enough evidence that she and Chance both used the room, on the dresser top was a man's hairbrush, black with a sturdy handle, and beside it a dainty, pearl-handled one.

Her face flushed with embarrassment, Fancy gave Molly a crooked grin and said, "We both use the room but not at the same time."

"I know." Molly grinned back at her. "Lenny thinks it's so funny, he told the whole class about your sleeping arrangements."

Fancy shook her head. "My cousin tells everything he knows."

"It's fortunate that he did in this instance. Everyone in camp knows that nothing is going on between you two," Molly said as they walked back into the kitchen.

Taking her shawl down from where Fancy had hung it, Molly arranged it across her shoulders, saying as she crossed the ends over her breasts, "I'm having a little tea at my house next Saturday afternoon so you can meet the other ladies. They're all anxious get to know you," she added on her way to the door.

Fancy was so surprised that she couldn't speak for a moment. The other camp wives wanted to meet her? She finally managed to say, "That's very thoughtful of you, Molly. I look forward to it." She followed the schoolteacher out onto the porch.

Good-byes were said, and as Fancy watched Molly turn onto the path that led back to her house, she hugged her arms around herself, shivering in the chilly air.

She was about to turn back into the kitchen when her name was called. She looked over her shoulder and smiled at the tall man walking toward her. "Hello, Gil," she said. "What do you think of this sudden weather change?"

"It could mean that we may get our first snowfall of the season soon." Hampton sat down on the edge of the porch and leaned back against a supporting post. "You're lookin' mighty fetchin' today, Fancy." He gave her a rakish smile. "I must say, though, that I like your little red dress better than the one you're wearin' now. The silk one shows more of your . . . charms."

Fancy's laughter rang out. She knew his remark was made in fun and that no insult was meant. Her mirth died abruptly. Chance and the boys, along with Pilar, were bearing down on them. The gray clouds gathering overhead didn't compare with the glowering looks on Chance's and Pilar's faces. In the Mexican's eyes was jealous rage, and in Chance's was cold contempt.

Gil stood up with lazy grace and said, "It was nice talkin' to you, Fancy." He nodded at

Chance, and taking Pilar by the arm, he led her away, paying no attention to her spate of angry words. As Tod and Lenny began excitedly telling Fancy about their day, Chance spun around and stalked off.

Fancy started to call him back, to explain that Gil had only stopped for a friendly visit, then changed her mind. She owed Chance Dawson no explanations. Let him think what he wanted to.

Chapter Ten

Chance stood on the banks of the Columbia, staring out across the water. Jealous anger still shook his insides. He had been blinded by it for a moment when he saw Fancy and Hampton on the porch sharing laughter, something that never happened between them. The only thing they exchanged were harsh, insulting words flung at each other. But most of the time there were no words at all, just cold, stony silence.

He kicked out at a rock half embedded in ankle-deep mud that had been churned up by countless hooves of oxen and mules dragging the huge logs to the river. Why did the one woman who had ever stirred his heart have to be one who had known other men? he asked himself. Fancy had him so twisted up inside that he no longer went to the dance hall because he couldn't bear the sight of her in the arms of the loggers. She always kept a respectable distance between her and the men, but he couldn't bear to think that she might slip off to her house during the day and meet Hampton there. She could, easily enough. The boys would be with Molly, and she'd have all the time she wanted to loll around with Gil while he was waiting between trees.

And there must be some reason that Pilar was so suspicious of the pair.

As Chance stood musing, late afternoon gave way to a shadowed twilight, heavy with the scent of snow. Thirty yards up the river, the huge saw was shut down, and an eerie silence settled over the mill yard. He could hear the muted talk and laughter of the loggers as they walked toward the cookhouse. When he thought they'd had enough time to wash up and file inside to eat, he started walking toward camp. Since he was in no mood to be around his men, and certainly not around Fancy, he would go visit with Luther and Big Myrt, who were sitting on a bench beneath an oak. When the men had finished eating and left the cookhouse, he'd go have his supper with Zeb.

Chance could hear Pilar's angry screeching before he reached camp. He hastened his pace, wondering what had set the dancer off this time. He burst into the clearing to see the loggers gathered around Pilar and Lenny. As he shouldered his way through the men, he saw Fancy come running from the house.

"That feeble-minded cousin of Fancy's tried to rape me," Pilar was yelling, pointing a finger at Lenny, who stood frightened and confused. "I gave him a friendly smile, and the next thing I knew he was throwing me on the ground and tearing at my clothes."

"That's a damn lie!" Fancy shouted, shoving her way through the gaping men and putting an arm around the shaken Lenny. "He would never do anything like that."

"Why wouldn't he?" Pilar shouted back. "He has everything a man has, and I'm sure he has the same urges. Look at the back of my dress."

She swept her gaze over the men, who looked on, uncertain about her claim. "You fathers with daughters had better think about this," she warned. "Molly Jackson allows that idiot to sit with your young girls. What if he should attack one of them some day? He's big and strong, and they wouldn't be able to fight him off. I say that he and Fancy should be made leave this camp. He's a danger to women."

Chance hadn't been aware of it, but he had moved to stand beside Fancy, giving her his silent support as she opened her mouth to defend Lenny again.

She barely got started when Blanche Seacat, her pale eyes snapping with anger, burst through the circle of loggers. Her long finger jabbed at Pilar's chest as she lashed out, "You whore, you're the one who should be run out of this camp. I was takin' down my wash and I saw the whole thing happen."

At the startled, uneasy look that came over Pilar's face, Blanche nodded her head in satisfaction. "You didn't think anyone was around to see what you were up to, did you? Well, I saw you. I saw you go up to that innocent boy and begin to fondle his crotch. I heard him say, 'Chance told me not to let anyone touch me there,' and with that he gave you a hard push. You stumbled and fell on your back. That's why you've got dirt on your backside and pine needles in your hair."

Everyone knew that the pious Mrs. Seacat wouldn't lie. The loggers began to mutter among themselves and to send angry, contemptuous looks at Pilar. Then, only moments after Blanche labeled Pilar a liar, Big Myrt stepped up to the dancer, her big hand raised. It popped like a pistol as it connected with the painted face.

Myrt grated out, "If you ever try a trick like that again, you bitch, I'll make sure you never work again." The big woman walked off then with Luther following her, and the loggers returned to their supper.

When Pilar had stamped away, the imprint of Myrt's fingers bright on her cheek, Fancy walked over to Blanche and held out her hand.

"Mrs. Seacat, I'll be forever in your debt for speaking out for my cousin. Things could have gotten pretty ugly for him if the men had believed Pilar."

"I wouldn't be a very good Christian if I'd kept my mouth shut." Blanche spoke through thin, disapproving lips. She looked at Chance, who had remained at Fancy's side with a protective hand on Lenny's shoulder. "Chance," she said sharply, gesturing toward Pilar, "you shouldn't let her kind in your camp. She's not like the other dancers, who know their place. She struts around, flaunting herself, always looking for a man, not caring if he's married or not."

Pity for the unattractive woman stirred inside Fancy. Blanche was probably thinking that her own husband was one of those married men.

"I'd send her packing in a minute, Blanche," Chance said, flicking a glance at the sky, "but by the looks of those clouds gathering in the north, we could get snow any time. I'd hate for her to get caught in a blizzard and freeze to death."

Blanche sniffed as if to say it would serve Pilar right if that did happen.

"Anyhow, she'll behave herself from now on. Big Myrt will see to that," Chance said, seeking to smooth the irate woman's ruffled feathers.

A pleased smile flickered on Blanche's thin lips. "Big Myrt did wallop her good, didn't she?" she said with satisfaction. When Fancy and

Chance grinned and agreed, she said, "I'd better get on home and put supper on the table."

"Thanks again," Fancy called after the raw-boned figure hurrying up the path to her home.

"There goes a very bitter woman," Chance said, mostly to himself.

"Can you blame her?" Fancy drew her shawl tighter around her shoulders; it was turning colder by the minute. "It must be very hard on so proud a woman to know that her husband prefers a whore's bed over hers."

"Maybe if she'd soften up a bit, get that prune look off her face, and act a little more feminine, Victor wouldn't look beyond his hearth for what a man needs."

"Ha!" Fancy snorted. "Trust you to find excuses for wife-cheating males. You men are all alike, never satisfied with what you've got."

"That's not true. There's Frank Jackson. He wouldn't dream of cheating on Molly. And Odie Snyder, and Henry Bedloe. Those three men wouldn't look at another woman." His lips curved in a crooked grin. "And don't forget Peter and Clarence. They're real true to each other."

Fancy ignored his attempt at levity. "I'll admit there are a few good husbands," she said reluctantly, "but they are few."

"What about wives?" Chance asked. "They cheat too. There's Alma Bandy. She's carrying on with one of the loggers."

"I don't want to talk about it," Fancy snapped. "We've saved you some fish. Do you want it?"

"I'm sorry to turn down such a gracious offer," Chance drawled derisively, "but I think I'll pass."

"It's up to you." Fancy shrugged indifferently and stamped off, her head held high.

"Go with her, son," Chance said to Lenny, who lingered at his side.

"Can't I stay with you, Chance?"

"You don't want to hurt Fancy's feelings, do you?"

"Oh, no. I'd never want to do that to Fancy," Lenny declared. "She loves me, and I love her."

"You'd better get home then, so she won't feel bad." The first snowflakes fell as Lenny walked away from Chance.

Chance entered the cookhouse and sat down at the long table. Zeb turned his head from the pan of dirty dishes he was washing, his wrinkled face showing his surprise when Chance asked, "You got any of your stew left over?"

"I guess I can scrape you out a bowlful," he answered, taking his hands from the soapy water and drying them on the towel tied around his thin waist. "Didn't they save you any of the fish up at the house?"

"Yeah, but the invitation to eat it wasn't very warm."

"When are you and Fancy gonna stop nippin' at each other?" Zeb plopped a tin plate heaped with meat and vegetables in front of Chance. "The two of you remind me of a couple of goats rammin' their heads together," he continued as he sliced bread from a sourdough loaf.

"She's a very difficult woman to get along with." Chance jabbed his fork into a piece of meat.

There was mischief in Zeb's eyes when he joined Chance at the table, a cup of coffee in his hand. "You mean difficult to get into your bed, don't you?"

Chance flushed uncomfortably, remembering the first time he'd seen Fancy and propositioned her. Looking away from Zeb, he mumbled, "I have no desire to take her to bed."

"Ha! Tell me another one. There ain't a man in camp who wouldn't give a winter's wages to sleep with that pretty little gal. If I was twenty years younger, I'd be one of them." The old man gave Chance a knowing look. "I think you've already tried and got turned down."

"Well, you think wrong." Chance kept his eyes on his plate to hide his lie. "She has too sharp a tongue for my liking."

Zeb shook his head. "That's hard to believe. She speaks real sweet to me. And I never hear a cross word out of her when she's with Tod and Lenny." He slid Chance a sly glance and said in deceptively serious tones, "I've heard her talkin' to Hampton, and she's just as sweet as can be."

Chance shot the cook a suspicious look. "Are

you taking little jabs at me, you old reprobate?"

"Who? Me? I wouldn't dream of it." The quiver of amusement on Zeb's thin lips belied the innocent look in his faded blue eyes.

"Like hell you wouldn't." Chance glared at his tormentor. Chuckling, Zeb returned to the pan of dishes waiting to be washed and changed the subject.

"I expect you'll be workin' farther down the mountain now that winter seems to have set in."

Chance set his empty coffee mug down and reached for the tobacco pouch in his shirt pocket. "I'll leave the upper tract of timber until next spring and cut in the lower foothills, where the snow is less deep.

"Even so," he said wearily, "I'll have to keep a road open through one of the passes so the logs can be dragged to the mill."

Zeb dried the last pot and hung his apron on a nail. "Stay as long as you want to, Chance, but I'm goin' to bed."

"I'll stay on a while," Chance said, "but I'm going to step outside and check on the snow." Zeb nodded and said good night.

Outside, Chance stood on the single step of the cookhouse's shallow porch and sniffed the air. It was heavy with the scent of wood smoke spiraling from nearly a dozen chimneys. Big flakes fell straight down, already covering the ground with a couple of inches of snow. He knew it would be much thicker higher up the mountain.

Chance looked toward the men's quarters, where most of the loggers would be sleeping until it was time to go to the dance hall at midnight. Off through the trees he could see the lamplight shining from Big Myrt's house. Maybe he'd go visit her for a while. He often visited the rough-spoken woman. He liked her. She thought like a man. She made a fine friend and a fierce enemy.

Ready to strike out toward the lamplight, Chance paused. Luther, the piano player, had just walked past the window, carrying a tray of something. Chance grinned to himself. It would seem that the gossip was true—Luther was courting Myrt. Or more likely, Myrt was courting Luther.

An ill-matched pair, one would think, seeing them together for the first time. But in a way they complemented each other. Luther, a southern gentleman at one time in his life, had a softening influence on big, brash Myrt, and she in turn showed him that in this wilderness he had to put a little more steel in his backbone.

"It's a damn shame a man can't sit in front of his own fire on a night like this," Chance muttered with a scowl. He couldn't believe that he was letting a little scrap of a woman with pale blond hair and dark blue eyes drive him from the comfort of his home.

Your home was never comfortable until she came along and made it that way, his inner voice reminded him. All you ever did in any of your houses was sleep in them. You never sat in front of a burning fireplace before, sneaking looks at a beautiful woman while you toasted your toes.

"Shut up," Chance growled and went back into the cookhouse.

Fancy had washed and dried the supper dishes and put them in their proper places. She yawned widely as she picked up the broom and swept out the kitchen. It had been a nerve-racking day, one that had left her as drained as though she had danced all night.

Her lips firmed in a tight line. She'd like to get her hands on Pilar and slap her silly, the trouble-making bitch. Thank God Blanche Seacat had seen what had really happened between the Mexican and her cousin.

Fancy yawned again as she put the broom away. Maybe she'd take a little nap, so she'd be refreshed when it came time to go to the dance hall.

She walked into the sitting room, where Tod and Lenny were doing their homework. Lenny was learning how to read and was so proud about it. "Fellows," she said, "I'm going to take a little nap, so please be quiet."

"We will," the two answered in unison.

In the bedroom she laid out her red dress, silk stockings, and black slippers. They would be ready for her to slip into when she awakened. When she had stripped down to her camisole and mid-thigh pantaloons, she pulled back the bed covers and slid beneath them. The snow beat against the window as she fell instantly asleep.

The cookhouse was cozy warm, the low flames and glowing coals shining through the window of the stove door the only light in the room. Chance lounged in a chair he had drawn close to the stove, dozing off and on while Zeb snored from his bed in the small room off the kitchen area. It was with relief that he finally heard the muted sound of Luther pounding on the ancient piano. He straightened up and yawned. At last he could go home and crawl into bed.

He wouldn't fall asleep right away, though, he knew. Fancy's scent would be in the room, and he would smell the rose soap she bathed and washed her hair in. His loins would stir and he'd get an arousal, hard and painful, keeping him awake for at least an hour.

Why in the hell do I let myself suffer like that? he grumbled to himself as he shrugged into his jacket and pulled the collar up around his ears. He could have any of the dancers he wanted, had used them often before the beautiful little vixen came along. But suddenly now he didn't want anyone but her, a woman who would just as soon spit in his eye as look at him.

An additional inch of snow lay on the ground when Chance closed the cookhouse door behind him and headed for home. It fell steadily, and his head and shoulders were white when he stepped up on his porch and stamped his boots before entering the kitchen.

The house was quiet, and he was careful not to make noise as he hung his jacket on its usual peg, then sat down to tug off his boots. He picked up the lamp to make his usual look-in on Tod and Lenny before retiring. In their room he held the lamp up so that its light shone on their sleeping faces. Hadn't Fancy made them wash up before going to bed? He frowned, holding the lamp closer to Tod's face.

His nephew's face was definitely dirt-smudged, and the hand curled under his cheek was none too clean either. Tomorrow he would have a few words to say to her. All her big talk about Tod needing a woman in his life was just that. Talk. She couldn't even see to it that he went to bed with a clean face and hands.

He carried the lamp back into the kitchen and blew it out; then, in the darkness, he made his way to his bedroom, stubbing his toe only once on a chair. He undressed down to his snug underwear bottoms and slid into bed.

As Chance stretched out and pulled the

covers up across his chest, he stiffened. He was not alone. A warm, soft body had rolled against him as his weight depressed the feather mattress. He bit back a soft gasp when a smooth thigh was thrown across him, a knee pressing against his maleness. And while he lay there with breath held, a slim arm came across his chest and a woman's breast pressed against his side.

Good Lord, he thought, his pulse leaping, Fancy hadn't gone to work tonight. She was right here, practically in his arms. All he had to do was turn on his side and she would be where he had dreamed she was so often—snug up against him.

Chapter Eleven

Fancy had had the same dream twice before. She was being held in a pair of strong yet gentle arms, and hot, urgent lips were covering hers. Her arms were clasped around broad shoulders and she was returning a passionate kiss, opening her lips to receive a rough, pointed tongue.

Hands were stroking her rib cage, moving nearer and nearer to her breasts. She gave a low moan when the fingers finally covered one, thumb stroking the nipple, making it hard and tingly.

Making an urgent little noise in her throat, she pressed her hips against male ones, catching her breath when she felt a full, hard arousal pulsating against her stomach. When the firm length bucked rhythmically against the short blond curls hidden under her pantaloons, she

169

began to writhe and dig her fingers into the muscular arms that held her. Seconds later she welcomed the removal of her camisole and sobbed her relief when a hungry mouth left her lips and settled over one aching nipple. Her dream had never gone this far before, she thought vaguely as Chance began to suckle the other breast.

When her pantaloons were stripped off and callused palms stroked her hips and thighs, she knew for sure that this hadn't happened in her dreams before.

In her dreamlike state, she wasn't aware when Chance removed his underwear, for all that time he didn't move his mouth from her breast. She frowned slightly as her legs were parted, and a lean, hard body positioned itself between them. Where was this dream taking her? She breathed a soft sigh. Wherever it took her, she wanted to go. Her loins felt as if they were on fire. She wanted this man's strength inside her so badly.

Her name was groaned against her breast; then she felt a full, hard maleness enter her moistness. She opened her legs to accommodate the intruder that felt so good, and it plunged deep inside her.

Fancy came fully awake with a painful cry. What was happening to her? Where had the wonderful feeling gone? What was tearing her apart?

In the snow-white light shining through the window, she stared up at Chance, who was staring down at her in utter disbelief. "Get the hell off me, you rotten bastard," she hissed, striking out at the broad shoulders over her.

Chance made no move to obey the order. He merely smoothed the hair off her forehead as he said softly, "I'm sorry I hurt you, Fancy. I had no idea you were still a virgin."

"Well, you know it now," Fancy whispered fiercely, "so get the hell off me."

"Oh, honey, you're asking the impossible." Chance dropped quick, small kisses on her face. "I'd rather cut my throat. Just relax," he coaxed, "the hurt will go away in a minute."

"Chance Dawson, you'd better get off me this minute or I'm going to start screaming. Do you want the boys to see you rape me?"

"Rape you?" Chance glared down at her. "What will they think of the marks you put on my back and shoulders, wanting me inside you?"

"I did not! And if I did, it was in my sleep."

"Sleep, hell! You knew what was going on and you wanted it just as badly as I did—still do. You just backed out because it hurt a little."

"A little?" Fancy grated, remembering to keep her voice down. "You've ripped me to pieces inside. And I *was* asleep. But I'm awake now, and I want to get out of this bed."

"Are you sure about that?" Chance looked

down at her with taunting, knowing eyes.

"Yes, I'm sure," Fancy answered his lazy taunt and shoved at his shoulders again. "Now move."

"I'm going to in just a minute." Chance lowered his head to rest between her throat and shoulder. "Just as soon as I prove something."

Fancy let out a smothered cry when suddenly his mouth was on her breast, his lips closing over the nipple. "Don't," she sobbed as he began to slowly draw on the hard little nub, his fingers stroking its mate. When his member began to swell and grow inside her, she was helpless against her body's response. God help her, but she wanted to feel him moving inside her. She slid her arms around his shoulders and brought up her legs and wrapped them around his waist.

"Oh, Lord," Chance moaned as the walls of her femininity flexed around him, doing much the same as he was doing to her breast. He began to move inside her, gently at first, knowing that she was sore. But when the rate of her breathing became faster and she began to buck her hips against his, he thrust deeper inside her and paced his rhythm a little faster.

His body grew slick with sweat as he worked over the slender woman who sheathed him so tightly, responded to him so completely. He wanted to reach that crest of no return and fall blindly off it, but at the same time he wanted to go on forever, moving in and out of the satin-smooth body.

He stroked inside her a few more minutes; then Fancy's feminine walls tightened about him and held. Placing his hands on her hips, he lifted them up in readiness to take a faster, harder ride.

The bed shook and creaked as Chance reached for that mindless release that would leave him weak as a kitten.

In seconds, their lips clinging, they were swept up and away.

Fancy slowly came back to earth, her body still throbbing from the heat of the passion that it had just experienced, even as her mind whirled with self-disgust. She had allowed herself to be added to the long list of Chance Dawson's women. Damn him to hell. How he must be gloating.

She was ready to push him off her when he raised himself on his elbows, taking most of his weight off her. As he traced a finger across one of her finely arched brows, he asked huskily, "Were you asleep just now?"

He didn't have time to duck the hard slap that smacked against his cheek. Stunned, he made no resistance when Fancy shoved him off her and bounced off the bed. Fingering the welts rising on his cheek, he silently watched her pull on her underclothes and reach for her robe. When she drew on her boots and began lacing them up, he sat up in bed.

"Why are you putting on your boots? They don't exactly go with your robe."

"I'm going home." She wheeled on him. "Surely you don't think I'd continue to live here with you now?"

"Why not?" Chance demanded, watching her closely. "Because of what just happened between us? If that's what's bothering you, forget it. I promise it won't happen again. It was just a thing of the moment, two bodies coming together in need."

His cavalier attitude was a raw blow. She had thought their lovemaking was the most wonderful thing that could happen between a man and a woman. It just showed how dumb she was about men, or at least about Chance Dawson. He hadn't been making love to her. He was only releasing his lust on her body.

Well, she thought, as she headed toward the door, he would never know how his words had wounded her. She would adopt the same attitude he had about taking her virginity. She, too, would act as though it was nothing. Chance, unmindful of his naked state, left the bed and caught her elbow as she was going to step through the door. "Don't think for a minute that you are taking Tod with you." His voice was hard and threatening.

"I most certainly am." She glared up at him defiantly.

Chance shook his head. "No, you're not."

"I'll just see what the loggers have to say about that. Tod needs me, and they know it."

"There's not one man in this camp who will say no to me," Chance pointed out confidently.

Fancy glared back at him, knowing that he spoke the truth. The wives might side with her, but they would have little to say in the matter. The anger that gripped her at the unfairness women had to suffer because of their weaker strength sounded in her voice when she said:

"Neither you nor your men can make *me* sleep here."

Chance made no response to her angry retort, but as he followed her into the kitchen his next remark brought her swinging around to stare at him in disbelief. "After what happened with Lenny today," he began coldly, "I think it best you stop dancing. The boys need all your time. They can't run around wild while you sleep all day."

Fancy continued to stare at him for several seconds before exploding in a torrent of words that stemmed from the resentment churning inside her. "You have gone too far this time, Chance Dawson. You are not about to run my life. There is no danger to Tod and Lenny while I sleep. They don't run wild either. The farthest they go from the house is to visit Zeb at the cookhouse and that's only a few yards away."

Her fists balled at her sides, she said defiantly,

"I'm not giving up my job and you can't make me."

"You think not?" Chance said, his eyes laughing at her. "I only have to have a few words with Myrt, and your dancing days are over."

In her indignation, everything went black around Fancy for a second. Why was he doing this to her? Was this his way of bringing her to her knees, of making her completely reliant on him?

Unable to come up with a rebuttal, she ran a scornful look over his naked body. "Why don't you put some clothes on before that thing you're so proud of gets frostbite?"

Chance flushed uncomfortably as he became aware of his naked state. While he was thinking what a picture he must make, standing in his birthday suit, issuing ultimatums to a fiery-eyed vixen who was dressed down to her boots and jacket, Fancy opened the door and stepped out into the night.

Chance returned to the bedroom and pulled on his bottoms, then drew on a woolen shirt. The room had grown damp and chilly, and frost glinted on the windowpanes. He walked into the sitting room, wide awake, his pulses still beating a little fast from his argument with Fancy. He poked up the fire in the fireplace, added a small log, and dropped into a rocking chair. With his feet propped on the hearth and his hands crossed over his stomach, he stared into the flames. He'd had his dearest wish come true tonight. He had finally made love to the beautiful Fancy and to his delight she had still been a virgin. Why then, he asked himself, did he feel so empty inside? Was it because it hadn't meant that much to her? Instead of nestling up to him in the afterglow of what had been the best lovemaking he had ever experienced, she had treated their loving as something to be ashamed of. And now she didn't even want to share the house with him.

Chance's face took on a look of self-disgust. He felt like a low-life, threatening to take Tod from her. She loved the boy, and he loved her. And he needed a woman's tenderness at this time.

He breathed a ragged sigh. He needed Fancy too. He couldn't deny it. He needed to hold her warm body in his arms at night, to make slow love to her. He had known countless women, but none had ever made him feel what she had.

"What do you feel?" his ever-present inner voice asked.

"Hell, I don't know." Chance squirmed in the rocker. "I know that I want her in my bed . . . for a long time."

"Can't you get it through your thick head that Fancy Cranson is not the sort of woman who will live with a man that way unless she's married to him? If you want her in your bed you'll have to marry her."

"Marry her! Are you out of your mind? Marriage has never been in my plans. Maybe later, when I'm in my forties and have grown tired of carousing. I've not reached that point yet, thank goodness."

"Haven't you?" the little voice sneered. "I think you have. You think of nothing else but that little miss who just stamped out of here. I think your long-range plans have hit a snag."

"Well, your thinking is way off center. I'm not about to ask that little witch to marry me. Can you imagine what it would be like, hitched to her for the rest of your life?"

"I have no idea. What do you think?"

As Chance mulled over the question, the pros and cons of it, the pros kept coming up on top. The thought of making love to Fancy every night brought a stirring in his loins, making him wish that he was in bed with her right now.

But the pesky voice taunted, "Chances are, though, she won't have you."

Chance jerked to his feet, muttering "Go to hell," and stamped off to bed. As he pulled the covers up around his shoulders, he wondered if Fancy was warm. Did she have enough wood in the wood box to keep her fire going all night?

He gave his pillow a whack. What did he care if she was warm or not? It would serve her right if she froze her little rump off.

Chapter Twelve

Fancy came awake to complete silence, a silence that only heavily falling snow could account for. A pale sun strove to shine through the snow's white curtain as she left the warmth of the bed and hurried to the window, curling her toes against the cold floor. She shivered in her nightgown as she scratched a patch in the frost on the window pane and peered through it. At least ten inches lay on the ground, with more snow steadily falling. Paths made by the loggers when they came to eat breakfast crisscrossed the area, then led off in different directions.

Her teeth chattering, Fancy hurried to the small sitting room. She found it as cold as her bedroom. The fire was almost out, no more than a bed of red-orange coals. She started to open the stove door to add more wood, then dismissed the idea. Whether she liked it or not, she had to go to the big house and make breakfast for the boys. And she must hurry, for they would be up and concerned about her absence. As she pulled on her robe and shoved her feet into her boots, she wondered what Chance had told them.

Most likely nothing, she decided as she slipped her arms through her jacket sleeves. The coward had probably sneaked away before they were up so that he wouldn't have to explain why she wasn't there.

The snow gave everything new shapes, Fancy thought as she fought her way through its thickness. The camp looked like a beautiful wonderland.

She was about to pass the cookhouse when the door opened and Zeb called out, "Come on in. Breakfast and the boys are waiting for you."

"That sounds real good, Zeb," Fancy called back, swerving in the direction of the building and stepping onto the path Zeb had shoveled. She noted that already the snow had partially covered the footprints of the loggers who had come in to eat.

When Fancy stepped up on the small porch and paused to stamp some of the snow off her boots, she saw Chance at the back door of the dance hall talking to Myrt. Her lips turned down in a sour smile. She didn't have to guess who they were talking about. Or rather, what Chance was ordering the big woman to do. Not to let Fancy Cranson dance anymore. And of course Myrt would do as ordered. She knew that if she didn't, Chance would order her and her girls out of camp.

She felt helpless and frustrated as she stepped into the warm kitchen and closed the door against the cold air that pushed in with her.

It was very difficult to smile and cheerfully answer the boys' questions without letting her ire come through. "I find my own bed more comfortable," she said to explain why she had slept in the small house last night and told them that was the reason she would be sleeping there from now on.

Lenny's handsome, childlike face looked doubtful as he said, "Our bed at Chance's house is much more comfortable than our old one at the little house, Fancy. It has a big, thick feather mattress on it."

"You can continue to sleep there, honey." Fancy bit back her disappointment. She had hoped that Lenny and Tod would say that they, too, would sleep in the little house. But the ready acceptance they both showed told her she had been mistaken.

She felt a little better when Tod said in a small, worried voice, "You're only going to sleep there, aren't you, Aunt Fancy? You'll be at the big house the rest of the time, won't you?"

"Yes, of course." Fancy smiled reassuringly at him. "Nothing will change. I'm just going to sleep in my bed. We'll carry on as usual."

The boys went back to eating their pancakes, and Zeb placed a plate of hot ones in front of her. After he had poured them a cup of coffee, he sat down at the end of the table and said in low tones, "You locked horns with Chance, didn't you?"

"Why do you say that?" Fancy gave him an innocent look.

Zeb stirred the spoon through his coffee a couple of times before saying, "As a general rule, Chance is very pleasant in the mornin's, more so than the rest of them grouches. But this mornin' ever time someone said somethin' to him they almost got their heads bit off. I figured his ornery mood had somethin' to do with a woman, and seein' that you're the only one he's interested in, I figured the two of you must have had a fallin' out."

"Well, you're mistaken on all counts. Number one, nothing is going on between us, so there is no reason for us to lock horns that way. As for his being interested in me, I've never seen any evidence of it. I have never in my life known a man who can irritate me like that one can, and I'm sure he feels the same way about me.

"I just feel more comfortable in my own home, in my own bed."

"Now don't go havin' one of your conniption

fits," Zeb said dryly as Fancy's voice rose. "I was just sayin' how it looked to me. Can't a feller express an opinion around here anymore? Ever time I said somethin' to Chance, he either ignored me or growled at me."

"You're lucky," Fancy said, trickling maple syrup over her last pancake. "All I ever get from him is an insult of some kind."

Zeb slid her an amused glance. "I take it you're all sweetness to him."

"I give him back the same treatment he gives me."

"It must be real pleasant, bein' around the pair of you. Maybe I'll move in with you and enjoy the jawin' you do at each other."

"We never argue in front of Lenny and Tod. It upsets them. Actually, we don't have much to say to each other."

The sound of snow being kicked off a pair of boots brought their attention to the door. Chance pushed it open and stepped inside, his face stony. He slid Fancy a quick glance, then managed a few pleasant words to the boys as he walked to the stove and picked up the coffee-pot. Taking a cup off a shelf, he filled it with the strong brew and sat down at the table.

"So, did you have a good night's sleep in your own little bed?" Chance slid Fancy a look, his eyes mocking her.

"I slept just fine," Fancy answered, but didn't look at him.

"I guess you didn't hear that big cat prowling around your house then."

Fancy couldn't help looking at Chance then, her eyes wide with the remembrance of the cougar that had nearly attacked her. When she saw the satisfied smirk on Chance's face, she wanted to reach across the table and slap him. He was deliberately trying to scare her.

Quickly wiping the alarm off her face, she answered coolly, "No, I didn't hear a cat walking around the house. And even if there was, he couldn't get inside."

"Is that right, Miss Know-It-All? As usual, you're wrong. I'm not trying to scare you, but there *was* a cat in camp last night. And if you don't keep your windows shuttered at night, he'll come through the glass to get at you."

Fancy looked at Zeb for confirmation. The old man nodded. "It's true, Fancy. There was cat tracks around the cookhouse this mornin'. I saw them when I went outside to fetch some wood in. I was gonna tell you about it, advise you to keep the boys inside until the men can track it down and shoot it. And those cats will go through a glass window pane if they're hungry enough."

"Does that mean no school today?" the cousins asked in unison, Tod hopeful, Lenny afraid they wouldn't be attending classes. He looked forward to the time spent with Miss Molly and the children.

Chance grinned at Lenny and reached across the table to lightly rub his fist over Tod's head. "You two forget that today is Sunday. No school."

Tod gave an exuberant shout and Lenny looked disappointed. But when Tod began making plans to build a snowman, Lenny joined in the excitement, telling Tod how he and Fancy always did that.

While Lenny and Tod chattered away, Chance looked at Fancy and inquired silkily, "What will you be doing today? Baking me a pie for supper?"

"Hah!" Fancy snorted. "I'd rather make you a hemlock pudding."

"Don't forget to put a lot of sugar in it." The corners of Chance's lips lifted. "I don't like sour food. Or sour people," he added after a slight pause. When Fancy made no response to his mocking quip, he let his eyes skim over her robe-clad body. "If you're going to wear that outfit all day, maybe I'll come home for lunch."

Fancy's answer was to jump to her feet, jerk on her jacket and slam out of the cookhouse. The boys sat a second, then stood up and followed her.

"You sure like to rile her, don't you, Chance?" Zeb grinned at him.

Chance scratched his head thoughtfully. "Actually, I don't like ruffling her feathers, but she's

185

so damned uppity and stubborn, I can't help tweaking her."

"I think you're both pretty much that way from what I can see—when you're together at any rate. The two of you rub each other the wrong way."

"She's going to find that I can rub a lot harder." Chance stood up and pulled on his jacket. Zeb followed him to the door, and when Chance stepped outside, his lips curved in the first real smile of the morning. It had stopped snowing. The blizzard was over for the time being.

"I guess I can put away the snow shovel for a while," Zeb said, peering around Chance's broad shoulders.

"Looks like." Chance looked up at the sky. The clouds were all gone, and a pale sun was shining. "If anyone comes looking for me, tell them I've gone up the mountain to check out the passes. We've got to keep one cleared to get down the logs we cut last week."

"I expect tomorrow you'll start a new track closer to camp."

"Yeah," Chance answered and struck off toward the men's quarters to roust them out to go tracking the cat. The big animal had to be brought down. There were too many children in the camp.

The falling snow dwindled away to a few scattered flakes as Fancy and the boys entered the big house. The sun shone through the kitchen window, its rays bathing the range that sent warmth throughout the room.

"Can we go out and build our snowman now, Aunt Fancy?" Tod asked.

"I guess so. But keep close to the porch. You heard what Zeb and your uncle said about the cougar." She watched the pair through the window for a minute as they romped through the snow. How she envied them their carefree laughter; the only thought on their minds was the snowman they were beginning to make.

Unlike the turmoil going on in her poor overworked mind, she thought, turning away from the window and taking off her jacket.

Fancy stayed in the kitchen another moment, girding herself to enter the room where she had known such bliss and such mental pain last night.

"But I can't stay in my robe all day," she told herself, "and to get dressed I must go in there."

The bed looked almost the same as when she had left it in her angry rush to flee the house. The covers were tossed about, the quilt hanging almost to the floor. She wondered if Chance had had a restless night and hoped that he had. She had certainly tossed and turned in the darkness.

But most likely he had slept like a hibernating bear, she told herself angrily. It wouldn't bother him that a momentary rush of lust had made him lose control.

"Why should he care that he took my virginity?" she added bitterly, seeing the proof of that on the sheet she was pulling from the bed. Her movements were swift and angry as she remade the bed with clean linens.

As Fancy straightened Tod's and Lenny's beds, plumping the pillows and smoothing the covers, she asked herself how she was ever to get out of this dilemma she found herself in. She had no one to go to, and the small amount of money she had saved was only a fraction of what she'd need to provide a home for the boys until she found employment.

She brushed a frustrated tear from her cheek, promising herself that she would think of something.

It was a slow and laborious climb through the unbroken forest, where the men had tracked the cat's prints to a jumble of large boulders, where the animal probably had his den.

Chance and his men kept their hands close to the guns strapped on their waists. In all likelihood the big cat was watching them from one of the weather-worn rocks, ready to spring at any minute.

It was Gil Hampton who spotted the snarling animal just as it came bounding off a tall crag. Its object was Victor Seacat, who was trailing a few feet behind the others. In one smooth motion, the scaler brought his Colt from its holster, aimed, and fired. The cat twisted in midair, then dropped at Victor's feet, a bullet between its eyes.

The men gathered around Hampton, congratulating him on his straight and fast shooting. Victor was practically blubbering his thanks as he realized that he had come near to being mauled to death.

"I was happy to do it, Victor." Gil grinned up from his kneeling position by the cat. "You'd have done the same thing for me."

"I'd have tried," Victor said in a voice still shaking, "but I doubt if I could have hit the animal. I'm not too good with guns."

Before Gil went back to examining the cat, he said, "You've got the spirit, Victor, and that's what counts."

"That was a good shot, Hampton," Chance said, though reluctantly.

"I learned how to shoot fast and hit my mark when I was a youngster, ridge-running and hunting for squirrels."

"He's a fine-looking animal." Chance nudged one of the haunches with his foot.

"He sure is." Gil looked up at Chance, a devilish grin tugging at his lips. "Won't his pelt look good laid out in front of Fancy's fire, inviting her to lie on it?"

Although the words were innocent enough, Chance knew they had a double meaning. Hampton was really saying that he would be lying there with Fancy. Chance stood a moment, his eyes narrowed, then said in threatening tones, "I don't want that thing in my house." He stalked away, Gil's mocking laughter following him.

"Come on, men," he called over his shoulder. "Let's go find the most favorable pass to clear out."

Gil glanced at the men tramping away, then looked at the two-hundred-pound cougar. "Who's going to help me get this cat down the mountain?" he called after them."

"I'll give you a hand," Victor said and started toward him.

"The hell you will, Victor," Chance snapped. "I need every one of you men to help me shovel. Hampton, if you're so interested in tanning its hide, drag the animal down the mountain yourself."

When Victor halted, undecided, Gil said, "Go on with them. It will be all down hill, so it's not going to be that difficult to get him to camp."

Victor still hesitated. Hadn't this man just saved his life? But he needed his job. If Dawson fired him, Blanche was liable to lock him out of the house. He made a helpless gesture with his hands, and Gil waved him on. "I'll manage, Victor," he said, his eyes boring a hole in Chance's back.

Chance chose a pass close to where most of the fallen timber lay, and he and the men pitched in with shovels, working doggedly at opening it up.

Meanwhile Fancy tried to keep herself busy in the house, but there was little for her to do. She went often to the window to check on Lenny and Tod, then stood there staring outside, wondering if this was how she was to spend the long, cold winter days.

She had about decided to go help the boys with the fort they were building when she heard them call a greeting to someone. She laid down a thin volume of poems by John Greenleaf Whittier and rose to go look out the window. She was startled to see Big Myrt, bundled to the nose, coming up their path.

"Hey, you fellers, come help me through the snow," the big woman called to Tod and Lenny.

After the stamping of feet stopped, Fancy opened the door and smiled at the red-cheeked owner of the dance hall. "Come in where it's warm," she invited her visitor.

Myrt stepped inside, and as she unwound a yard-long scarf from around her head and throat, she said, "I guess you know why I'm here."

"Yes." Fancy helped her off with her heavy coat, then hung it up on a peg. "You've had your orders that I'm not to dance anymore."

Myrt nodded. "I got the word this morning. But I tell you this, Fancy, I don't like being told what I can or can't do." She pulled a chair away from the table and sat down. "So if you want to continue dancin', you can. I'll chance bein' sent out of camp."

"Oh no, Myrt, don't take that gamble," Fancy exclaimed as she filled two cups with coffee and set them on the table. "Chance is just ornery and stubborn enough to make you and the girls leave. Winter is here, and it's no time for you to pick up and try to get settled somewhere else. Thank you for your kind thought, but I'd feel awful if I were the cause of you and the others having to leave."

"We women have to stick together in this man's world," Myrt said.

"Most of the time, though, when we do fight for our rights, we lose." Fancy sat down at the table and pulled the sugar bowl toward her. "If they don't succeed with brute force, they find other ways to control us. Like seeing to it that you lose your job. That's a fine way to control a woman, not letting her earn enough money to get away."

"Chance does want to control you, doesn't he?" Myrt lifted her coffee to her lips.

"Yes, and it's out of pure meanness. He wanted sole custody of Tod, and I wouldn't stand for it."

"I think it's more than that." Myrt watched Fancy's face as she added, "I think he wants you in his bed in the worst way. I think he'd use any means in his power to keep you here in camp."

Fancy wasn't about to tell Myrt that Chance had already had her in his bed once, that she knew he wanted her there until he got tired of her. Her response to Myrt's last remark was, "What the big man wants and what he gets are two different things."

"I could let you have a little—"

"No, no, Myrt." Fancy didn't let her finish her sentence. "I won't take your money. I'll think of something. As for Chance and any ideas he may have, he can forget them. I'll be sleeping in my own bed, in my house—with the doors locked."

"Good for you, Fancy. I wish I'd had your determination at that age. I probably wouldn't be keeping herd on a bunch of man-crazy fools today." Myrt gave a short, harsh laugh. "I'd probably still be in that run-down farm with worn-out soil, working from dawn to dark for a man who was lazier than sin and drank up every penny he could get his hands on." She shook her head. "God, but he was a mean bastard. Always beatin' on me. Didn't even have an excuse to do it.

"I had three miscarriages in the five years I was married to him. It was the happiest day of my life when he got into a fight with one of his drinkin' buddies and wound up with a knife in his heart."

Myrt paused, a smile of remembrance coming over her rough features. "Believe it or not, I was good-lookin' in my youth, with men always hangin' 'round me. After I buried my rotten husband, and those men started comin' 'round the shack wantin' to get in my bed, I saw a way to get off that dirt-poor farm. They would not pleasure themselves on me for nothing. They would pay for my favors. When I had saved up enough money to go west, I packed up my duds, got a place in a Pleasure Wagon, and landed in San Francisco. I stayed with the girls from the wagon train for a while, then struck off on my own. I entertained men until my looks started goin'. That's when I started up my first dance hall. I did that in the city for ten years; then I heard about the money that could be made in timber camps. And"—she grinned—"here I am."

Fancy gave a sly grin. "With Luther, right?"

Still smiling, Myrt nodded. "With Luther. The piano player who came up here with me caught pneumonia and died a month after we settled in. When Luther came and asked me for the vacant job, a softness I hadn't felt in years came over me. If ever I'd seen a person who needed watching over, it was him.

"He's from a different world than we know, Fancy. He's from the South, where men are gentlemen and respect women. What drove him clear across the country, he's never said and I've never asked. He's never questioned me about how I lived all the years before meeting him, and that's how it should be. It's an unspoken agreement between us that everything in our past remains the past. The only thing important to us is the future."

"I envy you, Myrt," Fancy said, a wistfulness in her voice. "You have a good man who loves you and treats you like a woman should be treated."

Myrt nodded and said, "But remember, Fancy, it took me many years to find such a man. I hope it doesn't take you as long."

Fancy shrugged her slender shoulders. "I haven't even been thinking about finding a man. I've got Tod to raise and Lenny to look after. I doubt if the kind of husband I want would take on a ready-made family. Especially my poor cousin, who will always be with me."

"I think you're mistaken, Fancy," Myrt said. "There are plenty of men who would take over the raising of your boys just to get you. I think you could even tame that wild Gil Hampton. 'Course he'll never amount to much. He's a drifter, always wanting to know what lies on the other side of a mountain. He'd be good to you, but he'd drag you and the boys all over the Northwest."

Fancy smiled at Myrt's apt description of Gil Hampton. That one would never settle down to one place. Why was it, she wondered, that some men worked hard at accomplishing something worthwhile, building their future, while others were satisfied to live from day to day, working at a job that would provide them no security in their old age?

Without intending to, Fancy was comparing Gil to Chance. When Chance reached the age of sixty or so, if he wanted to he could sit back and enjoy the rewards of his hard work. She wondered what Gil, and others like him, would do when they were no longer able to work the timber.

"I guess I'd better get back to my quarters and make some lunch for Luther," Myrt interrupted her musings. "I'm tryin' to put some weight on his bones," she added with a laugh.

"I expect Tod and Lenny are getting hungry too." Fancy rose to help Myrt on with her coat. "I've enjoyed our visit, Myrt. Will you come again?"

Myrt hesitated a minute, then said, "Yes, I will. I get tired of the girls' inane talk about men all the time." She looked at Fancy with a thin smile. "I don't expect you'd care to drop in on me and Luther sometime, have coffee with us."

"Of course I will. I get hungry for the company of women lots of times. Always having to talk to eight-year-olds gets tiresome too."

"My girls have about the same intellect. Sometimes I don't answer the door when they knock. Especially that Pilar. That's the meanest bitch that ever drew breath. She's never happy unless she's got the others into some kind of uproar or other. It's a wonder someone hasn't killed her by now."

"The one thing I'm glad about not being able to dance is not having to be around her anymore," Fancy said, walking out onto the porch with Myrt.

Tod and Lenny came running up, their noses and cheeks red from the cold. "Do you want me to help you home, Miss Myrt?" Lenny asked, and with a smile the big woman crooked her arm for him to take hold of.

"Come straight in for lunch when you get back, Lenny," Fancy called after the aging ex-whore and the man-child.

A lunch of warmed-over chili had been eaten and Fancy had gone outside to help Tod and Lenny finish their their fort when Gil Hampton walked tiredly into camp, dragging the big cat behind him.

"Hey, Zeb!" Fancy pounded once on the cookhouse door. "Gil just brought in the cat. Come and look at the size of him."

While she and the boys squatted down to look in awe at the dead animal, Zeb came running up, still pulling on his jacket. "Would you look at the size of him," he exclaimed. "I knew he was a big one from the size of his tracks. I see you got him right between the eyes, didn't mess up his fur."

"I tried not to." Gil gave Fancy a crooked smile. "Do you think its cured pelt would look nice spread out on the floor in front of a fire, or beside a bed to step on when you crawl out on a winter morning?"

"I should think so," Fancy answered before realizing that Gil was talking about her floors. She hurried to add, "I'm sure Pilar will be very pleased with it."

"Pilar?" Gil scoffed. "That one wouldn't appreciate the beauty of this skin."

Before Fancy could respond to his remark, Chance and his men walked into camp. They stopped briefly to take another look at the cat, then went on into the cookhouse to see what Zeb had prepared for lunch.

Ignoring Gil and the cat, Chance looked at Fancy and asked coolly, "What's for lunch?"

Fancy stood up from her examination of the slain animal and answered, equally cool, "I have no idea what Zeb has made for you and the men."

Chance was sure he heard Hampton snicker as Fancy walked away, but when he turned his head to glare at him, the scaler's face was bare of any emotion. A moment later, however, when he entered the cookhouse, he knew in his bones that the man was laughing like hell at him.

Fancy felt some guilt as she washed the bowls and spoons she and the boys had used. She should have served Chance some of the chili. After all, he paid for the supplies that came into the house. It was the attitude he'd taken in front of Gil that had provoked her anger. He had acted as though she was paid help and he could speak to her any way he wanted to. If he had asked in a normal voice, she would have served him some chili.

Her chin squared determinedly. Chance Dawson was going to learn that she was not hired help and that she didn't intend to be treated as such. She would, however, make a roast from the side of beef one of the farmers had delivered today and bake an apple pie for dessert. A kind of peace offering.

When the pale winter sun was about to sink behind the mountain, the sawmill was shut down and the men took off for the cookhouse to eat and thaw out their cold flesh.

Chance lingered behind them, walking slowly. Should he eat with the men, he asked himself, or go home and see if the little vixen had set a place for him at the table? He couldn't much blame her if she hadn't, considering how he had spoken to her. But she and Hampton had looked so cozy together, Hampton giving her that lazy smile of his, probably telling her that the fur was for her floor, and God knew what else the damn womanizer was saying.

His feet, as though propelled by their own power, walked past the cookhouse. Inside, the men laughed and joked with each other as they washed up before sitting down to eat at the long table that would be loaded with bowls of steaming vegetables and platters of meat.

The light from his kitchen window seemed to welcome Chance, and he hurried forward. When he walked into the kitchen, Fancy looked up from taking the tender roast from the oven. He gave her a tentative smile and said, "It sure smells good in here."

"Thank you." Fancy gave him a quick smile, then said, "There's warm water in the reservoir for you to wash up."

Chance didn't immediately fill a basin with water but stood looking through into the family room, where a cheery fire burned in the fireplace. Tod and Lenny sat on the large, brightly colored Indian rug spread before the hearth, looking quite comfortable as they shot marbles. This rug he had provided for Fancy was more handsome and would be just as warm for her to sit on—or lie on—as any animal pelt. He would point that out to her if the occasion should arise.

The roast, with the potatoes cooked in its juices, was delicious and Chance ate until he was ashamed of himself. But when Fancy brought out the apple pie, heavy with the aroma of spices, he was still able to eat two pieces. When she poured their coffee, she was surprised he had room for it.

Did he eat like this all the time? she wondered. If so, the side of beef and the sugar-cured hams in the larder wouldn't last long.

"That was a fine meal, wasn't it, boys?" Chance finally pushed away from the table.

"Fancy is a real good cook," Lenny said, ready to rise and follow Tod into the family room. "Uncle Buck always said so."

"He still misses his uncle, doesn't he?" Chance said when Lenny had left the kitchen.

"Yes, he does," Fancy answered sadly.

"And you still miss him too," Chance said, a softness in his voice.

When Fancy nodded, her eyes moist, Chance asked, "Was he the man you said would never be replaced in your heart?" Fancy nodded again, too choked up to speak.

A slow, pleased smile crept into Chance's eyes. There really wasn't a man of importance in her past. He had to work hard not to let his relief sound in his voice when he said, "I'll give you a hand with the dishes."

"No," Fancy said as he started stacking the plates. "Go on into the family room and sit with the boys. You've been out working in the cold all day."

There was no caring in Fancy's words, just plain facts and Chance found himself wishing they had come from some concern that he had put in a hard day. He put the plates down, muttering, "If you're sure," and left the kitchen to join Tod and Lenny. Sitting down in the large rocker that Fancy had in mind for him the day she chose it, he stretched his stockinged feet to the fire, curling his toes in its warmth. His stomach replete and his flesh warm again, he yawned widely, and a few minutes later he was nodding, then was in a deep sleep.

Lenny and Tod giggled when occasionally a soft snore escaped from between his lips. He was still sleeping soundly three hours later when Fancy quietly told the boys it was time to go to bed.

He didn't wake up when a little later she put on her heavy jacket and let herself out the back door to walk the short distance to her house.

Chapter Thirteen

As Fancy walked toward her house, the snow crunching coldly beneath her feet, she had the eerie feeling that someone, or something, was following her. Yet every time she turned around in the moonlit night and looked, she could not see anything that would cause the shivery feeling inside her.

She was thankful when she reached the small house and pushed open the door, not taking the time to stamp the snow off her boots. Nor did she remove them until she had barred the door. There might be another cat out there. Maybe the mate to the one Gil had killed.

As she struck a match and held its flame to the wick of the lamp sitting on the kitchen table, she noted that the house was still warmish from the fire she had built in the potbellied stove in the afternoon. She added two more sticks of wood to the bed of red coals, then went into her bedroom and changed into her gown and robe. She shoved her feet into the fur-lined moccasins her father had given her last Christmas, then turned back the bed covers to warm before she crawled beneath them.

Back in the family room, she picked up a newspaper that was two weeks old from San Francisco. She had not been reading long when she lifted her head to listen. Had she heard the crunch of stealthy footsteps in the snow? Thank God she had barred the door. One of the lumber men might have seen her enter the house, and knowing that she was alone decided he would call on her. She wasn't afraid of any of the men if they hadn't been drinking, but sometimes too much raw whiskey turned a man into something that even he wouldn't recognize in a sober state.

She stood up and took the rifle off its rack on the wall, thanking God that she knew how to use it. She was ready to step into the kitchen when she remembered that she hadn't closed the shutters there. The blood seemed to freeze in her veins as she remembered Zeb saying that a big cat would come through glass if he was hungry enough.

Fancy paused in the doorway to check if the rifle was loaded, and when she looked up a muted scream tore from her throat. Peering through the window was a woman's face, pale and wild-eyed. Fancy's outburst of terror hadn't died away when the woman spun around and darted off, disappearing into the tall pines in back of the house with an eerie laugh.

With cold sweat seeping from her pores, Fancy rushed across the floor and slammed the shutters closed. It seemed like forever before her shaking fingers could fasten them with their heavy latch. Every bone in her body still shaking, she went back into the family room and hovered over the stove, spreading her ice-cold hands over its warm top.

Who was the woman? she asked herself. No one from the Dawson camp. She began to wonder if the face she had seen was real. Maybe she was an apparition, the ghost of a woman who might have been killed by an Indian years ago in the very forest that grew so close to her house.

I'll never fall asleep, she thought, but nothing could make her walk back to the big house tonight. She added more wood to the fire and dragged the rocker up close to the stove. As the hours passed, she started violently at every little sound—the house creaking from the cold, the flap of an owl's wing as it flew past the window, the squeak of a small animal that would be a larger one's supper.

The night dragged on, and finally a gray dawn crept in. But Fancy sat on until she heard the men leaving the dance hall. Then, looking as if she hadn't slept in days, her eyes bloodshot and her features pinched, she got dressed. On her hurried walk to the big house, she looked often behind her.

Chance was building a fire in the range when Fancy burst into the kitchen. He took one look at her drawn face and asked anxiously, "What in the world is wrong? You look like you've seen a ghost."

"I think maybe I have." Fancy dropped into a chair.

Chance closed the firebox door and sat down also. "What are you talking about?"

In short, jerky sentences, Fancy told him of her scare and how the woman had disappeared into the forest.   .

"You must have imagined it," Chance said when she had finished. "It was probably the reflection of your own face in the glass pane, and in your nervous state you mistook it for some other woman's."

"I'm not apt to mistake my face for someone else's, Chance. I'm telling you that a face not familiar to me was peering through that window."

"All right." Chance held up a calming hand. "I'll go take a look around your place. In the meantime, go to bed and get some sleep. I'll keep an eye on the boys."

"I appreciate your offer," Fancy said at the

end of a jaw-breaking yawn. "Make sure you look real good. I didn't imagine that woman."

"I will. Don't worry about it. Now scat."

Chance immediately spotted the footprints under the kitchen window. Fancy hadn't been imagining things. He hunkered down to examine them. They were almost the size of child's; those of a small woman. He rose and followed the tracks. Judging from the distance between the footprints, the woman had been running. Then, right before his eyes, the prints disappeared as though their owner had grown wings and flown away.

Chance turned back, his brow furrowed in concentration. Who was the woman and where did she come from? Fancy had said that she was a stranger, and she had been here long enough to recognize every female face in camp.

Smoke was pouring from the cookhouse window, and Chance could see Zeb through the window as he cleared the dirty dishes left from the men who had eaten and then gone off to work. He turned onto the path the old man had shoveled clear of snow.

Zeb looked up from wiping the table when Chance opened the door and stepped inside. "Mornin', Chance," he said. "What brings you out so early? I saw Fancy high-tailin' it to your house a few minutes ago. Has she kicked you out already?" He grinned slyly.

"No, she didn't *kick* me out of the house."

Chance gave him a dark look as he poured himself a cup of coffee and sat down at the table. "Did you hear or see anything strange or unusual last night?"

"You mean like an animal prowlin' about?"

"No, a human—a woman."

Zeb started to shake his head, then stopped with a thoughtful look on his face. "Come to think of it, just before I went to bed last night I did see a woman walkin' 'round the dance hall, peerin' through the windows. I figured it was probably Pilar lookin' for Hampton. She gets fightin' mad when he spends some time with one of the other dancers."

The old man could be right, Chance thought, but if it was the Mexican woman, why did she run off through the woods instead of returning to the dance hall? Besides, Fancy knew Pilar and she had said the woman she saw was fair.

"Why are you concerned about a woman walkin' around at night?" Zeb asked.

"A woman, a stranger, was peering in Fancy's window last night. Scared the daylights out of her."

"You don't say. Do you think maybe it was a ghost?" Zeb's eyes grew round. "They do say there's a woman's spirit that roams around sometimes, moanin' and wailin'."

"You don't believe that nonsense, do you?" Chance said impatiently.

"Well, a lot of people have seen and heard her

over the years. They say she and her husband got separated in a flood long time ago and they both drowned. The story goes that the woman is still wanderin' around, lookin' for his spirit."

"I've heard that outlandish tale," Chance scoffed as he pushed away from the table. "I thought you had more sense than to believe such tripe."

"Well, I don't, not really. But just the thought that it might be true makes shivers run up and down my spine."

"Don't think about it then." Chance walked to the door. "I've got to get up to the house and make breakfast for the boys. I think that Fancy went straight to bed. She hadn't closed her eyes all night."

"I bet she won't be eager to sleep in her house anymore."

"I wouldn't be surprised." Chance's eyes kindled, and a slow smile crept across his face. Little Miss Vixen would welcome his bed now.

As if he had read Chance's mind, Zeb said slyly, "I reckon you'll be sleepin' on the floor in front of the fire."

"You reckon that, do you?" Chance grinned at him as he opened the door and stepped outside.

"I sure do reckon it," Zeb said to the empty room as he started washing the dishes. "And you're gonna reckon it too, Bucko, when she hands you your blankets and a pillow tonight."

Chance stepped along, his spirits high. Bit by bit he was getting what he'd set out to accomplish. Fancy no longer danced, making her dependent on him for her and the boys' welfare, and now, through no effort of his, she would be sleeping under his roof again. He might have to sleep on the floor a couple of nights, but if he made just the right moves, said the right words, he'd soon be back in his bed with her at his side.

Fancy awakened to a twilight-darkened room and the low murmur of voices coming from the kitchen. What time was it? she wondered, peering at the clock on the bedside table but unable to make out the hands. Whatever the time, she felt quite refreshed.

She remembered then why she had slept the day away and shivered. As though it was printed on the backs of her eyes, she could see that white face staring at her with maniacal eyes. There was no way she was going to sleep in her house again.

But where was she to sleep in this house? Not with Chance, that was for sure, although he probably had that in mind.

She lay in bed pondering her situation and finally smiled. She had come up with the perfect solution. Tod would sleep with her, and Chance would share Lenny's bed. She slid out of bed and hurriedly dressed, telling herself that tomorrow she must go to her house and get her gown and robe and slippers.

Three pairs of eyes looked up when she entered the kitchen. Chance and the boys were eating a supper of leftovers—chili and roast beef and sourdough bread.

"How are you feeling, Fancy?" Lenny asked. "Is your headache gone?"

Fancy glanced at Chance, who shrugged as if to say he didn't know what else to tell the boys, since the truth might scare them.

"I'm feeling fine," she answered the questioning looks directed at her. "And I'm starved. Did you all leave me anything to eat?"

"Uncle Chance has your plate in the warming oven," Tod answered her. "He got it from Zeb."

"You should all have eaten your supper there." She looked at Chance.

"I thought it best the house not be empty when you woke up."

There was surprise in Fancy's voice when she said, "Thank you, Chance. That was thoughtful of you."

Chance gave her a rakish smile. "You'd be surprised at how thoughtful I can be sometimes."

Fancy blushed at his meaning and was saved from making a retort when Lenny said, "Chance says you'll probably not be sleeping in the little house anymore because it's too cold. That's how you got your headache."

"Oh, he said that, did he?" Fancy arched an

eyebrow at Chance. "I didn't know he was a doctor. Did you fellows know that?"

"He's not a doctor, Fancy," Lenny said soberly. "He's a lumberman." This last was said proudly.

"I see. One of those, huh?" Fancy curled her lips in a pretended sneer.

"You're feeling pretty frisky, aren't you?" Chance grinned at her. "A big change since this morning."

"Please, I don't want to talk about this morning," Fancy said shortly and went to the stove to take her meal from the warming oven.

She felt guilty as she cut into a thick slice of baked ham that was surrounded with sweet potatoes and buttered turnips and a fresh sourdough biscuit. But the boys didn't seem to mind that her meal looked so much more appetizing than theirs, so she dug in, putting her supper away as fast as any hungry logger.

Chance's lips curled in amusement as he watched her, but he didn't voice it. He was seeing a new side to Fancy tonight, a softer side, one that he liked very much and he didn't want to change by a careless word. The trick now was to keep her in this genial mood. He must handle her as carefully as though she was a fine piece of china.

When Chance stood up and started clearing the table of dirty dishes, Fancy told him that she would clean the kitchen.

"Maybe I'll go play a few hands of poker with the husbands then," Chance said and took his jacket off the peg next to the door. "I won't be gone long."

"Stay as long as you like." Fancy started stacking the dirty dishes.

Zeb's small clock showed quarter to ten when the poker game broke up. Bill Bandy and Victor Seacat said good night as they stepped out into the cold night, leaving Chance to help Zeb push the chairs back in place and clear the table.

"You seemed kinda fidgety tonight, Chance," Zeb said, putting the cards away in a drawer. "You got somethin' on your mind? Like where you're gonna sleep tonight?" His eyes twinkled humorously.

"No, you old reprobate," Chance growled as he pulled on his jacket, "I haven't been thinking about where I'll sleep. I'll sleep under my own roof like I always do." As he slammed the cookhouse door behind him, he heard Zeb's devilish chuckle.

A lamp burned in the family room when Chance entered the house. His eyes went straight to the sofa, and his lips curved in a wide smile. There were no blankets and pillow laid out for him. Pehaps no seduction was going to be necessary.

But even as the thought entered his mind, Chance knew he had to be mistaken. Fancy

Cranson wouldn't fall into his bed that easily. She had gone back to her house after all.

As he stepped quietly toward his bedroom, Tod, half asleep, stepped through the door. "I have to use the chamber pot in the kitchen," he mumbled as he walked past Chance.

"What were you doing in my room?" Chance followed him into the kitchen, but turned his back when the boy lifted his nightshirt.

"Me and Aunt Fancy sleep in there now," came the sleepy answer. "You're to sleep with Lenny from now on."

When the lid clattered on the pot, Chance turned around and said, "Why don't you sleep with Lenny? I'm sure you'd rather be with your pal."

Tod shook his head. "Lenny snores too much."

Chance watched his nephew pad off to crawl into bed with his aunt. "Damn." He rapped his knuckles on the table. Not only was he not going to sleep with Fancy, he had to share a room with her cousin. It looked as if he'd have to start his seduction as soon as possible. Each day he wanted Fancy a little more.

Chapter Fourteen

Fancy stayed in bed until she heard the kitchen door click shut behind Chance. She avoided him as much as possible, for she felt herself softening toward him. She was afraid she'd fall prey to his smiles, the way he gave her those slumberous looks, the raw desire in his eyes as he touched her every chance he got. And how was one to remain cool toward a man who was always polite, soft-spoken, and anxious to please?

She rolled over onto her back, a knowing smile curving her lips. Chance wasn't fooling her, though. She knew what his sweet talk was all about, and she knew it wouldn't last once he realized that he was wasting his time. He'd quickly go back to his old, insulting ways again.

This new Chance had lasted a week now, and

she was sure that he would be making his move soon. That was when smooth talk and easy laughter would disappear, and friction and tension would be felt in the house again.

A long sigh feathered through Fancy's lips. How was it all going to end? How long could she continue to live in the same house with a man who only wanted her for his mistress, who weakened her resolve not to become so with every silky smile he gave her? How was she ever to get a loving husband and children of her own? She saw no chance of that in this camp.

Tod stirred and Fancy leaned up to gaze down on his sleeping face. She smiled tenderly. The cause of her dilemma, the stick Chance Dawson held over her head. She ran her hand lightly over his curly head. In order to keep him, she could put up with much worse than the threat of seduction. He was a part of her sister, a piece of Mary that Fancy would always have. Sooner or later something was bound to happen that would remove the obstacle of a tall, dark man with eyes that turned from brown to black when he was in a temper or in passion's grip.

"That's enough thoughts wasted on that man," Fancy grumbled as she got out of bed. She would think about the visit she was going to make to Molly Jackson's this afternoon. Today she would formally meet the other camp wives, and she hoped that they would be friend-lier than they had been in the past. Blanche Sea-cat had seemed a little cordial the day she stepped in and branded Pilar a liar. But the woman had been so irate at the Mexican dancer that she'd have seemed friendly to anyone else at the time.

Anyhow, Fancy assured herself, Molly was too kind to ask her to join them for coffee and cookies if she thought her neighbors would be rude to her.

Nevertheless, when four hours later Fancy stood in front of the dresser looking at her reflection in the mirror, she was a little nervous. She was remembering the disapproving looks she always received when she met any of the women on one of the many paths that criss-crossed the camp clearing.

She leaned forward to examine herself closely. Of the two nice dresses she owned, this dove-colored woolen was her favorite. Its bodice hugged her slender rib cage, then followed the rich curves of her breasts up to a demure neckline edged with a narrow lace ruffle. Its long sleeves narrowed at the wrists, and the skirt fell in soft folds to her feet. Her pale blond hair lay in soft curls on her shoulders.

I guess I look respectable, she thought, then gave a gasp. Chance's face had appeared behind her in the mirror. "You look lovely," he said, coming up behind her and putting his hands on her shoulders. "But you know, I'll always remember how you took my breath away the first time I saw you in that little red dress that showed your pretty knees."

Fancy remembered well that night. It was the first time a man had so blatantly insulted her. She met his eyes coolly. "Do you mean the time you decided that I was a whore and that I should be pleased that you wanted me to move in with you to be your private plaything until you tired of me?"

"Yes, damn you!" Chance spun her around to face him. "What was I to think? You were all fancied up in that red dress, your long legs clad in black silk stockings, your face painted, and that white hair almost blinding a man. Of course I thought you were like the rest of them, and my blood ran hot with wanting you.

"And I still burn for you," he said in a husky whisper. Before she could move, he jerked her up against his hard body and his hungry lips were on hers, hot and demanding that she respond.

Fancy fought the desire the drugging kiss was building inside her. This man only wanted to use her body. He cared nothing about what she thought, how she felt about the universe, the inner core of her being.

She hated herself as her body won out over her mind, and her arms came up to wind around his shoulders. She curled her fingers in his hair and pressed closer to him. She felt his lean body stiffen and heard his low gasp as her tongue came out to meet his probing one.

His hand had slipped into her neckline and was caressing her breast when Tod called from the kitchen, "Aunt Fancy, all the other ladies have gone to Miss Molly's house. You'd better hustle up."

Tod's young treble was like a dash of cold water in Fancy's face. She pushed herself out of Chance's arms and rubbed the back of her hand across her lips. "Don't you ever do that again!" she whispered fiercely.

"Why not?" Chance grated back. "You wanted it—you liked it."

"I did not! I hated it!"

"You lie, Fancy Cranson. If Tod hadn't called you, another minute and I would have had you on the bed with your skirts up around your waist."

"Oh, you crude devil, I hate you," Fancy fumed, straightening her bodice with trembling fingers. "I would have never gone to bed with you."

Chance gave her a knowing look and said huskily, "Should I send Tod outside and prove to you how fast I can have you on your back?"

The air around Fancy fairly crackled with her outrage. "Don't you dare talk vulgar to me like you do to your whores," she hissed. And before he could dodge it, her hand swept up and cracked across his cheek. He blinked and reached for her, but she had spun around and hurried to the kitchen where Tod waited for her.

"You look angry, Aunt Fancy." Her nephew peered at her face when she joined him. "Your cheeks are all red and your eyes are glittery."

"That's because I've been hurrying," she said, pulling a smile to her lips. As they went out the door, she reminded Tod to stay close to the house, that his uncle would be looking after him and Lenny until she got home.

Fancy felt the battery of eyes focused on her as Molly ushered her into the Jacksons' family room and wondered nervously if there was any remnant of passion on her face.

Her tentative smile was answered freely as she was introduced to each woman. Blanche Seacat said in her shrill voice, "I think you should know, Fancy, that we've broken our rule about lettin' single women join our little group." She looked at Molly as she continued, "Molly pointed out to us that you didn't have any decent young women to visit or become friends with. So"—she paused and smiled widely— "welcome to our little . . . club, I guess we can call it."

Everyone echoed Blanche's welcome, with Mavis Bedloe adding with a laugh, "Henry calls it a gathering of cackling hens."

"Well, whatever you ladies call your group, I'm pleased to be a part of it. Thank you for inviting me," Fancy said gravely.

Molly had no sooner put cookies on the table and poured coffee than Blanche wanted to know all about the face Fancy had seen at her window.

As the women waited with their eyes fastened on her, Fancy told of the woman peering in at her, how wild her eyes looked, how her skin had crawled when the creature ran off through the night, her crazy-sounding laugh floating behind her.

"You must have been scared out of your wits," Mavis Bedloe said when Fancy had finished. "Henry caught a glimpse of her the next night down by the mill yard. Only this time she was making a wailing noise as she disappeared into the woods. He said his whole body shivered, he was that shook up."

"Victor saw her too, just last night," Blanche said, bringing all eyes swinging to her. "Yes, he did." Blanche nodded. "She was peering into the cookhouse. When she saw him, it was like she just up and disappeared in the air."

"Did he see her face? Did he recognize her?" one of the women asked, her eyes, like the others', showing her uneasiness.

"He couldn't see her too clearly because the moon wasn't very bright last night. But he could make her out enough to know that he had never seen her before."

The old story of the dead woman's spirit looking for her departed mate was repeated; then other tales about 'haints' and ghosts were told. By the time Molly's clock struck four, the ladies had scared themselves close to hysteria. When they looked out the window and saw that the sun was setting, a mad rush was made for their wraps. Hurried good-byes were said, and Molly's kitchen emptied in seconds. Only Fancy lingered to thank Molly for inviting her to meet her neighbors and assure her hostess that she had enjoyed herself.

Chance saw Fancy hurring toward the house, and he quickly left the kitchen to join Tod and Lenny in the family room. He wasn't about to let the little hellcat know that he had been watching for her—had made half a dozen trips to the window. His cheek still stung from the wallop she had given it, and if she ever slapped him again, he was going to put her across his knees and blister her little rear end.

And someday she was going to admit that she enjoyed their kisses just as much as he did, the stubborn little mule.

But when was that day going to come? he wondered as he sat down and stared moodily into the fire. They'd known each other for a month now, had made love once, and Fancy still treated him with a cool disdain that made him want to grab and shake her until those white curls flew all over her head.

"That's not what you'd really like to do," his

inner voice said slyly. "What you want to do more than anything else in the world is to take her to bed and make love to her until neither one of you can move."

Chance didn't deny the charge. It was all too true. He wanted to make love to Fancy so badly he could almost taste it. It was pure hell living under the same roof with her, knowing that only a wall separated them at night when they lay in separate beds, knowing also that it might as well be a mountain keeping them apart.

He heard Fancy open the kitchen door and wondered what attitude he should take with her. He was getting desperate because he had tried everything he could think of that would make her warm up to him.

He decided that he would go back to treating her coldly to give her little digs whenever he could. She would snap back at him and make him angry. When he was in a rage at her, he didn't want her so badly.

Yet, when Fancy called out, "I'm home, fellows, what do you want for supper?" Chance was just as eager as the boys to go into the kitchen and sit at the table watching her fly about, making what she pleased for the evening meal.

Chapter Fifteen

Fancy had been up since the first pink of dawn preparing the cornbread dressing she would stuff the Thankgiving turkey with.

Two days ago Zeb had gone hunting and shot two wild turkeys and had given her the smaller one. It was a hen and would be more tender than the big twenty-pounder he had kept for the loggers. The fourteen-pound bird would be plenty for them and their two guests, Peter and Clarence. Brothers, supposedly.

She hoped that the two pumpkin pies that she had baked yesterday and now sat in the larder had turned out well. She hadn't planned on making them, but when the farmer's oldest son delivered the milk, eggs, and butter on Monday he had given her the big pumpkin. "Maw thought you might like to bake some pies for your Thanksgiving dinner," he said shyly.

Fancy had mixed emotions as she loosely packed the cavity of the plump bird. It would be her first holiday without her father, but at the same time she was grateful that Tod had escaped death in the floodwaters that had taken his parents. She wasn't happy with their living conditions, but they did live in a warm house and had plenty to eat.

It griped her, though, that Chance Dawson was responsible for that. Had he left her alone, not made her lose her job, she and the boys would have fared all right in their little house. At least she wouldn't be walking around all the time filled with tension, always trying to avoid Chance.

Sometimes that seemed an impossible endeavor, she thought as she lifted the turkey into the roasting pan she had borrowed from Zeb. It seemed that every time she turned around she was bumping into him; it was as if he watched and waited for the right moment to pounce on her. She wished he'd spend more time with his men, tend to business, and stay out from under her feet.

When she had placed the turkey in the oven, Fancy poured herself a cup of coffee and sat down at the table to watch the sun come up. When it cleared the tree line, sending out its rays, she was surprised to see them glistening on freshly fallen snow. Sometime during the night two or three inches had fallen.

A couple of hours passed during which Fancy straightened the family room, changed out of her nightclothes, and brushed her hair until it shone like silk, spilling down her back, the curls almost reaching her waist.

She was standing at the dry sink peeling potatoes, the roasting turkey sending out a delicious odor, when Chance walked into the kitchen and sniffed the air. "It sure smells delicious in here." He sniffed again and said, "I haven't smelled anything so good since my ma passed away."

"My sister Mary taught me how to stuff and roast a turkey," Fancy said, a note of sadness in her voice as she remembered those days before her sister married and moved away.

"You know," Chance said, half serious and half teasing, "you're going to make some man a fine wife someday."

Fancy bit her tongue to keep from saying that since he had carelessly taken her virginity, she had little chance of marrying a decent man, and if she couldn't wed an honorable man such as her father had been, she'd remain an old maid the rest of her life. She contented herself with giving Chance a scorching look and continued peeling the potatoes.

"Why the dirty look?" Chance came and stood beside her.

"I wasn't aware I gave you such a look."

"You know that you did. Don't you intend marrying someday?"

"Not if I only have a bunch of loutish loggers to choose from."

"What's wrong with loggers?" Chance gave her a frowning look. "I'm one."

"Exactly," Fancy snapped and brushed past him to check on the turkey.

"Are you saying that you're too good to marry a *loutish logger*?"

"Exactly." Fancy picked up an oven pad and pulled the roaster forward until she could baste the big bird with its own rich juices.

"You're a lady of few words this morning, I see." Chance gave her a dark frown. "Nothing I say strikes you right."

When Fancy only shrugged, he asked, "How do you expect to find a prissy gentleman here in the big timber?"

"I don't expect to find him here," Fancy answered shortly.

"I'd like to meet this perfect man when you meet him." There was sarcasm in Chance's voice.

"You'd be the last person I'd introduce him to." Fancy slammed the oven door closed and straightened up. "Anyway, he won't be from around here so it's unlikely you'll ever see him."

"So, you've decided you don't want to be burdened with Tod after all." Chance watched her face through narrowed eyes.

"Don't you wish that was true?" Fancy flared out at him. "I'll never tire of looking after my sister's son, and you might as well get that through your thick head."

"Then you're stuck here with me whether you—" Chance clamped his mouth shut. How had they gotten into this hot argument? All he had said when he walked into the kitchen was how good it smelled. Five minutes later they were taking pieces out of each other.

The heated words would have had to cease at any rate. Tod had walked into the kitchen, and it had been agreed between Fancy and Chance that he and Lenny would never hear them sniping at each other.

Fancy forced a cheerfulness, talking and joking with them, but Chance went around in a moody silence, prowling the house from kitchen to family room, then back again. Finally, in desperation, Fancy whispered to Tod, "Why don't you ask Uncle Chance to help you and Lenny build a snowman?"

Excitement glittered in the boy's eyes as he left the kitchen on the run. A tickled smile lifted the corners of Fancy's lips as she listened to Chance trying to beg off, saying it was too cold out, that they should stay in and pop some corn. But Tod and Lenny insisted they'd rather build a snowman, and he reluctantly gave in.

As they took their jackets off the pegs beside the door, Chance grouched, "Which one of you fellows dreamed up the idea of making a snow-man?"

"Neither one of us." Tod grinned, pulling a stocking cap over his curls. "Aunt Fancy thought of it."

"I should have known it came from you." Chance gave Fancy a black look. When he caught her grinning with devilish glee, he slammed the door so hard behind him and the boys that the wall shook.

"How do *you* like being manipulated, Bucko?" Fancy muttered, still grinning as she finally found the time to go make up the beds.

It didn't take her long to smooth the covers on her and Tod's bed. They were both quiet sleepers. But Chance's bed looked as if a battle had been fought in it. All the top covers lay in a crumpled mass on the floor. As she remade the bed, she hoped Chance had been awake half the night.

Peter and Clarence arrived precisely at three o'clock, the hour Fancy had invited them to come. Peter, the more talkative one, handed her a bottle of wine. "Say," Chance said, "that looks like homemade. Where'd you get it?"

"We made it from wild grapes we picked in the foothills this past summer," Clarence an-swered. "It's got a powerful kick, so be careful or you'll be under the table while the rest of us sit at it eating Fancy's mouth-watering turkey."

"I know about grape wine." Chance grinned. "Don't worry, I'll treat it with respect. Let's go into the family room and have a glass while Fancy puts the meal on the table."

"I'll stay here and give Fancy a hand," Peter said quietly.

"You don't have to, Peter." Fancy smiled at him. "I can do it."

"At least I can lift the turkey out of the oven. It's bound to be heavy."

When Fancy agreed that, yes, it was a little heavy, a startled look came over Chance's face. It quickly changed to one of discomfort, however. No wonder Fancy thought him a lout, he thought. He was one. He should have realized that she could have used some help cooking such a large meal. And the big turkey would be heavy for her to lift from the oven.

"See what happens to a man when he only associates with whores," his inner voice scolded. "He loses all his finer senses."

Chance stood uncertainly for a moment; then, as he was ignored by Fancy and Peter, he turned and followed Clarence into the family room.

"Now, how can I help?" Peter rolled up his shirt sleeves. "I'm quite handy in the kitchen."

"You can mash the potatoes." Fancy smiled at him, taking in the sharp crease in his trousers, his smoothly ironed shirt and polished boots. She had always noted that Peter and

Clarence were neater than the other single loggers. They changed their shirts and trousers every other day and they never smelled of sweaty body odor.

"You come from back East, don't you, Peter?" Fancy asked as she handed him the potato masher. "How did you wind up out here?"

"I was studying medicine back in New York when I met Clarence. I . . . was thrown out of school after we began living together. We decided to come here to the Northwest where no one knew about the scandal."

"And do you like it here?"

"Yes, very much. A man is mostly left to live his life the way he wants to."

That's so important, Fancy thought, wishing that she was allowed to live her life the way she wanted to. It wouldn't involve Chance Dawson in any way.

When Peter had finished preparing the potatoes, Fancy handed him a couple of pot holders. "If you'll take the turkey out and carve it, I'll put the rest of the dinner on the table."

A few minutes later, after Fancy had called that dinner was ready, everyone was so enthusiastic in their praise of Fancy's culinary expertise that she blushed with pleasure.

"You're a lucky man, having Fancy in your kitchen, Chance," Peter said, reaching for another biscuit.

Fancy glanced at Chance and saw the wicked

look in his eyes; she knew what he was thinking. He'd rather have her in his bedroom. She wanted to kick him when he drawled, "Yes indeed, I am a lucky man to have Fancy living with me." He made it sound as though they were living together in the biblical sense.

More praise was heaped on Fancy when she served the pumpkin pie and poured coffee for the three men. When everyone sat back, fully sated, Peter said, "It's been a long time since we've sat down with a family to eat a holiday dinner."

"Then you must eat Christmas dinner with us." Fancy smiled.

"Thank you, Fancy, we'd be pleased to," Peter said and Clarence nodded. "I'll give you a hand with the dishes; then we'll be on our way."

Fancy couldn't hide her surprise when Chance said, "I'll help her clean up."

When the brothers had gone, and Fancy and Chance were clearing the table, Tod and Lenny pitched in and helped, getting in the way more than aiding them.

When the last dish had been put away, Tod reminded Chance that he had promised to take him and Lenny over to the Daniels' home to play with the children of Sukie and George. Fancy held her breath, waiting for Chance's answer. She was tired, sweaty from being around the stove so long, and she longed for a warm, soaky bath in the big wooden tub hanging on a peg in the storage room. If he would only go with the boys for a couple of hours, she could have it.

Chance agreed, though reluctantly. As soon as they left the house, Lenny and Tod bundled up to their noses, Fancy brought the tub into the kitchen. She barred the door, then filled the tub half full from the warm water in the reservoir.

She had soaped her entire body with her rose-scented soap and was lazily rinsing the suds off her shoulders when a knock sounded at the door. "It's me, Fancy," Zeb called. "I've run out of sugar. Can you spare me some?"

"Can you come back a little later, Zeb?" she called back. "I'm taking a bath."

"Sure. There's no hurry."

It seemed to Fancy that barely five minutes had passed when she heard the old man step up on the porch again. He must be in a hurry for that sugar, after all, she thought, standing up in the tub and reaching for the robe she had hung over the back of a chair. She supposed she was lucky she'd had half an hour to herself. Privacy was a rare thing in this household.

She tied the robe's belt around her waist and opened the door, then grabbed the robe together at her throat. Gil Hampton stood smiling down at her, his eyes raking over the curves the clinging robe emphasized.

Hampton's features creased in a smile of pure

pleasure. "Aren't you something," he said admiringly.

"Gil, you know you shouldn't be here," Fancy squeaked. "Chance would have a fit if he knew you were here."

"He's always having a fit about something or other. Anyhow, it's said around camp that you're not his woman, so you should have men callers if you want to."

"I'm not his woman, but he runs most of my life because of my nephew. If he found you here, and me in my robe, he'd claim that I'm loose and unfit to raise Tod."

"If he has such control over you, in a sense you are his woman."

Fancy shook her head. "I suppose it looks that way, but as long as I live under his roof, I must abide by his rules. My nephew is very dear to me, and I'll put up with Chance's high-handedness for the time being in order to keep him."

"You might not belong to Dawson," Gil said, "but everyone knows he wishes that you did. If two men get together, they talk and laugh about it. Up until you came along, he could have had any woman he wanted."

"And that's probably why he wants me. He's the type who would want what he can't have."

"No, not in your case." Gil trailed a finger down her cheek. "He'd want you anyway. Every single man and half the married ones in camp would like to have you for their woman."

"Does that include you, Hampton?" Chance had stepped quietly up on the porch.

Fancy's heart began to beat in heavy thuds as several tense moments passed before Gil turned around and answered lazily, "Maybe. What business would it be of yours if I did?"

"It would be my business if my nephew was going to be dragged all over the Northwest as you went from camp to camp."

Hampton ignored Chance's insulting remark and smiled down at Fancy. He held out a cloth-covered plate, which in her nervous state she hadn't noticed, and said, "Big Myrt asked me to bring you this cake she baked for you."

"How nice." Fancy took the plate from him. "Thank her for me, will you?"

"I sure will." Gil smiled at her; then, giving her a little salute, he stepped past Chance and walked away, his hands shoved in his jacket pockets as he whistled a merry tune.

Chance muttered a swear word and slammed the door closed. "Are you in the habit of answering the door in your robe—naked beneath it at that?" he demanded.

"I thought it was Zeb. He'd said he'd be by to borrow some sugar earlier."

"I wish I could believe that," Chance said, his eyes skimming over her body, stopping at her breasts where the nipples pressed against the material, hard nubs from her nervous state.

"I don't care whether you believe it or not." Fancy spun around and headed for the bedroom. "I'm going to get dressed."

Chance knew deep in his heart that Fancy was telling the truth. He had found her to always be open and honest. Sometimes so honest it hurt.

"Fancy," he called, going after her. "I shouldn't have said that to you. I know you're no liar." He caught up with her and took her by the arm. "I'm so tired of fighting with you." He swung her around to face him. "Can't we stop this bickering and live in some kind of harmony?"

If only he meant it, Fancy thought, giving Chance a pensive look through long dark lashes. She, too, was tired of having to always wonder what his mood would be from day to day, having to watch what she said in order not to start an argument.

A slightly humorous smile curved her lips. "Do you think it's possible?" she asked. "We get along like two strange bulldogs."

"We can do it, Fancy." Chance took hold of her other arm and drew her forward until their bodies were only inches apart.

She could feel the heat of his palms wrapped around her arms, and her heart beat faster. She lifted her gaze to his face and trembled at the leashed hunger in his eyes. She looked at his lips, soft now, and suddenly wanted his mouth on hers, unaware that it showed in the way her expression grew soft and waiting. She didn't resist when, with a muffled groan, Chance transferred one arm to her waist and drew her tight between his slightly spread legs. As his hard arousal throbbed against her stomach, his lips moved coaxingly over hers.

Fancy didn't resist when Chance swung her into his arms, their lips still fused together, and carried her into the bedroom. He stood her on the floor and, lifting his head, he untied the robe's belt and slid the garment over her shoulders to crumple around her feet.

Chance laughed softly when she instinctively brought her hands up to cover her breasts. He gently took her hands and held them to her sides and gazed at the perfect beauty of her body.

The hot raking of his eyes mesmerized Fancy, and she could only stand helplessly, letting him look his fill. Then a low cry was wrenched from her when he bent his head and took her breast into his mouth. The tug and pull of his lips made her forget everything but him and the desire that was beginning to simmer inside her. When he moved his head to claim the other breast, every nerve ending tingled with the desire that blazed through her.

When Chance finally raised his head and looked down at her, his eyes silently questioning, there was acceptance in hers. He scooped her up and laid her down on the bed, coming down beside her.

Little mewling cries fluttered through Fancy's lips when he again suckled a breast, then moved on down her body, his tongue and mouth laving every inch of it. She held her breath when he came to the apex of her thighs and lingered there. She gasped when he gently parted her legs, his tongue searching for the hard little nub hidden in her silky curls. She thrashed her head back and forth when he found it and stroked and nibbled.

"Don't hold back, little fox," he lifted his head to coax. "Ride the tide that's trying to be free inside you."

Fancy mutely shook her head. She would not let herself lose control like that. She never dreamed that a woman could be loved like that. But when once again she felt his tongue doing its wicked work, she was powerless to hold back the waves of passion that washed through her. She moaned his name and clutched his shoulders, mindlessly kneading her fingers into his hard, muscular shoulders.

Her spasming body finally lay still, leaving her so weak that she was sure she couldn't so much as lift a finger. She watched Chance through slumberous eyes as he tugged off his boots, then stripped off his clothes. When he turned to face her, her eyes were drawn to the long, hard arousal standing stiff and proud, and her excitement grew as she remembered how it felt inside her.

Chance moved up to the bed and rasped, "Look how much I want you, Fancy. Please hold it, stroke it."

She reached out and curled her palm around the thick hardness and slowly stroked her hand up and down the long length. When he suddenly came down on his knees beside her shoulder, she lifted questioning eyes to him.

"Please," he begged softly.

It took her a moment to realize what Chance was asking her to do. And since there was nothing she wouldn't have done for him at that moment, she leaned over and opened her mouth over him. He lifted her hair, which had fallen forward, so that he could watch her love him.

Fancy's adoration of Chance lasted but a short time. He wanted her too badly, had waited to long to have her. He slowly freed himself and lifted her head to lay her back on the pillow. As she opened her legs to receive him, he entered her slowly, filling her tight sheath with his largeness.

When he had buried himself until her blond curls meshed with his dark ones, he held still a moment, savoring the feel and heat of her. When her hips nudged his, he placed his hands on her hips, holding her steady for his thrusts. When she wrapped her legs around his waist and her arms around his shoulders, he began a rocking rhythm that made the headboard bounce against the wall. A few minutes later, the house rang with their cries of release.

When Chance's breathing returned to near normal, he raised his upper body from her and smiled into her eyes. She lifted a languid hand and traced the fine lines around his eyes, put there from exposure to the sun and wind. She loved the way they crinkled when he smiled.

Chance softly stroked her cheek and smoothed the tangled curls off her forehead, then whispered huskily, "I feel like I just experienced a little piece of heaven." When Fancy nodded agreement, a teasing smile hovered at the corners of his lips. "Do you think you can bear up under so much loving every night . . . and day?"

Before Fancy could smilingly agree that it would be her pleasure, his next words shattered her belief that he was thinking of marriage.

"We'll move Tod back in with Lenny and take over this room." He dropped a kiss on her nose. "We're going to have some fine times in it. I think this passion we share will last a long time. Maybe even a year or more. What do you think?" He stroked a finger across her bottom lip, which she was trying desperately not to let quiver as she strove not to lash out at him in bitter denunciation. She wanted to tell him exactly what she thought of his smug assurance that she would gladly be his whore.

Keeping her features as bland as possible and lowering her lids to hide the fury in her eyes, she answered in what she hoped was a normal tone. "I don't think that's a good idea. After all, it's only passion that we share. If we don't like and respect each other, which we don't, any kind of relationship between us couldn't last more than a week, if that long."

When Chance opened his mouth to say that she was wrong, Fancy hurried on. "I don't want this to happen again, so I'll go back to sleeping in my house."

"Come on, Fancy, you don't mean that," Chance protested as she scooted out from beneath him. "Have you forgotten about the woman who was peering in your window?"

"She can't get through barred doors and shuttered windows," Fancy said as she walked across the floor, deliberately naked, to the dresser and opened the top drawer.

"I still don't think you mean it," Chance said in a thick voice, his loins stirring as he watched her pull lacy underclothing from the drawer.

"Yes, I do," she answered, stepping into mid-thigh pantaloons, then pulling a camisole over her head. "I couldn't sleep with you in front of Tod even if I wanted to. He'd know it wasn't right and might grow to dislike me, lose his respect for me."

Chance was silent as Fancy pulled on a dress, then sat down to slide stockings up her lovely legs, followed by ruffled garters to keep them in place. Anger and resentment were building inside him. When Fancy stood up, ready to leave the room, he said in a hard voice, "I know what you're thinking, you know. You think that I'll offer marriage just to keep you. But you're mistaken, lady. There's not a woman alive who's going to put a permanent ring in my nose."

When Fancy made no response, only walked toward the door, he called after her, "You aren't all that good in bed anyway."

Chapter Sixteen

Chance hated himself the moment the lie left his mouth. Fancy was the best. He doubted that there was another woman alive who could send him soaring the way she could. It had been a cruel taunt he'd made, saying that she was lacking in the art of lovemaking. He had sounded as if he thought her a whore who hadn't performed her job well.

He heard the kitchen door close and left the bed to hurry to the window from where he could see Fancy's little house nestled among the tall pines. A moment later he saw Fancy's bundled-up figure hurrying toward it. When she paused on the porch and filled her arms with wood from the pieces stacked against the wall, he knew she was going to build a fire in her stove to warm the place up for when she returned at bedtime.

A sigh escaped him as he thought of the strained silence that would once again exist between them. It wasn't as though they were in the habit of talking to each other as they sat in front of the fire in the evenings. They were usually angry at each other for some reason or other. But even at those times, her presence was a comfort to him. He derived a good feeling just watching her help the boys with their lessons, read a story to them, or just sit quietly, staring into the flames. Sometimes she wore a contented look; at other times she looked pensive, and occasionally there was a sadness on her lovely face. He imagined that she was thinking of her father and sister at those times.

I'm going after her, he decided. He'd apologize for his words spoken in anger and promise to keep his hands off her. But God, what torture it would be, keeping his hands off her, he thought as smoke began to rise from Fancy's chimney. He ached to have her in his arms right now.

Chance was getting into his clothes when he heard Tod and Lenny's noisy entrance into the kitchen. He frowned. Had they came home alone? It was almost dark. He'd have a few words with George Daniels tomorrow. Not only could there be wolves lurking about, that crazy woman was still being heard of once in a while. The woman could very well be dangerous, for he thought she was real, not a spirit looking for her dead mate.

She was another reason he didn't want Fancy sleeping in her house. Although he hadn't told Fancy, he had found the woman's footprints under her window a couple of other times.

As Chance opened the door for the boys, Zeb called from the cookhouse, "Send one of the boys over with some sugar, will you, Chance?"

By the time Chance found the sugar container and sent Tod to bring it to Zeb, he had changed his mind about coaxing Fancy to give up her plans of sleeping at her place. He felt sure that after a couple of nights alone, she would come back on her own. Meanwhile, she need never know how he had weakened, until he was almost willing to beg her to return.

Fancy finished turning back the bed covers to warm in preparation for crawling under them later in the evening, and glancing out the window, she saw the boys walking home. Sukie Daniels walked with them, carrying a club in her hand. Why wasn't her husband bringing them home? she wondered. As she watched, Sukie stopped a few yards from the house and waited until the boys stepped up on the porch. She turned around then, and with shoulders slumped, walked toward her house.

I bet George is drunk, and she's afraid he will beat her when she gets home, Fancy thought angrily. She started to ask herself why Sukie put up with her husband's cruelty, then shook her head. What could the poor woman do? Her looks were gone from twelve pregnancies in as many years, four resulting in miscarriage. Where could the poor woman go with eight children, all under the age of twelve? She was bound as tightly to George as though she were in prison. In order to keep a roof over their heads and food in their bellies, she must endure whatever her husband chose to do to her.

As Fancy walked back to the big house, she was still pondering on Sukie's misfortune. If she had married a man like that, the first time he beat her would have been the last time. She would wait until he fell into a drunken stupor, tie his hands and feet, then take a whip to him. She'd strip the hide off him. He'd think twice before he struck her again.

Fancy had been sleeping in her house for a week. And though both doors were barred and the shutters fastened over all the windows, she was uneasy, jumping at every little sound. She kept the lamp on the bedside table lit all night, for twice someone had rattled the kitchen door knob, then moments later did the same thing to the front door. She had been too frightened to get up and peek through the shutters at who-ever was trying to get inside.

But with the rising of the sun, her fears of the

night always disappeared, not to return until she was back in bed, the covers pulled up over her head.

The first time she had decided to sleep in her own bed again, Tod and Lenny had complained about it. It made no sense to them, they said, that she would want to sleep in the little house, and wasn't she afraid to do so?

Fancy smiled wryly. She couldn't tell them that she was more afraid of sleeping in the big house, that she was afraid she'd succumb to Chance's charms and end up in bed with him any time he felt like making love to her. She had learned that where he was concerned she was a moth to his flame.

She hadn't had to worry about that recently. Chance was back to his usual cold self, barely talking to her. When he did speak, it was to make some cutting remark that made it very difficult not to snap back at him.

He left the house each evening right after supper and didn't return until after midnight. This didn't surprise her. It was his way of punishing her for not going along with his plans. He intended that she lose sleep; he made sure she would have to walk to her house when no one was out and about.

Fancy didn't know that every night Chance stood at his bedroom window, watching until she was safely inside and had lit her lamp.

Fancy had smoothed the quilts over the boys'

beds and was on her way to do the same to Chance's when someone knocked on the kitchen door. When she swung it open, her eyes lit up. "Gil!" she exclaimed, "I haven't seen you for ages, it seems. Come in."

"Where's the big man?" Gil peered over her shoulder, grinning. "I wouldn't want to make his mood worse than it is. He's been like a mad bull all week. I've been keeping out of his sight as much as possible."

"I'm not sure where he is, but I think the grouch went with one of the men to grease the skids."

Gil held up the hammer he carried in his hand. "The reason I'm here is to check the shutters on your house, make sure there's no loose nails and that the latches are sturdy. I just finished going over Myrt's windows. If we get a strong wind and the shutters aren't fastened tight, they can whip about and come loose in their frames."

"I certainly wouldn't want that to happen." Fancy shivered. "I don't like to think that crazy woman could get inside my house."

"I doubt that she'll be out much anymore, it's so cold," Gil said quietly as he helped Fancy on with her jacket. "I don't think anyone would prowl around in this freezing weather."

"I feel sorry for the poor soul," Fancy said as she and Gil crunched through the snow. "Has anyone found out where she comes from, if she has anyone to look after her?"

"I don't think there's been any inquiries made. Most everyone thinks she's a spirit, a 'haint.' " Gil gave a disparaging laugh. "But I'm sure there's someone who tries to look after her."

"Maybe all she's looking for is a friend," Fancy said.

Gil stopped short and grabbed her shoulders, making her look at him. "Don't try to be her friend, Fancy," he said soberly. "The woman is unbalanced and could do you serious harm, if not kill you. Promise me you'll not try to help her." Gil looked so frighteningly solemn that Fancy could only gaze at him and nod her head.

She followed Gil around the outside of the house as he examined the windows. She called his attention to the tracks made by a woman under her bedroom window as well as the kitchen. "Some of these tracks look pretty fresh, Gil, like they might have been made last night."

"Maybe," Gil answered as he hammered a loose nail firmly into place. "Why don't you go back to sleeping in the big house if you feel uneasy? It might be better if you do."

Fancy shook her head. "If she can't get in, I'll not worry."

"She'll not be able to get in if your inside latches are tight. Let's go check them."

Fancy led Gil through her house, he checking all the latches. "All are in good order," he said after examining the last one in the kitchen. "Not even a hungry bear could get in to to you."

"Nevertheless, I'm glad the bears are hibernating." Fancy grinned at him. "Thank you, Gil, for checking everything. I'll sleep much better tonight." When a mischievous smile hovered around his lips, she hurried to say, "Shall we go have a cup of coffee?"

"That sounds good." Gil opened the door and stepped back for her to precede him.

Fancy had slipped on a piece of ice and she and Gil were laughing as he caught her arm, when they saw Chance walking up from the river. "I'll have that coffee some other time, Fancy," Gil said, his eyes sparkling humorously, taking his time releasing her arm. "I've got a feeling my boss wouldn't welcome me in his kitchen."

"Probably not," Fancy laughingly agreed. "You do seem to get under his skin."

"I hope so. I try to."

"Shame on you," Fancy scolded, her tone light as she walked on to face a wrathful Chance and Gil took the path to the cookhouse.

Chance had taken off his jacket and was standing at the stove pouring a cup of coffee when Fancy pushed the door open and walked inside. She breathed a relieved sigh when he didn't start right in on her, but sat down at the table as though she wasn't there. She had unwound the heavy scarf from around her head and shoulders, thankful there would be no sparring between them, when Chance exploded.

"That bastard didn't lose any time getting over here when he saw me leave, did he? I wonder how many other times he's sneaked over here."

"What are you talking about? Gil didn't know whether or not you were home. He was here to check the windows in my house to make sure they were tightly shuttered. And he has never *sneaked* over here."

"Like hell he hasn't. I bet he hightails it over here every time I leave the house."

With her hands on her hips and her eyes blazing, Fancy said in a fury, "Just for the sake of argument, let's say your charges are true. It's none of your business what I do or who I see. You're not my father or my husband. I don't have to answer to you about any of my actions."

It took Chance a minute to digest the angry words shot at him. Fancy spoke the truth. He didn't have any rights over her. There were only those that he had imposed by holding the loss of Tod over her head. And if she only knew it, that threat wasn't very strong. Tod loved his aunt and needed her at this time in his young life. Chance knew he'd never be able to take the child away from her. He jerked to his feet and slammed out of the house.

Later that evening, as the four of them ate supper, Tod and Lenny didn't seem to notice the charged silence between Chance and Fancy, and chattered on as usual. They looked disappointed, though, when the meal was over and Chance stood up and said coolly in Fancy's direction, "I won't be home until morning. Plan on spending the night here."

Fancy started to object, then closed her mouth. In all fairness, she had no right to. Chance had been staying in with the boys for over a week. It was only natural that he'd want a little entertainment in his life. She wouldn't let herself think what that entertainment would probably be and ignored the little voice that jeered, "Do you think that dancing is all he's going to do?"

Chance paused at the door for one last word. "If I hear that Gil Hampton was here while I was gone, I'll fire him."

"Don't you ever get tired of making threats?" Fancy said wearily. "I'm sick to death of hearing them."

"You might as well get used to it. You're going to hear them every time you step out of line." Chance jerked the door open, stepped outside, and slammed it behind him. A furious Fancy flew across the room and kicked the shuddering door hard enough for him to hear it.

Satisfaction glittered in his eyes. He had broken through that cold shell she had encased herself in during supper.

*   *   *

Sometime in the early hours of morning, Fancy's house burned to the ground.

It wasn't discovered until five o'clock when the dance hall closed and the men walked outside. Chance's face blanched as he looked at the smoking ruins of Fancy's little house. Dear God, what if she had been sleeping inside it? And who had started the fire? There hadn't been a fire built in her stove for over twenty-four hours.

The married men came running up, astonishment on their faces as they stared at the charred timbers. "Did any of you men see anybody prowling around Fancy's house last night?" Chance's questioning gaze ranged over all of them.

They all shook their heads; then Frank Jackson said, "Around three o'clock this morning, I heard that wild cackling laughter of that crazy woman."

"I heard it too," Bill Bandy spoke up. "Gave me the shivers, it sounded so unnatural."

Gil Hampton's face was as white as Chance's. Something had to be done about the unbalanced woman.

"Well," Chance said, his face grim, "There's nothing we can do, so you men may as well eat breakfast and get on to work. I'll go give Fancy the bad news. She's going to be mighty upset."

Chance was ashamed of the elation that sang through his blood as he walked home. Fancy would have to live with him now. She had nowhere else to go.

None of this showed when, an hour later, Fancy walked into the kitchen, tying the belt of her robe around her trim waist.

"I'm sorry I overslept," she apologized.

"That's all right," Chance surprised her by saying.

She was more surprised when he poured a cup of coffee from the pot he had brewed while waiting for her to get up. He placed the cup on the table and said, "Sit down, Fancy, I have something to tell you."

He looks so grave, Fancy thought as Chance took a seat across from her. What had happened that he thought might upset her? Chance returned her questioning gaze, searching for the right words to tell her that her home was gone. But when he realized there was no easy way, he said bluntly, "Fancy, your house burned down last night."

Fancy blinked, sure that she had misunderstood him. But as he continued to look steadily at her, she knew she had heard him right. "I don't know how that is possible." Her voice trembled. "I didn't make a fire in the stove yesterday."

"I know." Chance placed his hand over her clenched one. "I think it was deliberately set afire."

"But by who?" Fancy half sobbed, the tears

welling up in her throat. Her mother and father's pictures were gone, as well as the little hoard of money she had kept hidden in her sewing box.

"I'm pretty sure it was set fire by that crazy woman who's been spying on you."

"But why me?" Fancy cried. "I've never done anything to the woman. I don't even know her." A thought that widened her eyes in alarm gripped her. "Something has to be done about her, Chance. When she learns that I didn't perish in the fire, she's going to set fire to this house"—her voice broke—"with Tod and Lenny asleep in their beds."

"Don't worry about that, Fancy," Chance soothed. "I'll have the house watched night and day. And in the meantime, that woman is going to be tracked down and put away in an insane asylum where she belongs."

For three days Chance and some of his men searched a mile in all directions of the camp clearing looking for the woman's tracks. They came up with no evidence that any female had been roaming around. Bill Bandy suggested that maybe it had been a man, and Chance gave that remark some serious thought. Chances were, Bill and Frank had imagined they heard the crazy woman. When he held a meeting and assured everyone, especially the women, that there was no evidence of a crazy woman, or a ghost, stalking the camp, the wives departed with relaxed nerves and smiling faces.

Nerves, however, were raw in the Dawson household. Every time Fancy caught Chance watching her with eyes narrowed in desire, which was often, her pulses leapt in answer to the passion in his eyes. She knew it was but a matter of time before he would catch her at the right time, say the right words, or give her one of his melting smiles and she would fall into bed with him.

One Saturday afternoon, Fancy accompanied Molly to the river to wait for the canoe express that brought the camp its mail. Molly was expecting her monthly letter from her mother and two sisters. Fancy wasn't expecting to hear from anyone, but it felt good to be out of the house for a while despite the raw bite in the air—also to get away from Chance's disquieting presence.

Most of the camp wives were gathered at the river, anxiously awaiting news from home. Several feet away, in their own group, the dance hall girls waited also. Fancy started to speak to them, but they turned their backs on her, the silent gesture saying she was no longer one of them.

Thankfully, they didn't have to wait long before the canoe was spotted nosing through the water. Using the paddles was a man called Long John, because he was so tall and lanky. It was doubtful if anyone knew his real name. He was a very genial man, always ready with a wide smile.

A friendly grin was in evidence as he hopped up on the pier and snubbed the vessel to a post. "I've got a lot of mail for you ladies," he said as he lifted the mail pouch from the bottom of the canoe. "I wouldn't be surprised if everyone of you has a letter or two in here."

Fancy knew there wouldn't be a letter for her as Long John started calling out names. No one ever wrote to the Cransons. There was no one to write to them.

Molly's name was the fourth to be called, and she was handed three letters and a small package. "I can't wait to read them," she said excitedly, clutching the mail to her breasts as she and Fancy turned toward camp.

They had climbed halfway up the gentle incline leading from the river when Alma Brady called after them. "Fancy, there's a letter for you."

"For me?" Fancy stopped and turned around. "You must be mistaken. I don't know of anyone who would be writing to me."

"Well," Long John said, grinning, "if your name is Fancy Cranson, I've got a letter for you. A thick one."

Her face a study of surprise, Fancy walked back to the pier and was handed the first letter she had ever received. Without looking to see where it came from, she shoved it into her pocket. Something told her to read it in private. She was glad that Molly was in a hurry to get home to read her own mail, for it was all she could do not to strike out running for the house.

Chance and the boys were right where she had left them when she went off with Molly. They looked very comfortable in front of the fire, as though they were dug in for the duration of the winter. She quickly invented a headache.

"I'm going to lie down for a while," she said, rubbing her temple. "Probably for only a half hour or so."

"I'll see that the noise is kept down," Chance said as she closed the bedroom door behind her.

Fancy's hands were shaking so that she dropped the envelope when she pulled it out of her pocket. Picking it up, she finally looked at the return address in the upper left-hand corner. It read: Mrs. Thelma Ashely, Nob Hill, San Francisco.

Who was Thelma Ashely? she wondered as she carefully unsealed the envelope and pulled the letter free.

Chapter Seventeen

The opening sentence of the letter so stunned Fancy that she reached for the rocking chair beside the bedside table.

"My dearest granddaughter," she read. "It has taken me half the year to track you down. Sadly, in the process I learned that my beloved daughter had passed away, as well as your father and Mary, my other granddaughter. But happily, I also learned that I have a great-grandson.

"I also know that you are caring for a cousin on your father's side, a young man who is not mentally matured. I think it is very commendable of you to take such a responsibility onto your young shoulders. It shows that you had a good solid upbringing.

"My dear, I want to help lift that burden from you. It would make an old woman very happy if the three of you would come make your home with me in San Francisco. In the hope that you will do this, I have sent you three tickets to board the sidewheeler, the *Fairy*, which will bring you to San Francisco.

"You must be wondering why it has taken me all these years to look for my daughter. The sad truth is that your grandfather forbade me to do it. It broke his heart when Sarah ran off with your father. He felt that if she still loved us she would write and all would be forgiven. But months, then years passed without a word from her. He grew very bitter toward her.

"I have always felt in my heart that Sarah never stopped caring for us but was too ashamed to write. So, when your grandfather passed away seven months ago, I hired a detective to begin to search for our only child.

"Please come to me, Fancy. I am eighty-two years old and I feel that it won't be too long before God calls me home."

The letter was signed, "Your loving and waiting Grandmother."

Fancy let the letter drop to her lap and fingered the tickets as she stared at the floor, her mind in a turmoil. Mama had lied about her parents. Had she also lied about Papa's relatives?

But no, she believed that set of grandparents were truly dead. She remembered Papa and Lenny's father talking about their dying. They had passed away of influenza back in Illinois when the boys were teenagers.

When Fancy's mind calmed down and she could think straight, it struck her that she no longer had to live with Chance Dawson. She would no longer have to fear falling prey to his seductions. She had a place to go, a relative who wanted her and the boys.

Two important obstacles confronted Fancy. How was she to slip away and how was she to get to the Sound in order to board the *Fairy?* However she managed it—and she would— Chance must not know her destination. He would come after her and take Tod away.

She looked at her little clock. She had been here for forty-five minutes and it was getting dark outside. It was time she started supper. She slid the letter and tickets back into the envelope and, walking to her dresser, hid them under her underclothing in the top drawer. She left the room, telling herself that she must carry on as usual, chat with the boys, and answer any comments Chance might make. If she acted out of the ordinary in any way, Chance would notice and immediately become suspicious.

It was while Fancy was peeling potatoes that it came to her who would help her get to Puget Sound. Big Myrt. The dance hall woman had told her that if she ever needed help, she should come to her.

It was hard for her not to break into song as

she bustled about finishing the evening meal. Chance would really raise a suspicious eyebrow if she did that. It was out of the norm for her to sound happy in his presence.

The next morning when Fancy got out of bed, her eyes were red-rimmed and burning. She doubted she had gotten two straight hours of sleep, her mind had been racing so. Would the boys be happy in a crowded city? she had asked herself as Tod slept peacefully beside her. There would be so many changes in their lives. She doubted that, other than the streets, there would be any place for them to play. And people would probably give Lenny strange looks, seeing him playing children's games. Everyone here knew about him and paid no attention to his playing games with Tod.

And Tod would be entering a new school, a school that would not let his friend attend. And what about herself? There would be changes for her too. She would have to dress and act like a lady all the time. There would be no more riding skirts and logger's boots, her hair hanging free.

"Stop fretting," she had told herself sometime in the early morning hours. "You have always wanted to go to San Francisco and everything is going to work out fine."

It was ten o'clock by the time a leisurely Sunday breakfast was eaten and Chance had taken Tod and Lenny with him to oversee the greasing of the skids. As soon as they were out of sight, Fancy hurried into her heavy jacket and walked briskly toward the dance hall.

Myrt must have seen her coming, for the door to her living quarters opened before Fancy could knock. "Come in, Fancy," the big woman invited with a smile. "Luther and I have just finished breakfast and are having our coffee. Give me your jacket and sit down and have a cup with us."

"Thank you, Myrt," Fancy said, then smiled a greeting to Luther, who was still in his nightshirt. She knew by the flush on his cheeks that he was embarrassed at being caught in his nightclothes. But Myrt wasn't bothered in the least; she wore only a robe that clung to her ample breasts and hips.

"What brings you here, Fancy?" Myrt asked as she poured a cup of coffee and placed it before Fancy. "You look concerned about something."

"I am," Fancy said and pulled her grandmother's letter from her apron pocket. She handed it over to Myrt, saying, "Read this. It will explain everything."

After a short hesitation, Myrt took the letter and as Fancy and Luther watched, she swiftly read the spidery handwriting. When she had finished and folded the letter back into its creases, she said, "It's what you've been wanting, girl. Why the worried look?"

"I guess I'm not so worried as I am uneasy. It hit me last night that I'd be entering a world entirely new to me, living with an old lady I know nothing about. What if she's crotchety and the boys make her nervous? They can be quite loud sometimes."

"Now, Fancy, you're only imagining that," Myrt scolded. "Maybe the old woman would welcome a little noise in her house. She's probably lonesome. I think you should go. There's no future for you here, Chance Dawson being such a mule-headed fool." At Fancy's surprised look, she explained, "I always hoped that he would want to settle down with you."

"Hah!" Fancy snorted. "I wouldn't marry that arrogant grouch under any circumstance."

Myrt and Luther slid each other a glance but didn't speak what they were thinking—that Fancy was covering up her real feelings for the timber boss.

"I do have another problem, though, one that you can solve for me if you will."

"What's that?" Myrt asked.

"I need a way to get to Puget Sound. Would you take me there? Secretly, so that Chance doesn't know where I've gone? He'd come after Tod."

Her brow furrowed in thought, Myrt stood up and carried her cup to the stove. When she had refilled it, she sat back down and reached for the sugar bowl. After she had spooned the sweetener into the coffee and stirred a few times, she looked across at Luther.

"Do you think the road to the Sound is clear enough for my carriage to get through?"

Luther nodded. "I'd say so. Zeb has made a couple of trips over it with his wagon."

"That's settled then," Myrt said, looking at Fancy. "Now we've got to figure out the best time for you to leave. It will have to be when Chance is gone from camp for a couple of hours."

"That will be a problem." Fancy sat forward, relieved that Myrt was going to help her. "He doesn't have any set pattern of how he spends a day."

Myrt took a sip of her coffee, then set the cup down. "You're just gonna have to be ready to leave at the first opportunity. Have your clothes packed and ready to go. And keep your luggage on the light side. You're gonna have to carry them when you arrive at San Francisco. Vehicles can't get up those hills."

"Thank you, Myrt." Fancy looked gravely at the rough-acting woman. "I'll never forget what you're doing for me, and I hope you don't get into any trouble with Chance for helping me."

Myrt's lips curved in a humorous grin. "I'm the last person he'd think that you went to for help. I wouldn't for the world miss giving Chance a good jab. He took my best dancer away from me; then he's too dumb to know what to do with her. And I'm not talking about taking her to bed."

Fancy's cheeks reddened. Myrt should know that he'd already done that. She rose from the table saying, "I'd better get home and start getting a few things together while he and the boys are out of the house."

Fancy suffered through Monday as Chance hung around the house all day, tracing her every movement through lowered lids. Tuesday was much the same, but that evening she overheard him telling Tod and Lenny that he couldn't take them to the mill yard after school tomorrow. He explained that he'd be gone until dark, checking out passes where he could get the last of the fallen timber down to the river.

When Wednesday morning arrived, it was hard for Fancy to go about her usual routine of making breakfast and getting the boys ready for school. She thought Chance would never leave, but when he finally did, she stood at the kitchen window, a wistfulness in her eyes as she watched him walk away. She was going to miss him, she knew, even his roughness in his treatment of her and the way he could send her temper soaring. If only . . . She let the thought dangle as Chance passed out of sight.

He would never change his thoughts about marriage and being tied down, and she would never be his kept woman until he tired of her.

It was best that she was leaving. It pained her, however, to know that he would forget her long before she forgot him. To Chance she was just another woman to charm into his bed, while her feelings had been much stronger. She had foolishly dreamed that he would grow to love her and never again think of another woman.

With a ragged sigh for what would never be, Fancy turned from the window, and pulling a smile to her lips, she said to Tod and Lenny, "I have a surprise for you fellows. You're not going to school today."

Tod gave a happy shout, but Lenny's face grew long with disappointment. "Why not, Fancy?"

"Because we're taking a steamer to San Francisco to visit Tod's great-grandmother."

Excited cries from both Tod and Lenny greeted this piece of news. "Is Chance coming with us?" Tod wanted to know.

"He can't get away right now," Fancy answered, then told them to hurry and finish breakfast before they could question her further. Twenty minutes later, she and Myrt had hugged each other good-bye and Luther was helping her into the carriage, then picking up the reins and heading toward Puget Sound. Fancy prayed that no one had seen them leave.

It was a dismal sight when, a couple hours later, they arrived at the Sound. The sky was gray and overcast, and there was at least six inches of trampled mud on the ground. Ice had formed on the mud flats and the mouth of the river. The conditions of the shore didn't stop vessels from coming in, however. The brig *John Davis* was just pulling in.

Fancy groaned inwardly as she stepped down into the icy slush, for waiting to disembark from the brig were four farm women, laden with heavy baskets. She knew that her milk and butter were in one of the carriers.

As she knew would happen, the women spotted her right away and called out greetings to her. "How are you, Fancy?" one asked, while another wanted to know if she was visiting someone on the Sound or was she going on to Seattle?

"We're going to Seattle," she called back and shushed Tod when he would have corrected her.

Before the *John Davis* had been unloaded of its passengers and general merchandise, the *Fairy* came churning in. "Come on, fellows." Fancy hurried Tod and Lenny out of the carriage. "Let's get aboard." She gave Luther a big hug then, kissed his cheek, and followed the boys up the gangplank, hoping nervously that no one else had recognized her.

While the boys chattered excitedly, Fancy watched Luther turn the carriage around and head back toward camp. She thought of Chance and of how angry he would be when he discovered that she had taken Tod and left. Everyone in camp would be questioned. She hoped that Myrt had been right when she said that she would be the last one he'd suspect of helping her. She would feel dreadful if the big woman was banished from camp on her account.

The small vessel was pulling out then, cautiously moving away from shore, dodging the ice and mud that floated back and forth with the tide. It was a serious undertaking getting in and out of the Sound in the winter. Fancy watched the small village receding and tears glimmered in her eyes. She was leaving behind the only world she had ever known. What lay ahead for her and the boys? she wondered.

The captain was standing beside Fancy as they chugged into San Francisco Bay. It was hard for her not to voice her disappointment at her first view of the city. Everything about it presented such a disreputable appearance.

The buildings were low and shabbily built of wood that was gray and warped from wind and fog. Each one had a bow window, which she learned later was to catch all the morning sunlight that managed to pierce through the thick mists.

The captain sensed her dismay, and with a chuckle he said, "You're not looking at the real San Francisco, miss. Raise your eyes to that cliff facing seaward. That's called Telegraph Hill, and it has lovely homes. And farther along is Nob Hill, where you're going. The wealthy live there. Then at the highest point is Russian Hill. Below all of that is the business district."

"That's a relief." Fancy smiled at the genial man. "I couldn't live in this mud and squalor."

"Where you're going, young lady, you'll live like a queen." As Fancy led the boys off the *Fairy*, she wasn't sure she'd like living like a queen. For one thing, she wouldn't know how to act like one.

When she and Tod and Lenny stood at the foot of the gangplank, uncertain of where to go, the captain called out to a group of dirty and ragged boys, "One of you lads come help this lady up to Nob Hill. I'm sure there'll be a coin in it for you."

An immediate fight broke out among the ruffians, each determined that he would help the lady and receive the coin. In just a few minutes, a dirty, freckled-faced boy of around fourteen came out of the melee, a wide grin on his face and a trickle of blood coming from his nose.

"Right this way, lady," he said as he took Fancy's bag from her.

San Francisco lay on a series of hills with lowlands between. The boy led them up four blocks by regular steps like a flight of stairs. All four were puffing when they reached Nob Hill and their leader stopped in front of a two-story house of classical Greek lines. As Fancy and her charges stood on the grassy lawn staring up at the imposing building, all the many windows seemed to stare back at them.

Fancy came out of her trancelike state and dug two quarters from her wrist purse and, with a smile, handed them to the boy. Evidently it was double what he expected, for a broad smile split his face. When he had gone, running down the hill, Fancy nudged Tod and Lenny forward, and they climbed the two steps to the small portico. Taking a deep breath, she lifted the heavy brass knocker on the white painted door, then let it drop.

The portal opened shortly and a very erect gentleman, in his late sixties, Fancy judged, looked down his nose at them. Before she could speak, he said coldly, "Go to the back and knock on the kitchen door. No doubt Cook will find you something to eat."

Bewilderment creased Fancy's forehead. Had their young guide brought them to the wrong house? Had he grown tired of climbing hills and just dumped them here? She looked to her right to read the brass plaque on the brick wall. The name Ashely was printed on it.

Fancy's back stiffened and her chin squared belligerently as she said coldly, "Thelma Ashely's granddaughter is not here to beg scraps from her kitchen."

The pompous man's jaw dropped as he stared at her. His mouth moved then, but no words came out.

"Who is it, Thomas?" a reedy voice asked from the end of a long hall.

Again Thomas tried to speak, but without success. "Well, Thomas, can't you answer me?" This time the voice was accompanied by the sound of a tapping cane.

The man's Adam's apple bobbed a couple times and finally he croaked, "It's your granddaughter, ma'am."

"Fancy?" The tapping became faster, and the haughty butler stepped aside to reveal a tiny, frail, white-haired old lady. And though her face bore the passage of time, Fancy could see the resemblance to her mother in the structure of the facial bones. And my own, she added. Everyone said she looked exactly like her mother.

"My dear girl." Thin hands reached out to Fancy when she stepped through the door. Trembling arms came around her in a fierce hug, an embrace Fancy eagerly returned. They pulled apart then and gazed at each other.

"It's like looking at my Sarah again," her grandmother said in a teary voice. When she had looked her fill at Fancy, she turned her attention to Tod. She smiled at him and said, "Come give your great-grandmother a kiss and hug."

"Gently," Fancy whispered as her nephew rushed forward to the relative who looked like his mother. She was afraid his strong young arms might break one of the birdlike bones of the little lady.

She glanced at Lenny and saw him waiting for his turn to have a hug. "Please welcome him too, Grandmother," she whispered silently. The man-child's face beamed when he was invited to come get a kiss from his great-grandmother too.

When the two pulled apart, Thelma said, "Thomas, take the luggage up to the rooms I had Katy prepare in the hopes they'd show up some day. And light a fire in the stoves. It's quite chilly today."

When a now very meek butler silently reached for the bags, Lenny stepped forward and picked up the two heaviest ones. "I'm stronger than you." He flashed his boyish smile. Thomas returned the smile, and they were friends.

"Let's go into the parlor where it's nice and warm, Fancy. I'll have Katy bring us some refreshments." She looped an arm through Tod's and leaned on him slightly as they walked down the hall that was almost as big as Fancy's house that had burned to the ground.

Fancy tried not to gape at the room Thelma led her and Tod into. Heavy blue drapes that matched the Hepplewhite sofa and chair's upholstery hung at the windows, and there were beautiful lamps and figurines placed about on delicate tables and on the marble fireplace mantel. She cringed inwardly. What if the boys should break one of the lovely pieces or spill something on the thick carpet?

"Come sit beside me, dear." Thelma patted the seat of the sofa she had eased herself onto. When Fancy was settled beside her, she picked up a small silver bell from the table next to her and gently shook it. When a red-headed Irish lass entered the room almost immediately, Thelma smiled and said, "Fancy, this is Katy. She'll be looking after your needs."

As Fancy wondered what "needs" she would have that Katy could take care of, the little maid dipped her head and said, "Pleased to meet you, miss."

She dipped her head again when Thelma said, "Please bring us some sandwiches and tea—and hot chocolate for Tod and Lenny."

Katy left the room and Thelma took Fancy's hand and said, "Tell me of the years I've lost."

Chapter Eighteen

The setting sun had a sullen look to it as Chance left the mill yard and walked through a heavy fog on his way home. He stepped along briskly, anxious to get to his house, to the cozy warmth of the kitchen, the good smells in it—and most of all to feast his eyes on Fancy's lovely face.

He had been thinking about her all day as the huge saw sliced through the Douglas fir five feet across, turning out fine pieces of lumber. This coolness and bickering between them was wearing him down. He wanted to make peace with her. If he couldn't share her bed, he'd settle for anything she would give him. A smile, a friendly word—for the time being, that was. A man couldn't just be a friend to Fancy Cranson for very long. Given time, and with patience, he felt he would be able to win her over. If he could get her in his arms again, nature would take over.

Lamplight was beginning to appear in the windows of the little houses among the trees. He noted that the smoke rose straight up from the chimneys, another indication that snow was on its way.

Chance stepped into the camp clearing and frowned. There was no lamplight coming from his house, nor was there any smoke coming from the two chimneys. "What the hell?" he swore under his breath and stepped up his pace, almost running.

When he burst into the kitchen, the room was cold and dark, with the stillness a house had when it was empty. With hands that were beginning to shake, he lit the lamp on the kitchen table, then hurried with it into the family room. The fireplace was a black, gaping hole. No fire had burned in it all day.

He knew he would find the same emptiness in the bedroom Fancy and Tod shared as he went and stood in its doorway. The bed had been carefully made up, and the room was neat. It was too neat. Fancy's robe didn't lie across the foot of the bed as usual, and her house slippers weren't sitting next to the rocker. And more glaringly, the dresser top was bare except for the lacy runner Fancy had brought from her house.

A bleakness in his eyes, Chance placed the

lamp on the small table and sat down in the rocker, his elbows on his knees and his hands dangling between them. Fancy was gone. She had left him.

And why shouldn't she? he asked in self-reproach. God knew he hadn't made things very pleasant for her. Because she wouldn't sleep with him, he had acted like a spoiled child, pouting and saying hateful things to her.

But as Chance continued to sit in the cold room, eaten with remorse and wondering where Fancy had gone, it began to dawn on him that she had also taken Tod away from him. She had no right to do that. They had struck a bargain.

He pushed back the guilt he was feeling and let his temper take over. She was like all women, he raged inside—selfish and lying, determined to have their own way. "Well, by God," he said aloud, jumping to his feet, "she's not going to get away with it." He'd find her, then take the boy back.

Chance left the lamp burning in the kitchen as he slammed out of the house and made his way to the cookhouse. Zeb was setting the long table for supper and looked up, startled, at Chance's noisy entrance.

"I'm glad you're home," he said before Chance could speak. "I ain't seen Fancy and the boys all day. Around noon I went and knocked on the door, but nobody answered. Do you think somethin' has happened to them?"

"Something is going to happen to Fancy when I get my hands on her," Chance growled. "She's taken the boys and run off."

"Run off?" Zeb asked incredulously. "Where would she go? She ain't got no house no more. None of her friends have the room to take three more into their home."

"I don't think she's gone to any of her friends. She knows I'd come after her and take Tod. She's managed to catch a brig or steamer to Seattle."

"Why would she go now? If she had enough money to run away, why didn't she do it a long time ago? Why would she wait until winter set in?"

"I haven't figured that out yet." Chance shoved his hands in his pockets. "There's no one in camp who'd have any spare money to give her, unless . . ." He opened the door, saying, "I'll be back later. I'm going to have a talk with Big Myrt. She always had a softness for Fancy. If I find out she's involved in Fancy's disappearance, I'll give her an hour to take her girls and get out of camp."

Myrt opened the door to Chance's pounding. "The girls are still sleeping, Chance." She frowned at him. "I don't think they'd appreciate being disturbed, even by you."

"I'm not interested in your girls, Myrt, and I

think you know it. I'm only interested in one little witch."

"That's nothing new, Chance. Everybody in camp knows how interested you are in Fancy." Myrt gave him a sly grin. "Have you come here to talk about your interest in her?"

"No, damn you, that's not why I'm here, and you know it."

"Like hell I do." Myrt raised her voice. "I wish you'd spit out what's on your mind. Fancy's not working for me again, if that's what you think."

"She's left camp, and I think you helped her to do it."

"She what?" Myrt made a great show of astonishment. "I talked to her a bit on Monday, and she didn't say a word about leaving." She plopped down on a kitchen chair as though she was so shocked she couldn't stand. "Where could that foolish girl have gone?" She shook her head, a worried look on her face. "Did she take Lenny and Tod with her?"

"Yes, she did," Chance answered, his voice grim, disappointment in his eyes. Myrt's performance had satisfied him that she knew nothing of Fancy's whereabouts. What did he do now? he asked himself. Who else might know where she went?

A thought entered his mind, making his teeth clench. He looked at Myrt and asked, "Do you suppose she might have gone off with Hampton? He's crazy to have her."

"You're out of your mind, Chance. A lady like Fancy would never hook up with a rogue like Gil, even though he is as handsome as the devil and words roll off his tongue like warm honey. Anyway, he's in Pilar's room. He's been there all day."

Myrt could almost taste the relief that flashed in Chance's eyes. When he left a moment later, her whole body shook with silent laughter. Mr. Chase Dawson had finally met a woman who would, in time, bring him to his knees. She went to the window to watch his slump-shouldered figure move toward the cookhouse.

"If I thought you were aware that you loved her," she said to herself, "I'd tell you where to find her. But right now you're too thick-skulled to know that you want more from her than hot lovemaking every night."

The news that Fancy had taken her small family and left spread through camp like a forest fire. Different opinions were expressed about where she had gone, but none were voiced to Chance. Everyone avoided his scowling person whenever possible. And he was too proud to question them about Fancy. The last thing he needed was pity or, in some cases, malevolent satisfaction.

A week had passed when Chance got his first lead on where Fancy had gone. It was after supper, when the men had cleared out of the cookhouse, that Zeb said, as he and Chance still sat at the table, "That farm woman who brings us butter and milk was here today. She said that she saw Fancy and the boys at the Sound last Wednesday and that Fancy said she was goin' to Seattle."

Startled, Chance looked at Zeb; then a frown etched his forehead. "You waited until now to tell me?"

"Hell, I didn't see you all day, and I didn't think you would want me to say it in front of the men."

"I'm sorry, Zeb. I'm at fault. Did the woman say where in Seattle Fancy was going?"

"No, just that she was going there. But Seattle is not so big that you can't find her."

"I'll find her, don't worry." Chance stood up and shrugged into his jacket.

His steps were lighter than they had been in a week as he walked to the dark, silent house, telling himself that soon there would be laughter in it again.

In a gray frosty dawn, Chance stood on the Seattle pier, waiting for the brig *John Adams* to come plowing up the river. He had the beginning of a beard, and there was a bleak hardness on his face. A mood of depression hung over him. He had been in Seattle a week, scouring the town, checking hotels and boardinghouses. Everywhere he asked he received the same answer: No, they hadn't seen a blond young woman with a boy and a young man.

In the alley in back of the hotel where he was staying, he had found a week's back issues of newspapers. He had gone through the want ads, finding but a few advertising for a maid or cook or such. It had taken him only an hour to check if the positions had been filled. They had, but not by a blond young woman.

So here he stood, muttering, "Why did Fancy Cranson have to come to my camp?" Why hadn't she taken a job filleting cod in the cannery? He would have never met her then, wouldn't now be out of his mind worrying about her. He didn't think about the fact that, with the arrival of Tod, they would have been brought together sooner or later.

As the brig neared camp, Chance wondered why he didn't hear the saw going at the mill yard. Had the men taken advantage of his absence to slacken off their jobs? None of them struck him as being that sort.

He had no sooner stepped off the *John Davis* and into the mud and slush than he was surrounded by six of his men. "Why isn't the saw going?" he demanded.

"The saw is broken," the men all answered together. "Two days after you left," the machine operator added, "someone took a hammer to it and nicked the blade in six different places."

Chance looked thunderstruck. "The crazy woman?" he asked.

"Naw, it couldn't have been her," Victor Seacat said. "That saw was hit hard with a sledgehammer. Anyhow, no one has seen or heard her for over two weeks. Her people have either locked her up, or she's frozen to death back in the pines somewhere."

"Well, luckily," Chance said wearily, "I have a new saw locked up in the tool shed. Couple of you men come along with me, and I'll give it to you." He looked up at the pale winter sun. "You should be able to get in a couple hours' work before dark."

When the two men left the shed, carrying the giant saw between them, Chance walked to the cookhouse. Zeb had a bowl of steaming chili waiting for him.

"Well, Chance, I see by your face that you didn't find Fancy, and you're gnashing your teeth about the saw," Zeb said by way of greeting.

"Right on both counts," Chance grunted, pulling a chair away from the table and plopping down on it. "I couldn't find a trace of her. She's not in Seattle."

As Zeb poured him a cup of coffee, he said, "Whether I like it or not, it appears I have an enemy in camp."

"Hell, Chance, you can't think that everybody here likes you. There's always some man who has a grievance of some kind. Every camp has its malcontent, never happy, never agreeable with the way things are run."

"I'm not talking about small things like that, Zeb. I've got two or three men who are always complaining about something. I'm talking about a real enemy. Some man who is out to cause me real trouble."

"Have you had hard words with any of the crew lately?"

"I tangled with Gil Hampton recently."

Zeb shook his head. "He don't seem the type who'd go behind a man's back to get even with him."

"I don't think so either," Chance agreed, "but you never know. A man can do some crazy things when a woman is involved."

Zeb lifted a significant brow at the man staring into his coffee but made no remark. Didn't Chance realize he'd been acting pretty crazy where Fancy was concerned?

No more was said as Chance dug in and finished the chili. "I'll see you at supper," he said a few minutes later, pushing away from the table. "I've got to shave, take a bath, and get into some clean clothes. I must smell like a bear."

"You sure as hell look like one," Zeb laughingly said as Chance went out the door.

The empty house was so cold and depressing that the first thing Chance did was build a roaring fire in the kitchen range. While two big pans of water heated, he hung up his coat and went into his bedroom.

He hadn't transferred his clothes to the other bedroom when Fancy moved him in with Lenny. He had told himself that leaving them in his room would aggravate her. But he admitted now that it had given him a good feeling to know that his things were neatly tucked in with hers. It was a kind of bond between them.

Where *was* she? he wondered later, clean shaven and sitting in a tub of hot water soaping his chest. Was she warm? Was she hungry? Did she miss him the way he missed her?

The bar of soap slipped from his hand, and he grew rigid as a thought hit like a bolt of lightning. He hadn't been running around like a crazy man looking for his nephew—it was Fancy he wanted back. He wanted her back in his house, back in his bed, and for the rest of her life. If he had to marry her, he would gladly do it. In fact, suddenly now, he wanted that more than anything he had ever wanted in his life.

But did Fancy want marriage with him? he asked himself, standing up, the water sluicing down his hard, muscular thighs. She certainly never acted like it; also, he had accused her of wanting to trap him into marriage. She never had a kind word for him unless they were in bed together, in each other's arms.

She whispered his name so sweetly then.

Chapter Nineteen

Dressed in a simple blue merino dress with linen collar and cuffs, Fancy sat curled up on a cushioned window seat in her anteroom—the room in front of her private bedroom.

It was large, running east to west along the north of the building with three wide windows that gave her a distant view of the bay and the ships that came and went. The furnishings, like those in the rest of the house, were Hepplewhite.

Tod and Lenny's bedroom was across the wide hall from hers. During their waking hours, she kept the boys with her when they were inside. It was too nerve-racking to let them wander around the house and possibly break some of the costly figurines. But they weren't inside too often. They preferred to entertain themselves in the long backyard in the afternoons. Mornings were spent with a tutor in a storage room that had been turned into a schoolroom. She and Grandmother had discussed the arrangement and thought it best for Lenny. He would be heartbroken if he were separated from Tod.

Her nephew and cousin weren't happy here, Fancy knew, even though everyone was so nice to them, especially Grandmother Ashely. But like herself, they missed the mountains, the fir trees, and the open sky—a place where boys could whoop and yell as they played some game.

Fancy sighed. And they missed Chance. She drew up her knees and rested her chin on them. She missed him too. How it was possible, she didn't know, since they had fought so. She smiled wryly. Maybe that was what she missed. But she also missed her friends, like Zeb, and the way of life she'd been born to.

Molly and the others would be preparing for Christmas now, a decorated tree in every small house. They would be secretly wrapping presents and hiding them away from their inquisitive families. She could almost smell the delicious aromas coming from their kitchens as they baked goodies for the holiday.

She and the boys had wanted to go looking for their tree, but the butler, Thomas, had bought a monstrous big one from the market.

It stood downstairs in the large parlor, stately and beautifully trimmed—also by Thomas. Gaily wrapped packages by the dozen lay beneath it. At Grandmother's orders, Thomas had, however, taken the boys beyond town to look for mistletoe.

There were delicious aromas drifting through the house here, also. Mrs. Hammer had been baking for a week. Fancy had wanted to help the cook, but Grandmother had said that the rosy-cheeked woman never let anyone but the scullery maid into her kitchen. It was her domain, and she was very jealous of it.

Fancy sighed again. All this idle time was driving her crazy. She wasn't cut out to be a lady, to wear silk, velvet and satin, and to have callers in the afternoon. She hated sitting at the marquetry table serving tea from a silver tea service to Grandmother's friends.

But worst of all, she hated trying to hold a conversation with their silly daughters, who could only chatter about parties, balls, beaux, and clothes. They bored her silly. As did the young men who came calling. She wanted to giggle every time she saw one of them in their ruffled shirt fronts, skin-tight trousers, and shiny black boots. Their skin was as pale and smooth as her own, and their hands were much softer than her own work-roughened ones.

Fancy had realized from the beginning that her grandmother had hopes that she would be

attracted to one of the male callers, for that as-
tute old lady was worried that some rough tim-
berman had a niche in her heart. What the kind
little woman didn't know was that even if she
didn't know Chance Dawson, the milksops who
came visiting would never interest Fancy. She
was used to big, brawny men who could protect
her if necessary. These young men from San
Francisco would run a mile if confronted with
danger of any sort. She would probably end up
protecting them.

To take her mind off Chance and her yearning for the tall pines and lofty mountains, Fancy
gazed down at the bay, at the great warehouses,
long piers, and many vessels. There were many
clippers, South Sea Island brigs filled with co-
pra, Chinese junks, an old whaler dripping oil
from a year of cruising in the Arctic, and a few
windjammers. And far out in the bay was a fishing fleet.

She transferred her gaze to the many people
moving about. Mingling up and down the beach
were black Gilbert Islanders, Kanakas from Ha-
waii, Lascars in turbans, thick-set Russian sail-
ors, Italian fishermen, Greeks, Alaska Indians,
and Spanish Americans. A veritable melting
pot, she thought. It was a place where few decent people went unless to board a ship.

And women never, ever went there alone, for
haunting the waterfront were the drifters who
stopped for a while to live by their wits before

moving on. The Barbary Coast was three blocks of dance halls and saloons and houses of prostitution. And shanghaiing was commonplace.

Grandmother had said that the Barbary Coast was a loud bit of hell.

Fancy looked next to Kearny Street, a wilder and stranger Bowery. It was the main throughfare for the dregs of humanity, the cutthroats and pickpockets. She shook her head in wonderment. Such a short distance lay between the squalor of the bay and the opulence of Nob Hill. Did a toss of the coin determine who should be wealthy, who should live in poverty? And were those living in plenty any happier than those who begged on the waterfront?

She decided that it was those people in between, the hardworking men and women who, for the most part, lived contented lives. Look at her friends back at camp.

A soft knock on the door brought Fancy's attention from the window. "Come in," she called.

The little Irish maid stuck her head around the door. "Your grandmother said to remind you that it is time to go watch the parade."

"Thank you, Katy. Tell her I'll be right down."

Every Saturday afternoon, she and Mrs. Ashely went to watch the matinee parade. From two to five, a long procession of young women passed and repassed the five blocks between Market and Powell and Sutter and Kearny. This function belonged to the middle class, more proof to Fancy that it was those people who enjoyed life more. The dance hall women and prostitutes weren't allowed in the parade, and it was beneath the "upper class" to put themselves on view like that.

Fancy placed a jaunty little blue felt hat on her head and tied its ribbons in a perky little bow beneath her right ear. If it was not anchored down, the wind would blow it off her head. The wind. She grimaced. She could not get used to the bother of it. But she guessed she'd have to try a little harder, since Thomas had said that the west wind blew steadily for ten months out of the year.

When she had donned a close-fitting jacket of dove gray and pulled on matching gloves, Fancy descended the wide staircase with its beautifully polished mahogany handrail that swept down to the hall below. A small sigh whispered through her lips. No doubt after the parade, she and Grandmother would dine at the Poodle Dog. Anyone who was anyone could be seen there. She would like to visit Chinatown, but when she had expressed that wish on first arriving, Grandmother had said absolutely not, that those people used opium and trafficked in slave girls. She had added that it was much too dangerous to walk those streets.

Fancy hid her discontent and smiled at the little woman waiting for her at the foot of the stairs.

Fancy

*   *   *

Christmas had come and gone with Chance hardly aware of it. He had vaguely noticed the decorated trees in the houses, and knew that Bill Bandy had played Santa Claus to the camp children, but other than that, it was just another empty day for him—a day like all the others when he was sick with worry about Fancy. Over and over he asked himself where she and the boys could be. Were they warm? Did they have enough to eat? How was Fancy earning a living? Time and again he reproached himself for not allowing her to continue dancing. She would still be in camp, in his house, where he could take care of her.

The old year passed and the new one arrived, bringing with it freezing temperatures and a new blizzard. In some places the snow was piled three feet deep and the temperature dropped to three below at night. For a full week, the wind howled, blowing snow about so wildly that no one went outside unless it was absolutely neccessary. The men spent the days playing cards in the cookhouse. Chance joined them occasionally, but mostly he sat in his house brooding and worrying about Fancy.

One night the wind died down, and it stopped snowing. At last the children could go back to school, out from under their mothers' feet, and the men could go back to work.

The next morning, however, Chance discovered that there was something new to worry about. Two of the sawyers came to him, their faces dark with anger as they showed him their cross-cut saw. Someone had deliberately taken an axe to it, nicking out several teeth. It was starting all over again.

"There's a man in this camp who is sabotaging you, Chance," Victor Seacat declared, his fists clenched.

"That's right," Frank Jackson agreed. "You've got an enemy who's out to ruin you."

"Did you find any tracks around the tool shed?" Chance asked, making no response to the men's angry remarks.

Victor shook his head. "The whole area is windswept. The bastard could have done this days ago."

Grim-faced, Chance said, "The low-life won't get away with his dirty work again. Don't say anything to the others in case you'll be warning someone off, but I'm going to keep watch on the camp every night, sleeping days, until I catch him. If anyone mentions not seeing me around, say that I have a bad cold. For now, I'll get a new saw for you from the shed."

Two long, cold nights passed without anything suspicious happening. On the third night, around two o'clock in the morning, Chance grew sleepy. He left the concealment he'd taken up in the lean-to in back of the dance hall where Myrt kept her team and carriage and hurried to the cookhouse to grab a cup of coffee from the pot Zeb kept warm for him.

The place was in darkness as he had ordered it should be, and he made his way to the stove by the bright moonlight coming through the window. He swallowed one cup of coffee in one long draught, then rolled a cigarette before pouring himself another.

Chance was ready to snub out his smoke and finish his coffee when he smelled smoke that wasn't coming from tobacco. It was wood smoke and nearby. He stood up. Had Zeb not fully put out his pipe before going to bed, maybe set something on fire?

He took one step; then his eyes widened in disbelief. Clouds of gray smoke were rolling from under the outside door. He stood a moment wondering if he'd be shot at when he stepped outside. Did this man want him dead, as well as ruined?

One thing was for sure, he wasn't about to stay there and be burned to death. He drew his gun, gathered himself to face whatever danger lay outside, then jerked the door open.

He saw no one, heard nothing, felt no bullet strike him. But he couldn't rush outside either. Not a foot away from the door, on the small porch, a healthy fire was burning, the flames licking closer and closer to the cookhouse. He turned and rushed to the workbench where Zeb kept the water pail. He prayed that it wasn't empty. He saw that it was half full, and aiming carefully, he splashed the water over the core of the fire. The red coals sizzled; then the flames died, leaving only wet ashes and charred wood lying in the large hole that had been burned into the porch.

Chance wiped the cold sweat off his brow. What if he hadn't been in the kitchen? Would the arsonist have built the fire anyway? Zeb could have never gotten out. There was only one entrance to the shack. Whoever this man was, he was dangerous and had to be caught before he killed someone.

Even as he went outside to inspect the grounds, Chance knew he would probably not find any track that hadn't been there already. How was he to differentiate his enemy's from the others? Hunching his shoulders in his jacket, he headed for his house. He might as well go to bed and get some sleep. He smiled a thin, mirthless smile—just as his enemy was doing right about now, he thought grimly. The man had no doubt done his dirty work for the night.

The next morning, when Chance stepped out of his house, all the crew and Zeb were gathered around the burned porch. He paused to watch the men's faces, to observe their reactions. All seemed sincerely angry and upset. Gil Hampton looked sick. Why? Why should he be more upset than the others? Did he know the terror of having been caught in a fire?

That night, shortly after midnight, every few minutes Chance stamped his feet and clapped his gloved hands together to help the blood circulate through his veins. It was a clear night, but bitterly cold. From inside the dance hall came the sound of Luther pounding out a tune on the piano and the stamp of dancing feet.

Damn the man who kept him out here in the cold.

It was around two o'clock, and a rest period for the dancers, when Chance saw the shadowy figure of a man slip past the corner of the dance hall. Aha! he thought, here was the culprit. What would he be up to tonight?

When the man turned toward the river, Chance left his post and walked silently behind him, keeping to the edge of the forest. The bastard was out to tamper with the big saw again, he guessed.

When the man stepped off the path and stood at the river's edge, the moon shone fully on his face. Chance was disappointed, but not too surprised to recognize Gil Hampton. Although he was jealous of the man, he had thought him too honorable to do a man dirt behind his back. But as he had said to Zeb before, a man did some strange things when a woman was involved.

What did surprise him, though, was to see Hampton pull a canoe from under some brush growing alongside the river. He watched the scaler step carefully into the vessel, pick up a paddle, and head toward the opposite bank. What was over there that would interest him? Chance frowned. As far as he knew, there was nothing there but an Indian village a few miles into the forest and an old abandoned shack a trapper had used three or four years ago. That tract of timber hadn't known the bite of an axe yet.

Hampton reached the opposite bank and jumped onto land. As soon as he had dragged the canoe out of the water, a slim, feminine figure burst from the trees and threw herself into his arms. The pair held their embrace a moment, then arm-in-arm disappeared into the pine forest.

Chance felt as if he had been kicked in the chest by one of the mules that dragged the big logs to the mill. He knew now where Fancy had been all this time. Hampton had her and the boys hidden away in that shack that was ready to fall down. They probably planned to leave the area, come spring.

As he settled himself on a rock to wait for Hampton to paddle back across the river, he asked himself how the man could continue to sleep with someone like Pilar when he had Fancy tucked away. More fool him, Chance hadn't been near another woman since Fancy moved into his camp.

A little over an hour passed before Chance

saw Gil emerge from the pines and push the canoe into the water. As he stood up and trudged toward home, his spirits were lower than at any time in his life. If Fancy preferred Hampton over him, so be it. But tomorrow he was going to cross the river and bring his nephew home.

Chapter Twenty

After a desultory walk in the small park a short distance from her grandmother's home, Fancy made her way back toward the grand house. At last, thankfully, the holidays were over—the parties, the calling on Grandmother's friends, entertaining those same people in return.

It had been an exhausting, nerve-racking time for her. Maybe if she felt better, didn't always feel so tired and sleepy, she'd have taken more interest in the festivities that everyone else seemed to enjoy so. But her lack of energy had kept her mostly on the sidelines, observing, pretending that she was enjoying herself for her grandmother's sake.

She sighed softly. The dear, sweet lady tried so hard to make her contented in her new home, and that was why she pretended a happiness she didn't feel. And Tod and Lenny tried equally hard to appreciate all that was done for them and to express pleasure in the opening of the numerous presents that had been placed under the beautiful Christmas tree.

But hoops, balls, drums, wooden soldiers, and marbles were not for boys raised in the north woods. A jackknife, bow and arrow, or fishing pole would have brought shrieks of pleasure from them.

As for herself, she had opened gaily wrapped presents of silken lacy underclothing, sheer muslin nightgowns with matching robes, shawls of cobweb thinness. There were also fancy house slippers, gloves and muffs, perfumes, and ribbons for her hair.

She had taken pleasure in her gifts, for what woman wouldn't love such finery—to feel silk against her skin, to dab floral scents behind her ears and on the pulse that beat in her wrist? She had caught herself wishing that Chance could see her in the sheer camisoles and underpants, to watch his pupils widen and his lids grow heavy with desire of her.

She had soon put a stop to such thoughts. She told herself, stepping up on the small porch and lifting the heavy knocker, that Chance Dawson was out of her life now and would remain so.

Thomas opened the door, and with a brief "Thank you" Fancy sailed past him and climbed the winding stairs to her private quarters. The butler's action the day she and the boys arrived still rankled her. She didn't like the way he ordered Katy around, and the way he frowned if Tod and Lenny made the slightest noise in the house angered her. She'd had words with the uppity servant about that. She had made it clear that only she chastised her young relatives.

That evening, when the boys had gone upstairs to bed and Fancy and Mrs. Ashely sat alone in the warm parlor, Thelma said, "Fancy, dear, tell me about Tod's uncle. He and Lenny are so fond of him, he must be very nice. Is he an older man?"

Fancy gave the old lady a startled look. She'd had no idea that Tod and Lenny had talked to her about Chance. They must be missing him terribly.

"Compared to my age," she answered, "he's an older man. He's thirty years old, hard in many ways as most lumbermen are because of the rough life they have to lead, but there's a softness in Chance Dawson despite the way he tries to hide it. It comes out when he's with Tod and Lenny." She could have added how gentle he was when he made love to her.

"And how does he treat you?" Thelma asked, startling her again.

After a moment, Fancy gave a short laugh and said, "He and I can't be together half an hour before we're snapping and snarling at each other."

There was a short pause before Thelma said, "I gather that *you* don't miss him, then."

Miss him? Fancy asked herself. Yes, she missed him. And there was a deep ache inside her every time she thought of him. Avoiding her grandmother's eyes, she lied and said, "Not in the least."

Mrs. Ashely studied the beautiful face, the lowered lids, and opened her mouth as though to speak, then changed her mind. She knew that Fancy had just lied to her. Whether the girl knew it or not, her granddaughter was in love with this man she described as being hard with a softness inside him. He was the reason she couldn't enjoy the luxurious life that was her birthright.

The old lady switched the subject to how they would spend the next day. Fancy withheld a groaning sigh when she said it was time they started returning some of the visits they'd received last week. Another boring round of calling on people she had nothing in common with. When the clock on the mantel chimed nine o'clock, she kissed the grandmother's soft cheek and wished her good night.

Katy had turned down the covers on the big four-poster when Fancy entered her quarters and was in the process of gathering up the clothes she would rinse out tomorrow. The way the girl kept hanging around, Fancy suspected that the maid wanted tomorrow off. Her young man worked on the docks, and he was off on Sundays. They planned to marry in six months, Katy had told her. Many times Fancy found herself envious when the Irish girl talked of her soon-to-be husband and the life they were going to have together, the children they would have. She wished that she, too, was making plans to marry a man she loved, one who loved her in return.

What the little maid wanted to say to her, however, brought the blood draining from her face. "Miss Fancy," the girl started hesitantly, "maybe I'm out of line to say what I'm about to say, but you are so innocent-like, maybe you haven't noticed."

"Noticed what, Katy? If it's something I should know, please tell me."

"Well, the thing is, in the six weeks you've been here, I've seen no evidence in your underwear that you've had your mense."

Fancy couldn't speak as she realized what that must mean. Had she had a monthly before leaving camp? She thought back. She couldn't remember that she had. It was suddenly clear to her why she was always tired and why her breasts were so sore.

Tears glimmered in her eyes. She was carrying Chance's baby, and it would be her ruination to have a child without first having a husband. What would her grandmother think of her? Katy went to where Fancy had sunk down on the bed and took her cold hands into her own. "Don't be upset, Miss Fancy," she soothed. "You'll marry the little one's father and everything will be fine."

"I'll never marry its father," Fancy spoke sharply and vehemently.

"But why not? You must have loved the father to have—"

"Love had nothing to do with our coming together," Fancy interrupted the girl. "It was only lust."

"But Miss Fancy, there's always a little lust mixed up with love. Are you sure there wasn't a little bit of love between you? A fondness at least?"

Fancy shook her head and said bitterly, "He doesn't even like me."

"When will you tell your grandmother?" Katy asked after a pause.

"Oh, God, I don't know," Fancy wailed, the tears falling freely. "What is she going to think of me? She will hate me for bringing shame to her."

"No, she won't," Katy declared. "Mrs. Ashely is the kindest person I've ever known, and she loves you dearly. She's not going to turn her back on you. I think you should tell her as soon as possible."

"But she's so old. Can she bear the shock of learning that she's to become the great-grandmother of a bastard child?"

"She's a strong old lady, Miss Fancy. She'll take it in stride like she's done all her married life. According to Cook, her husband, your grandfather, was a philanderer of the worst kind. She bore up under the shame and embarrassment of that."

Fancy stared at Katy, surprise and anger in her eyes. How had her grandfather had the nerve to dictate to his daughter whom she should marry while he was sleeping with other women, shaming his lovely wife? She wasn't surprised that her mother had cut all ties with the old lecher.

She looked at Katy and said with biting contempt, "The father of my baby is the same kind of man. The only difference is that he plans on never marrying. He admits that no one woman holds his interest for very long."

"A child sometimes changes a man. Makes him want to settle down."

"That may be in some cases." Fancy took the handkerchief Katy handed her and mopped at her tears. "But it wouldn't be that way with this man. He'd love the child and be a good father, but he'd make an awful husband because he would continue to chase women."

"I'm sorry to hear that," Katy said, "but you owe it to your child to marry its father so that no man can ever call it a bastard."

Katy left her then with a pat on her shoulder, and Fancy moved in a mental fog as she changed into her gown and crawled into bed. She prayed that she could sleep, to escape for a while this new burden she must wrestle with.

She lay awake half the night, going over what the little maid had said. She would have to tell her grandmother because a pregnancy could be kept secret only a short time. But could she gather the courage to go to Chance and demand that he marry her so that her baby would have his name?

It was near dawn when she finally fell asleep, the same worries on her mind.

It took two days, together with Katy's urging, for Fancy to get up the nerve to talk to her grandmother, to tell the gentle old lady that she was going to be a great-grandmother again, that this child wouldn't have a father. The telling of it was helped along by some leading questions from Mrs. Ashely.

They were having after-dinner coffee in the parlor when Thelma looked at Fancy, concern in her eyes. "Something is bothering you, child. Do you want to talk about it?"

Fancy nervously fingered the strand of pearls around her throat. Was Katy right, would her grandmother be understanding? What if she told her to take the boys and leave tomorrow morning? That would mean returning to camp in shame and defeat. There would be no place for her to live except with Chance.

Finally she looked at Thelma and said what she must. "I don't want to talk about it, Grandmother, but I know that I have to. I have a problem that I can't keep to myself for very long."

When Fancy faltered, looking for the courage to go on, Thelma rose and sat down beside her on the sofa. "What is it, dear? Do you long to go back to the north woods? Do you not like it here with me?"

"If only it was that simple, Grandmother." Fancy clasped her hands together to stop their trembling.

"Then tell me what it is. I'm sure we can fix it somehow."

Fancy shook her head as a tear slid down her cheek. "My problem can't be fixed. It has to be solved on its own." She took a deep breath and added in a low, strained voice, "I'm going to have a baby in seven months."

To say that Thelma looked stunned would have been an understatement. She looked as though she had been delivered a fatal blow. Of all the problems her granddaughter could have told her she had, this was the last confession she had thought to hear.

She stared down at her own clasped hands. In seven months, Fancy had said. That meant she was expecting when she came here. Did she know then? She prayed that the girl hadn't. She loved her granddaughter and didn't like to think that her pregnancy had driven her here. She wanted to believe that Fancy had come because she wanted to.

"How long have you known, Fancy?" she asked quietly.

"Two days." Fancy sobbed. "Katy called my attention to the fact that I haven't had a mense since I came here. When I thought back, I realized that I had missed a monthly back at camp."

Thelma's relief showed on her face. She wasn't being used. Fancy was here because she wanted to be. She looked at her granddaughter and said quietly, "Chance Dawson is the father, isn't he?"

"Why do you say that?"

"Because of the soft tone in your voice when you speak of him. Love for the man comes through even when you tell of how the two of you are always sparring."

"But he doesn't love me, Grandmother, and worse, he wants no part of marriage, to being tied down to one woman."

A sadness came into Thelma's eyes. She well knew about such men, and she didn't like the idea of this dear child being tied to such a man. But the baby must have a name. If Chance Dawson wasn't good husband material, Fancy could quietly divorce him after the baby was born. It would be a scandal for a while, but better that than a lifetime of hell.

She put her arms around her sobbing granddaughter. "Dry your eyes, honey, and go up to your room. I must think awhile, plan for the future of your babe."

When she heard Fancy's door close, she rose and sat down at her desk. She opened the top drawer and drew out a sheet of paper, ink, and quill. She sat a moment in thought, then began to write. When she had finished, she sealed the letter and summoned Thomas.

"Make sure this is posted tomorrow," she said, then made her way to her bedroom, the fire of battle in her eyes.

Chapter Twenty-one

Chance was in a black mood. Breakfast was two hours late. His enemy had struck again last night, even as he kept watch over the camp. Someone had poured water over the wood Zeb kept stacked on the porch, soaking it through. No matter how the cook coaxed it, it was slow to catch fire.

Besides being hungry, the delay in the morning meal was keeping him that much longer from rowing across the river and tracking Fancy down.

He slid a fast glance at Gil Hampton sitting at the other end of the table. The man looked absolutely sick. Why? His lips lifted in a sneer. He was probably wearing himself out trying to satisfy two women.

Zeb finally managed to cook a large pot of

oatmeal, fry a platter of bacon, and brew a pot of coffee. The skimpy meal was quickly eaten and the men hurried off to work. Chance gulped down his second cup, eager to get across the river. He stood up and reached for his jacket hanging on the back of his chair.

"Hold on a minute, Chance," Zeb said as he started walking toward the door. "This came for you yesterday." He handed Chance an envelope. "I forgot to give it to you, there's been so much upheaval goin' on around here."

Chance looked at the left-hand corner of the white square and frowned. Who was Thelma Ashely? He sat back down to read the single sheet of paper.

"Dear Mr. Dawson," the letter began. "It is imperative that we meet and discuss my granddaughter, Fancy Cranson, who has been living with me for nearly seven weeks.

"I am eighty-two years old, so please don't make me come to you." It was signed "Thelma Ashely."

The letter dropped from Chance's hand as the blood surged through his veins with an elation he hadn't known in years. It wasn't Fancy who lived across the river; she had been in San Francisco all this time. Evidently Hampton had an Indian woman he visited once in a while.

But who was this Mrs. Ashely who claimed to be Fancy's grandmother? Fancy had never mentioned having such a relative. In fact he had gotten the idea that she had no relations except for Tod and Lenny. If she did know of this old woman, why hadn't she gone to her after her father's death?

That was all immaterial, he told himself. The important thing was that he finally knew where Fancy was. But what did Mrs. Ashely want to discuss about her?

A dark frown creased Chance's brow suddenly. What if it had something to do with Tod? What if she wanted him to give up his rights to the boy? She was in for a big surprise if she thought that. He would never agree to it.

"But you're not his blood relative," his inner voice pointed out. "If this woman wants to take you to court, there's no way a judge would let you have the boy."

"Is it bad news?" Zeb asked, squinting at the wild look that had come into Chance's eyes.

"This letter is from Fancy's grandmother in San Francisco. That's where Fancy went. The old lady writes that she wants to discuss her with me."

"Say, that is good news." Zeb sat down at the table. "You can bring Tod home now."

Chance nodded, the elation gone from his face. He had forgotten that he had told Zeb he only wanted his nephew back. What would the old cook think if he now told him it was really Fancy he wanted? Wanted with every fiber of his being. But chances were, he wouldn't get either one of them back.

"Do you suppose the old lady wrote to you to come take Tod back with you? Old people don't like the noise youngsters make."

"I doubt that. Fancy would never agree to giving the boy up."

"She might have met some fancy gent she wants to marry, but he don't want Tod around. He'd want his own children."

The pit of Chance's stomach curled in a knot. It hadn't entered his mind that Fancy might be thinking of getting married. He mentally shook his head in self-derision. It went to show how thick his head was. He should have suspected that grandmother of hers would see to it that Fancy met a lot of bachelors. Wealthy men in high places. Everyone in the Nob Hill area was filthy rich.

"When will you be goin' to get the little feller, Chance?"

"Hell, Zeb, we don't know for a fact that's what the old woman wants."

"I think you'd better face it, son. What else could she want?"

"Yeah, you're right. I'll go talk to Frank Jackson about keeping an eye on during the night. Maybe he'll have better luck than I've had catching the bastard who's determined to ruin me one way or the other."

Frank readily agreed to do night watch, and

Chance prepared to make the trip to San Francisco. In his hurry he nicked his jaw as he drew the razor over it, then spent fifteen minutes looking for his white shirt, then another ten searching for his black string tie.

He finally found the shirt folded neatly in a dresser drawer holding Fancy's blouses, and the tie among her hair ribbons. It took but a few minutes then to get into his black broadcloth suit, the one he hadn't worn since going on business to that city on the bay two years ago. Nor had he worn the highly polished black ankle boots. When he left the house, walking toward the river where he'd board the first brig that came along, Zeb thought him to be as handsome and stylish as any man Fancy would meet in the city.

Chance's pulse quickened as the *John Davis* nosed its way among the many seagoing vessels and found a spot to pull in to shore. In however long it took him to climb to Nob Hill, he'd be seeing Fancy again. How would she greet him? He decided that whether it be with a smile or a scowl, he would react the same way. If she showed him her usual coolness, he wasn't about to let on that his heart wanted to jump out of his chest at the sight of her. He had his pride after all.

But would he even see her? he asked himself as he stepped on shore and started pushing his way through the press of humanity that always hung around the docks. The old lady had only written that she wanted him to discuss Fancy, not necessarily see and talk to her.

How could people live like this? Chance asked himself as he climbed hill after hill. He'd feel smothered if he had to live any length of time in one of those houses squashed in between its neighbors like sardines in a tin. He looked with scornful eyes at the little patches of grass in front of each brick mansion, the absence of trees to soften the stern, dignified-looking buildings.

At last he found the address he was looking for. This house had more grandeur about it than the others. Fancy's grandmother must be very wealthy, he thought, lifting the heavy brass door knocker.

Chance was about to lift the knocker a second time when the door opened and a stern-faced butler asked, "Whom shall I say is calling, sir?"

When Chance gave his name, there was a slight flickering of the eyelids of the elderly man as he invited, "Step in, please. Mrs. Ashely is in the parlor."

So, the snobbish fellow knew about him. Chance grinned wryly, following the stiff back down a wide hallway. And probably knew why Chance was there, he guessed. Family servants usually knew everything that went on in the houses where they worked.

The butler opened a set of double doors and stepped aside for Chance to enter a large, high-ceilinged room. "Mr. Chance Dawson, madam," he announced.

Chance walked across the deep-pile carpet and looked down on a tiny figure that was almost lost in a big chair. The pleasant-looking face that was lifted to him was at odds with the cold, stern letter he had received. He had no doubt, however, that despite the softness of the delicate features, Thelma Ashely could be a tough combatant to come up against.

"Mrs. Ashely," Chance said, bending over Thelma and taking the hand she offered in his. "I came as soon as I received your letter."

"Thank you for being so prompt, Mr Dawson. Please take this chair beside me."

As Chance settled himself in a big wingback, Thelma surreptitiously studied his face and liked what she saw.

He had a strong face, broad forehead, high cheekbones, straight nose, and firm jaw. He was very handsome and that bothered her. Women chased men like him. How did he react to that? she wondered. Did he take everything that was offered to him? According to Fancy, he had no interest in marriage, so most likely he did.

Thelma felt Chance's eyes on her and hurriedly said, "May I offer you some coffee, or something stronger? A whiskey perhaps?"

Chance wondered if the old lady was trying

to find out if he was a drinker. "Thank you, but neither," he answered quietly. "I had a drink with the captain of the *John Davis* before pulling in to port." Actually, he'd had three belts of whiskey, pumping up his courage for whatever lay before him.

"How are Fancy and the boys?" he asked, resting an ankle on top of his knee.

There was a pause before Thelma answered, "Tod and Lenny are well. I think, however, that they miss you and their friends in the north woods. I'm afraid they're finding it hard amusing themselves here. They don't have much freedom, and not room enough to burn off the energy that the young have."

Here it comes, Chance thought. She's going to say she wants me to take Tod home with me.

But what Mrs. Ashely added, brought him sitting forward in his seat, was, "As I said in my letter, it's Fancy I want to discuss with you."

"Is Fancy ill?" The anxiety in his voice didn't escape Thelma. Maybe he did care for her granddaughter.

"Fancy is well enough, considering everything."

"What everything? I don't know what you're talking about. She was fine when she ran off and left my camp."

"She was in the same condition then as she is now. Fancy is going to have a baby. Your baby."

Chance couldn't move, couldn't speak for a

moment. He could only stare at Thelma open-mouthed. Then he was speaking, the words tumbling out of his mouth, most of them not making any sense. "Now hold on, Mrs. Ashely. Fancy and I don't want a baby. We don't even want to get married."

"Well"—Cold steel entered Thelma's voice—"Whether the pair of you want to or not is not your decision to make. Fancy is carrying your baby, and you're going to marry her and give the little one your name."

Give the little one his name. Chance liked the sound of it. Imagine, he was to become a father. Fathering a child had entered his mind a few times. He liked children. The only thing that had held him back was the thought of marriage. But that was before he met Fancy. And what about Fancy? How did she feel about getting married?

He put the question to Thelma. "Fancy knows nothing about her coming marriage. She doesn't even know that I wrote to you."

"What!" Chance gripped the chair arms. "Why didn't you tell her, sound her out? She's not going to like this."

"Perhaps I should have told her," Thelma agreed, "but I wanted to check you out first. If I didn't approve of you, or thought you were unfit for my granddaughter, or wouldn't make a good father for her child, then she would never know that you had been here."

"I see," Chance said tersely. "You've got it all worked out. Don't you think that regardless of what you might think of me, it would be dishonorable of you—and Fancy—not to tell me I was to become a father?"

"Not at all. I've seen men who shame the name father."

"Well, I'm not one of those men. Whether or not Fancy will marry me, I intend to raise the child and give it my name. No son or daughter of mine will ever be called bastard."

"Don't be too sure of that, young man." Thelma bristled. "I can always send Fancy to Europe, out of your reach, if I thought you unworthy of her and the babe."

"You can't play God like that," Chance rasped his indignation.

"I don't see it that way. I'm only looking after my granddaughter's welfare." Thelma picked up a small bell from the table at her elbow and gave it a shake. "However, I think you could be good husband and father material. I'm sending for Fancy now. We'll see what she feels about it."

Chance grimaced, but kept his thoughts to himself. He was pretty sure how she was going to react to her grandmother's dictum.

Upstairs, in her small sitting room, Fancy sat in her favorite place, the padded window seat, staring gloomily out the window. She was careful not to crease the skirt of her pale blue silk dress. Grandmother had said to put on her prettiest one today, that they might have a caller. She hadn't bothered asking who the expected caller was; she didn't care. All she could think about these days was the impending birth of her baby, a little one who would never know its father. Of that she would make certain.

She had no doubt that Chance would marry her if he knew of her condition, but it would be out of a sense of duty. She closed her eyes as though in pain. How hellish it would be to live a life without love. Perhaps, with Grandmother's help, she could move to a town where she wasn't known and claim to be recently widowed. Her child wouldn't bear the stigma of being born out of wedlock then.

Her spirits rose. She must ask Grandmother's opinion on her idea. When a knock sounded on her door, she turned her head from the window and sang out, "Come in."

"Your grandmother wishes to see you in the parlor, miss," Thomas said in the very formal manner he used with her.

"I'll be right down," she answered. Rising, she walked into her bedroom to check the curls Katy had pinned to the top of her head. Grandmother was a stickler for neatness.

The curls were still secure. Smoothing down the soft folds of her skirt and pulling a pleasant look to her face, she descended the curving staircase.

Her steps were light and the smile on her face was genuine as she stepped into the parlor. Hadn't she found a way to solve her problem?

She stopped in midstride and her lips lost their soft curve. Sitting beside her grandmother was the man she had run from and was planning to run farther yet. He looked so good, she thought, even as he scowled at her.

Fancy advanced into the room and sat down on the sofa across from Chance and Thelma. "So, Chance, you have tracked me down," she said coolly. "It's not going to do you a scrap of good. You are not taking Tod away from me."

"He has come for Tod, and for *you* too, Fancy," Thelma spoke up before Chance could answer.

"He's made a wasted trip then." Fancy glowered at Chance. "We're not going with him."

"You're going." Chance raked hard eyes over her, wanting to take her in his arms and kiss her sneering lips.

"Oh? And who says so?"

"I say so, Fancy," Thelma said gently. "For the sake of your baby, you are going to marry Mr. Dawson."

Fancy looked at Thelma, hurt and betrayal in her eyes. "Grandmother, you told him when you knew I didn't want him to know." Anger grew in her dark blue eyes. "You sent for him, didn't you?"

"Fancy, dear, I felt that I had to." Thelma rose

and took a seat beside her distraught granddaughter. She covered Fancy's clasped fingers
with her thin hand and continued, "If you find
that the two of you absolutely can't get along
and there's no way you can make your marriage
work, then after the baby is born you can come
back to me and I'll arrange for you to get a divorce."

"Hold on there!" Chance held up a protesting
hand, a deep frown creasing his forehead. "I
don't hold with divorce. There's never been one
among the Dawsons."

"Well, then"—Thelma pinned him with stern
eyes—"see to it that you treat your wife right or
you'll be breaking a family tradition."

"She'll get back the same treatment she gives
me." Chance glowered at Fancy.

"It never worked that way before." Fancy
glared back.

"Like hell it didn't. Every time I—"

"Stop it, the two of you!" Thelma interrupted,
throwing her hands up in the air in disgust.
"You sound like a couple of squabbling children." She rang the little silver bell again, and
when Thomas appeared, she said to him, "Go
tell Katy and Father Marcus that we're ready for
them."

"Grandmother!" Fancy wailed, "do you mean
for us to get married today? Can't I get used to
the idea for at least a week?"

"Today or a week from now, what difference

will it make?" Thelma asked gently. "I want you married as soon as possible. When your little one comes seven months from now, you can claim it came early."

"No one will believe it." Fancy looked near tears.

"They'll have no way of disproving it, will they?" Thelma smilingly pointed out.

"As if any of our friends will give a damn when we got married," Chance growled. "They don't put on airs or have false pride like you wealthy do. When and why a couple get married is immaterial to them."

What Thelma was going to answer wasn't voiced. The priest, followed by Katy and Thomas, stepped into the room.

As Fancy stood beside Chance, listening to the old priest speak of the sanctity of marriage and how they must forsake all others and cling only to each other, she told herself that the words meant nothing to Chance. He'd not change his life one iota. He'd still have his women and stay out all night.

She thought of caustic-tongued Blanche Seacat and felt pity for the woman. How she must suffer on those nights when she knew that her husband had slipped away to spend an hour in the arms of a dance hall woman. Would she, Fancy Cranson—Dawson—be able to bear the pity she would see on her friends' faces when the man standing stiffly beside her continued in his same fashion?

She knew that she could, that she would have to until her baby was born.

Every word the priest said sank into Chance's mind. He remembered his mother and father, how close they were in their marriage, and he wanted the same with Fancy. If she would just learn to care for him a little, they could have a good marriage. God knew he loved her, but a one-sided love could not make a very successful marriage. Nevertheless, he would try with every beat of his heart to making their marriage a lasting one.

Fancy came back to the present when Chance nudged her with his elbow. She said "I do" to the priest's questioning look, and a moment later Thelma was removing a thin wedding band from her finger and handing it to Chance. As he slipped the ring on Fancy's finger, he said after the priest, "With this ring I thee wed."

It was over then, and Thelma was drawing Fancy's head down to kiss her on the cheek. To Chance, who stood stone-faced, she said, "Some day you'll forgive me for this. You will realize that marrying Fancy was the best thing you ever did in your life."

Chance gave her a sour smile. "I suppose you think your granddaughter will feel the same way."

"I think that she will." Thelma smiled wisely.

Tod and Lenny were called in from the back-yard, where they had been trying to entertain themselves. As they whooped their joy at seeing Chance, Fancy and Thelma said their good-byes.

"Do you think you could make the trip to be with me when it's time for my baby to be born?" Fancy asked wistfully. "I'm a little nervous about it."

"I'll be there, honey, I promise. Besides, I want to see that country you and the boys think so highly of."

Chance was hurrying them along then, ex-plaining that he wanted to get back to camp as soon as possible.

Tod hugged Thelma; then Lenny did the same. Katy and Thomas had brought down four bags and placed them beside the door. Katy had wisely not packed all the finery Thelma had bought Fancy. The little maid had reasoned that they would be out of place in a rough lumber camp and besides, Fancy wouldn't be able to wear them much longer.

Thelma and Katy stood on the small porch waving good-bye. "Do you think Miss Fancy will be happy with that handsome man, Mrs. Ash-ely?" the little maid asked.

"Not at first, but later she will be extremely happy. Neither knows it about the other, but they are madly in love."

Chapter Twenty-two

Fancy sat alone in the rear of the brig, staring out over the water, her fingers playing with the unfamiliar weight of Thelma's wedding ring on her finger. Up on deck she could hear the exuberance in Tod's and Lenny's voices as they talked to Chance, asking questions about camp. She hadn't realized just how badly they had missed their old life. She suspected now that they had missed more the lean, muscular man who had grown so important to them.

She heaved a troubled sigh. They would be devastated when she took them and left Chance a second time. For there was no doubt in her mind that their marriage would fail. When she had stood beside Chance during the ceremony, she could feel the resentment flowing out of him.

She supposed she shouldn't blame him. No man would like being forced to marry a woman he didn't love. But she didn't like having to marry him.

A mirthless smile curved her lips. They were both paying dearly for two nights of wild passion. Chance had made clear his unhappiness when they left the mansion by walking at least two yards ahead of her, his broad back stiff and his strides long. She hadn't made an effort to keep up with him. She was so angry herself at the time that she wouldn't have cared if he took the boys and went back to camp without her. She was sick to death of his swinging mood changes.

It was Lenny who had waited to help her down the gangplank of the *John Davis* in Seattle. Chance had completely ignored her during the last few days as they sailed north. She told herself she didn't care, but she lied. Evidently the words spoken by the old priest hadn't meant anything to the man who was ignoring her as though she wasn't sitting next to him.

Fancy hunched her shoulders against the air that had grown colder and colder as they neared the Sound. She was feeling a little nauseated. She hadn't experienced the dreaded morning sickness yet, but she imagined it felt something like she was feeling now.

Chance absentmindedly answered the questions Tod and Lenny pelted him with. He was regretting his churlish behavior toward Fancy during the past few days. The thing that had set him off was hearing the maid, Katy, tell Fancy that she hadn't packed any of her finery because she wouldn't be needing it in a north woods camp. He had realized then what he was taking Fancy away from—a life of luxury that he'd never be able to give her.

But, he asked himself, did Fancy really mind giving up that soft life? There had been no tears, no longing backward looks when they left. Maybe she was glad to get away from it. After all, she had been born in a lumber camp and had lived in one all her life. She had never seemed unhappy with her lot. There was always a glow to her face and eyes and a smile on her lips—unless she looked at him.

He turned his head to shoot Fancy a fast glance and got a shock. Her face didn't wear a glow now. It had a greenish tint. Had she been seasick?

As he took her other arm to help her disembark, Chance swore to himself that this marriage of theirs was going to work. If they could just be civil to each other during the day, the nights would take care of themselves. They set fire to each other when their bodies touched.

A stirring began in his loins as he thought of tonight, their wedding night.

Fancy gave a startled little squeal when, at the end of the pier, he scooped her up in his arms and carried her across the ankle-deep mud and set her onto the hard, frozen ground.

"Thank you." She half smiled when he set her on her feet.

"Let's go see about rooms at the hotel," Chance said, taking her arm and leading her toward the weathered, unpainted building, Tod and Lenny following along behind them.

Surprising to him, Chance derived a pleasurable satisfaction from writing Mr. and Mrs. Chance Dawson in the hotel's guest ledger. He had never expected to add a Mrs. to his name.

The clerk handed him two keys and explained that their rooms were at the top of the stairs, the first two on their left. Chance passed the keys to Fancy, saying, "You and the fellows go on up and get settled in; then meet me in the dining room in about an hour. I'm going to walk around a bit, say hello to a couple of men I know. I may stop in and visit with Al Bonner a minute."

As Fancy and Tod and Lenny climbed the stairs, Fancy knew by Chance's softened attitude that he expected to sleep with her tonight. A grim smile curved her lips. He'd better get that notion out of his head. Their sleeping arrangements were going to be the same despite the old priest's words. She was not about to put up with his insults by day, then let him use her body at night.

Fancy laid out her and Tod's nightclothes in

one of the rooms, then took Lenny to the other room and did the same for him. "Will I be sleeping with Chance again?" Lenny asked.

"That's right." Fancy smiled at him. "Don't you like sharing a bed with him?"

"It's all right, but he does a lot of tossing and kicking."

"Maybe he's having nightmares," Fancy suggested.

"Maybe, but I think he dreams of you a lot. He says your name kinda sleepy-like, or in pain."

Fancy blushed, then said jokingly, "Maybe he was dreaming that I was kicking him."

That tickled Lenny, and he said, "I'm going to ask him if he dreams that."

"Oh, no, honey, I don't think you should do that," Fancy said in some alarm. "You might embarrass him."

"Oh, I wouldn't want to do that," Lenny exclaimed gravely. "I won't say a thing about how he sleeps."

"Good. Let's go back to my room and wait until it's time to go eat supper."

While they waited, Tod and Lenny talked excitedly about going home and seeing their old friends again. Fancy had mixed feelings about returning to camp. She looked happily toward it, at the same time dreaded it. She would be asked so many questions—such as why she had left without saying good-bye.

She looked at the small watch pinned to her

bodice and saw that it was time to meet Chance. She and the boys descended the stairs and saw Chance waiting for them in the small lobby. He rose from a chair and as he joined them he said smilingly, "They're serving chicken and dumplings tonight, with chocolate cake for dessert."

Tod and Lenny loudly expressed their approval, and taking Fancy's arm, Chance led them into the dining room. He was disappointed that he could only show Fancy off to two other diners, an older married couple.

They were a merry group, talking and laughing as they ate supper. While Chance and Fancy were having coffee, Fancy asked, "How are the Bonners?"

"They weren't home. Al's foreman said he thought he had taken his wife to San Francisco to spend the winter. I guess she had been complaining a lot about it being so cold here in the winter."

"It seems strange that Mr. Bonner didn't tell his foreman where he'd be. What if an emergency arose?"

Chance shrugged. "He left a note saying that he was taking Clare away for the winter. That he'd be back in the spring."

Full darkness had descended when Chance led his small party out of the dining room. "Shall we sit down here in front of the fire a while before going up to our rooms?" he asked as they stepped into the lobby.

Fancy had caught Tod yawning a couple of times over his cake and answered, "I'm pretty tired and I think the boys are too. But why don't you stay and have a drink with the men at the bar?"

There was a slow curl in Chance's loins. She wanted some time alone to change into her nightclothes, to be waiting for him in bed. He nodded and said, "Maybe I'll have a couple. I know that fellow at the end of the bar." But as he watched the graceful sway of Fancy's hips as she climbed the stairs, he decided that one drink would be sufficient.

The man Chance had recognized was a garrulous fellow, and he started a long-winded tale as soon as Chance stepped up beside him. Half an hour passed before he could get away. With anticipation racing through his blood, he took the stairs two at a time.

He found the first door he tried locked. He moved to the one beside it, and the door knob gave when he turned it. The room was dark as he stepped inside it, lit only by the moonbeams shining through the window. He walked quietly over to the bed and gazed down on Fancy's sleeping face.

How lovely she was, he thought, her features in repose, her long lashes casting a fan shape on her pink cheeks. He reached down and stroked one of the blond curls that spilled over a bare shoulder, thinking that it felt like silk.

And so did her skin, he remembered, and in a rush to feel that softness again, Chance jerked his shirttail free of his trousers and began to undo the buttons. It was then that the lump of bed covers bunched up next to Fancy stirred and a small arm flung free of them.

Chance stared at his nephew's arm, his eyes turning from brown to black with the anger that swept through him. "Damn you, Fancy," he grated out in a whisper, "you don't intend this marriage to work, do you?" He stood a moment longer, then muttering, "To hell with you," he turned and stalked out of the room, not caring that the door hadn't closed very quietly.

It was a surly-faced Chance who met Fancy and the boys in the dining room the next morning. As they were eating ham and eggs and fried potatoes, Lenny asked, "Where did you sleep last night, Chance?"

Chance wasn't about to answer that he had spent the night getting drunk with the man who talked nonstop, so giving Fancy a cool mocking look, he said, "I spent the night with an old friend."

Fancy looked away from him, hoping that the pain that jabbed her chest didn't show in her eyes. She told herself that she had better grow a thick skin because this was going to happen again and again. There would always be a *friend* her husband would find to sleep with.

Half an hour later they boarded the brig *Franklin* and headed upriver toward home. Home, Fancy thought, sitting where Chance had led her, a spot sheltered from the cold wind—lumber camp would always seem home to her in spite of the discomforts she had to put up with occasionally. But the fresh piney air, the open blue sky, a people who were rough, yet caring, was the most wonderful place in the world to her.

Fancy placed her hand on her flat stomach and made a decision. Let Chance go his own way; she'd somehow live with his philandering. She wanted her baby to grow up in the big timber that was its heritage.

In the cold, still air, the sound of the big saw tearing through a log reached half a mile down the river. Tod and Lenny could hardly contain themselves when they rounded a bend in the river and the mill yard came in view. As soon as the big vessel docked, they clambered ashore, yelling a greeting to Victor Seacat, who operated the saw.

Victor shut the big machine down to an idle and walked to meet them, a broad smile on his face. The three had been missed in camp. He slapped Lenny on the back, ruffled Tod's hair, and held out a hand to Fancy. "Sure am glad to see you back, miss," he said sincerely.

"She's a Mrs. now, Victor," Chance said gruffly, but with a proud note in his tone. "We got married in San Francisco."

"Well, don't that beat all." Victor beamed. "Blanche is sure gonna be happy to hear that. She's always said that you belong together. You have my heartiest congratulations."

While Fancy smiled her thanks, Chance asked, "Did everything go all right while I was gone? Any visits from that sneaking skunk?"

"I don't think so. I ain't heard of any mischief bein' done."

"That's a relief," Chance said, then struck off after Tod and Lenny, leaving Fancy to walk alone. Victor watched them a moment, thinking that Fancy and Chance didn't act like newlyweds.

Victor must have broken all speed records spreading the word that Chance and Fancy were married, for Fancy hadn't been in the house more than half an hour when her friends came tromping through the snow to welcome her home and to express their happiness for her marriage. To her surprise and relief, nothing was said about her secret departure so many weeks ago.

She thanked them, then laughingly said, "I can give you ladies coffee, but that's about all. There's not even a loaf of bread in the house."

They all laughed at that, with Blanche Seacat saying that she wasn't surprised. That Chance had been like a mean bear coming out of hibernation all the time Fancy was gone. "I think cookies and such was the last thing on his mind. We all hope that he will mellow now that you're back."

"I don't think my being gone had anything to do with his grumpiness," Fancy said. "He's worried about all the vandalism that's been going on in camp."

"That bothers us all," Molly said. "While you were gone the cookhouse was set on fire one night. We're afraid to go to sleep for fear our houses will be set afire."

"We keep a couple of pails of water handy just in case," Sukie Daniels said. "We've got all them younguns of ours to think about."

The other women said that they, too, kept extra water in the house, and Fancy made a note to do the same. She had Tod and Lenny to think about. Not that Chance wouldn't be concerned for them too. She must give the devil his due. He cared deeply for the boys.

Her neighbors didn't stay long, saying that they knew how much work lay ahead of her. She answered that other than the kitchen, the house only needed a good dusting; the first thing she was going to do was get a batch of bread dough rising. And look in the larder to see if there was anything she could cook for supper.

Molly was the last to go, lingering to say how happy she was that Fancy was back, that she had missed her. She also asked, with concern in her eyes, if her friend was truly happy in her married state.

"Oh, yes, I'm quite content." Fancy forced a wide smile to her lips as she told her lie.

"I'm glad." Molly smiled back. "A woman should have a husband's strength to rely on."

Fancy watched Molly hurry toward her house a few minutes later, wishing that she could depend on Chance always being there for her.

She turned from the window and started gathering the ingredients she'd need for the breadmaking. Her husband wasn't like Molly's, who adored her. Chance didn't even like her, much less worship her.

Chapter Twenty-three

Fancy stood on the porch waving good-bye to Tod and Lenny as they joined the other children on their way to school. She hugged the heavy shawl closer around her shoulders. It was so good to be back. She loved this land of mountains, forests, and fog-hung cliffs.

Away in the distance she could see the Olympic Mountains, full of wild beasts and ferns that grew twenty feet tall in the saturated clouds that usually hung over the peaks. Some days the clouds were so low that a stranger wouldn't know the mountains were even there. But today they stood out crisp and clear.

And the wind was just right to hear the savage music of the whining saws coming from Puget Sound twenty miles away. The scent of fresh sawdust was strong in the air from their own saws as Fancy turned back into the house.

Zeb called to her before she could close the door. She hadn't found the time to visit him yesterday, what with the neighbor women stopping by, the unpacking to be done, then preparing supper. But she had planned to stop by the cookhouse first thing this morning, right after she made out her grocery list.

The old man looked at her with fond, aged eyes. "It's good to have you back, girl." He grinned, pumping her hand up and down. "It sure wasn't the same around here without you."

He pulled out a chair when Fancy motioned him to sit down. "Chance hasn't been fit to be around. We all stayed away from him if we could. 'Course, I got stuck with him the most, the cookhouse bein' so close to his house. Seemed like he couldn't go or come from his place without stopping there with his long face. I don't know which was worse—when he was rakin' someone over the coals, or when he sat like a wooden Indian not sayin' a word."

"I doubt if my absence had anything to do with his actions," Fancy said as she poured Zeb a cup of coffee. "I'm sure all the happenings in camp have him worried."

"Oh, he's concerned about that all right. He's angry about the lowlife who's givin' him so much trouble. But you're to blame for his black moods."

"Well, he has Tod back now, so he can be his

usual grumpy self again."

"He wasn't always grumpy, as you call it," Zeb said, pulling the sugar bowl toward him. "I've known Chance most of his life. I worked for his paw until he got killed in a logjam; then I worked for Chance when he took over. Chance was always a hellion, drinkin' and courtin' the wimmen, and you'd never find a more devil-may-care fellow anywhere.

"Nope, young lady, it wasn't until you came along that his personality changed."

"Well, I'm sorry if I upset him because I wouldn't turn my nephew over to him."

"Why do you keep bringin' the boy up? I know Chance is right fond of the boy, but you're not so dense that you don't know how he feels about you."

"Of course I know how he feels about me." Fancy's eyes snapped angrily. "He wants to sleep with me. The first time he saw me at the dance hall, he asked me to move in with him, be his private woman for a while. The arrogant fool thought I'd jump at the chance and he's been like a wounded bear ever since when I turned him down."

"But he married you in the end, Fancy," Zeb pointed out. "Doesn't that show that he cares for you?"

"No, it does not!" Fancy was so upset and angry now that the truth of her marriage came tumbling out. "He didn't marry me because he loves me, he married me because I'm carrying his child."

It seemed the wrinkles on Zeb's weathered face deepened as he stared at Fancy. Several seconds passed before he managed to say in a shakened voice, "I'm sorry, girl. His father would take a whip to him if he was alive. How did it happen?"

Fancy's outburst had relieved some of the repressed resentment that had roiled inside her ever since her forced marriage. She couldn't help the half smile that tugged at her lips as she said, "The way all pregnancies happen, Zeb."

"Dad blame it, Fancy, I know that. I meant how come you weakened and went to bed with him?"

When Fancy only shrugged helplessly, he said, "You don't have to explain. He could coax a nun into his bed if he wanted to."

As Fancy stared discontentedly out the window, Zeb tried to console her. "I've got a good feelin' that your marriage is gonna work out fine. You're both fine people and you're gonna work it out."

Fancy didn't respond to Zeb's prediction. Instead she said, rising to her feet, "I'd better make out the list of what I need for when the brig comes in."

As she watched Zeb walk back to the cookshack, she mulled over what he had said and concluded that the old fellow was mistaken.

Nothing was going to work out in this farce of a marriage. Last night, after the boys had gone to bed, Chance had left the house and hadn't returned until this morning when she was making breakfast.

She wondered which of the dance hall women he had slept with. She tried to ignore the pain that thought gave her. She didn't want to think of Chance being in bed with another woman. It tore her apart with jealousy.

While she sat at the kitchen table trying to think and write down the household items she needed, the picture of Chance's strong body making love to another woman kept entering her mind. When tears glimmered in her eyes, the voice inside her spoke. "You could make him welcome in your bed. After all, he is your husband and has a right to be there."

"But he doesn't love me. I refuse to be used like a whore."

"He's your husband. How can he treat you like one of those women? He hasn't done so yet. Do you think he gives them tender kisses and loving words the way he does you when you're making love? I think you should give this some serious thought, young lady."

Half an hour later, hurrying down to the river to board the brig that brought in merchandise for the camp, Fancy had decided to take the advice of her other self. If it took sharing a bed with her husband to keep him home nights, she was going to do it. But she would not share him. He had better crawl into *her* bed every night. The first time he didn't, it would be the end. She would go back to Grandmother's, and he'd never lay eyes on his child.

When she returned to the house, she would transfer Tod's clothing to Lenny's room.

Chance finished greasing the skids, then leaned back against a pine, his mouth open in a wide yawn. He hadn't slept much last night, rolled up in a couple of blankets on the cook-house floor. With the cold air seeping from under the door and Zeb's thunderous snoring, it had been a long, miserable night.

He had asked himself a dozen times why he didn't get up and take advantage of a warm bed in back of the dance hall. At the same time, he could rid himself of the gnawing hunger he felt for his wife.

How much longer could he go on? he asked himself, wanting her so that his whole body hurt. One thing he did know, he wasn't helping the situation by making Fancy think that he was sleeping with one of Myrt's girls.

Foolishly, it had been his intent last night to make her jealous. But how could he do that if she didn't love him? The only chance he had of that ever happening was if he could make love to her on a regular basis. She was a different woman when he held her in his arms.

So there would be no more acting like a greenhorn trying to get back at a girlfriend.

Chance straightened up when he saw Fancy come hurrying along, walking toward the river. He knew she was going after supplies. He had just decided to go with her, do the husbandly thing by carrying her purchases home, when Gil Hampton came from the mill yard and fell into step beside her. It was all Chance could do not to step forward and knock the smile off the scaler's handsome face.

Only the fact that Fancy would give him one of her cool, disdainful looks stayed him. But Hampton must have felt the hot bore of his eyes in his back.

When Lenny and Tod got home from school, the kitchen held a mixture of delicious odors. There were two apple pies cooling on the workbench, a spicy steam wafting from them. In the oven a big piece of beef was roasting with potatoes browning in its juices. There was a pan of string beans waiting to be heated, and a sheet of sourdough biscuits to go into the oven at the proper time.

The table was set for four, although Fancy had no idea if Chance would show up for supper. He hadn't come home for lunch, and she had seen him go into the cookhouse with his men.

The sun set and Fancy lit the lamp on the

kitchen table and two in the family room for Tod and Lenny to see to do the lessons Molly had assigned. Lenny had learned how to print his name and knew quite a few words in his primer. Fancy wished that her nephew was as studious as her cousin. The roast was done, sitting on top of the stove, and biscuits would be ready to take from the oven in about fifteen minutes.

Fancy's nerves tightened when she heard the crew coming in, laughing and talking as usual as they tramped into the cookhouse. Was Chance among them? she wondered, but she was too proud to peer through the window and find out.

Ten minutes passed and Fancy gave up on Chance eating supper with them. She was taking the biscuits from the oven when the door opened and Chance stepped inside. She gave him a searching look to see what mood he was in as she placed the hot bread on the table. He looked pleasant enough, she decided, and gave him tentative smile as she said, "By the time you wash up, supper will be on the table."

Much praise was heaped on Fancy as the three males dug in with hearty appetites. "It sure is good, the four of us eating together again, huh, Chance?" Tod looked at his uncle, a white rim of milk circling his mouth.

"It sure is." Chance ventured a smile at Fancy and nearly choked when she smiled back.

"Did you miss us, Chance?" Lenny asked. "Me and Tod sure missed you."

Chance looked at Fancy again. Had she possibly missed him also? Her lowered lids hid what she was thinking. "I sure did," he answered Lenny. "It feels real good to have you all back home."

"I'll help you with the dishes," Chance offered when the meal was over and Tod and Lenny had gone back to the family room.

Fancy shook her head. "Thanks, but I'll do them. You've been working out in the cold all day. Go on in with the boys and warm up."

Chance didn't know how to respond to this new Fancy. She had been more genial to him this evening than she had all the other evenings put together. "It was cold out there today," he said finally and left her clearing the table.

When a short time later Fancy followed him into the comfortable room, she thought how cozy Chance and the boys looked- Chance with his long legs stretched to the fire, Lenny sitting on the raised hearth mouthing the printed words in the primer he held in his lap, and Tod stretched out on the rug in front of the fireplace, staring into the flames. Was he thinking of his parents? she wondered as she sat down in the rocker on the other side of the table that separated it from the one Chance was relaxing in.

"What do you see in the flames, honey?" She playfully nudged Tod's shoulder with her toe.

351

"He sees Ruthie Daniels's face." Lenny looked up from his book, a teasing light in his eyes.

"Do not." Tod glared at him.

"Do too. You write notes to each other."

"Do not."

"Do too."

Fancy interrupted the growing argument by saying to a grinning Chance, "How did you happen to end up in the Washington Territory?"

"My mother and father were part of the fifty-one settlers who first came to Oregon. The group called themselves The Great Enforcement. I was fifteen when we settled in the Willamette Valley and my father started cutting timber. Ever since then, I've lived in lumber camps.

"My mother died in one of them, then Pa and I came up the Columbia to the Walla Walla region. When Pa was killed in a logjam, I left there and came here."

Tod and Lenny had listened intently as Chance spoke briefly of his past, but now that he was finished they both yawned widely.

"I think it's time you two went to bed," Fancy said.

"Can't Uncle Chance tell us one last story?" Tod begged.

"Not tonight," Fancy said firmly. "Maybe tomorrow night."

Tod and Lenny had just said good night to Chance when someone knocked on the kitchen door. Chance went to answer it, and as Fancy herded the boys out of the room she heard him talking to Frank Jackson. When Tod would have gone into her room, she called him back. "You'll be sleeping with Lenny from now on, honey."

Tod looked surprised for a moment; then understanding flashed in his eyes. "That's right," he said, " 'cause you and Uncle Chance are married now, you'll sleep together just like Ma and Pa did."

"That's right, honey. Now you two get to bed and go right to sleep. I don't want to hear any talking in here."

In her room, as Fancy changed into her night-gown, her stomach curled with the memory of how good it had felt when she had made love with Chance. To her embarrassment, she could hardly wait to experience again that mind-shattering release of passion. She could almost feel his hands and lips on her body, making her lose control, doing things that made her blush when she remembered them in the daytime.

She was in bed, waiting, when it occurred to her that Chance might not even plan on sleeping in the house tonight. What if he didn't go into Lenny's room and discover Tod had taken his place in the bed? What if his sleeping arrangements were the same as they were last night? Maybe one of the dancers was waiting for him to join her in bed right now.

Finally, Fancy heard the outside door open, then close, and it grew quiet in the kitchen. When several seconds had passed and she could hear no movement in the house, depression gripped her. Chance had left with Frank Jackson. She turned on her side, fighting back tears. All her plotting had come to nothing.

She was telling herself to get used to a lonely bed when she heard a rustling close to the bed. It sounded like someone was taking off his clothes. She grew still when a heavy weight tilted the feather mattress, rolling her toward its center. She recognized then the lean hand that placed itself on her hip.

Chapter Twenty-four

Chance closed and barred the door behind Frank; then, cupping his hand over the lamp chimney, he blew out the flame. By the light of the moon, he moved quietly into the room where he guessed he'd be sleeping the rest of his life.

He pulled his shirt free of his trousers and was about to sit down on the edge of the bed to remove his boots when he noted that two bodies already occupied the bed. He peered down at the sleeping forms to make sure he wasn't mistaken, and his lips stretched in a wide smile. In the semidarkness he made out Tod's freckled face.

When and why had Fancy changed her mind about sleeping with him? He didn't care what the reasons were, he told himself, and in his room he undressed to his skin. Then, his heart pounding, he slid in beside Fancy, laid a hand on her hip, and whispered softly, "Does this mean what I think it does, Fancy?"

Why is he making it hard for me? Why does he have talk, ask questions? Fancy stared at the gray shape of the window. Why can't he just take me in his arms and make love to me? Why make me admit that I want him?

What she finally blurted out surprised her as well as Chance. "Tod thinks that we should sleep together, like his mother and father did."

The hand that had been stroking her hip grew still, and a bitterness clouded Chance's eyes. Fancy hadn't let him into her bed out of great desire or love for him. He stared down at her, trying to read her face in the darkness.

He was telling himself to leave the bed, put his clothes back on, and leave the house—that he didn't care what his nephew thought they should do—when Fancy turned over, her body soft and warm against his. Conscious thought became impossible as his body's desire took over. He said her name in a rasping whisper and drew her into his arms.

Fancy awoke to find the sun streaming through the window. She wondered what time it was and looked at the small clock on the table. Twenty minutes after nine. She couldn't believe it. She scrambled out of bed, then discovered her nakedness and grabbed for her robe. Tod and

Lenny were going to be late getting to school.

She hurried to their room and found the bed empty. Becoming a little alarmed, she hurried to the kitchen and relaxed. There were three plates on the table, sticky with syrup, and two glasses with a bit of milk left in them. An empty coffee cup sat beside one plate.

Chance had made breakfast for the boys and got them off to school. Why hadn't he awakened her to do that? She sat down at the table, a bleak look coming over her face. He hadn't wanted to face her this morning. They had made wild love half the night, but in the daylight he regretted the ecstasy they had shared.

She sighed and stood up. Was her plan going to work? She would know if he came to her tonight.

When Fancy had dressed and straightened up the house, she sat down at the kitchen table and wrote a letter to her grandmother. The dear old lady would be waiting to hear from her. She didn't write about her unhappiness with Chance—that would upset this grandmother she had learned to love deeply. She wrote that everything was going well and that she was feeling fine. She added that she missed Thelma and looked forward to her visit.

When she had sealed the envelope, Fancy put on her jacket and fixed her shawl around her head and shoulders. She planned to pay Myrt a visit before walking down to the river to wait for the postal canoe.

"So, you married that wolf," Myrt said after they had hugged and were sitting and having coffee and a piece of cake that Luther had baked. "I've got to say that surprised the hell out of me. Not that I didn't think Chance wanted it to happen, I just thought he was too mule-headed to ask you."

Fancy gazed out the window a moment, then turned her head and looked at Myrt. "He didn't ask me."

"Are you telling me that you asked *him*?" Myrt couldn't keep the disbelief out of her voice.

"Of course not," Fancy denied indignantly. "My grandmother ordered him to."

"Ordered him to? Do you mean . . ."

"Yes. I'm carrying his child. It will be born in mid-July."

Myrt sat stunned for a moment. Finally she spoke. "Shall I congratulate you or give you my sympathy?"

"I really don't know, Myrt," Fancy answered frankly. "If things were different between me and Chance, I'd be real pleased. I've always wanted children of my own. But if I have to raise it alone, with no father about, that would be hard on a little one, especially if it's a boy."

"What makes you think you'll have to raise it alone? If I know Chance Dawson, he'll be right there helping you with the little one. He's not one to shirk a responsibility."

"I wouldn't want him to be there because he felt like he should be."

"Nor would he feel that way. He'll be crazy about a child of his. Wait and see."

Fancy didn't tell Myrt that if things didn't change between her and Chance, she'd be going back to her grandmother after the baby came.

She and Myrt talked of other things then, Fancy telling about her seven weeks in San Francisco, what a nice old lady her grandmother was, but how she hated dressing up every day and visiting people she had nothing in common with. Myrt said nothing much had changed in camp, except for the man who seemed to have it in for Chance. "We're all scared to death of fire now."

"Chance says he has no idea who the man is."

"Nobody does, but it's my thought that it's somebody from a different camp. Some man who has it in for Chance."

Fancy gave a short laugh. "Probably some husband."

"No, you're mistaken there, Fancy. Chance has had a lot of women, but he never touches a married woman. And he's had plenty of opportunities."

Fancy finished her coffee and stood up. "I'd better get down to the river before I miss the canoe. I'm sending a letter to my grandmother."

"It's good to have you back, Fancy. Stop in again."

"I will. And you know the way to my house."

Fancy was halfway to the river when she saw Gil and Pilar coming toward her. As soon as the Mexican woman saw her, she looped a possessive arm in Gil's and gave Fancy a smug smile when they met. Resentment, however, flickered in her eyes when Gil said warmly to Fancy, "It's good to see you back. The camp will be a little brighter now."

"She's a married woman now, Gil, so don't go flirting with her." Pilar pretended to be joking, but her voice was a little too shrill to pull it off.

"So I heard." There was accusation in Gil's brown eyes. "I must say I was some surprised when I heard it." When Fancy didn't make a response, only looked helplessly at him, he disengaged his arm from Pilar's and, stepping forward, said, "I didn't get to kiss the bride." Before Fancy could move, his arm was around her waist and his hand was tilting her chin.

Rather than a customary congratulatory kiss, swift and on the cheek, Gil chose Fancy's lips and took his time with the kiss, like a hungry bird sipping nectar from a flower. Fancy heard Pilar give an angry gasp, and she brought up her hands and pushed against Gil's chest, at the same time jerking her mouth away from his. He stared down at her swollen lips a moment, then released her and walked away.

"Bitch!" Pilar hissed at Fancy, then ran to catch up with Gil.

Her fingers on her lips, bruised from a kiss that had held punishment as well as hunger, Fancy looked after them until they were out of sight. She hadn't known that Gil's feelings for her ran so deep. She had known he had a fondness for her, but thought that most of his caring actions had been designed to irk Chance.

If only Chance cared as much for her, she thought unhappily and walked on down to the river to join her friends waiting there.

Chance, taking a short cut through the forest from the mill yard to the camp, was ready to step onto the path when he saw Gil put his arms around Fancy and kiss her. "What the hell," he muttered and came to a halt. That man had more brass than a brass monkey. Kissing Fancy right under Pilar's nose! He started to move forward, to tear Fancy out of Gil's arms, when she herself tore away from the scaler.

She took her sweet time, he thought darkly, and wondered if Fancy would have pushed away from Hampton at all if Pilar hadn't been there.

The lighthearted mood he'd been in all day darkened. Was this an omen of what he had in store? Men always hungering after his wife? Would he always have to worry that one of them might take her away from him?

Chance wheeled around and walked back in the direction of the mill. He had intended to go to the house and have a cup of coffee with Fancy and maybe coax her back into bed for a little lovemaking before the boys returned home from school.

He dismissed the thought from his mind. The less he was around Fancy, the easier it would be when she left him and returned to her grandmother.

Fancy was so occupied with thinking of Gil and the shock of his passionate kiss, that it took her a moment to realize that she was nearing the river and that she was being hailed by her friends.

"Mavis has a wonderful idea," Alma Bandy said when Fancy joined them. "She thinks we should have a party."

"Sounds good to me," Fancy said, and meant it. A get-together would break up the monotony of their long evenings. "Where would we have it? None of our houses is big enough to hold us all."

"We'll use the bachelors' quarters," Alma said. "It's plenty big. There'll even be room to dance."

"Who'll make the music? Are you going to bring Luther and his piano over? I don't think Myrt would approve of that," Fancy joked.

"We've got some good musicians among us," Blanche Seacat said. "Victor plays the banjo right well, and Frank Jackson is a real good fiddle player. And believe it or not, old Zeb can make a body cry with the beautiful tunes he can play on his mouth-harp."

"When are you going to have the party?"

"We thought maybe this Saturday," Alma said. "The men don't work on Sunday so they can stay up as long as they want to."

By the time the mail canoe pulled into shore, everything had been planned, down to who would bring what to eat. "And make sure you bring plenty," Blanche reminded everyone. "Remember, the bachelors will be joining us and they eat like a bunch of hogs."

"What about Myrt and the dancers? Will they be coming too?" Fancy asked the question of anyone who wanted to answer.

"They'd better not!" Blanche's eyes blazed like a cat's ready to spring on its prey.

No one was surprised at Mrs. Seacat's impassioned words. They all knew what made her speak so, and none of them faulted her for it. Victor was like an old hound dog sniffing after the dancers, especially Pilar. And the Mexican dancer, bitch that she was, flaunted Victor's weakness for her by flirting with him in front of Blanche. Everyone waited for the day that the big raw-boned woman would wipe up the camp with her tormentor.

Later, as Fancy walked home, she wished that Myrt could come to the party. The women would like her if they got to know her.

The children were coming out of the makeshift school when Fancy walked into the camp clearing. She stopped to talk to Molly, to discuss the party with her. She was saying that she thought she would bake a cake for the event when Molly smiled and said, "Hello, Chance."

Fancy turned her head to look over her shoulder at Chance, who had come up on silent feet. The smile he had given Molly was not bestowed on her. He wore the same stony look he always wore when around her. She gave an inward sigh. What she had suspected this morning was true. Nothing had changed between them.

She hoped that Molly hadn't noticed Chance's coolness as she said good-bye to her favorite neighbor. She didn't want anyone feeling sorry for her as they did Blanche Seacat.

That night as she and Chance and Tod and Lenny sat in the family room, Fancy slid Chance many looks from the sides of her eyes and always found him staring moodily into the fire. She in turn never caught the quick looks he darted her.

Both dreaded going to bed, to lie suffering beside the other. For if they hadn't been civil to each other in the daytime hours, how could they make love at night?

But when they went to bed and Chance lowered the lamp's wick, enclosing them in darkness, they turned to each other as though it was the most natural thing to do. It was as though two different couples shared the house. The daytime pair were cool and aloof, while the nighttime couple were passionate and loving.

Chapter Twenty-five

A new moon had risen the night of the party, lighting everyone's way to the bachelors' quarters. Chance and Fancy hurried along, Chance holding Fancy's arm so that she wouldn't slip and fall. They would be the last ones arriving at the party.

Chance grinned, remembering the reason. Fancy had changed dresses three times before one fit her around the waist. It wasn't evident to their neighbors yet that his wife carried his child, but at night, holding her naked body in his arms, he could feel the gentle swelling of her stomach. And as the babe grew beneath her heart, the more he grew to love the baby the two of them had created.

As they neared the long building, Fancy wanted to ask Chance if tonight he would pretend that they were a normal, happy couple, but she couldn't get up the nerve. The evening would be spoiled for her if he gave her some cutting answer whose hurt she couldn't hide.

Her heart skipped a happy beat when Chance continued to hold her arm when they joined the merrymakers. She gave him a grateful smile when he helped her off with her jacket and hung it up. Greetings were called to them, and as always happened at gatherings the men gravitated toward each other at the far end of the room and the women stayed around the warmth of the fire. The children ran about like wild things let out of a cage, getting into everyone's way, filching sweets from the long table practically groaning from the weight of the many dishes the wives had brought.

Fancy took her fruitcake from Chance and placed it on the table, then joined the women chattering away. Sukie Daniels was explaining how she had received her black eye when the strains of "Camptown Races" played on a mouth-harp rang through the room. A fiddle was added and then a banjo. Feet began tapping; then husbands were grabbing wives and whirling them around the room, sending their skirts flying above their knees.

Fancy was wondering if Chance would dance with her when suddenly he was there before her, smiling and opening his arms to her. She couldn't remember ever being so happy, flying around the room in her husband's arms.

After the first dance, the bachelors moved in, tapping husbands on the shoulder. They good-naturedly relinquished their wives; after all, who else were the single men to dance with?

Fancy wondered if Chance would turn her over to one of the lumbermen and found that he would as a bearded sawyer claimed her.

The next hour, as Fancy danced with one man and then another, Chance leaned against the wall, watching her graceful movements. He was so proud that she belonged to him that he was hard put not to stand there and smile like an idiot.

Chance's proud smile of ownership faded when, from out of nowhere it seemed, Gil Hampton was claiming his wife for a dance. When the scaler took Fancy in his arms, Chance started forward, then stopped. Every man there had danced with Fancy at least once, and eyebrows would be raised if he put up a fuss.

Fancy made sure she kept a decent distance between herself and Gil as they circled the floor, although it was a little difficult. He stubbornly tried to draw her closer into his arms even as she strained against them. Knowing that Chance's eyes would be upon them, she finally whispered, "Gil, behave yourself. You might make Chance angry, but you would make me look bad in the doing."

Gil's arms immediately loosened around her,

and he said contritely, "I'm sorry, Fancy. I never thought of that."

When Fancy and Gil swept past Chance, she smiled and waved at him. She received a cold stare in return. Resentment flared inside her. She had done nothing differently with Gil than she had with the other men. So what was Chance blaming her for? She was sick to death of trying to figure her husband out and walking on eggshells in order not to rile his temper.

She was debating pressing her body up against Gil's and giving Chance something to really get angry about, when the music stopped and Blanche called out that it was time for refreshments. Everyone made a rush to the table, each person loading the plate that had been brought from home. Zeb had brought a stack of tin plates for his and the bachelors' use.

It was relatively quiet as everyone settled down to eating. It grew deadly quiet then, when the door opened and Pilar stepped inside. As everyone stared with open mouths, the dancer scanned the room, clearly looking for someone. No one was in doubt whom she looked for.

Pilar stepped farther into the room and suddenly Blanche stood in front of her. "What are you doing here, slut?" she demanded. "Nobody wants you here."

"Speak for yourself, Mrs. Seacat," Pilar sneered, her hands on her hips. "Victor over there is happy to see me."

All heads swerved to look at Blanche's embarrassed husband. "Tell her, Victor," Pilar ordered. "Tell her how happy you are to see me here."

Victor looked at his tall, unattractive wife and saw the suffering on her face. For the first time, he was ashamed of how he had shamed her over the years. He walked over to Blanche, put an arm around her shoulders, and said clearly, so that all could hear, "I'm not in the least happy that you are here, Pilar."

"Is that right? Well let me tell you that—"

Whatever the angry dancer was about to say Gil interrupted by grabbing her arm and marching her to the door. No one could hear what he said to her before opening the door and jerking her outside.

The men picked up conversations that had been dropped, pretending that nothing unusual had happened. The women, however, stood around Blanche, their voices loud in what they thought of the bitch, Pilar.

The party lasted another hour, the pleasure of it waning, thanks to Pilar. Empty plates and flatware was gathered up by owners, and children were bundled into coats. It was noted that Victor gave Blanche a hand and that when she left the party, he went along with her. It was also noted the pleased, proud look Blanche wore.

"Do you suppose Victor is turning over a new leaf?" Fancy asked Chance as they walked home later.

"It looks like it, but Pilar is going to use all her wiles on him, just to get back at Blanche. I hope Victor is wise enough to see through her."

"I don't know why Blanche has put up with him as long as she has. I'd have kicked him out the first time he went to bed with another woman."

A wry smile twitched the corners of Chance's lips. Was Fancy warning him that if he strayed from her bed, he could stay strayed? "That's easy for you to say." He helped her over a piece of ice. "You'd be aware that there would always be someone waiting to replace the one you'd kick out. That wouldn't be the case with Blanche. Besides being as plain as a mud-hen, she's got a disposition like a green persimmon. She'd never be able to find another husband."

"I bet she she didn't have that sharp tongue when she and Victor got married. I'm sure he made her the way she is today."

"You women sure stick together." Chance chuckled.

"No more than you men do." Fancy jerked her arm free from Chance and then would have fallen had he not laughingly caught her around the waist. She tried to pull free, but his arm only tightened around her and stayed there until they walked inside the house.

That night something new entered Chance and Fancy's lovemaking. There was a tenderness, a lingering that had never been there before. Fancy fell asleep in Chance's arms and was still there the next morning.

Chapter Twenty-six

Fancy awakened to her bedroom awash with sunshine. She stretched and smiled. At last the rain had stopped. Three days ago a storm that had hung for hours, threatening dark clouds in the south, had finally moved north around sundown and broke with a vicious fury. When morning came, the downpour had subsided to a gray and steady rainfall. Old Zeb had been right when he said it had come to "stay awhile."

The Columbia had risen several feet, as had all its lesser streams. Bodies of drowned farm animals floated out to sea. If it weren't for the many layers of pine needles, the camp would have been a quagmire of mud. Fancy was thankful that they sat high enough from the raging river so that they were in no danger of being flooded.

It was May, Fancy's favorite time of the year. The salmonberries were blooming and the frogs now sang in the marshlands, their voices chiming together. On the last day of winter, meadowlarks had flown in and settled down in the fields, with the robins coming next, then the crimson-headed linnets. All day long the camp was serenaded with their song.

Fancy clasped her hands over her well-rounded stomach. In another two months it would be flat again, and she could hardly wait. She was tired of her awkward movements, her back aching. Sukie Daniels told her she was fortunate that her hands and feet weren't swollen. All in all, she imagined she'd had an easy pregnancy so far. She hadn't gained too much weight; in fact she had only begun to show a couple months back.

Of course there was also the fact that she was being well tended to by the men in her family, as well as by old Zeb. Most evenings for the past two months, they had eaten supper with the old man in the cookhouse. And if that wasn't being spoiled enough, Chance had hired an Indian woman to wash their clothing. Fancy had written to her grandmother that she was afraid she was being envied by some of the women in camp.

Fancy's thoughts stayed with her grandmother. The dear old lady would be here in another month, a month before her granddaughter's baby was due. For the past three weeks, the house had rung with the noise of saw and hammer as Chance added a new room to the house. It was a large one with two purposes. Grandmother would use it during her visit; then Tod and Lenny would take it over, each with his own bed. And the baby, when it was old enough, would sleep in the boys' old room.

Fancy folded her arms behind her head and gazed up at the ceiling, a smile on her lips. How many rooms would Chance have to build over the years? she wondered. She wasn't going to stop with just one child. She wanted at least six.

A tiny frown worried her forehead suddenly. Maybe Chance wouldn't want six. Maybe he didn't want any more after this one. They had never discussed the size family they would have. Come to think of it, they never discussed anything—for instance, the Indian woman who came once a week to scrub the clothing. She had shown up one morning announcing that she had come to wash the Dawson family's clothes. When Fancy said that she washed their clothes, the woman had shaken her head. "Dawson come to village yesterday. Hire me. One silver dollar he give my husband."

Then there was the room he had built for Grandmother. The first she had known of his intention was when he started hammering. She had gone outside, walked to the back of the house, and inquired what the noise was all about. "A room for the old grandmother," he explained. "She can't sleep on the floor, and if she tried to sleep with Tod and Lenny, they would kick her to death in their sleep." Before she could say anything, he warned, "I'm not giving up my place in bed."

She had not known quite how to take that remark. Had Chance meant that his bed was too comfortable to give up, or that he wasn't going to give up sleeping with his wife? They didn't make love very often anymore. Chance was afraid of hurting her, even though Sukie claimed there was no danger to her or the baby if they were careful. He still held her in his arms, however, while they slept.

Actions like that told Fancy that Chance cared for her, yet the word love hadn't passed his lips.

Fancy sat up and swung her feet to the floor. "Count your blessings, woman," she scolded, "you could be much worse off. Your husband respects you at least, and surprisingly doesn't seek out other women the way you thought he would."

That had been the biggest surprise of all in her marriage. She had been so sure Chance would continue his old ways, and she couldn't believe it was true when days passed into weeks and then into months and Chance hadn't strayed from her bed. It appeared that her plan to keep him happy in bed to keep him home nights was working. Even now that her time was drawing near and lovemaking was curtailed drastically, Chance's nights were still spent with her.

She remembered that Zeb had said once that Chance was an honorable man. Was that why he was honoring his wedding vows? Did he expect, and want, her to divorce him once the baby was born? She hadn't thought of what his feelings might be. She had only concerned herself about how she could divorce him if their marriage didn't work out. Maybe he felt the same way. Maybe he planned on dissolving the marriage once the baby came.

She felt an emptiness in the pit of her stomach. She didn't want this marriage to end. She loved her strange husband more today than the day she married him. She wished the two months would hurry by so that she would know one way or the other what the future held for her.

"Please, God," she prayed, "don't let it be a future without Chance in it."

With a long sigh, Fancy pulled on a robe that would be two sizes too large for her a couple of months from now and went to the kitchen. As usual, the sunny room was spotless. Chance always left it that way when he went to work. She poured a cup of coffee from the pot, still warm from a low-burning fire, added sugar, then carried it into the bedroom where she sipped the strong brew while getting dressed in the sack-type dress she wore these days. She'd be glad to see the end of them for a while.

The clock was striking ten when Fancy stepped out onto the porch and stood breathing deep of the rain-washed terrain. Stepping carefully to the ground a minute later, she walked to the corner of the house to check the holy-leaf bayberry that Zeb had dug up and transplanted for her. He had done the same with some wild raspberries she had found in the meadow. She had always felt that a few shrubs and wildflowers gave a house a permanent appearance, as if it wouldn't be abandoned when a new tract of timber was sought out.

Fancy was thinking that now that school was out until next fall, she would go visit her friend Molly for a while, when she heard a loud commotion coming from the direction of the river. From the shouts coming from alarmed throats, something serious was wrong. Someone had been hurt.

She had reached the floodwaters when Chance came splashing through the water, shouting, "Go back, Fancy!"

"What has happened?" she asked anxiously as Chance came to a panting stop before her.

"Al Bonner's body just washed ashore."

"You mean he's . . ."

Chance nodded. "Yes, he's drowned."

"Oh, dear." Fancy clutched at Chance's arm, feeling faint.

"Come on, let me take you back to the house."

His arm went around her waist.

"No, I'm all right now, Chance. I suppose he and his wife were coming home from their winter stay in San Francisco. Did the heavy rain cause a shipwreck? Is his wife all right?"

"I'm afraid he and his wife never made it to San Francisco. From the looks of the body, it's been in the water all winter. Evidently it got hung up in some driftwood that kept it from washing out to sea. But as for his wife, I'm afraid she's been washed away. The men are getting ready to row up and down the river looking for her, but we don't hold much hope of finding her."

Fancy joined the women who had come running at the sound of the men's loud voices and stood beside Myrt, watching as three boats were rowed away, the men looking for the body of Clare Bonner.

"Poor little thing. She didn't have a happy marriage, you know," Alma Bandy said.

"I didn't know that," Molly Jackson said, and the other women remarked that they hadn't either. "How do you know she wasn't happy in her marriage?" Molly asked.

"I went with Bill to the Sound one day last spring and got in on the tail end of a big ruckus between Al Bonner and one of his crew. Seems Mr. Bonner caught the man kissing his wife. He fired the man and slapped Clare around a little."

"I'd say she deserved it if she was cheatin' on her husband," Blanche said, giving Alma a knowing look. It was common knowledge that Alma was meeting one of the sawyers every chance she got.

Alma's face had reddened guiltily when she blustered, "Al Bonner should have expected his wife to cheat on him. He was old enough to be her father. He was forty-two, and Clare was only eighteen when they got married."

"She shouldn't have married a man that old," Blanche argued back. "There's plenty of young men she could have picked from."

"From what some of the people were saying that day, her pa made her marry Bonner to settle a debt of money he owed Al."

The women all agreed that was a shame, with Myrt adding that both of the men should have been shot, using a helpless girl like that.

The group broke up shortly, the women going home to take up whatever they were doing before being interrupted. Fancy said good-bye to Myrt, and as she walked homeward she decided that she would cook supper tonight. She wanted her family around her, safe and happy.

As she went about cutting a chunk of beef into bite-sized pieces of stew, she kept thinking of Clare Bonner, of how unhappy the young girl must have been, married to her stern-faced husband. Marriage without love must be pure hell.

Fancy stopped suddenly, the knife poised over a piece of meat. Chance didn't love her. Was he living in hell? The question hit her so hard that she had to sit down. All this time she had been feeling sorry for herself, but what about his feelings? It wasn't his fault if he couldn't return her love. A person couldn't help who they loved or didn't love. She'd give anything she owned not to love Chance, but she loved him just the same. And no matter how he might wish he could love her, there wasn't anything that could make it so.

Tears smarted the backs of her eyes as she gave up her dream of making her marriage last. It wouldn't be fair to Chance. Nonetheless, she promised herself that for the next two or three months that they would be together, she was going to be more pleasant to him.

The men gave up the search for Clare Bonner's body when the sun went down and they could no longer clearly see the riverbank they rowed the boats along. It was agreed among them, however, that Al Bonner's wife wasn't in the Columbia.

In the meantime, Bonner's remains had been wrapped in a sheet of canvas and Victor had taken it to Puget Sound by wagon, where he turned it over to the stunned men there.

Supper was a quiet meal that evening in the Dawson home, even Tod and Lenny having little to say. That night in the darkness of their room, Chance drew Fancy into his arms and made slow, gentle love to her. She had never felt so close to him as she did when he brought her to a shuddering climax.

Chapter Twenty-seven

Fancy pushed open the door and breathed deep of new lumber and furniture oil. What would Grandmother think of the room built specially for her? Would she like it? She would if she knew of the long hours Chance had put in building it.

And what would she think of the furnishings? Although new, they were very plain, a far cry from the Heppelwhite that graced Thelma Ashely's mansion. All the pieces—bed, dresser, nightstand, wardrobe and rocker—were constructed of pine, hand rubbed to a satin sheen.

Chance had purchased the beautiful, brightly colored quilt that covered the bed from one of the farm women, and Fancy had made the blue ruffled curtains that hung at the window overlooking a small creek whose water ran freely all year round. The cushion on the rocker matched the material of the window covering. The three Indian rugs placed about the floor gave the room a welcoming coziness.

Fancy walked over to a corner adjacent to the wood-burning stove and folded back a free-standing screen. Chance had even bought Grandmother her own beautiful hip-bath. Placed discreetly behind the tub was a dainty little chamber pot. There would be no going to the outhouse for Mrs. Ashely. Fancy grinned.

She certainly couldn't find fault with Chance for the way he treated her relatives, Fancy thought, giving the room one last look before closing the door behind her. Grandmother was arriving today and would be with them for several weeks, and he didn't seem to mind having her stay for such a long visit. In fact, he seemed to be looking forward to it.

Then there was Lenny. Chance had acted the big brother to him from the start. There weren't many men who would take on such a respon-sibility, considering her cousin's retardation. It would break Lenny's heart to be torn away from the man who had taken his Uncle Buck's place. As for Tod, she had no idea how it would affect him to lose a father again, so to speak. For the lean lumberman had taken over that role and played it well, if not better than the blood fa-ther, Jason Landers.

Not that Jason hadn't loved Tod—she was

sure he had—but he had never given the child the stability of the carefree life that every youngster deserved.

"Please, God," she prayed silently, "if you can't convince Chance to love me, at least don't let him send Lenny and me away. We both love him so deeply. I can't imagine a life without him."

The mantel clock struck three times. Fancy pushed away her unhappy thoughts and went to the kitchen door to call Tod and Lenny in. It was time to wash up and change into clean clothes. The sidewheeler, the *Fairy*, would be docking in a little over half an hour. Her dear old relative would be on it.

Sitting in the cookhouse killing time talking to Zeb while waiting for Fancy and the boys to join him, Chance saw Fancy walk out onto the porch and call to Tod and Lenny. He shook his head in admiration. Eight months into her pregnancy, big with his child, yet she had never looked more beautiful. His desire for her hadn't lessened one whit.

Of course he kept a tight rein on that these days, had done so for the past two weeks. He sighed. He had a long wait ahead of him. According to Sukie Daniels, and she should know with that brood of hers, there was to be no foolin' around for six weeks before the baby came and six weeks after.

But would Fancy still be with him six weeks

after the baby arrived? For all he knew, she might still be planning to leave him as soon as she was able to travel. She had made it clear that she was only marrying him to give her child a name. Nothing had been said about the marriage being a permanent one. She could very well be planning to leave with her grandmother when it came time for the old woman to go home.

Chance's lean hands clenched into fists. That didn't bear thinking about. A life without Fancy by his side would be no life at all.

Lenny and Tod could hardly contain their excitement as the *Fairy* came close enough for them to see Thelma's smiling face as she waved to them from the deck. "I hope she brought us some candy." Tod smacked his lips.

"Now don't go asking her," Fancy warned. "If she did, she'll give it to you when she's ready. You know how she is about good manners."

The *Fairy* docked and Chance was there to put his hands around Thelma's tiny waist and swing her ashore. Fancy and the boys were around her then, hugging and kissing, Tod's rough embrace knocking her perky little bonnet askew on her white head.

"You all look so healthy and happy," Thelma exclaimed, a little breathless from the enthusiastic greetings she had received. She studied Fancy's smiling face, her shining eyes, then looked at Chance. "Well, from the looks of her,

Chance, I'd say she's been well treated."

"I've done my best." Chance grinned, his tone saying it hadn't been all that easy sometimes.

"I guess we'll have to forgive her shortcomings these days," Thelma teased as she patted Fancy's rounded stomach. "A woman is allowed to be ornery occasionally when she's in waiting."

"Will you stop talking as if I'm a hundred miles away," Fancy said in sham annoyance. "Let's get up to the house now. You look tired, Grandmother."

"I am, a little. The sea breeze, I expect." Thelma took the arm Chance crooked for her. "I haven't felt so alive, though, in a long time."

Even though her little home would fit inside her relative's grand mansion, Fancy was proud of how it looked as they approached it, drowsing in the sun, its windows sparkling clean, the kitchen curtains fluttering gently in the cooling breeze blowing off the river.

To the left of the house, a few yards away was a wilderness of purple fireweed that grew taller than a man's head, and spreading up toward the foothills was a tangle of wild roses and honeysuckle. On a quiet evening, their delicate scent perfumed the whole area as well as the inside of the house.

"What a charming home you have, Fancy." Thelma stopped and leaned on Chance's arm as she gazed at the little domicile. "It looks like it just stepped out of a picture book."

"Wait till you see your room." Tod tugged Thelma in motion again. "Uncle Chance built it for you."

"He did?" Thelma looked up at the man who had more or less been forced into marrying her granddaughter. Her opinion of him was improving by the minute. However, she wouldn't capitulate too quickly. She'd wait, see how he treated Fancy. Good surface manners and actions didn't mean a thing. They could be hiding how the big lumberman really felt about the whole situation he found himself in.

"It is delightful!" Thelma exclaimed as she stood in the doorway of her room, running her gaze around the room that would be hers for several weeks.

Chance's and Fancy's faces flushed with pleasure at Thelma's praise of the room. "It's not what you're used to, Grandmother, but I think you'll be comfortable," Fancy said.

"Oh, my dear," Thelma said, a little sadly, "I've not always lived on Nob Hill. Before your grandfather struck it rich in the gold fields, we lived in some awful places—dirt floors, roofs that leaked when it rained. To have had a place like this would have been paradise."

"Why don't you change into some comfortable clothes and try out the bed, maybe take a little nap," Fancy suggested.

"I just might do that." Thelma nodded. "But

first I want to give you each a little gift I've brought you."

Tod and Lenny rushed forward, Tod stepping on Fancy's foot and Lenny almost knocking Chance over. "Which bag are they in, Grandmother?" Tod hurried over to the corner where Chance had put the fancy luggage.

"Tod!" Chance frowned at the excited boy and Tod's face reddened with embarrassment.

"It's all right, Chance." Thelma gave her great-grandson a hug. "Can't you remember back to his age, when excitement overran your tongue?" She pointed to a medium-sized bag. "Put that one on the bed, Tod, and we'll see what I've got inside it."

The first thing Thelma pulled out was the hoped-for candy, followed by a bag of marbles for each boy. Fancy expressed her pleasure over a bottle of heavenly scented toilet water and the fancy bowl of talc bearing the same scent. Chance was equally pleased with the bottle of brandy Thelma handed him. "I'll let Zeb have a nip or two of this." He grinned. "I doubt if he's ever drunk anything this smooth before." After a moment, however, he changed his mind.

"Maybe I won't. He wouldn't appreciate it. His palate is too used to that raw whiskey he drinks."

"Who is this Zeb?" Thelma asked.

"He's the crew cook," Chance answered. "He's more family than hired hand, though. He's worked for the Dawsons since I can remember."

"I'd like to meet him." Thelma looked interested.

"Oh, you will." Chance laughed. "I'm surprised he didn't tag along with us to meet you at the river. He sticks his nose in my business all the time."

Fancy saw a tiredness in her grandmother's eyes and ushered her family from the room. She lingered a moment, however. "I'm so glad you're here, Grandmother." She took Thelma's delicate little hands in hers. "I'm beginning to get a little nervous now that the time for the baby to be born is drawing near. I'm a little afraid too."

"Don't be. You're going to do just fine, honey. And that big handsome husband of yours is going to be beside you all the time, lending you his strength and support."

"Do you really think so, Grandmother?" Fancy asked wistfully.

"Don't you think so, child?" Thelma cupped Fancy's face between her hands and looked deeply into her eyes. "Doesn't he treat you well? Is he harsh with you? I know he'd never strike you. He's not that kind of man—I can tell that about him already."

Fancy paused a moment before answering. Those were good questions to ponder. Ones that she had never given any thought to. Finally, she said, "It's true Chance has never struck me, and

I can't say that he treats me harshly. It's just that there is no closeness between us. I get the feeling that he's just biding his time, waiting for the baby to come, and then he expects me to leave."

Thelma looked at Fancy and shook her head impatiently. "I hope that you're not thinking that Chance Dawson would let you walk away with a child of his. If anything, he's probably scared to death that you'll try that."

Thelma sat down on the bed and patted the space beside her. When Fancy sat next to her, she asked, "Have you given your all to make your marriage what you want it to be? Do you ever make the first move toward that closeness you speak about?"

Fancy looked down at her clasped hands lying in her lap. "I try to, Grandmother, I really do. But Chance is so remote, so polite, I can't even bring myself to flirt with him, to break down that cold wall he has built around himself where I'm concerned."

"I'm going to ask you a delicate question, Fancy, and if you don't want to answer it, I'll understand." A flush spread over Fancy's face. She had a pretty good idea what the question was going to be. She looked up at Thelma and waited.

"At night, in bed, is Chance still remote and polite, or does he leave that wall you speak of outside the bedroom door?"

Fancy's lips twisted wryly. That wall crumbled once Chance took her in his arms. They were as one then, their bodies speaking what they were unable to say. And that intimacy lasted throughout the night—until the coming of dawn. It was then that Chance crawled back into his shell, to remain there until it was loving time again. Even now, though that part of their marriage was put on hold, there was still a tenderness in the way Chance held her through the night, her head resting on his broad shoulder.

Fancy looked up at Thelma, and with a decided red in her cheeks, she said shyly, "I can't fault him there."

"Well, my girl, you've got more than half your battle won then." A sadness came into Mrs. Ashely's eyes. "A wife has to worry when a husband doesn't care whether she finds fulfillment in the marriage bed. Even though that couple might stay together, the wife suffers untold agonies when over the years her husband doesn't make a pretense of wanting her, and before she knows it, they aren't even sharing the same bed. She sheds many bitter tears, knowing that he is finding pleasure in another woman's arms."

Fancy got the distinct impression that her grandmother was talking about herself. Had her husband withheld his love from her? She wanted to put her arms around the narrow shoulders touching hers, hug her, and tell her that she was deeply loved by her granddaughter.

But Thelma Ashely was a proud old lady and wouldn't accept sympathy from anybody. So she kept her hands in her lap and, smiling at the white-haired old lady, said, "I'm so glad I had this talk with you. For the first time, I have hopes for my marriage."

"Marriages have started out with a lot less, Fancy. Good relations in bed give you the beginning. Respect comes next, then a liking for each other. Love is sure to follow. Now"— Thelma stood up—"I think I'll take that nap you suggested earlier."

Fancy rose also. Kissing the soft cheek raised to her, she left the room, closing the door quietly, a smile on her face.

Chapter Twenty-eight

Supper was late, simply because Zeb insisted that they eat with him. He hadn't "tagged along," as Chance had put it, to meet Thelma simply because he had gone fishing to prepare a grand feast for Fancy's grandmother. He had caught a string of trout that when fried up were fit for a queen to eat.

But first he had to feed the crew; then he had to clean up after them. He hurriedly prepared some hush-puppies, then thinly sliced cabbage for coleslaw. And finally he had fried the fish.

The old fellow had unearthed a white tablecloth from somewhere—or maybe it was a sheet, Fancy thought—and sitting in the center of the table was an Indian pot crammed full of wild roses. Fancy grinned to herself. She would have never guessed that rough old Zeb was a romantic.

The romantic blushed with pleasure when Thelma took a second helping of the fish, declaring that the trout was the best she had ever eaten.

There had been an instant affinity between Zeb and Thelma, which was a big relief to Fancy. If their crotchety old friend decided he didn't like a person, he could be very cantankerous toward that man or woman. A couple of the crew members had learned that by getting on the wrong side of the ex-sawyer. If stew was being served for supper, they got fewer pieces of meat dipped onto their plate; their pieces of steak would just happen to be smaller than the other men's; and dessert was always smaller portions for those Zeb did not like.

"Maybe you'd like to go fishin' one day." Zeb was moving around the table, serving peach cobbler.

"I'd love to, Zeb," Thelma answered quickly. "I can't remember the last time I sat on a riverbank and dangled a line over the water."

"We'll go one day next week." Zeb grinned widely, then poured the adults coffee and offered Tod and Lenny more milk. Before he sat back down, he lit a lamp and brought it to the table. An early dusk had descended because of the dark clouds that had gathered overhead.

"It looks like we might have a storm tonight,"

Zeb said, cutting into his dish of cobbler.

"I hope so," Chance agreed. "The forest is getting pretty dry. I've given the men orders that they're not to smoke away from the camp. It would only take one spark and everything would go up in flames."

"Let me help you with the dishes," Thelma said when everyone sat back, groaning with replete stomachs.

"No, no, you go along with Chance and Fancy. Tod and Lenny will give me a hand."

"Will you tell us about the good old days?" Lenny wanted to know. "When you fought the Indians—how you killed thirty in one day."

"Zeb!" Fancy gasped, appalled. "What kind of stories are you telling them?"

Zeb slid Thelma a glance, and when he saw the merriment in her eyes he grinned and said, "Who says they're stories?"

"You know they are, you old scallywag. I won't even ask what other kind of nonsense you've been filling their heads with."

"I ain't told them anything that will keep them awake nights, if that's what you're thinkin'," Zeb said defiantly.

"I've got my doubts about that." Chance rose and helped Fancy out of her chair. "You used to tell me some hair-raising tales, as well as some big whoppers. One whole summer you had me looking for a two-headed buffalo you claimed you had seen. The crew had a lot of fun at my expense that season."

When Zeb assisted Thelma to her feet, she looked up at him and smiled. "We'll have to get together some afternoon and see who can tell the tallest tales."

"I look forward to it." Zeb smiled back.

As Chance walked between the two women to the house, lightning pierced the darkness, followed by a loud clap of thunder. "Let's sit on the porch a while," Thelma said. "It's been a long time since I've watched a storm roll in."

Fancy eased herself down onto one of the four cane-bottom chairs that always sat on the porch unless it looked like rain. They would be brought into the kitchen then.

Fancy made a disgruntled sound as she eased onto a chair and tried to make herself comfortable. "What's wrong?" Chance asked anxiously.

"Nothing, really," Fancy answered. "I'm just tired of carrying this weight around. I've had a nagging backache all day."

"Where about is it aching?" Thelma sat forward.

"My lower back." Fancy put her hands on either side of the spot that had bothered her all day.

Thelma frowned. "Usually that's an indication that you're going to go into labor."

"It couldn't be that, Grandmother. I have a full month to go yet."

"You can't go according to a due date with the

first baby. It can come two weeks early or two weeks late. It comes when it's ready. I hope your midwife lives nearby."

"We don't have a real midwife, Grandmother." Fancy revealed what she had been dreading since Thelma's arrival. "One of the camp wives knows all about delivering babies. She's had eight of her own."

"Having them doesn't make you an expert in bringing them into the world."

"I'm strong and healthy. I'm sure everything will be all right," Fancy assured her grandmother.

"I'm sure it will, honey," Thelma hurried to agree, seeing the uneasiness that had crept into Fancy's eyes despite her firm declaration that everything was going to be fine. And Chance's face had turned as white as snow. She had upset them both. Unnecessarily, she hoped. Still, she wished her doctor was within a short traveling distance.

During one flash of lightning, Chance called their attention to a porcupine scuttling across the yard, no doubt hurrying to get to cover before the storm broke.

The next time the camp was lit up, it revealed Pilar running after Gil, her voice shrill as she berated him about something. "Oh dear, that one is angry." Thelma laughed. "Who is she? The man's wife?"

"Hardly," Chance said with dry amusement.

"Pilar would like for him to be her husband, but no one woman will ever tie Gil Hampton down."

"Pilar is one of the dance hall girls," Fancy explained to Thelma, "and the man, Gil Hampton, works for Chance. He's a scaler, and Pilar is crazy about him and very jealous. He probably smiled at one of the other dancers." Fancy gave a light laugh. "He does like to torment Pilar."

"He'd better not aggravate her too much," Chance said. "That fiery little Mexican will put that stiletto she keeps in her garter into his heart."

"Or maybe into the poor woman he decided to tease her with," Fancy pointed out in angry tones. "You should speak to Gil about riling her up. Point out to him how dangerous she could be."

"I expect he thinks he can handle her." Chance dismissed Fancy's concern.

Pilar's irate voice was heard once more before the storm broke, the pounding rain drowning out all other sounds. Tod and Lenny came sprinting to the porch and Chance yelled, "Grab a chair, boys."

Inside the kitchen, Chance took a sulphur stick from his pocket and raked his thumb nail across its red tip. When it flared, he lit the table lamp. Its illumination showed Fancy's features pinched and pale. When she said, "Come on, you fellows, let's get you washed up and ready for bed," Thelma took her arm and turned her toward her and Chance's bedroom.

"I'll see to them," she said. "You look tired— go on to bed."

Fancy smiled weakly. "Thank you, Grandmother, I believe I will."

Chance watched her leave the kitchen with worried eyes. Her hips were so narrow. Would she have a difficult birth?

Fancy had just changed into her gown and crawled into bed when Chance entered the bedroom. She listened to the rustle of his clothes as he undressed, silently telling him to hurry, that she needed the comfort of his arms.

A flash of lightning lit up the room for a split second as Chance climbed into bed. After the deafening roll of thunder died away, he asked softly, "Shall I rub your back?"

"Would you, please?" Fancy rolled over on her side, her back presented to him.

Chance's hands were like coarse-grained leather, his palms callused from years of handling an axe. Still, they worked with incredible gentleness on her back.

It was raining a steady downpour when Fancy closed her eyes and slipped off into a light sleep.

The clock had struck two when the household was awakened by a pounding on the back door. "What is it?" Fancy asked, leaning up on an elbow as Chance left the bed and fumbled his way through the darkness.

"I don't know," he answered, swearing when he stubbed his toe against Fancy's rocker. "It's still pouring rain and whoever it is must think it's important to get me out of bed at this hour."

"Be careful," Fancy warned. "Don't forget you have an enemy in camp."

"I don't expect it's someone who wants to kill me, making this kind of racket," Chance said, amusement in his voice.

In the kitchen, fumbling for the tightly capped jar Fancy kept the sulphur sticks in, Chance yelled, "Hold your horses," as the knocking sounded again.

When the lamp was finally lit and Chance jerked open the door, a white-faced Gil, drenched to the bone, looked at him from uneasy eyes.

"I'm sorry to bother you at this hour, Chance, but I'm afraid something has happened to Pilar. She didn't show up for work tonight. I've looked around camp some, but I haven't seen any sign of her."

Chance opened the door wider. "Come in. I'll get dressed and we'll look some more. The two of you had an argument earlier, didn't you?"

"Yeah, she got mad because she caught me talking to one of the other dancers. I'm getting pretty fed up with her tantrums. She's probably hiding somewhere, laughing her ass off while I run around in the rain looking for her."

Chance didn't doubt that for a minute. It was just such a trick as Pilar would pull, he thought, entering the bedroom and closing the door.

Fancy had lit the lamp they kept on their bedside table and was sitting up in bed, her eyes questioning him.

"It's Hampton," he said, drawing on his trousers, then sliding his arms into his shirt. "Pilar didn't show up for work and he doesn't know if anything has happened to her or if she's hiding somewere pouting, making him look for her."

"I hate for you to go out in this weather to hunt for that nasty, evil woman." Fancy's eyes flashed. "I hope she drowns."

A slow, elated smile crept across Chance's face. Fancy had never before shown any concern about his welfare. Did this mean that she was beginning to care for him?

He bent over and dropped a kiss on her cheek. "As his boss, I'm obligated to help Hampton look for her. I'm sure it won't take long to find the bitch."

Back in the kitchen again, Chance found Thelma standing in her doorway, dressed in her robe and slippers, her white hair in a single braid hanging down her back. "What's wrong, Chance?" she asked. "Is Fancy all right?"

"She's fine, Grandmother," he used that title for the first time. "This is Gil Hampton." He motioned toward the scaler. "One of the dancers is

401

missing and I'm going to help him look for her."

Thelma nodded her understanding, and when Chance finished lacing his caulk boots, he and Gil left, their heads bent against the slash of the rain.

Thelma turned to go back into her room, then swung back around when a low cry sounded from Fancy's room. She hurried to the other room to find her granddaughter standing in the middle of the room holding the bottom of her wet gown away from her legs.

Her voice full of fear and anxiety, Fancy cried, "I think my water has broken, Grandmother."

"Oh dear," Thelma murmured. "Let's get you into some dry clothes and get you back into bed. Have you had any pain yet?"

"I've had one." Fancy's words were muffled by the fresh gown Thelma was pulling over her head. "I thought I probably had indigestion from eating too much fish."

"How long ago was it?"

"Quite a while—before Gil knocked on the door."

"I'm going to send Zeb after that Sukie woman," Thelma said as she helped Fancy into bed and pulled the sheet up around her shoulders.

"You musn't go out in this rain, Grandmother." Fancy sat up in bed. "You'd catch your death of cold."

Thelma pushed her back down, then looked over her shoulder and said, "Lenny there is going to go for me."

Lenny and Tod stood in the open doorway, blinking the sleep from their eyes, a little bewildered. "Are you sick, Aunt Fancy?" Tod took a step into her room.

"No, she's not," Thelma answered. "She just has a little tummy ache." She looked past Tod to Lenny. "Lenny, put on an oil duster and go tell Zeb to come over here."

Lenny nodded and a few minutes later, they heard the kitchen door close behind him. It was then that Fancy had her second contraction. She held back her cry of pain, not to worry Tod, who looked so scared already. She knew he had a fear of losing her as he had his mother.

It was only a matter of minutes before Zeb burst into the room, his shirt unbuttoned and his gray hair plastered to his head. "Lenny says you've got a bellyache from eating too much fish." He gazed down at Fancy, worry in his faded blue eyes. He took a bottle from his pocket and placed it on the small table. "I brought you some pepsin. It helps digest food."

Thelma shook her head at him and said in a low voice so that Tod and Lenny couldn't hear, "It wouldn't help. Fancy needs Sukie Daniels's help."

"Oh, I see." Zeb's eyes grew round as he realized that Fancy didn't have a common bellyache. "I'll hurry right over to Sukie's."

"And, Zeb"—Thelma followed him into the kitchen—"I'll want you to take Tod and Lenny home with you when you return."

"Oh, sure." Zeb nodded, then said, "By the way, where is Chance?"

When Thelma finished telling him how Pilar had seemed to disappear, he shook his head in disgust. "It would be a blessing for everyone if she disappeared forever. She's a trouble-making bitch."

No one has a good word for the Mexican dancer, Thelma thought as she went back into her granddaughter's room.

Chapter Twenty-nine

Chance and Gil could hardly distinguish each other through the rain that still poured down. They had gone over every inch of the camp, looked behind each house; they had even gone through the long building that housed the bachelors. The had found no sign of Pilar. Wherever she had hidden herself, she was well dug in.

I hope she drowns, Chance thought tiredly as they now searched the fringe of trees and brush surrounding the camp. They had been looking for the dancer for over two hours and were drenched to the skin, their boots squishing water with each step they took.

They were in back of the dance hall now, protected from the rain somewhat by the towering Douglas firs. Holding the lantern waist high and shining it ahead of them, Chance could hear Luther pounding on the piano, the tune he played almost drowned out by the laughing and stamping of the dancers. Why weren't the bachelors out here in the rain helping to look for the woman they had lain with countless times, he griped to himself.

The music and laughter faded as the two men came to a path leading to the river and the mill yard. The narrow way triggered Chance's memory of the night he had followed Hampton and watched him row across the river to rendezvous with the Indian woman. He was tempted to ask the man plodding along behind him if he still met the woman sometimes. He had noted that every once in a while Hampton disappeared from camp for a couple of hours.

He decided that it was none of his business how many women Gil Hampton slept with and kept his mouth shut. He was about to suggest to Gil that they give up the hunt, that the kerosene was getting low in the lantern, that they would soon be looking in the dark for Pilar, when from the sides of his eyes he glimpsed what looked like a body lying alongside a rotting tree trunk a few feet off the river path.

"Look!" He grabbed Gil's arm and pointed.

"Oh, dear God," Gil moaned and started running through the mud and puddles to kneel beside the inert form of the dancer.

Chance was right at his heels, and they both gasped and stared at the handle of a butcher knife sticking up from between Pilar's shoulder blades.

Who had killed her? Chance wondered as Gil removed the knife and turned Pilar onto her back. The woman had so many enemies that it could have been one of a dozen different people. He looked around for tracks, knowing he would find none. The rain would have washed away any sign of footprints.

"You know," Gil said, looking down at the bloodless face of the woman whose bed he had shared for the past several months, "I always felt that she would die a violent death at someone's hand. I wonder who did it?"

"We'll probably never know."

"Yeah, and no one will care enough to try and find out," Gil said. His observation spoken so coolly made Chance wonder if he was counting himself as one of those uncaring people.

"I guess we should take her to Myrt." Gil scooped up the lightweight figure.

"I expect so. Maybe she'll know if Pilar has any relatives who should be notified," Chance answered, then led the way to the living quarters of the dance hall.

Myrt must have been waiting for them, for she answered their first knock. She ran her gaze over Pilar's lifeless face and said, "I figured only death would keep her away from the dance hall." She swung the door wide. "Take her to her room. You know where it is, Gil." There was no censure in Myrt's voice, just a statement of fact.

When the scaler had disappeared down the narrow hall, Pilar's limp arm swinging in time to his heavy step, Chance looked at Myrt and asked, "Do you know where she came from? Does she have any family?"

Myrt shook her head. "She was always very secretive about her past. She appeared here one day, asked for a job, and I hired her. Much to my sorrow, I soon found out. She didn't have any friends, didn't want any. She wasn't even friendly with the men she slept with."

"What about Hampton? She was awfully jealous about him."

"She wasn't jealous. She was possessive. Gil satisfied her in bed, and she didn't want to lose him."

"What should we do with her body? Should we take up a collection and send her to San Francisco to be buried in Potter's Field?"

"I guess that's the logical thing to do." Myrt nodded. She looked out the window where the gray of dawn was trying to penetrate the clouds and rain. "I'd better go pass the hat around right away. The dancing will stop soon, and the men will be gone. If I give them time to think about it, they won't contribute a dime."

"Let me know if you don't collect enough," Chance said. "Zeb should have a pot of coffee

made by now, so I'm going to drink a quart of
it, then go home and get into some dry clothes."

"Do you have any idea who done Pilar in?"
Myrt followed him to the door.

"I don't have the slightest idea. Probably
some man she stole from."

"Or some woman," Myrt pointed out.

"Well . . . yes, I suppose. I never thought of
that."

"Think about it," Myrt said as he stepped out
into the rain.

Fancy lay on her back, her skin and hair soaking wet with perspiration. She had just suffered
through a contraction that felt as if it was tearing her apart. The pains were harder and coming more often now, but nothing was
happening. How much longer would it go on?
How much longer could she bear it?

During the lull before before she was gripped
with pain again, she gazed up at her grandmother, who was bathing her face. The house
was swelteringly hot, for all the windows and
doors had been closed against the rain, as well
as the cries of pain that she was no longer able
to hold back.

"How long does this go on, Grandmother?"
she asked weakly.

Thelma hid her concern as she dropped the
cloth back into the basin of water, then stroked
Fancy's forehead. "Sometimes it takes a while

for the first one to enter this world, honey," she said gently, "but I don't think it will be too much longer."

But Sukie Daniels, sitting on the other side of the bed, ready to let her hand be squeezed the next time Fancy had a contraction, knew better. Something was wrong, and she was afraid this delivery would be beyond her capability. Her own babies had been born easily, with no fuss. Her body, however, was built for carrying and birthing babies, whereas Fancy was delicately made and narrow of hip. She was afraid the little one was trying to come out feet first.

Sukie sighed deeply. If that was the case, Chance Dawson was going to lose his young wife as well as his child. Already Fancy was worn out from the loss of blood. And when was Chance coming home? He'd been out in this downpour for close to three hours, helping hunt that dancing whore. He should be in here with his wife.

She looked down at Fancy's waxen face and thought angrily that Chance should be here holding her hand. In all fairness, though, he didn't know that his wife was in labor, trying to bring his child into the world. Sukie made up her mind that if Fancy called for him again, she was going out to look for Chance. Let Gil Hampton search for his whore alone. She wasn't worth a man's getting wet over.

*　*　*

Zeb looked up from chucking a stick of wood into the firebox of the big black range when the door opened. Relief washed over his worried face when he saw Chance standing there, dripping water onto the floor. Before he could speak, Chance said, "We found her. Dead. She'd been stabbed in the back with a butcher knife."

"You don't say!" Alarm replaced the relief on the old man's face. "I never liked the woman, but I never wished her dead. Whoever done it must have really hated her."

"There are a lot of people who did."

"You know somethin', Chance, I'll bet it's my knife that was used on her. I've been lookin' all over for it. I needed it to slice the bacon for breakfast." He shoved more wood into the fire. "It fair gives me the shivers, thinkin' a murderer sneaked in my kitchen and went through my tools while I was asleep."

Chance had poured himself a cup of coffee while Zeb chattered on. He took a long swallow of the strong hot coffee, relishing the feel of it hitting the bottom of his stomach, then said, "I'm sure Fancy will let you use hers until you can get another. Come up to the house with me and I'll give it to you."

Zeb closed the range door and gave Chance a solemn look. "Fancy is in labor, son, and having a hard time of it. I guess it started only minutes after you left with Hampton. Thelma sent me after Sukie, and the boys are asleep in my quarters. . . ." Zeb's voice trailed off. Chance had bolted from the cookhouse as soon as he said that Fancy was in labor.

Chance rushed into the kitchen; then his feet were rooted to the floor by the agonized cry that rang through the house. When it died to a low moan, movement returned to him and he rushed into the bedroom, his face almost as white as Fancy's. His mouth pinched and his eyes full of tortured concern, he knelt down beside the bed and took Fancy's hand in his. She looked up at him through pain-dulled eyes and said hoarsely, "I'm glad you're here, Chance. It hurts so. I'm so tired."

Chance brought her hand up to his lips. "I know, honey, and I'm so sorry to be the cause of it. If you will stay with me, I promise you'll not have to suffer this pain again."

Sukie touched Chance on the shoulder. "Move aside, Chance. I want to examine her the next time she has a contraction."

Chance had no sooner sat down in Sukie's chair than Fancy's body was wracked again, her stomach lifting and contracting as she fought the unbearable pain. Chance ran his fingers through his hair, a sound like a groan issuing from his throat. Thelma looked at his drawn face and rose to massage the tense muscles in his neck and shoulders.

*   *   *

Fancy

A white sun had risen as the men filed into the cookhouse for breakfast, their faces somber, their voices quiet as they discussed Pilar's death. Who had killed her? they asked among themselves. It had been none of them. The driving rain had kept everyone inside the dance hall. No one had left until after Myrt announced that Pilar had been killed, then took up a collection to send her body to San Francisco.

So that left the married men, one of the lumbermen said.

"Or maybe a woman," another suggested.

That started a new subject to discuss, the popular opinion being that if a woman had done Pilar in, the most likely suspect was Blanche Seacat. She was big and strong and hated Pilar with a passion. Despite all the talk about it, no one seemed to really care that the Mexican was dead, or who had killed her.

The rain had lost some of its power, as well as its noise. The men were having their coffee when everyone went still as the sound of pain, like an animal's cry, cut through the cookhouse. "My God, what was that?" one of the sawyers exclaimed as his spoon dropped from nerveless fingers, clattering onto the table.

"Fancy is in labor and havin' a hard time of it," Zeb said in the stunned silence. "I guess it's pretty much touch and go with her makin' it, accordin' to Sukie. I guess the baby ain't turned right."

"Chance must be out of his mind with worry,"

one of the men said. "He's plumb crazy about Fancy."

"He is that," Zeb agreed. Then looking out the window, he said, "It's only drizzlin' now. Don't you men think you should get to work?"

The crew nodded, drained their cups, and shuffled outside.

Chapter Thirty

The hours dragged on, noon came, and still there was no baby. Weak from exhaustion and loss of blood, Fancy was no longer able to cry out her agony. She could only lie and look at Chance, her eyes pools of pain. And he, sick with fear of losing her, felt as if he was collapsing inside.

"Chance," Sukie said gently, "do you want Zeh to bring Tod and Lenny here . . . to see Fancy?"

"Oh, Sukie, do you mean . . ." Thelma couldn't bring herself to ask if Fancy was near death.

His eyes wild, Chance knelt down and cradled his wife in his arms, his voice agonized as he called her name. He was rocking her back and forth, whispering endearments to her, when a knock sounded on the kitchen door. Sukie, tired circles around her eyes, went to answer it.

She returned almost immediately, Peter walking behind her. She looked at Chance. "Peter thinks he may be able to help Fancy."

"What can you do, man, that Sukie hasn't already done?" Chance looked up at the "brother" of Clarence, hope and doubt warring in his eyes.

"I don't know that I can, Chance, but I'd like to try. I'm told that the baby is trying to come out feet first. It will never make it. As brutal as it sounds, if I can't help your wife, she'll go with your child."

"What will you do?" Chance laid Fancy's limp body back onto the bed.

"My training as a doctor taught me how to deal with situations like this. I want to try turning it until its head is in the birth canal. If necessary, I'll pull the little one out."

"Oh God, man, do you think you can?" Chance looked at him hopefully.

"I'll try my damnedest, boss," Peter said, then turned to Sukie. "I need to scrub my hands in hot water and some lye soap if you have it." Sukie nodded, and he followed her into the kitchen.

"Oh, Chance, I pray the man can save her," Thelma said, "I don't know if I could bear losing her when I just found her."

Chance could only lay his head next to Fancy's and sob.

Fancy

In the kitchen, Sukie frowned at Peter as he trimmed his nails down to the quick. "Why are you wasting time paring your nails?" she asked sharply.

"My hands and nails must be scrupulously clean, for I'll be putting them inside Mrs. Dawson. She must not get an infection. She is much too weak to fight one off."

Sukie looked down at her own dirt-rimmed nails and was thankful she hadn't made an internal examination of Fancy. As Peter dried his hands on a clean towel, he said, "Would you please fold a clean sheet and slip it under Mrs. Dawson."

He walked into the bedroom then, saying briskly, "Chance, if you and Sukie will hold her hands, I'll see what I can do."

With hands as gentle as a woman's, Peter slowly reached inside Fancy, found the tiny feet, and ever so gently turned the little body until he could feel the small head, liberally covered with hair.

"Fancy, girl," he said gently, "when you get your next contraction can you bear down once more?"

Fancy looked up at Chance through pain-glazed eyes, barely conscious now. "Just one more time, honey," he coaxed. "Peter will help you."

A contraction came almost immediately, and with her last strength, Fancy bore down and Peter caught the tiny little girl in his hands.

When he gave the little red rear a slap and the baby cried weakly, but angrily, Chance exclaimed, "You did it, Fancy—you have a little daughter!"

Fancy didn't hear him. She had fainted.

"Dear Lord, Peter, she's dead!" Chance's voice was wild with his mental pain.

Peter handed the baby to Sukie and hurried to pick up Fancy's limp wrist. After holding his fingers on her pulse a moment, he looked up at Chance and smiled. "She's fainted. She's going to be all right."

"Thank God," husband and grandmother said in unison.

"It's going to take a while for her to recover, though," Peter said, rolling down his sleeves and watching Sukie bathe the newborn. "She's lost an awful lot of blood and it must be replenished. She must drink a lot of beef broth and eat a lot of steak."

"She'll do that," Chance said, his eyes shining as he stroked the damp hair from Fancy's forehead. "I'll see to it that she drinks broth by the gallon."

"Take a look at your daughter, Chance." Sukie laid the blanket-wrapped baby in his arms. "She's got your hair."

Chance's heart swelled with love for the tiny piece of humanity, whose weight was so light he could hardly feel it. "She's so little," he said in awe, gently tracing an eyebrow that arched the same way her mother's did.

"She's not so little," Peter said. "I'll bet she weighs close to seven pounds."

"Peter." Chance looked up at the soft-spoken man. "There aren't words enough to thank you for what you've done today. Fancy and I will be forever in your debt."

"Hey, that's all right, Chance. I'm just glad that I could do it."

"There's one other thing I wish you'd do." When Peter looked at him questioningly, Chance said soberly, "I'd like for you to be my daughter's godfather. I'm sure Fancy will feel the same."

"I know I do." Thelma lifted her eyes from admiring her great-granddaughter. "If not for you, this little one wouldn't be lying in her daddy's lap right now."

Surprise didn't describe the look that sprang to Peter's face. Stunned was a more apt description. He swallowed hard, then said, "I'd be honored, Chance, but are you sure? You know what's whispered about me and Clarence."

"I never listen to whispered words, Peter. Will you be our daughter's godfather?"

There was a slight pause; then Peter spoke in a grave voice. "I will gladly take on that responsibility. You and Mrs. Dawson need never worry that I wouldn't take care of your daughter if the need ever arose."

Norah Hess

Chance stuck his hand out to Peter and it was shaken warmly. "I'll go spread the good word," Peter said, "If Sukie hasn't beaten me to it."

"She will have told all the women," Chance laughed, "but I doubt that she's told Myrt. You might stop by and tell her before you give the news to the crew. I'll tell Zeb when I go to collect Tod and Lenny."

Chance didn't get to tell Zeb his good news. Sukie had stopped at the cookhouse on her way home. Thelma had just taken the infant from him when Tod and Lenny came bursting into the room, Zeb right behind them.

Zeb carried a hand-crafted cradle. "Boy, I had to work some last night to get it finished." He placed the cradle beside the bed. "I thought I had another month."

"You did a real good job, Zeb." Chance inspected the small piece of furniture—its sturdiness, the smooth hand-rubbed polish. "Grandmother Ashely has made a little mattress for it, and little blankets and quilts. Fancy will be real pleased."

"Well, let me see the little scutter who took so long to get into this crazy old world." He pushed in between Tod and Lenny, who were staring in awe at what looked like a doll. When he had studied the baby a minute, he looked up at Chance, his eyes twinkling. "You done real good at your first try. You'll improve with each new one."

"There will be no new ones," Chance said harshly, his lips in a firm line. "I almost lost her, Zeb, and I'll never chance her life again."

"I guess I understand how you'd feel that way. But a son would be nice."

"I can live without one," Chance said, "but I couldn't live without Fancy." He looked at Thelma as he said the last, as though warning her not to try taking Fancy away from him.

Thelma smiled gently at him and said, "I'm sure she feels the same way, Chance. She has no intention of leaving you."

Chance wished he could be that sure as he watched Thelma make up the cradle, then lay his daughter in it.

"I'd better get back to my stove," Zeb said. "I've got a big piece of beef simmering so we can start Fancy right in drinking the broth she needs. You folks come down and eat your supper about an hour before the men come in."

"Thanks, Zeb. Now that it's all over, I'm starving. What about you, Grandmother?" Chance looked at Thelma.

"I'm looking forward to it, Zeb." Thelma smiled at the cook.

When Zeb was gone, Tod asked, "What's her name, Uncle Chance?"

Chance had no idea what Fancy planned to name the baby. Like all intimate things, they had never discussed names for the infant. He privately thought that Ruth Ann was a pretty name, but it would be left up to Fancy to choose what the little one would be called.

He answered Tod, "We haven't made up our minds yet."

When the boys started suggesting names, some quite ridiculous, Chance told them to go outside before they wakened Fancy. Zeb left shortly after them, and Thelma announced that she was going to her room and catch a nap before suppertime.

Chance picked up Fancy's hand again, and holding it, fell asleep in the rocker he had pulled up close to the bed. He slept until Thelma gently shook his shoulder and announced it was time to go eat the evening meal and did he want to go first, or should she?

"You go on, Grandmother," he said, then grinned. "But hurry up—my stomach is growling like a hungry bear."

Fancy didn't awaken until nightfall. The lamp on the table beside her bed had been lit, and the cool breeze that had followed the rain fluttered the curtains at the open window. She started to lace her fingers over her stomach, as had been her habit for the past few months, and they fell several inches from what she had expected.

It came to her then in a joyous surge that her stomach was almost back to normal because she'd had her baby. She tried to sit up, but was too weak. She could barely lift her head. Had she delivered a boy or a girl? Whatever the sex, was it all right? She vaguely remembered that Peter had come to help her, and that finally the nightmare was over.

And where was the baby?

She called Chance's name, but doubted that he heard her, her voice was so weak and hoarse.

But Chance had heard her. He was sitting on the porch, his chair right beneath her window. He was beside her almost immediately. They smiled at each other as he sat down in the rocker. "How are you feeling?"

"Like someone has beaten me with a stick." She tried to squeeze Chance's hand, but was able only to tighten her fingers a fraction. Chance felt it, however, and gently squeezed her fingers in return.

"The baby—is it all right?" Fancy looked at Chance anxiously.

"She couldn't be better," Chance answered proudly. "She has all her fingers and toes, and a lot of brown hair."

"A little girl," Fancy whispered, her lips curved in a soft smile. She looked up at Chance with a guilty flush. "I was hoping it would be a little girl, even though I figured that you would want a son."

"But that's where you were wrong, young lady. I wanted a little girl too. One that would look like her beautiful mother."

Fancy lifted a strand of her sweat-matted hair

and said sourly, "I'm sure I'm not very beautiful now."

"Yes, you are. You'd look beautiful if you lost all that hair and grew a wart on your nose."

"All these compliments are going to swell my head." Fancy laughed. "Don't you think it's time I see my daughter?"

Chance leaned over and lifted the sleeping infant and laid it in her mother's arms.

Fancy's gaze roamed over the tiny red face, studied its features, ran a gentle finger down a satin-smooth cheek. Then, lifting her glowing, damp eyes to Chance, she said, "She *is* beautiful."

"What will you name her?" he asked.

"If it's all right with you, I'd like to name her Mary, after my sister."

Chance hid his disappointment and said he thought Mary was a grand name and it pleased him to have his daughter named after his sister-in-law.

Thelma entered the room then and was equally pleased that her great-granddaughter would bear the name of her dead granddaughter.

"I've come to give you a sponge bath and to change your bedding and gown. This little miss will be wanting a meal before long." She smiled, taking the baby from Fancy's arms and placing her back into the cradle.

Chance stood up. "I'm going to go have a few

words with the men, see how things went to-day." Actually, as he stepped out into the darkness, he decided he would go visit Big Myrt, to see if Pilar's body had been sent down to San Francisco for burial. He knew that Frank Jackson would have seen to it that the men would be kept busy in his absence.

Chance found Myrt and Luther sitting outside, enjoying the cool breeze coming from the river. Myrt asked after Fancy and teased him, calling him daddy. When he left fifteen minutes later, he had learned that Myrt and Luther had seen to it that the dancer's remains had been put on the *John Davis* near sunset, and that no one but Gil Hampton had shown up at the river to see Pilar off.

When Chance walked into the house, he found that Thelma had sent the boys to bed and had retired herself. It had been a very tiring day for the old woman. He turned the wick down in the lamp on the kitchen table and walked quietly to the bedroom. The lamp there had already been lowered, its soft light bathing Fancy and the baby in a golden glow.

He stood silently in the doorway a moment, unnoticed by Fancy as she nursed their daughter. Never had he seen a more beautiful sight than the baby they had made together taking nourishment from her mother's full breast.

Fancy became aware of his presence and smiled sleepily at him. He crossed the room and knelt beside the bed. He stroked her hair, then lowered his head to kiss her softly on the lips. Fancy ran her fingers through the long hair at his nape when he bent his head further and kissed the corner of the tiny sucking lips, including a part of her breast.

Chance raised his head and whispered, "You're tired. I'll get my bedroll, and we'll turn in when this greedy daughter of ours gets her little belly filled."

Fancy grabbed his hand when he would have stood up. "You're not going to sleep on the floor, Chance Dawson. You're going to sleep with your wife the way you're supposed to."

Chance's heart gave a great leap. Did Fancy know what she had just said, that he belonged in her bed? "Are you sure?" he asked, his voice shaken. "I might roll on you, hurt you."

"Nonsense. You never did before, so you're not likely to now." She looked down at the infant, who had released her nipple and was now sound asleep. "Mary is finished now. Put her back in the cradle; then come to bed."

The baby transferred to her own little bed, Chance stripped down to his underwear—there would be no sleeping naked with his little girl in the room—and climbed into bed, being careful not to jostle Fancy. As he lay on the very edge of his side of the bed, Fancy teased, "Are you going to make me stir my tired body and come to you?"

Chance didn't need a second invitation. He scooted over beside Fancy, his weight tipping the mattress, rolling her up against him. He slid his arm under her shoulders and she snuggled up to him, her head nestled under his chin.

Such a rush of love for her moved through Chance that it flowed out of his mouth. "I love you so much, Fancy Dawson. I have loved you from the first time I saw you in your little red dress and black silk stockings."

"And I have loved you from the first, even though you insulted me minutes after meeting me. I was so jealous when you danced with other women."

"But did you know that after meeting you, I never went to any of the dancers' rooms?"

"Truly, Chance?" Fancy whispered against his throat.

"Truly," he answered.

After a few moments of silence, Fancy said, "Grandmother told me about Pilar. "I never liked her, but I never wished her dead."

"Someone sure wished her dead. They used Zeb's butcher knife to make their wish come true."

"Grandmother said that Zeb threw the knife in the river." After a moment Fancy asked, "Do you think we'll ever know who did it?"

"If it's the same person who's been sabotaging

the camp, and I think it is, we'll catch the culprit eventually and then we'll know."

The silence between them lengthened and soon both fell into a deep, peaceful sleep.

Chapter Thirty-one

It was mid-July, an unusually hot day, as Fancy sat on the back porch, looking out over the camp, hoping for a breeze. But the leaves on the hardwoods were motionless, and the wash the Indian woman had hung on the clothesline hung limply. The whine of the big saw down at the mill yard was loud on the quiet air.

Fancy released a long sigh. Grandmother had caught the *Fairy* to San Francisco yesterday and already she missed the gentle old relative. She had been such a source of strength for her when she was riddled with doubts that Chance cared for her. It had been Thelma Ashely's assurance that her husband cared deeply for her that had kept her spirits up.

And Grandmother had been right. She smiled

to herself. She knew now that Chance loved her deeply.

She felt a tightening in her lower body. She couldn't wait for the six weeks to be up, to feel Chance inside her again, to thrill at the weight of his body as he came down on top of her. They pleased each other often with lips, hands, and fingers, but it wasn't the same somehow.

Her lips twisted wryly. That wasn't necessarily true in Chance's case. He loved it when she parted her lips over his straining arousal and brought him to a shuddering climax. Last night, when he lay replete beside her, he'd whispered that he hoped she would continue loving him in that special way occasionally, even when they were able to go back to their usual bed activity.

She had teasingly answered that she would give him that treat when he had been a very good boy.

"In that case, then," he'd answered, humor in his voice, "I'll be good every day."

Fancy smiled when she saw Chance, Lenny, and Tod leave the cookhouse and walk toward home. The boys were begging him to take them fishing, looking at him with expectant eyes. She knew he would give in to them. He loved to fish as much as they did.

As she had expected, Tod gave an excited whoop and he and Lenny left Chance to run to the storage shed for the fishing equipment, leaving Chance to walk on alone. He sat down on the edge of the porch when he reached the house and, grinning up at her, asked, "How do you feel about a mess of trout for supper?"

"It sounds fine." She smiled back. "I'm sick to death of my meat diet."

"Ah, but look how it brought the roses back to your cheeks and the strength to your body." Chance's eyes lingered on her high, proud breasts, a wicked look in his eyes when he asked, "Is Mary sleeping?"

"Yes, I put her down about half an hour ago." Fancy worked hard to keep the amusement out of her voice. She knew what her husband had in mind—the hard ridge in the front of his trousers alerted her to that. Staring significantly at his full fly, she said with twinkling eyes, "Isn't it too bad you're going fishing?"

"I could put the boys off for half an hour or so."

"You think so, do you? Here they come now."

"Let's go, Uncle Chance," Tod called, wildly waving a fishing pole.

"Have a good time." Fancy laughed at Chance.

"You're a hard woman, Mrs. Dawson," Chance said reproachfully as he stood up.

Fancy only smiled as he walked away, a fishing partner on either side of him, both chattering about the fish they were going to catch.

Fancy sat on, thinking how blessed she was.

She leaned her head back on the top of the rocker and nodded off.

A fly lit on her nose, then trailed over her cheek. Even in sleep she automatically brushed it away. When it returned and insisted on fluttering around her lips, she came awake, brushing at her mouth. A low chuckle brought her eyes flying open. The "fly" was a long blade of grass handled by Gil Hampton. Giving him a warm smile of friendship, she said, "It's about time you came to see me and my baby."

Gil sat down where Chance had sat earlier. "I've been busy tying up some loose ends, getting ready to move on."

"You're leaving? How come?" There was surprise and regret in Fancy's tone. "I thought you were happy here. Everybody likes you."

"Do you like me, Fancy?" Gil watched her closely.

"Yes, I do. Very much."

Gil looked away from her, his lips twisted in a bitter smile. "Where you're concerned, Fancy, liking is not enough for me. I want your love. That's why I've hung around here as long as I have. I thought, hoped, that your marriage wouldn't work and that you'd turn to me." He sighed. "I know better now, so I'm moving out. I'm not one to beat a dead horse."

"I'm so sorry, Gil," Fancy said sincerely. "If I hadn't met Chance first, who knows what might have happened."

Gil nodded. "I knew all along that you loved him, but I couldn't tear myself away." He stood up, "So I'll say good-bye to the only woman I ever loved." He gave a self-derisive laugh. "And I didn't even get to sleep with you."

Fancy broke the silence that fell between them. "When are you leaving?"

"Day after tomorrow. The other scaler is laid up with a wrenched back. I promised Chance I'd top some trees before I left."

"He knows you're going then?"

"Yes, I told him. I told him why too."

"You did?" Alarm grew in Fancy's eyes. "What did he say?"

"He thanked me for being honest with him and said there were a lot of other good women out there, that I should stay away from whores. That there's no future with them."

"He's right, Gil. There's lots of nice women out there who would love you and be happy to be your wife."

"I'll think on it," he said tonelessly. Then, with one last look at Fancy, he walked away without another word.

Tears glimmered in Fancy's eyes as Gil disappeared down the river path. She wished he would find a woman, settle down, and raise a family. There was so much good in him.

It wasn't until Mary fussed that she realized Gil hadn't looked at her baby. She realized then that the last thing he would want to do was see the baby another man had sired on her.

It promised to be another hot day as Gil fastened the wide belt around his lean waist and adjusted the heavy rope that would hold him secure while he sawed off the top of a Douglas fir that rose three hundred feet in the air. He was good at his job and could almost do it blindfolded.

As he climbed the huge tree, his special spiked boots biting into the bark, he thought of tomorrow, when he would leave. He would make a last trip across the river before daybreak, bring her back with him, then board the first brig that came by going to San Francisco. When he had seen to her care, he would go on to the desert in southern California to mend his heart and mind there. When he felt healed, he would start a new life, maybe take Chance's advice and settle down. In truth, he was tired of always floating from place to place, never amounting to anything.

He reached the top of the tree, leaned back to decide where to start sawing, and the rope, his life line, came apart. With a startled yell, he was plummeting to the ground.

Shocked voices rang out; then there was a stampede of feet rushing toward his crumpled body.

Chance reached him first. As he lifted Gil's

head and saw the thin trickle of blood running from the corner of his mouth, a tight feeling in the pit of his stomach warned him that the scaler would not survive the fall. Not only was his body broken, he was broken inside.

It was when he laid Gil's head back down that he saw where the rope had been cut in half. His lips firmed in a grim line. This predator in camp had murdered two people, for Gil would never make it. Who would be next? Him? His wife? His baby? A chill ran down his back at that thought.

Chance felt a tug on his sleeve and, looking down at Gil, saw his lips moving. He lowered his head almost to the fallen man's lips in order to make out his softly spoken words.

"She's . . . across the . . . river. Crazy . . . go . . . get her . . . maybe kill . . . again."

"Who is she, Gil?" Chance urged him to speak again, to say the name. But the man, a mixture of good and bad, had said his last. His head fell sideways, his eyes staring, unseeing.

Shaken, Chance started to stand up from his kneeling position when a wild-eyed woman broke from among the pines and threw herself down beside Gil. As she lifted his upper body in her arms and cradled it against her breast, someone exclaimed, "Why, that's Clare Bonner! No wonder we couldn't find her body. She's not dead."

The men talked among themselves, remembering the time Al Bonner had fired a man he'd caught carrying on with his wife. Was Gil Hampton that man? they asked themselves. Had Hampton killed Bonner?

Meanwhile Clare was sobbing hysterically, the words tumbling out of her mouth almost unintelligibly as Chance strained to put the broken sentences together. When she finally exhausted herself and only sat quietly, rocking Gil back and forth in her arms, Chance managed to piece her story together. He learned that Gil Hampton was the man Al Bonner had fired, and that it was Clare who had written the glowing letter about his ability to scale the big pines.

Gil had promised to return and take her away, but days and weeks followed and he hadn't showed up. It was then that she shot her husband and dragged his body to the river, where she had managed to push it into the water. She had been sure that Gil would come to her then, but he hadn't.

She had then heard that Gil was working in a camp twenty miles up the river from the Sound. She had followed him there. He had been very angry with her for following him and had become very upset when she told him she had killed Al. He had secretly settled her into the abandoned cabin across from the mill yard.

But Gil wasn't the lover she had expected him to be, nor had he offered her marriage. He only crossed the river once a week to bring her food and to tell her to go away before winter set in.

She had stayed on, however, hoping that he would change his mind and that it would be as it used to be between them. When that hadn't happened, she had taken out her anger at him by doing what damage she could to the camp.

Then one day she had seen him with Pilar, kissing the dancer. She knew that the Mexican was keeping him away from her and that she would have to kill the woman in order to get him back. But still he hadn't come back to her, she had wailed—not as a lover, at least.

She looked up at Chance, her eyes wild and bright, pleading for him to understand as she said, "He was going to take me to San Francisco tomorrow and put me in an asylum for crazy people. It's an awful place. I've been there before. I knew I had to kill him.

"So I cut the rope."

She had laid Gil back on the ground then, and as Chance told the men what he had gleaned from her garbled words, she gently stroked Gil's head.

The men looked at each other, dumbfounded. "I guess we can sleep peaceful in our beds now," Victor Seacat said.

"What are we going to do with her, Chance?" Frank Jackson asked.

"We'll have to turn her over to the authorities in Seattle, let them handle her future."

No one had noticed that Clare had turned her

head and was listening intently to them. They never became aware of it until she jumped to her feet, gave a wild cry and, running to the river, threw herself into it. They gaped helplessly as the rushing water swept her into an undertow. The last they saw of her was her bobbing head as she was swept away.

"Should we try to save her?" one of the men asked.

Chance shook his head and said, "It would be a useless undertaking." He was thinking that the poor crazed soul would be better off dead than in an asylum for the rest of her life.

"What about Gil?" Victor asked. "Do we turn his body over to the authorities in Seattle?"

"That's the only thing we can do," Chance answered. "After all, he was murdered. I'll take his body there on the next barge that comes along."

Fancy stood on the kitchen porch, looking up at the mountains that were wrapped in haze as Indian summer approached. There was a chill in the air and a bite in the light breeze that had sprung up. It was a warning that soon winter would descend on them once again.

She dropped her gaze to the hardwood trees. They were bare, their leaves now spilled to the ground. She watched a couple of chipmunks scampering about in them, looking for food to store away for the winter. She smiled when every once in a while they lifted their small heads to stare at her.

Leaning against a supporting post, Fancy thought back over the past months. She had suffered mental pain when she thought that Chance didn't love her; then she had known joy at finding a grandmother that she hadn't known existed. And the most joyful of all, she had given birth to little Mary and at the same time learned that her husband did indeed love her.

A sadness came into her eyes. Gil. How sad his wasted life had been. She prayed that he was in heaven looking down at her with his crooked smile and teasing eyes. And poor Clare. She hoped with all her heart that she had finally found peace. And Pilar, what had God done with her? Had she found forgiveness with Him?

Fancy straightened up when she heard the saw shut down in the mill yard, then saw the men coming up from the river. Her eyes grew smoky when Chance separated himself from them and walked toward her, desire shimmering in his gaze.

When he came up to her, she glanced down to where his trousers molded his sex, and giving him a teasing, sly look as the bulge there grew right before her eyes, she said, "Something tells me you have something on your mind. Something that can only be solved in the bedroom."

"Little witch." Chance put an arm around her waist and walked her into the kitchen. "I don't suppose you would care to help me clear my mind?"

"I might if you promise it will be worth my time." She slanted him a flirty smile as he turned her to face him, to feel the heavy weight of his maleness.

"It will be, I promise." He took her hand and shoved it beneath his waistband. "Feel the culprit that drives my mind crazy with wanting you."

"I can't get to him, your pants are too tight," Fancy teased, deliberately allowing her fingers only to touch the top of him.

"I can take care of that," Chance said huskily, his fingers going to his fly. In an instant all eight inches of him had sprung free. As usual Fancy grew damp between her legs, knowing the joy his largeness would soon be bringing her.

When she gave him a sultry look from beneath lowered lids, he folded back his fly and, spreading a hand on either side of his throbbing manhood, he bucked his hips at her, asking huskily, "Do you want to go to bed and decide if it's worth your time to help me out of my dilemma?"

"Maybe," Fancy answered, then bent forward a bit and cupped her hands around his heavy sacs. "These feel like it would." She gently squeezed them.

Chance gave her a devilish grin. "I thought

you'd think that." He swept her up and carried her into the bedroom.

Bare of clothing within seconds, as they climbed in bed, Fancy thought how wonderful it was that they could have these naughty exchanges of words and actions. She felt sure there were few married women who acted the whore for their husbands.

They didn't know what they were missing. She smiled lazily as Chance climbed onto her and sent his hardness plunging inside her. "I love you, Fancy," he whispered as he rose and fell against her.

"And I love you, Chance," Fancy whispered, backlifting her hips to take all that he could give her. "And I love this monster that gives me such pleasure." She leaned up on her elbows in order to watch the 'monster' slide in and out of her.

Dusk had settled in while they made love again and again. When Fancy feared she'd never get her legs together again she teased huskily, "Let's save some for tonight."

"I'll be ready." Chance playfully slapped her small rear as she scooted off the bed.

He smiled up at the ceiling. Truth be told, he'd be ready for her anytime, any place.

Dylan

Norah Hess

Dylan Quade is a man's man. He has no use for any woman, least of all the bedraggled charity case his shiftless kin are trying to palm off on him. Rachel Sutter had been wedded and widowed on the same day and now his dirt-poor cousins refuse to take her in, claiming she'll make Dylan a fine wife. Not if he has anything to say about it!

But one good look at Rachel's long, long legs and white-blond hair has the avowed bachelor singing a different tune. All he wants is to prove he's different from the low-down snakes she knew before, to convince her that he is a changed man, one who will give anything to have the right to take her in his arms and love her for the rest of his life.

Whirlwind

CINDY HOLBY

As the last remaining bachelor among all his friends, Zane Brody can always be counted on for irresistible charm. So when he sets out for New York to retrieve a valuable thoroughbred mare to Laramie, he has no doubt he can handle any female he encounters, whether equine or human. What he doesn't reckon on is an independent-minded schoolteacher named Mary Dunleavy. A goat butts him off the train and eats his hat, while the woman bats her eyelashes and appropriates his heart. As Mary takes off across the plains, Zane finds his head spinning, and his love life in a...

Whirlwind

CASSIE EDWARDS

SAVAGE BELOVED

Terrified and alone, Candy huddles beneath the trapdoor in the floor of her father's cabin, listening to the blood-curdling whoops of attacking Indians. When she finally creeps outside, it is to find a fierce-looking Wichita chief thundering toward her. Surely Two Eagles has captured her in retaliation for the atrocities her commander father committed against the Wichita. But as he slowly awakens her virgin desires, she begins to hope there is something more in his heart. For she no longer thinks of this proud, handsome man as her captor, but as her…

Savage Beloved

A Texan's Honor

LEIGH GREENWOOD

Bret Nolan has never gotten used to the confines of the city. He'll always be a cowboy at heart, and his restless blood still longs for the open range. And he's on his way back to the boundless plains of Texas to escort a reluctant heiress to Boston—on his way to pick up a woman destined to be a dutiful wife. But Emily Abercrombie isn't about to just up and leave her ranch in Texas to move to an unknown city. And the more time Bret spends with the determined beauty, the more he realizes he wants to be the man in Emily's life. Now he just has to show her the true honor found in the heart of a cowboy.

Hawk's Passion

Elaine Barbieri

Jason will do whatever it takes to bring down Simon Gault, the corrupt shipping magnate. The supposedly upright citizen betrayed Galveston during the war, causing untold deaths. But even more disturbing is his twisted desire to seduce innocent Elizabeth Huntington. No matter how determined she is to make her own way in the rowdy, war-ravaged city, Jason swears he will protect the daring young beauty from Gault, help find her missing family and then win her heart.

Hawk's Pledge

Constance O'Banyon

Whit is a gambler by necessity, a loner by choice. Ever since the orphanage had gone up in flames, Whit Hawk has been searching desperately for what remains of his family. Instead he finds Jacqueline Douglas, a rancher in need of a good hand, a woman in need of the right man. Wildly beautiful, she is as untamed as the Texas he loves, and Whit knows that no matter what else life holds in store for him, the fiery redhead must be his.